State of Denial

Andi Marquette

Quest Books

Nederland, Texas

ISBN 1-935053-009-4
978-1-935053-09-5

First Printing 2008

9 8 7 6 5 4 3 2 1

Cover design by Mari SanGiovanni
Cover concept byDonna Pawlowski

Published by:

Regal Crest Enterprises, LLC
4700 Hwy 365, Suite A, PMB 210
Port Arthur, Texas 7764

Find us on the World Wide Web at
http://www.regalcrest.biz

Printed in the United States of America

Acknowledgments

Thanks to Cathy LeNoir and Angel Grewe at Regal Crest for taking another chance on me, and for working so hard to get this book into this format. A big shout-out and thank you to editor Sylverre, who bravely took another one of my manuscripts on and helped me turn it into something even better. Thanks to the proofreader who went through it as well, mopping up after us all. And to Mari SanGiovanni, thank you so much for lending your humor, kindness, and artistic talent in the cover design. No word from the Pope yet on whether there's a patron saint of book covers and freaky authors. If there is, I'm nominating you.

Thanks to all the people who have read various parts of this and commented extensively on it and offered encouragement along with critique. You know who you are, and this is a better book because of you.

A monster shout-out to my friends, parents, and my sister, who continue to listen to my nutso ideas and who offer advice and support in myriad forms. I'm so fortunate to have the friends and family I do (the two not necessarily mutually exclusive), and I only hope that you continue to listen to my nutso ideas and that you never run out of advice or patience.

My gratitude to my muses, who continue to lead me in search of stories and characters. I think they rather enjoy the travels we're taking and I hope that never stops.

And many thanks to you, the reader, for spending some time with Chris and company. Hope you enjoy the journey.

Chapter
One

CHRIS SQUATTED BY the shallow grave. A cold late January breeze ruffled her hair as she studied the body within. He lay face-down, hands tied behind his back with what looked like electrical cord. The odor of human decomposition wafted under the edge of the bandanna she held against her mouth and nose and she automatically stopped breathing through her nose.

A crime scene tech ducked under the yellow tape that surrounded the perimeter of the clearing. He carried a clipboard and a plastic tackle box. If only this was a fishing trip, Chris thought as he set his box down near the perimeter and started writing on the form attached to his clipboard.

Dale Harper hunched across from her, pressing a handkerchief to his face. Two crime scene techs were engaged a few feet away, carefully screening the dirt that a third tech was gingerly removing from around the body with a small trowel and emptying into a stainless steel pail.

"Nasty," Harper intoned. Chris's fellow detective spoke with the accent of the upper Midwest, a blend that sounded like Chicago-meets-Canada. He rubbed the fingers of his left hand on his knee, as if the fabric of his trousers was some sort of cleansing agent.

Murder always is. Chris didn't vocalize the thought, waiting for him to make an inappropriate comment about the naked man in the grave. He seemed to have a penchant for doing that and it grated on her nerves. Gallows humor was one thing. Harper's comments were another.

He shifted his weight forward to get a better look, careful not to dislodge soil from the grave's edge. "I'm guessing sexual assault," he began, holding the handkerchief over his nose. "Probably a gay thing. No normal guy would end up like this."

"No *normal* guy goes out and kills another guy, either, and then leaves him naked in a hole in the bosque." The cloth blunted the hard edge in Chris's voice. She didn't look at Harper, instead continued studying the dead man between them, silently apologizing to him for Harper's remark, as if he still lived and was only sleeping or comatose. As if he could still care what anybody said about him. She apologized to him again anyway.

"Well, I seriously doubt a chick killed him," Harper muttered with what sounded like distaste.

Chris stared at him. "We don't know that yet."

He shrugged. "Oh, right. Women can do everything men can do."

Typical male cop crap, trying to get a rise out of her, most likely. Chris counted backward from ten before responding. "Yeah, we can. Unfortunately." She looked down at the body again. "But I agree that the perp in this case is most likely male. Still, the evidence isn't in."

Harper muttered something that she didn't pick up. She looked back at the man in the grave. He appeared to be Caucasian, mid-twenties. Maybe he had been thought handsome when he was alive, though she couldn't see his face. She considered his pale form and tried to imagine his last day of life. Maybe he went to work, as usual, thinking about all the things he had to do that day and the next. And maybe he went out after work with friends. Or maybe he went to a party somewhere. A night of fun, hormones, drinking. And then he'd ended up here.

Chris adjusted her weight to better balance on the balls of her feet as she leaned over, assessing. He was maybe six feet tall, about one-seventy-five. Dark-haired, this young man thrown away with no more ceremony than a bag of dead leaves. He had been somebody's son, somebody's grandson. Maybe somebody's brother. Did he have friends? Was he missed? What drove someone to put an end to this vibrant young man? What could he possibly have done to warrant this?

A little prickle raised the hairs on the back of her neck. As much as she hated to admit it, Harper was probably right. The young man in the grave was most likely gay. Why she thought that she wasn't sure, since what happened to him here didn't feel like a hate crime. She'd seen what happened to the victims of hate crimes. They were horrendously brutalized, often beaten beyond recognition, and sometimes stabbed numerous times. Here, the perp had undressed the victim, tied his hands, and placed him face-down. Without the electrical cord around his wrists, he might have just been sleeping. From her vantage point, Chris didn't see any bruising or stab wounds on his body or any kind of marks that would indicate he had been knocked around. So why did she think he died because he was gay?

A ring graced the third finger of his right hand but she couldn't get a good look at it without touching him and possibly disrupting the scene before the team started processing it. Animals had been gnawing on his fingertips, which might hinder identification. She checked his feet. Something had been chewing on his heels, which made sense since those, like his fingers, were closest to the surface. She picked out faint ligature marks on his neck. So he'd been strangled. That was a crime of intimacy, requiring close contact and physical strength. He might have known his killer.

Chris stood, brushing at her khaki trousers, and looked around the clearing. The main trail was to her right, past a tangle of bushes and stands of massive cottonwood trees and from there, the distance from the grave to the parking lot of the Rio Grande Nature Center was about three hundred yards, down a sandy path toward a paved bike path that ran perpendicular to the trail. About twenty yards from the bike path, the trail wended between what looked like huge metal jacks strung with wire to keep mountain bikers and hikers from walking in ecologically sensitive areas.

She studied the clearing in which the body had been found. Six feet from the gravesite ran one of the numerous hard-packed BMX bike tracks that spiderwebbed the bosque. The Rio Grande was located just a few minutes west, through underbrush and cottonwoods. Chris glanced east, back toward the Nature Center. The Sandia Mountains bordered Albuquerque's eastern edge, looming above the city like giant pointed teeth, and the setting sun splashed their western flanks a pinkish red, like the flesh of a watermelon, the fruit for which the mountains were named.

Chris returned her gaze to the crime scene. She noted bike tracks in the dirt not two feet from the grave and a large disturbed swath of soil and dry leaves that nearly touched one side of the grave. A sloppy killer? In a hurry? Or someone who wanted the body found? Why not just dump him in the river? Too awkward to lug a body the extra yards? If so, the vic might already have been dead when he was brought here.

Sam Padilla, head of the Albuquerque crime lab, approached, smiling apologetically. His heavy boots *thwumped* in the soft dirt and his reddish hair looked like he had just rolled out of bed. His face bore a perpetually bemused expression. "We've gotta start processing the body," he explained. "You guys need to see anything else at the moment?" He set his equipment box carefully on the ground and pulled a pair of latex gloves out of the pocket of his mid-weight jacket.

She shook her head. "No. Go ahead and do what you need to do. The perimeter's been processed, but I might do another walk-around." She liked working with Sam, a tall, thin guy with a calm demeanor. Nothing rattled him, an extremely helpful personality trait when dealing with the press as well as the decedent's friends and relatives.

"Cool," he responded, marking time on the triathlon watch

around his right wrist and writing it on his checklist.

"Who was first on the scene?" Chris addressed Harper as she shoved the bandanna into her jacket pocket though she still watched Sam. She heard Harper flip through his notebook.

"Um, Halstead." He closed the small notebook and took a few steps away from the grave. "I'm gonna check in with the canvass team."

"Good idea. I'll talk with Halstead." Any excuse to limit her interaction with Harper. Unfortunately, for whatever reasons, Sergeant Jerry Torrez wanted Harper working with Chris on this one and he'd cleared it with the area commander. For Jerry, Chris would deal with Harper. She'd do the best damn job she could. The young man lying face-down in the grave deserved no less, and his friends and family deserved no less than everything she could do to find his killer.

She ducked under the crime scene tape and followed Harper around the bushes to the path, one of the official routes from the Nature Center to the river. About three feet wide, stones lined it and occasional signs informed passersby about native vegetation. The path intersected at a near right angle with a paved bike route that ran north-south the length of Albuquerque here on the east side of the Rio Grande. She automatically checked for cyclists and roller-bladers before crossing, though the police had blocked it off for a tenth of a mile on either side of the Nature Center. Harper split off and headed north on the bike path.

Chris turned right on the path and went down a short rise to a pedestrian bridge that crossed an arroyo, mostly dry this time of year. On the other side of the bridge stood the entrance to the Nature Center. She took the dirt path through the grounds toward the parking lot, where Officer Erin Halstead leaned against the driver's side of the closest police car. She was facing Chris, talking animatedly to another uniform Chris recognized from the back as one of the rookies. Andrews, she catalogued as she passed Maria Geddes, part of the crime scene investigation team. Maria wore two older cameras slung over her neck and she carried a newer digital. "Hey," Maria greeted her, headed toward the gravesite. Chris waved at her and continued toward Halstead and Andrews.

To Chris's left stood the walled enclosure of the interpretive building for the Nature Center. Chris knew the area well. When she was a beat cop, she had broken up numerous illicit parties along the banks of the river, usually involving drugs, alcohol, and teenagers. More people used the park for legitimate reasons, fortunately. Even in winter months like now, the bosque was popular with runners, cyclists, and assorted sportsters taking advantage of dry weather for athletic pursuits. The Nature Center wasn't necessarily easy to find, though, because it wasn't marked on any major thoroughfares in the city. The perp probably knew the Albuquerque area, which might narrow the field of inquiry.

The Nature Center closed around five but the bosque was always open, accessible by a hundred-yard walk down a paved path from Candelaria, a sleepy residential street lined by a mixture of old money and older haciendas and new money and newer multi-storied residences behind high adobe walls. The street dead-ended in a turn-around in front of the Nature Center. After dark, the cottonwood forest could be dangerous, as homeless people and tweakers often used the area as a campground in spite of park patrols. Had the killer known that? The body hadn't been hidden well, so whoever put the vic in the grave was probably looking for a quick body dump, after dark.

Erin raised her sunglasses and perched them on her head. Uniforms milled around the parking lot, keeping curious onlookers at bay. The mobile crime lab—a tricked-out RV—was parked closest to the trailhead at the Center.

"So I understand you're the lucky winner," Chris said, tone dry. She nodded in greeting to Andrews, who moved away, suddenly engaging himself with dissuading a few curious spectators from getting too close to the path into the bosque. Chris looked past Erin toward the turn-off into the Nature Center's parking lot as a media van eased in, avoiding a huge rut at the entrance. She turned her attention back to Erin, who could easily have passed for a California surfer girl, all long blond hair and blue eyes. She kept her hair tied back in a pony tail when she was working, but she still attracted lots of attention from the straight male cops on the force. And a few not-so-straight females. Not really Chris's type, but Chris could see why people of both sexes allowed their gazes to linger much longer than necessary on Erin. Especially when she was in uniform.

"Yep. Got the call at thirteen thirty-six." Erin's tone broadcast calm professionalism. Smooth. Chris knew the tone. The younger ones always had it. A detached, almost military cadence. Confident but cautious, especially when interacting with older cops like her.

"Fill me in." Chris joined Erin at the car, leaning her right side on it, arm braced on the roof, demeanor as casual as ever. In spite of her easygoing manner, Chris was focused entirely on Erin and what information she had.

"Teenager found him. One of those BMX racers. He was down here practicing and took a jump—you probably saw it. A pile of dirt between the grave and river. About ten feet tall."

Chris nodded once. She *had* seen it, top packed hard and smooth beneath myriad BMX bike tire assaults.

"He took the jump and landed it, but his front wheel caught on a rock and he endoed. When he got up, he looked to his right and damn if the back of our vic's head and a few of his fingers weren't sticking up out of the dirt."

That would explain the disturbance on the ground near the body. The teenager's bike wreck. Chris pursed her lips, thinking. "Where is he now?"

"Over there, with Jenkins." Erin turned her head to the left and gestured with her chin. Chris saw a lanky blond-haired young man standing next to another uniform, talking. He wore a bright yellow long-sleeved shirt with anime designs all over it and black padded leggings, typical of BMX racers. Extra padding puffed out the elbows and knees. A big white bandage covered his chin.

"His name's Paul Woodfin. I told him he had to hang out awhile because some of the bigger department guns would need to shake him down for info." The expression in her eyes was sly though her tone was neutral.

"That's right. I'm the biggest damn gun on the force." Chris took the jibe and tossed it back at her. "When there're teenagers to interrogate, they wheel me out of my cage, like Hannibal Lecter."

Erin's mouth twitched in a smile.

"So walk me through it." Chris settled in against the car.

"Arrived on the scene at thirteen forty-two. I was just off the Plaza over there on Rio Grande and Central when the call came in. Woodfin met me in the parking lot, actually. His chin was bleeding pretty badly, so I called for an ambulance, which arrived at thirteen fifty-one. They cleaned him up and at fourteen-oh-seven he led me to the body. He had left his bike there with his friend, Rodney Garcia."

"Garcia still here?"

"Yep. He's the kid over there behind Woodfin."

Chris followed Erin's gaze over the top of the patrol car and saw another teen, mostly hidden behind Woodfin's greater height. "And?"

"Garcia was not near the body. He was standing by the bike jump to make sure nobody else rode it. Smart kids, actually. Woodfin didn't follow me to the body. He stayed on the perimeter and pointed. I did a quick visual, then retreated in my footprints and called it in. I took photos and roped it off, then put a uniform over where Garcia was and took 'em both to the parking lot with me. I've already interviewed 'em but you'll want to do your own follow-up."

"Other witnesses?"

"Nope. Garcia tells me nobody else was riding the trail. No surprise, really. It's January and gets dark early. Plus it's a school day." She arched an eyebrow.

"Our boys missing classes?" The thought amused Chris.

"They both admitted they skipped out at lunch. Woodfin drives.

That's his truck by the meat wagon. They're students at Highland."

A Southeast Heights high school. Middle- and working-class neighborhoods that abutted Albuquerque's War Zone, an area known for drugs, gangs, and violence. The Nature Center was part of the northwest quadrant of the city, generally a better area. It provided easy access to the trails along the river and a place to park.

Chris pushed off the car and stood regarding Halstead. "What's your take?"

Erin looked surprised, as if no one had ever asked her opinion. "From the look of the dirt when I got there, I don't think he'd been in the ground that long. A few days tops. The perp was either sloppy or in a hurry. I think both. I'm surprised coyotes or dogs didn't dig him up, actually."

"What else?"

Erin was quiet for a moment before answering. When she did, she sounded thoughtful. "I think the vic was dead when the perp brought him here. Maybe he was looking for a quick body dump. I don't think he had much time to really think this through. I mean, shallow grave, close to a trail? I don't think he had a light with him or decent tools. So maybe he didn't mean for the vic to die. Or if he did want to kill him, something made him do it before he could really plan it out. Depending on what kind of homicide this is."

A slow smile pulled the right side of Chris's mouth up. "My thoughts exactly. What's your take on Woodfin and Garcia?"

Erin relaxed at Chris's encouragement. "They're good kids, doing what kids do on a reasonably nice January day in Albuquerque. They get their gear and go tear it up in the bosque before they have to get home. Except this time, their folks are gonna bust 'em for ditching school." She shrugged and Chris saw a tiny smile edge the corners of Erin's mouth. It softened her features.

"I take it you've — ah — engaged in such behavior?" she teased.

Erin snorted and smiled. "Who hasn't?"

Before Chris could respond, Harper's voice interrupted the conversation. "Hey, Gucci, I got nothin'." The nickname grated across her nerves. He was originally from North Dakota and couldn't pronounce Spanish to save his gringo ass. In addition to his insensitive and often sexist and homophobic remarks, he felt compelled to grant everyone he knew a nickname. The one he bestowed upon Chris was his attempt at her last name, which he mangled as "goo-chee-hair-eez" when he deigned to use it.

"Jesus, Harper, I hate that name." Chris made a disgusted noise in the back of her throat.

"Not to mention, the detective ain't exactly a Gucci girl," Erin added innocently. "She's more Eddie Bauer, maybe."

Harper ignored them both and zipped up his windbreaker. A

big, raw-boned man with broad features, pale blue eyes, and
strawberry-blond hair he kept cropped in a military buzzcut, he fit
Chris's idea of what a corn-fed Midwestern male should look like. "I
think our boy took a straight shot with the vic from parking lot to
grave. He did what he had to do, then went right back to the parking
lot."

"Detective Gutierrez and I were just discussing that," Erin said,
putting a deliberate emphasis on her correct pronunciation of Chris's
last name.

Chris swallowed a laugh.

If Harper caught the dig, he didn't acknowledge it. "On the
other hand," he said slowly, looking at a page in his little pocket
notebook, "could be the perp put the vic in a busy spot like that so
trace around the grave could get wiped out. Maybe he's done this
before. Or maybe he's just some loser perv getting his rocks off."

Chris looked at him with grudging interest. "Not a bad idea."
She braced her hands on her hips, pondering. "Yeah. I can see that.
Still, it's risky because so many people and dogs come through here
that the body could have been discovered faster than the perp liked.
But it's something to think about." She turned her attention back to
Erin. "Thanks for the update. I'd appreciate a copy of your report,
and I want to compare notes on Woodfin and Garcia with you."

"No problem. Let me know." Erin pushed off from the side of
her car and moved quickly to head off a group of reporters who were
bee-lining for the trail into the bosque.

"I'm going to talk to the guys who found the body. You'd better
be in on this, too," Chris said to Harper as she headed across the
parking lot. He grunted a response and followed her.

Chapter
Two

CHRIS SAID GOODBYE to Paul Woodfin's mom, then hung up and handed the cell phone back to him.

"Thanks," he said, grateful. "She was probably gonna have a major freak-out. I'm already in trouble for ditching school."

Chris smiled at him. "The trick is, keep your grades up and your nose clean and the ditching stuff—" she shrugged noncommittally.

Rodney's father pulled into the parking lot to pick his son up. Chris went over to chat with him and make sure he understood what was going on to spare Rodney some parental displeasure. The teen loaded his bike into the back of the SUV and waved at her as he climbed into the passenger seat. Chris stepped back and watched them leave, then checked her watch. Nearly seven. The chill winter night descended quickly in the dry air and she was glad she had brought her mid-weight jacket with her. Nice kids, she decided. Funny and articulate. The stories both teens told matched what they had said to Erin, so Chris had given them each one of her business cards with instructions to call if they thought of anything else.

Harper had let Chris handle the interviews with Woodfin and Garcia. She had worked with him twice before this and he generally played silent straight man to her casual cop approach. She appreciated it, actually, and she was hard-pressed to find much to appreciate about him.

After she finished with the teens, she checked in with security at the Nature Center and got the names of all the bosque rangers. She'd have to talk with each of them, but it would be best to do so if she had a clearer idea of how long the vic had been dead. Harper offered to find Sam about identifying the body and then to check in with Nature Center staff. Chris didn't protest. He could be an ass, but he was patient and generally meticulous in his work. Maybe that's why Jerry wanted him on this. Chris wished they had the staff for another homicide detective based out of Valley Area Command. APD generally preferred three detectives on a murder, but they didn't have the staffing. Jerry, thus, would be operating as the third man *and* case leader. Double duty for him again. And more work for her and Harper. *Ah, the glamorous life of APD law enforcement.*

She slid into the front seat of her personal vehicle, a silver sporty Pontiac Vibe, and started the engine. Just another fourteen-hour day. She was tired, hungry, and chilled. *And another romantic evening with* Nuestra Señora de Pizza. As if on cue, her cell phone rang. She pulled it out of her jacket pocket and smiled when she saw the ID.

"Hey, *esa*," she answered.

"Detective Supah-fly, your presence is required at our house right now."

Chris laughed. She couldn't help it. K.C. Fontero, her longtime best friend, had that effect on her. "Oh, really. What if I had an ultra-shitty day?"

"All the more reason to get your hot ass on over here."

"Does Sage know you talk dirty to me?" Chris asked, teasing.

"Please. She's standing here feeding me lines. And speaking of feeding, we've got dinner and I know you haven't eaten yet."

Chris sighed. "Watched the news again, huh?"

"Yeah." K.C.'s voice took on a more serious tone. "Tough day, *mujer.* So put it away for a couple of hours and chill with us."

"Actually, that sounds great. I'll see you in about a half-hour."

"Excellent. Roger that, Houston. Out."

Chris smiled as the line went dead. She put her car into reverse and backed out of the space, then headed for the exit, driving slowly to avoid press and bystanders still milling around. Andrews waved at her as she passed. She waved back and turned onto Candelaria, feeling a sense of relief to be leaving a scene of death behind. Chris stayed on Candelaria, driving east toward Carlisle. She flicked on her iPod and Norah Jones's voice filled the car, smoothing the jagged edges of the day.

She turned right onto Carlisle and stopped at a small upscale liquor store on the corner of Lomas and Carlisle where she bought a bottle of wine, a local cabernet from Casa Rondeña vineyard. She then jagged onto Monte Vista and turned onto Berkeley to park in front of the house. A string of red plastic chile lights hung from the roofed porch, lending it a festive and typical Albuquerque air. She grabbed the wine and locked up.

As she climbed the five steps onto the covered porch, K.C. threw the front door open.

"¡Ay caramba! Bienvenidos, tall, dark, and handsome!" She put her hand on her heart and staggered, then quickly recovered, laughing. She was wearing her usual faded sweatshirt, jeans, Birkenstocks, and a baseball cap, bill to the back.

Chris laughed as well and leaned in to peck her on the cheek. "With friends like you, who needs lovers?" She handed the bottle to

K.C., who took it and pulled her into the big front room that served as both living and dining areas.

"Hi, Chris," Sage called from the kitchen. "Sit down!"

K.C. shrugged, an "uh-oh" expression on her face. "Better do it. You know how she can get. You working tomorrow?"

"Technically, no."

"So, you want a glass?" She held the wine bottle up.

"Yes, please." She put an emphasis on the please.

K.C. grinned and headed for the doorway into the kitchen. Chris tossed her jacket onto the closest couch, one of two that sat at right angles in the center of the room. The back of one served as a divider between living room and dining area. She took a seat at the big comfortable Mexican-style table near the kitchen doorway and allowed the warmth in the house to wash over her. The soft strains of Brazilian chill music emanated from the sound system hidden in a rustic armoire that Sage had painted with bright designs reminiscent of Oaxacan folk art.

"Hey," the artist in question greeted her as she emerged from the kitchen carrying a big plate of food, brown hair pulled back, exposing her sparkling brown eyes and elegant cheekbones. A bundle of energy and mysticism, Sage proved a perfect counterpoint to K.C.'s inherent analytical streaks and research bent.

"Sage, you're a goddess."

"So K.C. tells me." She winked and put the plate on the placemat in front of Chris, then handed her a fork and knife.

"Well, she's right." Chris shook her head in wonderment at the tamales, rice, and *chilaquiles* that graced the plate. "God, this is unbelievable. Thank you *so* much for hooking up with my best friend."

Sage laughed and leaned over to plant a kiss on the top of Chris's head. "Well, you know. Tough job, but *someone's* gotta do it."

"That's the truth." K.C. appeared, carrying two glasses of wine. One she handed to Sage, the other she put on the table next to Chris. She looked questioningly at Sage, as if to say "anything else?" Sage took K.C.'s hand and brought it to her lips for a quick kiss. "I'm good," she said softly.

K.C. smiled. "Well, then, I think I'll join you." She retreated to the kitchen only to return seconds later with a glass of wine for herself. She and Sage took chairs at the table, chatting with Chris and each other while she ate.

Chris finished, feeling more than contented, and moved the plate carefully out of her way. Sage was an excellent cook. The masa of the tamales practically melted in her mouth and the *chilaquiles* exploded with flavor and spice.

"More?" Sage reached for her plate.

She shook her head. "I'm good, thanks. That was superb. It'd give *Abuelita* a run for her money."

"Hardly," Sage said, giggling. "I've had *Abuelita*'s cooking. But I do like talking food with the both of you. Thanks for sharing your grandma." She took Chris's plate into the kitchen and returned with the bottle of wine, refilling all three glasses and setting the empty bottle on the table before sitting down again.

"So how'd you know I had a bad day? Did the media manage to catch me this time?" Chris reached for her glass.

"Nah. I just had a feeling it was a case you'd have to deal with." K.C. picked up her own glass. "Dead guy. Bosque. And you've worked homicides, if that's the situation."

Chris nodded slowly. "It's a sad one. Ugly."

"You have to work on it this weekend?" K.C. took a sip of her wine.

"Yep. Some, at least. Once the crime lab gets a time of death and hopefully an ID, we'll be able to really rock n' roll." Chris picked up her glass and leaned back in her chair.

A cell phone rang from one of the bedrooms. Sage bounced out of her chair. "That's mine."

Chris heard her answer the phone in the other room. She reappeared, talking animatedly.

"River?" K.C. asked softly, looking at her.

Sage nodded and grinned, talking a mile a minute to her brother.

"Tell him hi for us." K.C. stood and picked up her glass of wine. "C'mon," she said to Chris. "Join me on the patio."

Chris retrieved her jacket, then grabbed her glass from the table and followed K.C. through the kitchen and mud room onto the back porch. K.C. had moved back to Albuquerque from Austin last summer and ended up living in the small mother-in-law cottage not ten yards from the steps of the back porch. That's how she and Sage had met two years ago. Now Jeff Abeyta, Sage's former roommate and good friend, occupied the cottage. From the looks of the darkened windows, he wasn't home.

K.C., Jeff, Sage, and Chris had installed a patio off the porch and built a ramada over it. Sage had planted grapes and honeysuckle with the hopes that the vines would climb up the posts and eventually wind their way around the two-by-fours set at six-inch intervals that served as a stylized roof. So far, the honeysuckle had tracked a couple of feet up the four corner posts. It'd smell great come spring.

"Nothing like a fire on a night like this." K.C. set her glass on a small wooden end table across from a large chiminea that dominated a corner of the patio. She took a book of matches out of her front pocket, struck one, and held it to the newspaper she had already stuffed into the opening beneath the kindling. Chris watched as tiny flames licked the paper, tentatively at first. K.C. struck another match for good measure and held it to another spot in the chiminea's opening. The flames spread, devouring the paper and moving hungrily to the wood. Chris settled into one of the chairs and stretched her feet out to the fire. Smoke and heat rushed out the chiminea's slender top spout. K.C. took a small log from a nearby stack and with a practiced motion placed it in the fire. She then sank into a chair on Chris's right.

A warm silence fell between them. Chris loved that about her friendship with K.C. It was easy and comfortable, like a favorite pair of jeans. K.C. was waiting for her to choose the topic of conversation, but if nothing was said, that would be okay, too. Chris leaned back and tilted her head to the sky, visible between the two-by-fours. No moon yet, so she could see stars.

On a night like this, she missed the sexual relationship she and K.C. had shared in the past, when neither was seeing anyone. Chris had no difficulty finding women to join her in bed every now and again, but sometimes she really needed the trust she had with K.C. to be part of that experience. And that was something Chris doubted she'd find with anyone else, though she'd gotten her hopes up last summer, when she'd met an attorney in Santa Fe at a law conference. Chris took another sip of wine. Dayna had gone to California in November to help her mom after an accident and...nothing since December. And since Dayna had left, Chris hadn't dated anyone. She actually missed Dayna. *Weird.*

"Lonely cop moment?" K.C. kept her eyes on the fire, her glass propped on her right thigh.

"You know me too well, *esa*," Chris said wistfully.

"No such thing. Have you heard from her?"

"Nope."

K.C. reached over and squeezed Chris's forearm. "She'll show up."

Chris managed a smile. "Says who?"

"Sage." K.C. leaned back in her chair then set her glass down before she poked at the fire with a two-foot long piece of rebar. "And she isn't wrong about shit like that."

"She felt a tremor in The Force, huh?"

K.C. set the poker down and picked up her wine. "You know how she is. She just *knows* shit."

"Doesn't really matter," Chris said, watching the fire. "Maybe it's not my path."

K.C. paused and took a drink. "Tell me about the victim."

Chris smiled against her glass. K.C. also knew exactly when to press her about her work, to "clear the bad ju-ju," as Sage liked to say. "Young white male." She thought about the ring on his finger and wondered if it had had any special meaning for him.

"Anything I can do to help?"

"Not sure yet. I only saw his back. I don't think it's a typical hate crime, but there's something about it that doesn't feel right. I think he was gay, and I think that played into this, but I don't know how." She stared into the flames. "I hate this shit. I hate that people die for being gay."

K.C. made a sympathetic noise and took another sip of wine.

"Your guys leave calling cards, for the most part," Chris said thoughtfully. She didn't recall seeing anything that looked remotely like a white supremacist symbol on or near the body, though since K.C.'s experience summer before last, when she returned to Albuquerque to help locate her ex's sister Megan, Chris made it a habit to check for such things when investigating certain cases.

"True. Swastikas especially. No mistaking what *that* is. Still, you don't have to be a white supremacist to do a hate crime. Or even white."

"No, but it helps."

K.C. chuckled. "A lot." She got up and put another piece of wood in the chiminea, returned to her chair, and looked at Chris. "If you find out this case needs my eyes, let me know."

"It's a murder, *chica*. Some things maybe you don't want to know."

"I love that you try to protect my sensibilities. But I'd be really pissed at you if this case turns out to involve my research topic and you didn't ask me for help. I *do* consult with APD and the local FBI since the Megan situation."

Chris sighed. "Why couldn't Megan just hook up with a nice, nerdy engineer? No, she had to go for the neo-Nazi. And not just any neo-Nazi. She had to go for the leader. The *cabrón* who was all into stashing major weaponry." She rubbed her forehead at the memories, thinking about how K.C. had ended up with a knife at her throat outside an Albuquerque tattoo parlor and, worse, getting shot at because her ex's younger sister fell in with the wrong crowd.

"Hey, whatever. It brought me back here. And we got Megan out of that group and on a better track."

Chris laughed softly. "Only *you* would say that about what happened."

"All the more reason to let me help you if this case turns out to involve the people I spend an inordinate amount of time researching."

"It's ugly, Kase. And you're one of the things in my life that I would like to keep untainted." K.C. opened her mouth to say something but Chris held up her hand. "But I know you're a big girl and, yes, if something pops up here that might need your expertise, I'll let you know."

"Thanks for being aware of my delicate nature," K.C. said with pronounced innocence.

Chris shot her a look and K.C. batted her eyes. Chris tried to glare, but K.C. only made kissing noises at her.

"C'mon, Detective Hotshot. You know I would never forgive you if that poor guy died at the hands of the assholes I study and you didn't ask for my input."

"You would *so* forgive me."

"Nuh-uh."

"You can't live without me," Chris said smugly as she lifted her glass to her lips.

"Well, *duh*. But I can still not live without you *and* never forgive you. I'd just keep you around so I could give you stink-eye, which would get boring after a while, but it's the principle of the thing."

Chris started laughing. "I love you, Kase."

"I know. I love you back." She leaned forward in her chair, watching the fire. "How's *Abuelita*?"

"Good. She's feeling much better. Nasty case of the flu. Not pneumonia, thank God. I'm supposed to go over on Sunday and do some stuff around the house for her." Chris took another sip of wine and glanced over at K.C. "You talk to your grandpa?"

"Yeah, actually. A couple of days ago. Things are about the same. He sounded good. You know how he is. Won't admit his arthritis bothers him. But Mom says he's actually getting around fine and he's got a couple of guys who help him out around the farm."

"Do you ever miss Texas?" Chris watched K.C.'s face, felt the way the past joined them. Like sisters in some ways.

K.C. turned to her and grinned. "Hell, no. I miss Grandpa, but I never could bond with Texas. You know that. You told me enough times when I came back to help Megan and Melissa. Besides, I just can't live without *you*," she teased.

"True," Chris said. "And speaking of Megan, what's she up to?"

"Doing well in school. Oregon's good for her. She called a few days ago, actually." K.C. stared into her wine glass. "I'm really glad she left Albuquerque. Melissa was acting more like a parent than a sister with her."

Chris nodded. K.C. was right. Megan's struggles with addiction had created a seriously unhealthy dynamic with Melissa. But then, addiction had a way of doing that. She'd seen it while pursuing her certification as a counselor and then as a police officer.

"Megan being out of state like this helps them both work on boundaries," K.C. continued. "And I'm really proud of Megan, working on her shit like that. She's still in therapy on her own, too. Chillin' with apocalyptic white supremacist gun nuts kinda messes with you," she said wryly.

"No argument there."

"You know, *amiga*," K.C. said softly, "you're responsible for how well a lot of that turned out."

Chris shrugged. "That's just what you do for your friends. And you're the best of the bunch. So how is Melissa?"

"Pretty good, too. It's weird for me, being friends with an ex like that, but I guess Megan kind of keeps us linked. Maybe I sort of adopted Megan as another sister." She stretched her legs out. "But Melissa's still in therapy too, and she's doing pretty well, last I saw. More relaxed than I've ever seen her."

"Good." Chris took another sip of wine.

"She asks about you when I see her."

"Huh."

K.C. flashed a grin at her. "I think she decided she might like you a little bit, after what went down with Megan and the freaks."

"I've always liked Melissa. I just didn't think she was right for you." Chris winked at her. "Sage. Now *she's* a good match." A completely goofy expression crossed K.C.'s features and Chris laughed. "Damn, *esa*. You are so in love!"

K.C. cleared her throat. "I am," she said quietly before motioning at Chris's glass. "You want more wine? We have another bottle."

"Nah. I have to go track some folks down tomorrow while things are still reasonably fresh."

"You okay? You can crash here tonight."

Chris smiled at her. "You take such good care of me."

"I told you I'd always have a room for you, Detective I'll-never-find-anybody-to-love-me. Even though I think your attitude is *such* a crock. And I know that deep down, you're a one-woman kinda gal."

"Kase—"

"I tease you because I can and because I know how you are and I know all the things you tell yourself to keep your walls up. You're an awesome catch. Just let someone hook you."

The back door opened.

"Jesus, you're starting to sound like Sage," Chris retorted good-naturedly.

"Good. I'm rubbing off." Sage descended the steps carrying two mugs. She handed one to K.C. and the other to Chris. "It's decaf."

K.C. stood and pulled a chair over, positioning it between her and Chris. Sage sat down.

"River's great," Sage said. "Hunting seasons are pretty much over but he made a shitload. He's working again at the gun store until this summer. He's thinking about spending some time in Cheyenne with Mom. And he sends his love to you both."

K.C. took Sage's right hand in her left and stroked her knuckles with her thumb. The look they exchanged echoed through Chris's heart and she smiled. K.C. had fought her attraction to Sage at first, then finally gave in, Chris providing pep talks like a coach at a big game. The photographer was good for Kase, Chris had figured out right away. And though she herself hadn't had much luck with relationships, she wondered what it would be like to share a moment like that with someone. Maybe K.C. was right. Maybe she just hadn't let anyone really get to know her. Or maybe she just wasn't meant to have a long-term relationship. She sipped her coffee. Sage had flavored it with cinnamon and chocolate. "Damn, this is so good. Sage, can I marry you?"

"I guess it's up to K.C." Sage threw a glance at her partner. "Honey, Chris wants to marry me. What do you think?"

"Sure. But only if she marries me, too."

Sage turned her head back to Chris. "Well?"

Chris took another sip before answering. "Oh, all right. But I get my own room. Christ, we sound like we're about to run off and join a polygamous cult or some shit."

"And your problem with that is...what?" K.C. waggled her eyebrows. "Maybe I'll start researching stuff like that."

Sage reached over and playfully smacked her on the arm. The conversation drifted to K.C.'s teaching contract in the Department of American Studies at UNM — it was good for two years — and Sage's upcoming trip to the Baja. She had been commissioned by *Adventure* magazine to do a shoot there in April. In the meantime, she was teaching two workshops through the Fine Arts Department at UNM.

Chris thought about her own work, wondered what it would be like to go to the Baja for a work assignment. *Maybe I need a vacation.* She listened to Sage and K.C. banter back and forth and interjected good-natured comments at K.C.'s ribbing until she finished her coffee and checked her watch.

"Uh-oh," K.C. said. "She's checking the time."

Chris stood. "Yep. I'm beyond tired. And you know how this goes. Crime doesn't stop, even on weekends." She picked up her wine glass and coffee cup. K.C. and Sage stood with one accord and preceded her up the steps to the porch. Sage held the door open and Chris set her cup and glass on the counter while K.C. wandered into the living room, probably on her way to the bathroom. Chris turned to Sage. "Thanks so much for dinner."

"You're always welcome." Sage pulled her into a hug, then released her. "K.C.'s right, you know."

"Oh? About what?"

"Letting someone hook you."

Chris smiled and shook her head. "You too, huh?"

She shrugged, a funny little smile at the corners of her mouth, like she knew the secrets of the universe but only revealed them at certain times to certain people. "You encourage in others what you bury in yourself. Maybe it's time to consider another channel. Or keep one open." She arched an eyebrow. "And sometimes what you're looking for is right under your nose."

"I don't know. And right now, I've got way too much going on at work."

"You *always* have way too much going on at work. But when the time comes, make room."

From the other room, Chris heard a door open and K.C.'s footsteps on the hardwood floor of the hallway between the bedrooms until she appeared in the doorway, waiting. "Good night," Chris said to Sage. "Thanks again."

"Of course."

"I'm walking you to your car," K.C. announced. "It's scary out there, you know." She looked at Sage, smiling. "Back in a few."

Chris rolled her eyes and brushed past K.C. "Yeah, I need an escort." K.C. almost always walked her to her car, a longstanding tradition between them.

"That's me. K.C.'s escort-a-cop." She followed Chris out of the house and down the steps to the car at the curb.

Chris stood next to K.C., hands in her jacket pockets. "Thanks, *esa*," she said. "I really needed this."

"I know." K.C. smiled mischievously. "So did you have a mystical Sage moment?"

Chris looked at her, surprised. "How—"

"I told you. Hurricane Sage."

"And I remember telling *you* she'd be good for you."

"So we're both right." K.C. wrapped her in a bear hug. "Call any time. And don't play that protective bullshit with me on this, okay? Sometimes it's okay to ask for a little help on the road of life."

"Good fucking God," Chris groaned against K.C.'s head. "Are you reading tarot now, too?"

"Nah. That's one of Sage's things." K.C. released her. "Go home and get some sleep. Let me know if you need *anything*."

"Yeah, yeah." Chris smiled and walked around to the driver's side. She unlocked the door and pulled it open. "Kase—"

She turned, waiting.

"Thanks."

"Damn right. See ya, Detective hard-to-reach."

"*Hasta*, Doctor know-it-all." Chris blew her a kiss and got into the driver's seat. She pulled away from the curb and threw a wave at

K.C. By the time Chris reached the end of the block, K.C. had gone inside. Chris turned her music on and headed home, thinking about the day and an unknown young man lying face-down in a makeshift grave.

Chapter
Three

CHRIS PUSHED BACK from her desk and stretched. She'd been working on her report for the past two hours and she needed a break. That morning, she had managed to catch three bosque rangers between shifts and she interviewed each at the Nature Center though they couldn't shed any light on the case. Nope, didn't see anything beyond the usual shit. Homeless, teenagers, junkies. And a couple of indefinable nutjob types. Nothing out of the ordinary, Chris had thought as she talked to them. Two other rangers had shifts in the bosque but Chris ruled out interviewing one because he'd been on vacation for the past week and before that he was at Coronado Monument up in Bernalillo. That left one more and she had already left a message with him. She hadn't heard from Harper yet, but he'd check in when he had something. He was trying to get an ID on the vic.

She let her gaze drift to the photos on her desk, framed and standing at the far left corner next to a small Mexican-style vase full of a variety of pens and pencils. One photo was of her with *Abuelita*. Another showed her in full dress uniform when she graduated from the police academy eight years ago, and another held the Gutierrez family portrait: Chris, her parents, and three brothers. Chris's father stood six feet, two inches and he had passed those genes on to Chris and her older brother Mike. Her two younger brothers, Pete and then John, stood about five-seven and five-six, slightly shorter than Chris. She and Mike still teased their younger siblings about it. The last photo showed Chris, K.C., and Sage on a hike last summer. They were posed at the trailhead, arms around each other. Another hiker had taken the photo for them. A guy with a black lab, Chris remembered.

"Whazzup, homes?" Detective Alan Mitchell popped his head into her cubicle, affecting a New Mexico *cholo* accent. He resembled actor Gary Sinise, especially in the hard line of his jaw and the boyish glint in his eyes. Al wore his light brown hair longer, however. It fell past his ears.

"Christ, Al. You sound like Cheech." Chris's desk faced the

doorway of her cubicle and she shook her head at him in a long-suffering motion.

"I try." He entered her office space and placed a cup of Starbucks coffee on her desk. "For you, *mi amor.*"

"Nice. But I'm not going to go out with you. Ever. But thanks." She reached for the cup and took a tentative sip. Black, with a tiny bit of sugar. *Yum.*

He grabbed the chair she kept against the opposite wall and slid it in front of her desk so he could plop into it. "Hey, can't blame a guy for tryin'." He wore jeans and a long-sleeved red tee today along with beat-up running shoes.

"Give it up, bro." She smiled at him. "I'm not into guys." She recited it like a mantra, though with him, it was more teasing than anything.

He grinned, and his brown eyes crinkled at the corners. "Me, either. See? We have things in common." He took a swallow of coffee.

"You are too much. What's up?"

"Heard you and Harper are workin' the bosque case."

"Must you remind me? I was enjoying the peace and tranquility of a Saturday afternoon here at the station." She frowned.

"Yeah. You and Buddha. Anyway, what do you think?"

Chris watched him over the plastic top of her coffee cup. "Not much at this point. We've got a young, presumably Caucasian male buried nude, hands tied behind his back. Nobody saw anything. Nobody I've talked to, anyway. Autopsy results won't be in for a couple of days, though Sam's trying to get it done. I'm waiting on an ID. Why?"

He shrugged, affecting an innocent air. "Oh, well, you know, I was talking to a buddy of mine down in El Paso—war stories and shit like that. We got to tossing cold cases around and he mentioned one he knew about in Las Cruces about six years ago that stumped him when he was there. White kid, early twenties. Buried in a shallow grave, hands behind his back."

Chris leaned forward. A familiar anticipation clenched her gut. "Naked?"

"As the day he was born, yep."

"No shit?"

"None at all."

She leaned back in her chair, tugging on her lower lip. "That sounds just a tad suspicious."

"Yeah, I thought so, too." He smiled angelically.

"Can you—"

"Done." He reached into his shirt pocket and took out a folded piece of paper that he tossed onto her desk. "Carl Maestes. Call him on his cell. Tell him I sent you. You never know. There could be a relationship." He put a slight emphasis on the last word.

"Between two dead men, yes. Between you and me, no."

He pretended to pout. "Damn, Detective. You're just so *fine*. You gonna let all that good stuff go to waste?"

She grinned wickedly. "Nope. There are a number of women who would assure you that *nothing's* gone to waste where that's concerned."

His eyes widened and a flush spread over his face. He quickly took a drink of coffee and she snickered. "Shit," he muttered.

"C'mon," she pushed. "Don't think I don't know about the bets. When are you guys gonna get tired of that? It's been four years since I made detective."

He shrugged, sheepish. "The bet changed, actually, when Halstead got here."

Chris stared at him in disbelief. "Oh, so now it's when I'm gonna bag *her*? She got here, what—two years ago?"

He looked like a kid busted with his hand in a cookie jar.

Chris shook her head. "Two fuckin' years and you *still* have a bet. For the record, she's straight and very happy with her boyfriend, who recently became her fiancé. Get with it, Cheech. You're not up on *all* the latest gossip." *Guy cop bullshit.* Good thing she grew up with brothers. She was used to dealing with men.

"But women are different," he pressed. "They'll do a chick even if they're straight."

"You're a *pendejo*," she snorted.

"What?" He looked hurt.

"I'm not even going to dignify that with a response. You want a bet? Here's one. How long before I haul off and smack the shit out of Harper for calling me 'Gucci'?"

Al picked at a thread on his jeans. "Yeah, he does come up with some bullshit, doesn't he? Mine's Donut."

"For?"

"Mitchell...Winchell. Donut. And you think *you've* got a bad one." He rolled his eyes and took a sip of his coffee.

Chris groaned in sympathy. "Okay, that just *might* be worse than mine. So maybe I should start a pool on when *you* smack the shit out of him." She began organizing the papers on her desk, knowing he'd take it as a signal to leave. He did.

"Thanks for the coffee. And the tip." She looked up at him.

"Hey, you know I was only kidding about—"

"Yeah. Don't worry about it. *Hasta.*"

He left and Chris watched his head bob over the wall of her cubicle as he headed toward his own office space. He was working on solving a series of bank robberies in the Northeast Heights. Chris knew he'd rather work homicide, but when Harper transferred in from Fargo, he actually had more experience than Mitchell. *Too bad. I'd rather hang with Donut.*

Chris had learned her methods working several homicides with Jerry Torrez, one of the senior detectives and current Homicide Sergeant. His by-the-book relentless pursuit of every lead ensured a case was solved. If it wasn't, his colleagues joked, it was because the perp was actually made of air and Jerry just hadn't found it yet to analyze its content.

Jerry had taken Chris under his wing, maybe because they shared deep New Mexican roots. He was a mentor to her and eventually, the work that she did made an impression on the higher-ups so she got called to more and more of the tougher cases. Jerry was proud of her and he told her so. She had also picked up some of his habits when approaching an investigation, including an almost obsessive attention to detail.

Chris smiled. She ragged K.C. about working too much and being too anal and here *she* was, doing the exact same thing. *Maybe I do work too much. Maybe Sage is right.* Chris's fingers hovered over the keyboard. *Or maybe I just need to get laid.* That was probably it. She continued typing but her mind wandered back to what Sage said last night. *"You encourage in others what you bury in yourself."* She stopped typing and stared blankly at the screen. Her desk phone rang, jerking her back to her office. She answered it.

"Hi. Gutierrez here."

"Oh, yeah. This is Marty Holmes? You left a message that you needed to talk to me?" The bosque ranger finished his sentences as if they were questions.

"Thanks for calling me back, Mr. Holmes —"

"Marty."

"Okay. Marty. Do you have a few minutes in the next day or so? I can meet you —"

"Now's fine. I'm at the Nature Center."

Chris pursed her lips in mild frustration. He also tended to interrupt. "Great. I'll be there in about thirty minutes." *Back to the Nature Center.* She'd been there more in the past two days than she had in the past year.

"Sounds good. See you then." He hung up.

Chris exhaled, irritated, and returned the phone to its cradle. Hopefully, he knew nothing. She didn't want to have to put up with his apparent lack of social graces too long. *Of course, I could always put Harper on him.* That thought made her smile. She saved what she was doing on the computer, logged out, and shut it down before she stood and pulled her black leather jacket off the top of the file cabinet, situated in a corner behind her desk, and slid her arms in before picking up the Starbucks cup.

"I'm outta here, Al," she called.

"All right. Catch you later," his disembodied voice responded from the opposite side of the room, most of which was a labyrinth of cubicles.

Must be a slow day. Usually at least four people worked on the weekends. Her office space was located opposite the door into the main corridor so she had to walk around the perimeter of the room to exit. She pushed through the door and headed down the broad, bright hallway to a set of double doors that locked from the outside. The administrative offices were off limits to unauthorized personnel. Chris held the handle down and pushed out into the lobby.

"Take it easy, Theresa," she said to the uniformed clerk behind the info desk.

"You, too. Have a beer for me." Theresa looked up briefly to catch Chris's eye before she continued with whatever she was doing. Chris paused and leaned over the counter. A crossword puzzle.

"Seven-letter word for idiotic," Theresa said as she tapped her pencil on the desk.

"In Spanish or English?"

"I'll bite. Spanish."

"*Gringos*. Or *hombres*."

Theresa giggled. "Oh, that reminds me. Dale called."

"And?" Chris rolled her eyes.

She picked up a scrap of paper and read, "He said he ran a missing persons check and has a few possibles on the vic. He's dropped them by the ME's today but he just wanted you to know."

"Why didn't he just call my cell or office?"

Theresa looked at the paper again. "He was calling from the ME's and left his cell in the car. Didn't have your direct line."

"Thanks. I'll call him back."

"I'm sure it'll be the highlight of your day," Theresa teased.

Chris flashed her a smile. "Oh, you know it. Later." She turned and walked across the clean but scuffed linoleum toward the front doors. This was a newer building and Chris appreciated the light, airy feeling the architects created. When she first started out as a cop, she had worked in an older sixties-style building with bad lighting, worse carpet, and ultra-crappy seventies-style furniture. It had looked like the set of a porn movie. Chris stepped into the cool January afternoon and took her shades out of her pocket. She put them on and unclipped her cell phone from her belt. As she walked across the parking lot, she dialed Harper's number. He answered on the second ring.

"Yeah. Dale Harper."

He didn't have her programmed into his cell. *Good. I'm not special enough.* "It's Chris."

"Gucci," he said in his bland baritone. "So did you get my message?"

Chris clenched then unclenched her teeth. She was convinced he called her that to deliberately get under her skin. "Yeah. So give me an update."

"Good news. We've got a dental hit on the vic. I'm at the ME's now. Can you stop by?"

"Negative. I'm on my way to the Nature Center to talk to our last ranger."

"All right. Let's see—hold on."

Chris stood next to the driver's side of her car, waiting. She heard what sounded like papers. Probably his notebook.

"Okay. Travis McCormick, twenty-four. Reported missing January twenty-second by—let me see—his roommate, Josh Hopkins." He said "roommate" with what sounded like a tinge of sarcasm. "Oh, here's something. Hopkins told us the mom's name. She's local. He said McCormick and the mom didn't have much contact but that McCormick had gone to his mom's house around the twentieth. Her name is Angela Griggs."

Chris let this information work through her brain. The twenty-second. Six days ago. But he might not have been dead since then. She squeezed her temples with the thumb and index finger of her free hand. Harper provided an address for Griggs that Chris knew was just past Tramway, the north-south boulevard that ran along the base of the Sandias. Smaller residential streets curved off Tramway into exclusive neighborhoods that followed the contours of the foothills. Massive, California-style villas with things like brick driveways and curved Spanish-like tiles on the roofs. New money. Lots of it.

"Does the mother know?" she asked.

"Not yet. Can't find her. We ran a check and found the father, who lives in Dallas, where the vic was born. Dad's name is Paul McCormick. Some kind of investment banker. As soon as we can track the mom down, we'll have her come in."

Chris sighed. This part of her job always sucked. "Okay. Keep me posted on that. I'll catch up with you after I talk to the ranger. Oh—"

"Yeah?"

"Do we have a cause of death?"

"Looks like strangulation, with the cord the perp used to tie the vic's wrists."

So perhaps the killer and the vic had been engaged in a little autoerotic asphyxiation when things went wrong? Possibly, but if there was a link to the Cruces case, there was more going on here than sex games. Why kill someone and *then* tie his hands? "Thanks. I'm on my way to the Nature Center. Oh, I've got a possible link to a cold case. I'll fill you in when I see you. Catch you later."

"Okay, then." He hung up after this, his signature sign-off.

Chris slid into the driver's seat and buckled up. *Damn. Twenty-four.* She put the car in gear and exited the parking lot, turning left onto Second. Chris hated this part of her job, when she was privy to someone else's grief, often a bearer of it. She'd had to break such news in the past, and it never got easier. For that, she was glad. If it ever did, it meant she'd lost part of her soul. She turned right onto Candelaria, hoping more than before that Marty Holmes didn't know anything so she wouldn't have to spend too much time talking to him.

BOSQUE RANGER MARTIN G. Holmes turned out to be a short, earnest man with a round, reddish, pudgy face and a slightly upturned nose, maybe in his early fifties. When he smiled, he looked like a thinner, clean-shaven Santa Claus. He was in full uniform, which he kept crisp and starched. It hugged his powerful, stocky build. Proud of his job, Chris thought. He wore his cap as if he was in the military, bill straight ahead, a half-inch above his eyebrows. The way he comported himself, Chris suspected he probably had been in the armed services at one time. He seemed entirely comfortable around her, though she stood a good six inches taller. He wore a wedding band on the ring finger of his left hand.

No, he told her, he hadn't seen anything out of the ordinary. And then he laughed, because, as they both knew, "ordinary" in the bosque could mean any number of things. He meant that he hadn't seen anyone dragging or carrying anything that might have been a dead person. He worked the noon to eight shift, and he passed the crime scene six times every shift. *Plenty of time to see something.* Unless the killer brought the body much later. That seemed more likely.

From their conversation, Chris determined that Marty knew the area extremely well and most likely would have noticed and recalled something that struck him as strange. She thanked him, which made him grin in obvious pleasure. Oh, he was so glad he could be of service and if she needed anything else, just give him a call. She handed him a business card, which he slid into his left breast pocket. He'd be sure to contact her if he saw or remembered anything. And he shook her hand warmly, tipping his hat.

Chris smiled at him as she left. She put her notebook into the inside pocket of her jacket and headed to her car, close to the parking lot entrance. Because it was a reasonably mild day, lots of people were making use of the Nature Center's easy access to the river and bike trail. Consequently, the lot was crowded with various vehicles, mostly sporty SUVs and hip Japanese sedans, bike racks on many of them. A few people wandered past, laughing and talking, some actually dressed in shorts. A dog barked from the other side of the lot.

Her shoes crunched on the gravel as she headed toward her car. Halfway there, she stopped and waited for a small blue Mazda to back out of a nearby space. From behind, she recognized the sound of mountain bike tires approaching too fast. She turned, prepared to tell the speed demon to slow down. Before she could get the words out, the rider braked suddenly, shooting a cloud of dust and dirt into the air, some of which settled on Chris's jeans. The bike's knobby front tire stopped barely a foot from her shins. The rider expertly jerked her right foot out of the pedal clip and braced it on the ground. She undid her helmet strap and pulled it off so she could shake out a wealth of curly light brown hair that fell around her shoulders.

"I'd know that ass anywhere," the rider said, laughing, as she took her sunglasses off. They hung around her neck with the help of a Croakies strap.

Chris took her own shades off, fighting a variety of emotions. "Hopefully, that's a good thing." She smiled broadly. She couldn't help it. Dayna Carson had that effect on her. "How are you?" *Damn. Ultra-sexy still.* Giddiness ricocheted through her heart. "Haven't heard from you in a while," she said, keeping her tone light though a question lingered in it.

Dayna was about to answer when a woman near a grey SUV called her name. She jerked her head in the direction of the voice. "What?"

"You wanna go with us for beers?" The speaker, a spiky-haired brunette, stood with two other female gearheads, bikes leaning against the SUV's back bumper. All three were watching Dayna and Chris with interest.

"No, not this time. I'll call you later. Thanks."

The speaker shrugged. "Okay. Take it easy." She lifted her bike onto the rack on the vehicle's tailgate.

Dayna waved and turned back to Chris. "Where were we?" she asked coyly, resting her helmet on her handlebars.

"How you are." Chris liked the way Dayna's thighs filled the black bike tights and how the garish long-sleeved jersey clung to her shoulders and breasts. She allowed lascivious thoughts to bounce around her head.

"Well, you'd know," Dayna said seductively. "In certain contexts, at least. But I believe we were discussing your ass." She grinned.

Her teeth reminded Chris of piano keys. Straight, white, clean. "True. And your verdict?"

The grey SUV passed and Dayna waved again. "Thanks, you guys!" she called as the spiky-haired brunette waved from the driver's seat. She shifted her attention back to Chris and a slow smile pulled the corners of her mouth up. "Mind-blowing."

"Why, thank you, Ms. Carson." *Flattery will get you everywhere. Especially in the mood I'm in.* She focused on Dayna's astonishingly blue eyes rather than her lips, which could put Julia Roberts' famous mouth to shame. Chris was a sucker for a well-proportioned mouth. Best to avoid looking at Dayna's lips.

"I could continue to stand here in this parking lot and flirt with you, but I think I'd prefer to do that elsewhere," Dayna said, breaking her reverie.

"Which? Stand? Or flirt?"

Dayna had a particular smile that could set stone on fire. It appeared at that instant.

"Well, *that* question just got answered," Chris said appreciatively as a jolt of warmth surged down her legs.

"Is it too forward of me to ask you to dinner tonight?" Dayna sounded hopeful.

"Not at all."

"I'd like to apologize for not talking to you for two months."

Chris smiled. "You had your reasons," she said, taking a shot in the dark with the statement. Dayna generally did have good reasons for what she did and said. Still, a little bit of anxiety lurked in the back of Chris's mind. What had happened? Why hadn't she called? *And why is it so important for me to know?*

"I did." She looked at Chris, an odd expression on her face, which dissipated as quickly as it had come. "So, Detective, how about it?" She offered another one of *those* smiles.

Chris felt her lasciviousness degenerate to lust. "I suppose it's way past the point where I could play hard to get."

"Afraid so," Dayna said with a laugh. "Given the last time I saw you."

Chris smiled again. "I'll be chivalrous. You pick the restaurant."

"Thai. Bangkok Café okay with you?"

"Always. When?"

"Seven."

"Excellent. See you then." Chris started to turn away, but Dayna reached out and grabbed her by her jacket's left lapel. She pulled her close and Chris automatically leaned in over the bike's handlebars for a soft, luscious, and demanding kiss. Dayna's tongue slid over her lips and chills raced up her spine. She'd forgive the two months of silence for that alone.

"Definitely," Dayna whispered as she pulled away and let go.

Chris put her shades back on, fully aware of the shit-eating grin on her face. She stood looking at Dayna for a few more moments, then turned and continued to her car. She could feel Dayna's eyes on her still and it gave her a little rush. *Just what the doctor ordered,* she thought as she settled into the driver's seat. A little distraction with a hot lawyer. She glanced at her watch. Four o' clock. She'd check in with Harper and give Al's El Paso connection a call. In her rearview mirror, she could see Dayna loading her bike into her Toyota truck and she breathed a thanks to Marty Holmes for having some time to talk to her that day. Chris turned her music on and headed down Candelaria, humming along to Bob Marley.

Chapter
Four

"DAMN," DAYNA GASPED as she collapsed back onto the pillows. "I need to call you more often." She was still breathing hard as she pulled Chris against her and kissed her languorously, causing all manner of sensations to race up and down Chris's nerve endings. Dayna Carson had to have the best lips in the entire lesbian universe.

"I'd have to agree," Chris murmured against her mouth, nearly losing her mind at how it felt to be naked with her. She slid her tongue between Dayna's teeth, eliciting another gasp. Dayna twisted her fingers in Chris's hair and strained against her lips while she wrapped strong, bike-riding legs around her waist. Another surge of moisture collected between Chris's thighs. *Oh, Jesus.* Dayna was beautiful clothed, but nude...*it's a world wonder that I haven't passed out.* Chris liked strong women with a bit of meat on them. She liked muscle, especially coupled with a woman's natural curves.

Dayna had that kind of body and she knew exactly how to work it. She broke the kiss first. "God, you're hot," she whispered, watching Chris's eyes. "I just look at you and want to take you to bed."

"And here we are," Chris said softly. "So what are you going to do about it?"

"Mmmm." She playfully nipped Chris's lower lip, then rewarded her with her granite-exploding smile. "Fuck you again, of course."

"By all means," Chris said with a soft laugh. She loved how Dayna could get a little racy, how she knew exactly what she wanted, and how she sensed exactly what Chris needed.

Some time later they lay sweaty and spent, twisted up together in the sheets. Dayna's head rested on Chris's shoulder and her left arm was thrown across her waist. Light from the huge pillar candle on a nearby bedside table cast a warm glow around the room. Dayna's lips brushed Chris's shoulder, an unexpectedly tender gesture that sent a delightful little pang through her torso.

"Thanks for having dinner with me," Dayna said softly.

"Thanks for inviting me." Chris closed her eyes as Dayna's

fingers tracked lightly down her arm. She was really liking the way Dayna's breasts felt against her. Actually, she was really liking everything about Dayna, even in the wake of the weird silence. The thought both scared and excited her.

"Will you stay?"

Dayna's tentative tone was not something Chris was used to hearing from the cocksure prosecuting attorney. "Of course. But I do have to take my grandmother to mass tomorrow at eight-thirty."

Dayna was quiet for a bit before answering. "That's really sweet of you."

Chris stroked Dayna's hair. "It's a bit early, but that's the Spanish service at San Felipe de Neri." And Chris loved spending time with *Abuelita*, whose wicked sense of humor never failed to make her day.

"Good thing she lives near Old Town," Dayna said as she nuzzled Chris's neck. "Because I'm afraid I've kept you up rather late."

"You did. But I helped."

"You know I'm a morning person," Dayna added. "I'll get up with you. I wouldn't *think* of sending my favorite law enforcement officer out the door without coffee, at least."

Chris chuckled. "Since you're one of those, fine. But it's Sunday and you don't need to worry about it." She felt an odd little kick in her gut at the word "favorite." She buried it immediately. Dayna kept a few regulars around for dating, so being her favorite was like being a favorite horse in a stable.

"I'm not. I'd just like to."

"Well, thanks." Chris hugged her close, enjoying the feel of her body and the way they fit together. "And thanks for dinner." She repositioned herself a bit so she could kiss her lightly on the nose. "I'm glad your mom's healed up."

"Me, too. I like San Diego, but for some stupid reason, I've sort of bonded with Albuquerque." She gently kissed Chris's cheek. "I was so glad when my sister could take care of Mom after New Year's. I've only been back here since then. Of course, tons of work to catch up with." She shifted and propped herself on an elbow so she could look at her. "I was actually going to call you this week." She sounded contrite.

"Oh?" Chris kept her tone level.

"To ask you to dinner."

"And?" she teased.

Dayna laughed. "Yeah. And for some of *that*, too. Though I thought I might be pushing my luck." She was suddenly serious. "Don't get me wrong. I really enjoy interacting with you physically." She rolled her eyes and smiled. "I mean, look at me here."

"Gladly." *I love looking at you, actually.* Chris pulled her gently down into a kiss, to which Dayna responded avidly before she pulled away.

"But—" Dayna put an emphasis on it. "I also like you as a person and I like being around you. So I'm sorry I didn't call you back after Thanksgiving. That was—that's not like me." She dropped her gaze momentarily, then looked into Chris's eyes again. "I know you called a few times while I was in California. And I'm sorry about not getting back to you. It wasn't because of anything you said or did." She brushed a strand of Chris's hair out of her face. "Shit came up," she finished softly. "As you know."

"You had things to do and people to see. I understand." Chris watched her eyes, knowing there was something else Dayna wasn't saying. She hadn't specifically mentioned what the shit was over dinner, either. *Don't go there.* Chris didn't want to dig any deeper at the moment, though she appreciated the apology, since it had stung a bit when Dayna hadn't called her back. Why, she wasn't sure, and she hadn't wanted to think about it and she tried not to, but she *did* think about it. Quite a bit.

"So I'm assuming you're in on the bosque situation." Dayna abruptly changed the subject and Chris thanked her silently for it. "The tape's still up," she explained. "And you know how lawyers gossip."

"Yep." Chris responded. "And yes, I do. You know the drill. I can't tell you much about it because when we find the perp, he or she will be funneled through your office."

"And we can't have you compromising anything," she said teasingly.

"Except your reputation." Chris ran her hands down Dayna's back, reveling in the softness of her skin. It seemed her hands burned as they touched her. *Damn.* Her heart rate increased.

"Hell, I'll compromise that for you any time," Dayna said softly, a strange expression in her eyes. She kissed Chris's forehead gently. "I'm so glad I ran into you today." Her breath was warm on Chris's face.

"You didn't. Though you tried." Chris grinned.

"Oh, ha ha." Dayna snuggled closer and kissed her on the neck. "Thanks for staying."

"You're very welcome. Thanks for asking." A little thrill chased itself through her gut.

Dayna made a contented noise. "Good night," she said softly against Chris's neck.

" 'Night." She felt Dayna relax into sleep against her and for the first time in a long time, Chris felt a peace of sorts settle over her. She didn't remember falling asleep.

CHRIS WASHED THE two Tylenol down with a swig of Diet Coke. She'd started working on a headache at *Abuelita*'s as she was fixing the bathroom sink. Harper called just as she finished tightening and caulking the last of it. He added to her headache with the "Hey, Gucci" greeting.

Angela Griggs positively ID'ed the body of Travis McCormick earlier that day and dental records confirmed it. The DNA results would come back from the lab within the next week or two, though that could vary. DNA analysis took a hell of a lot longer than people realized. What Griggs might not know is that her son had been tested six times for HIV since the age of eighteen, according to his medical records. Which, on the surface, might mean he was an IV-drug user. Except the autopsy noted no track marks or drug-related sores on his body, something that long-term users tended to have. What the autopsy did find was rectal trauma, both old and new. Travis McCormick had most likely been gay, though it wasn't unknown for heterosexual men to have sexually-induced rectal trauma.

Chris's instincts didn't lean that way, however, and she wondered as she showered at *Abuelita*'s and changed into the spare set of clothing she always kept handy in her car whether Travis's mom knew her son was gay. Chris inspected herself in the bedroom mirror, making sure she was presentable. She favored casual cotton trousers like Dockers and button-down shirts and that's exactly what she had on. Black pants, white shirt, and a pair of urban hipster black Doc Martens. Her colleagues teased her about her Docs, but they were sturdy and comfortable and looked better than the standard-issue police footwear.

Chris arrived at the station an hour before Griggs was scheduled to get there. She went through the preliminary autopsy report, though she'd go through it again later when she had more time, and checked her messages on her desk phone. Still nothing from Carl Maestas, Al's El Paso connection, either here or on her cell. She'd call again after finishing up with Ms. Griggs.

She took another swallow of Diet Coke and twisted the cap back onto the bottle before setting it on the table in the windowless conference room. The lighting, though, was good here and the newer berber carpet gave it a more informal feel than one of the police interrogation rooms. Plus, the chairs were more comfortable. Chris glanced over at the autopsy file to make sure it was closed just as Harper opened the door and stood waiting while Angela Griggs brushed past him, trailing a cloud of some kind of floral perfume that filled the room. Chris thanked whatever deity might be listening that she had just taken Tylenol.

Plump but athletic-looking, Angela Griggs stood about five-three and exuded a junior league air. Exceedingly blond, she wore enough gold jewelry around her neck and wrists to star in a hip-hop video. Her high heels matched her pink track suit and that bore the Chanel label. Older straight men probably found her attractive, Chris thought, as she assessed Griggs and estimated her age as around fifty. From Griggs's sense-of-entitlement demeanor, Chris had a feeling this interview might not go well. *It's going to be a long rest of the day.*

"Ms. Griggs, I'm Detective Chris Gutierrez." She motioned to one of the chairs pulled slightly out from the table. "Please, have a seat. Would you like something to drink?"

"Coffee," Griggs said somewhat imperiously.

"Comin' right up." Harper placed a few forms on the table, then ducked out of the room, expression impassive.

Chris watched him leave then turned her full attention back to Griggs, figuring she was someone who tended to get right to business, so Chris sat down to her left, praying that her olfactory nerves would mutate so she could survive while breathing whatever the hell it was Griggs had bathed in.

"Thank you for coming in," Chris continued. "I'm sorry about your son—"

"Thank you," Griggs interrupted, waving a dismissive hand. "Let's get to it." Her voice had a slight Texas twang. She set her expensive-looking purse on the table and opened it, then pulled a photograph out that she handed to Chris. "That's the most recent picture I have of him. He was eighteen then."

Nice, Chris thought sarcastically as she took the image and placed it on top of the autopsy file. She'd study it later. "All right. When was the last time you saw Travis?" She tended to humanize victims, which helped with interrogations because people would relax into the personal aspects of their relationships with the decedent.

"January twentieth. He came by the house around two. I know that because I was just coming back from a golf game and I had to get ready for a neighborhood meeting at five."

"Where do you play golf, ma'am?" A woman like this no doubt expected to be accorded some sort of formal address.

"On that day, at Arroyo del Oso. It's closer than the others. I've already provided a list of my foursome to Detective Harper."

"Thank you. That's very helpful. Did Travis have any brothers or sisters?"

"No. My ex-husband and I tried, but I couldn't get pregnant again." She held Chris's gaze, as if daring her to say something more about that.

"Why did he stop by that day? Was that something he did often?" Chris kept her tone smooth and professional, which generally worked on most people she interviewed.

Here the muscles in Griggs's jaw tightened.

Ah. They weren't close.

"No," she said, answering both Chris's spoken question and silent observation. She looked down at her hands, which were in her lap.

"Ms. Griggs, I have to ask you some rather personal questions about your relationship with Travis. It's standard procedure and helps us track his movements and figure out who he came into contact with prior to his death."

"We didn't get along," she announced in a tone like the winter wind that curled rare snow off the tops of the Sandias.

"So why did he come by that day?"

She let out an exasperated breath. "He did that every now and then. To try to talk to me about his —" a look of disgust crossed her features and she frowned. "Lifestyle."

So he was *gay.* "I'm sorry, Ms. Griggs, but could you elaborate?"

She sat back, glaring at the ceiling. "Homosexual, Detective. He was one of *those*."

Harper chose that exact moment to enter the room. At the term "homosexual," he hesitated, then seemed to catch himself and his jaw clenched.

Oh, lovely. He's more homophobic than I thought. Chris had a feeling she'd need more than Tylenol when this was over. Harper closed the door behind him and moved to the table, setting the large Styrofoam cup near Griggs's right hand. He took several packets of sugar and fake creamer from his inside blazer pocket along with a plastic stir-stick and set them on the table as well before easing his big frame into the chair to Griggs's right. She gratefully began to open sugar packets and pour them into the cup. Her nail polish matched her track suit.

Chris continued. "And he would come by to do what, exactly?"

She made an irritated noise in her throat. "Try to 'make me understand'." She stirred her coffee with long, manicured fingers. Harper watched her ministrations with interest. "His father and I tried everything to get him to stop being that way. We sent him to Out of Darkness while we all lived in Dallas and that didn't work. He was still in high school then."

" 'Out of Darkness'?" Harper interjected softly. He had his notebook ready.

Chris knew it was an ex-gay ministry, but she wanted to hear Griggs's take.

"It's to help people stop being homosexual." She said it matter-of-factly, like she was talking about her golf game.

"And how long was he involved with the organization?" Chris

kept her tone neutral, an act worthy of an Oscar.

"Not even three weeks," she scoffed. "Had he just given it a chance—" She stopped and took a careful sip of coffee.

"How old was he then?" Chris leaned forward, hoping she still sounded non-judgmental.

"Seventeen."

"So he left the group and what happened after that?"

"It was a mess for a while. Travis's father and I—it wasn't working. I moved here a couple of months after Travis ran away." She poured more creamer into her coffee.

"So Travis stayed in Dallas for a while?"

"Yes. He lived with his father's sister."

"How long?"

She made a vague motion with her hand and her heavy gold bracelets slid up her wrist. "Until he was twenty. Then he went to Los Angeles, convinced he was going to be some kind of big star."

"Why did he come to Albuquerque?" Chris pressed.

"He had friends here and it was cheaper than L.A. That's when he started visiting me every now and again." She took another drink. Her lipstick left a perfect impression on the cup's rim.

"Ms. Griggs, walk me through that last time you saw Travis. He arrived around two. Where were you?"

"Inside. The doorbell rang. I went to see who it was."

"So you saw it was Travis. What did you do then?"

"I opened the door and asked what he wanted. I also told him I didn't want to hear anything about his sick lifestyle."

Chris ignored the comment. "What did he do?"

"What he usually did. He told me he'd keep trying until I'd talk to him. Oh, and he gave me a flyer about one of those godawful perversions he performs in. Then he left."

"Flyer about what?"

She clicked her tongue against her teeth disapprovingly. "Those—you know. Where men dress up like women and parade around like sluts. Disgusting."

Travis was a drag queen? "Ms. Griggs, did you ever happen to see on the flyer where these shows took place?"

"Some horrible place. 'Push.' Or something," she said with obvious disgust.

Chris regarded her for a moment. "Pulse?"

Harper glanced up from his notebook, then down again.

"Yes, that's it." She looked at Chris sharply.

"Was anyone with him when he stopped by?" Chris prodded.

"I don't know. I did see his car at the curb, but as soon as he turned around to leave, I shut the door." She made another dismissive motion.

Her own son. "Did you hear from him after that?"

"No. He never called. He would just show up every once in a while." She looked at the gold watch buried amidst the bling on her left wrist.

Chris bit back her remonstration. "Did Travis have any contact with his father?"

"I don't know. You'll have to ask him." Her tone indicated that she was done here.

"All right, Ms. Griggs. Detective Harper here has some forms you'll need to fill out. They'll include a list of Travis's friends and acquaintances — if you know of any — and the type of car he had. And anything else you can think of that might help us find the person who did this to him."

"I don't know who his friends are," she said petulantly. "I never talked to him and barely saw him."

Harper stepped into the conversation. "Regardless, ma'am, maybe as you're filling these out it'll jog your memory." He pushed the forms toward her and held out his own pen. "And if you could please leave contact information, that'd be helpful. If you'd like to put a request in with the District Attorney's office for your son's personal effects once we conclude this investigation, the number is on this sheet." He slid another piece of paper next to her hand.

She sighed with resignation, as if trying to find her son's killer was the most annoying thing she had to do that week. "I told him that nothing good could come of his lifestyle. His father and I told him when he was still in high school." She huffed. "I was right, of course."

Chris barely stifled an urge to smack her on the back of her perfectly coiffed head. She stood. "Thank you for your time. Detective Harper will show you out." She gathered up the autopsy files and left without looking at either of them again, disgust crawling up her throat like bile.

CARL MAESTAS HAD called while Chris was interviewing Angela Griggs. He left a message on her cell phone, apologizing for not getting back with her sooner but he'd been out of town for a conference. He told her to call him back on his cell. Deciding that might help get her mind off smacking the shit out of Travis McCormick's mother, she went to her desk and dialed Carl's number. He picked up on the third ring.

"Hello?" He had a slight accent Chris pegged as Mexican.

"Hi, Mr. Maestas. Chris Gutierrez, with APD."

"¡Muy bien! Al's colleague. Call me Carl. Sorry about not getting back with you."

"No problem. Listen, I'll just get right to it. Al told me you worked a homicide in Cruces a few years back and the scene sounds a bit like one we've got here."

"Yeah, Al told me a little bit about that. Not much, though," he added quickly. "Let's see—winter of 2000. The case we had was a white male, twenty-three. Face down in a grave that you could barely call a hole in the ground. Hands tied behind his back. Oh, and naked. Kid's name was..." he trailed off into silence for a bit. "Henderson. Yeah. Robert Henderson. But his family said he went by his middle name. Tyler."

"Huh. Anything else you remember that struck you at the time?"

"Yeah. The kid had a crucifix stuffed in his mouth, under his tongue."

"That's interesting." Chris opened the autopsy file on her desk and started scanning the paperwork.

"On a chain. Like it was a necklace. His family and friends didn't recognize it, so we figured the perp put it there. Here's the other fucked-up thing. Somebody carved 'John three-sixteen' on his chest. You know. The Bible verse. The one about God sending his son so all us sinners will have eternal life."

"Carved it? With a knife?" Chris reached for a pen and legal pad.

"That's what it looked like. Autopsy confirmed it was a sharp blade. ME thought it might be an exacto-knife."

"Any trace on the body?"

"Not much. ME figured he'd been washed before he was buried. Autopsy indicated he was dead before burial."

"Where was he found?" Chris abandoned the paperwork and instead furiously wrote what Carl was saying down on one of her legal pads.

"Right outside town, near Mesilla. You familiar with the area?"

A small, artsy community just southwest of the Las Cruces metro area, Mesilla's historic Spanish plaza attracted locals, artists, and lots of tourists. "Yeah. In a well-traveled area?"

Carl was quiet for a moment, probably thinking. "Not really. But it wasn't isolated, either. A party spot. Horny teenagers, mostly. He'd been there about five days when some hippie dude happened upon him. Henderson's hair, fingers, and part of his ass got uncovered. And chewed a bit. You know how the wildlife is." His tone was dry.

"Do you recall—" Chris wondered how to put it delicately, then decided not to worry about it. Carl was a cop, after all. "Did the autopsy note any anal trauma?"

He answered without missing a beat. "Yep. Henderson was a

grade-A *joto*."

Chris winced at the derogatory Spanish term for "faggot," though Carl's tone didn't sound malicious. She knew how these older male cops could be. Especially the Latinos. That's just how they referred to gay men.

"Family and friends confirm that?" she asked, hoping he wouldn't use the term anymore.

"Family didn't want to talk about it much. The friends knew, though. The parents did admit they tried to save him." He put a sarcastic inflection on the word "save."

"Define 'save'."

Carl laughed then, a hearty sound from his gut. Chris pictured him as a typical macho Mexican guy, dark hair graying at the temples. Probably a mustache. And probably the kind of guy you'd like to have on your side. "Ay, you know. *De uno Nuevomexicano a otra*," he said, calling on their shared New Mexican background. "You know how these crazy Protestants are."

Chris stifled a laugh of her own.

"Shit, at the first sign of anything, they're running to some damn preacher about it. Henderson's brother said the parents shipped him off to one of those 'heal the gays' things when he was in high school."

Warning bells went off in Chris's head. "Do you know which one?" She tapped the tip of her pen against the tablet.

Carl was quiet again for a few seconds. "Ah, hell. Don't remember. Sorry. The brother said Henderson finished the program but it didn't do a damn thing except drive him away from his family."

"Anything else you can remember?"

"No. Hey, but I did some extracurricular research when I was working this case. Didn't find anything else that looks like this. So could be the Cruces case was the first, if yours is related."

Chris was glad to hear that. Though Henderson had been gay, it sounded like Carl didn't hold that against him, slur notwithstanding. "I appreciate your time here," she said. "Thanks."

"No problem. You know, when Al called and we got to telling war stories, I hadn't really thought about the Henderson case in a while. I was pissed 'cause we didn't solve it. You know how that goes. It's like the perp throws you the finger when you don't. *Pues...*" he stopped, then continued. "Everything should still be on file in Cruces. My notes and write-ups, too. And if you have any more questions, call. Always willing to help a brother of the badge. Or sister," he corrected himself.

"*Mil gracias*. And I just might be doing that. *Buenas tardes*."

"*De nada. Adios*." He hung up.

Chris replaced the phone and reached for the autopsy report. The picture of Travis McCormick still rested on top of it. Chris had carried it to her desk that way. She picked it up. A head shot, it showed him from the chest up, dressed in what appeared to be a tuxedo. Prom night, maybe? He had been a good-looking kid. Dark hair and blue eyes. A nice, square jaw. His smile didn't show his teeth. She looked for a resemblance to his mother and found it in the shape of his nose and eyes. Thinking about Angela Griggs's rejection of her son—her only child—brought a lump and a sour taste to Chris's throat. She put the picture down and turned her attention to the autopsy report.

Trace evidence on the body was minimal. The medical examiner conjectured that the body might have been washed prior to burial. She read on but stopped at one paragraph and re-read it: "Upon inspection of the oral cavity, a gold crucifix measuring one inch long and three-quarters of an inch across affixed to a matching chain was found underneath the tongue." *Fuck*. She read more and came across another paragraph: "Medical Examiner noted an inscription intentionally carved postmortem into chest, above nipples and across sternum area. 'John 3:16,' letters and numbers measuring 1 and 5/8 inches tall." She skimmed through the tissue descriptions and supposition that an extremely sharp blade had been used. *Holy shit. We've got a match.*

She then logged into her computer and Googled "John 3:16." She'd probably recognize the text, given years of mass with her family as a child, but it had been a while. She found it and read it onscreen then printed it out on her small desktop printer so she could read it again: "For God so loved the world that he gave his one and only Son, that whoever believes in him shall not perish but have eternal life."

Chris placed the sheet on her desk and pulled the autopsy photos out of the file. She found a series that showed the verse name and number carved onto Travis's body. Then she found the photo that showed the crucifix under his tongue.

Most likely the killer put it in his mouth right before he buried him. Chris doubted the perp waited too long postmortem to transport the body. When rigor starts setting in, it's damn near impossible to move a body's limbs. Plus, if the killer inserted the crucifix before taking the body to the grave, there was a chance it could fall out *en route*. No, most likely the perp put Travis in the grave, put the crucifix in his mouth, carved the verse, then turned him over and buried him. She put the photos back into the folder. Right now, she needed to make a call to Mark Aragon, lead detective on the gang unit, so he could activate K.C. as a consultant. She reached for the phone.

Chapter
Five

CHRIS LISTENED TO the message on her cell phone again. It helped put the day out of her mind. She stood in the carport of her house, located in the near Northeast Heights, an area of Albuquerque best described as "mixed." The neighborhood consisted of older retired people, middle-class, working-class, and college students plus a smattering of young hipsters buying up property reasonably close to Albuquerque's Nob Hill, a cool and funky arts district along Central Avenue. Best-known as part of the original Route 66, it bisected the city into North and South. Chris liked this part of the city, liked the variety of people in it and the reasonable quiet in the evenings.

She leaned against her car, grinning at Dayna's message on her personal cell: "Hi, Chris...God, I hate leaving messages. I'm not any good at it. Hell. Anyway, thanks. Jesus, that sounded stupid. What I mean is, thank you for—well, for last night—" Here she laughed, a rich, throaty sound. "I—you blow my mind." She laughed again. "I also wanted to thank you for giving me another chance. It was really shitty of me not to call you after I left for San Diego..." Her voice trailed off, as if she wanted to say more about that but decided against it. "Anyway, I would really like to see you again. This week's crazy, but maybe Friday? If you want. Your call this time. Talk to you later, I hope."

Chris saved the message and grabbed her gym bag off the roof of her car. She unlocked the side door that led from the carport into her kitchen, flicked on the light, and put her bag on the small island in the center of the room. The insistent beep of the alarm pulled her through the intimate dining room just off the kitchen to the living room, where she entered the code to disarm it. Chris wasn't a fan of alarms, but when she became a cop, she decided it was probably a good idea to have one because no doubt she'd piss somebody off. Cops always did. She picked up the mail from the floor near the front door. The slot was in the wall, an old-school mail drop, but Chris liked it because she didn't worry about her mail sitting out by the curb or in a box on her front porch. And it beat having a post office box.

She flipped through the envelopes. A couple of bills, credit card offers, invitation to a conference in Los Angeles, and a copy of *The Advocate*, in its opaque white plastic wrapper. They still had her last name misspelled. She sighed and took the mail with her into the bedroom she used as a study and set it next to her computer.

Twenty minutes later, clothed in sweats and sweatshirt, Chris stretched out on her couch after firing up the jar candles on her mantel. She turned on her stereo with a remote and the soulful, longing voice of Susana Baca filled the living room. *Ah. Much better.* She loved her house. The small, two-bedroom bungalow-style structure had been built after World War II, and its original hardwood floors were still intact. She had bought it ten years ago and, with the help of her brothers and father, re-did the wiring and plumbing. Chris's father owned a construction business, which made home improvement easy. She had also replaced the appliances in the kitchen, put saltillo tile on the floor, and also tiled the counters. She had painted the interior walls in bright, festive colors and filled the rooms with furniture and folk art she bought primarily in Mexico on trips with *Abuelita*, who was originally from Chihuahua.

K.C. had helped Chris re-do the back yard about six years ago. They took out most of the grass and created a meandering, meditative haven with rock paths and a few native trees and bushes. They'd also put up a seven-foot "faux-dobe" wall, as K.C. referred to fake adobe. This consisted of cinderblock covered with tan stucco. Chris had created a private courtyard in the back. She'd added a ramada of her own two years ago and expanded her patio as well. After dealing with the shit, it was nice to come home to this little peaceful corner of the world.

Chris leaned over and picked up her cell phone. She checked the time. Nearly eight. She called K.C. first.

"Hey, sexy! How are you?"

"Long fucking day, *esa*," Chris groaned. "I'll be able to tell you more about it in a day or so because I've asked Mark to activate you on this one."

"Well, all right. Can you tell me why yet?"

"Remember when you were in grad school back in the day and you were doing that research on the fundamentalist right?" Chris settled into her couch.

"Oh, hell no."

"*Sí. Los cristianos locos.*"

"Jesus," K.C. quipped. "Pun intended. You think crazy Christians might have something to do with this?"

"Well, at least one did. You published that article, didn't you? Some sociology journal?"

K.C. chuckled. "Of course. I'm the bomb. I'll bring a copy for you next time I see you."

"That'll be sooner rather than later," Chris said. "Mark should call me tomorrow. He'll probably call you, too."

"No problem. As soon as I know more, I'll check in with my peeps." She added an emphasis to make it sound mysterious.

"I'm not sure I want to know who those are," Chris said, laughing.

"Can't tell you, 'cause then I'd —"

"Have to kill you," Chris finished for her.

"Please. No, I'd have to take you to boring department meetings. Which might be almost as bad for you."

Chris heard her smile. "What'd I do to get so lucky to have a friend like you in my life?"

"Um, I believe you asked me out after a party. Hello!"

"You didn't have to say yes."

"Whatever. Some hot-ass wanna-be cop asks you out, you do *not* say no." K.C. started laughing.

"I wasn't a cop then. Hell, I was barely a psychologist."

"You were well on your way. Shit, you went to the police academy the next year."

Chris fell silent for a moment, remembering, before she continued. "I love what I do, Kase. But sometimes I'm not sure I made the right call."

"What's up?" K.C. shifted into serious mode.

"I don't know. This case...it's gonna be hard. I can't tell you much more than that right now, but you need to know that it's not pretty."

"Murder never is, *amiga*," K.C. said quietly. "You okay? Want me to come over?"

"No. I'm good. But I am actually glad that you'll be on board with this. Although, you know why I worry." She thought about what happened a year-and-a-half ago, when a group of skinheads nearly shot K.C.'s ass off. She felt her guts clench. If anything happened to K.C., she'd never forgive herself. Ever.

"Hey, we've been through this. Would you stop with the guilt thing? Damn. Put your inner Catholic to rest. I'm an adult. For the most part, anyway. And I want to help. All this shit in my head, geez. Let's put it to use."

Chris grinned and relaxed. "You're the best. How's Sage?"

"Unbelievable," she said softly. "For the life of me, I sometimes wonder what the hell she sees in me."

"I'm not even going to respond to that. You're one of the most beautiful people I know. Wait. I think you could possibly be the *most* beautiful, next to me, of course."

"Oh, of course." K.C. laughed. She abruptly changed topics. "So are you busy the eighteenth of next month?"

"Shit, I don't know."

"Well, clear your big studly calendar. That's Sage's birthday party."

"And does she know?" Chris teased.

"Duh. I can't keep stuff from her. You know how she is."

"True. You can't. Sounds like a blast. What should I bring?"

"Yourself and a guest, if you have one." K.C. was trying to keep her tone innocent but she failed and Chris smiled.

"We'll see." Chris immediately thought of Dayna but didn't want to talk about it with K.C. just yet. "What time?"

"Six."

"Most excellent. All right, *esa*. I have to prepare for yet another day in the trenches. I'll be in touch. Tell that mystical girlfriend of yours hi."

"Will do. See ya."

"Bye."

Chris smiled as she hung up and set the phone on the nearby coffee table. The candlelight made her think about the previous night and her stomach flip-flopped at the memories of Dayna's naked, sweaty body sliding over hers. And her *lips*. God, that woman could use those lips. On Chris's mouth. Neck. Nipples. Then lower. *Damn.* She had tried not to think about Dayna the two months she'd been in California, but invariably, she did. Who else was Dayna seeing? *And why does that bother me?* Normally, Chris preferred open dating relationships. And when she hooked up with Dayna, both were forthright about what they wanted and neither had specified exclusivity. Dayna had a lot going on, she told Chris. She was dating around and she had just gotten out of a three-year relationship six months earlier. She was in her mid-thirties like Chris, after all, and she wasn't interested in falling into something right off.

And Chris was okay with that. They had a good time together. They liked to do the same things and they shared political views and worked in fields that dealt with law and criminalistics. Plus, Chris felt extremely comfortable around her. And surprisingly, they didn't sleep together until they'd been dating a couple of months. Chris interlaced her fingers behind her head and stared at the ceiling. Sex with Dayna was beyond belief. She was as free in bed as Chris and very attentive to both their desires. The time they spent out of bed was a hell of a lot of fun, too. A couple of times, Chris almost saw herself wanting something more committed with her, but she had shut that thought down. A cop's life is no place for a relationship. No matter how much K.C. argued with her about it.

So why the hell does that commitment thing keep coming up? Like Dayna would ever go there. Chris shook her head at the irony. She had met a woman who really piqued her interest and that woman was quite possibly more relationship-shy than she was. She grimaced. *A taste of my own medicine.*

Chris suddenly reached for her phone and flipped it open. She speed-dialed Dayna's cell and waited, nervous, while it rang.

Dayna picked up on the third. "Hey! I was just thinking about you."

Chris shut her eyes as a wave of butterflies raced through her stomach. "Something good, I hope." Thank God. She sounded steady.

"Where you're concerned, always."

She smothered a groan. Dayna had the best voice. Just the right timbre. A radio voice. "Friday looks good."

Pause. "Really?" She sounded tentative, like she had the night before when she asked Chris to stay.

"Really. What time would you be able to join me for dinner?"

"Before I answer that, can I just say that you are the sexiest woman I've ever had the good fortune to meet?"

Chris's voice got stuck in her throat. Somehow, she managed to respond. "So you're buttering me up now, huh?"

She laughed, that wonderfully spicy warm-as-red-chile-sauce laugh. "If that's what it takes to see you again, yes. But it's true. Six sound good to you?"

"Hmmm. I'm not sure..." she affected an "I'm extremely busy" tone then laughed as Dayna giggled. "I'll block it out on my calendar."

"Wow, thanks," she said with an "I'm not worthy" inflection. "Where?"

"My place." Chris waited. She could hear Dayna breathing.

"You're amazing. I would love to."

"Remember how to get here?" Chris was only half-teasing.

"I never forgot," she said softly.

"Then I'll see you Friday at six." Her stomach was now doing full floor routines.

"This is going to be the longest workweek in recorded memory," Dayna groaned. "Thanks for calling."

"Thanks for leaving a message. And thanks for breakfast."

"I'll leave more messages. And hopefully I'll have other opportunities to make you breakfast," she said.

Chris heard Dayna's smile through the phone. It threatened to propel her out the side door and into her car to barrel up to the North Valley and bang on her door in the middle of the Goddamn night. "I hope so," she breathed.

"Count on it. I'll talk to you later. Good night, Chris."

"Same to you. Later." She listened as the line went dead.

"*Sometimes what you're looking for is right under your feet.*" Chris swung her legs onto the floor. Dayna? Was Dayna what she was looking for? *Bullshit.* Fun, yes. Sex, definitely. Something else? *No way.* But the thought lacked conviction. Sighing, Chris stood up from the couch. She blew out the candles and headed for bed. Another long day awaited her.

PAUL MCCORMICK KNEW even less about his son than his ex-wife did and demonstrated an even more detached demeanor. Even Harper looked frustrated after the interview. "Well, that was about as helpful as a Speedo at an ice-fishing tournament," he said when Chris returned from showing McCormick out. She laughed. Sometimes he let loose with something like that. It almost made her stop disliking him. But not quite.

"Did you look at the report?" she asked, taking the chair next to him at the big conference table.

"Yeah. What's all this with the crucifix and the Bible verse?"

Chris filled him in on what she'd learned yesterday from Carl.

"What are you thinking?" He folded his big arms over his chest and leaned back in his chair.

"I'm thinking I need to have a look at the Cruces case. I called down there to see how much material they have. They're checking. I figured I'd head down tomorrow night and come back Wednesday afternoon or Thursday morning, if there's a lot."

He nodded slowly. He had the kind of face that never really aged. He probably looked the same at twenty-five as he did now at forty. And when he was working a case, he developed extra gravitas in his persona, which was a little off-putting because it made him seem both aloof and passive. Chris knew, though, that he observed a hell of a lot more than he let on. *Probably a North Dakota white guy thing.* She wasn't entirely sure what to make of him, though he'd been with APD nearly two years, transferring to homicide from the drug squad. Chris could not picture him as a narc, though he had a good record as one. He seemed like a good detective. If he'd just quit with the stupid remarks about women and gay people, she might actually be okay working with him. But then she'd still have to contend with his damn nicknames.

"Let's head over to Travis's place and talk to the roommate," she said. "He might know more of the friends. Take the photo of the crucifix. I want to see if anybody recognizes it." She stood. "Let me check in with Cruces and I'll meet you out front."

"Okay, then."

Chris left him gathering up the autopsy report pages off the table. She walked down the hallway to the cubicle room, as she called it, so she could check her phone messages. Full house today. The buzz of several conversations and the hum of computers accompanied her to her desk. She dialed her message code. Laura from the Las Cruces Police Department had called to tell her they had two standard-sized boxes of materials from the Henderson case. Chris called her back and managed to catch her before she left for lunch. She asked Laura how long it might take to go through the materials.

"Oh, I'd say a few hours, if you really want to check it out. Less if you know what you're looking for."

"Sounds good. I'll leave here tomorrow night and check in Wednesday morning."

"Sure. We'll have the stuff ready. Just let us know if you can't make it."

"Will do. Thanks."

"You're welcome. See you Wednesday."

Chris hung up and shut her computer off.

"*Esa,*" came Detective Mark Aragon's deep voice from the entrance to her space. He filled it. Mark was bigger and taller than corn-fed Harper, even when he didn't wear his customary cowboy boots. Today he had them on, along with black jeans and a faded red button-down shirt. Mariachi colors, Chris thought.

"Hey, *amigo. ¿Qué pasa?* I was just gonna stop by your office." Chris motioned over the top of the cubicle toward his space, which was near the far wall.

He laughed. "Yeah, just make sure you call ahead to schedule an appointment. Anyway, K.C.'s activated as a consultant and expert witness if necessary. I need your signature and hers on this stuff ASAP." He waved some papers.

Chris shrugged into her jacket before she took the forms.

"So you've got a freak link to the bosque case, huh?" He let his arms rest on the top of Chris's cubicle walls.

"Looks that way. This one's more fundamentalist Protestant. K.C.'s got experience with them, too."

"*Ella esta loca,*" he said, shaking his head. "But I kinda like her anyway. I'll have a look at the file since I'm supposed to be coordinating information on fucknut groups." He moved aside to let Chris through, then followed her toward the main door. "Let me know if you need anything else," he said as Chris exited.

"Will do. *Gracias.*" She smiled at him and headed down the main corridor for the lobby.

TRAVIS HAD SHARED a two-bedroom apartment at a complex named, jokingly, "The Beach." Located on west Central just past Old

Town, it edged the east side of the Rio Grande next to an odd little urban recreational area called "Tingley Beach," which offered three small fishing ponds built in the 1930s using water diverted from the river. A stretch of sand provided a beach-like experience for desert-dwellers and proved extremely popular in the summer for picnics and barbecues. Tingley Beach had become part of the Albuquerque Biopark, a complex that included the aquarium, zoo, and botanic gardens, all located near Old Town and the river.

The Beach apartment complex's architecture was a mixture of art deco and Pueblo, which those in the know called "pueblo deco." It mimicked the stepping stone look of Puebloan dwellings but its paint scheme and neon edging evoked South Beach. The place proved popular with young urban types and artsy college students. Josh Hopkins met Harper and Chris outside the main entrance. He stood about Chris's height but his spiky blond hair added an extra two inches to him. He was long-limbed and extremely thin. The kind of thin that made Chris want to run out and buy him a bag of hamburgers and fries. He was wearing a pair of loose-fitting jeans and a baggy button-down shirt under a baggy fleece vest, which only served to accentuate how skinny he was. Chris estimated his age as early twenties.

"Hi. Josh?" Chris approached and extended her hand.

He took it and squeezed lightly before releasing it. "Yes, ma'am." His accent sounded southern. He managed a smile but Chris could tell he'd been crying. As she stood looking at him, his eyes started to tear up.

"I'm Chris Gutierrez and this is Dale Harper. Thanks for meeting with us."

He nodded and gestured vaguely at the building. "It's still roped off. I'm staying with friends at the moment."

Chris followed his gesture with her gaze. The crime scene team was no doubt at work in the apartment. She and Harper would need to have a look as well. Harper motioned at a nearby cement bench. "Why don't you sit down?" He sounded almost compassionate. Josh did as suggested and sank despondently onto the bench. Chris sat next to him as Harper pulled his notebook from his jacket pocket and took a position to Josh's left, close enough to be involved but far enough to be unobtrusive. Chris had to admit that the technique worked. Harper wasn't the best at interviews, but he was very good at recording things and making observations that others might miss. He would say as little as possible throughout this process. She took the high school photo of Travis out of the manila case folder and handed it to Josh.

"Is this Travis?" she asked gently.

He stared at the image. Tears rolled down his cheeks. He

nodded and handed it back.

"I'm sorry," she said. "This is hard for you. But we need your help to find the person responsible for what happened." She slid the photo back into the folder and set it on the clipboard she had brought, which she had placed on the bench next to her.

He sniffed and pulled a wad of Kleenex out of his shirt pocket and wiped his eyes and nose. "Okay. I'm ready."

"How long did you know Travis?"

"Two years ago. We met at Pride—" he flashed a look at Chris and she nodded in understanding. He continued. "I needed a roommate and he needed a place to live. He was staying with friends because he'd just moved from L.A. We got along pretty well." He wiped his eyes. "And no, we weren't ever anything but friends and roommates." He stopped and his eyes teared up again. "He was like my brother."

"What day did you last see him?" Chris kept her tone gentle though it wasn't hard to do with this delicate young man.

"Last Friday. Not the one we just had. The twentieth. He said he was going to do his duty and try to talk to his mom again."

"How often did he do that?"

Josh shook his head, staring at the ground. "Too often, if you ask me. Since I've known him, he's tried five times."

"Did you know his mom?"

"I never met her, but I did go with him once to try to visit her. She barely opened the door and then she told him to get the hell away from her with his 'perverted lifestyle.' I didn't want to know much more than that." He wiped his eyes again with the tissue.

"Why did he keep trying to have a relationship with her?"

"I have no fucking clue. She's a complete bitch. And, honey, I have been around some bitches in my day." He sniffled and looked up at Chris. "Sorry. That's not a gentleman's language."

"It's okay. Did he talk about her much?" she asked.

"No. But when he did, he'd say shit about how Jesus taught love, and he would always love his mom no matter what she thought of him. His parents are super Christian. Like, James Dobson Christian."

"James Dobson?" Harper asked.

"Yeah," Josh answered. "That right-wing Christian group Focus on the Family. Dobson's the director of it. They basically imply that if you're not Christian and straight, then you're a target. They don't just leave you alone if you don't agree. They go after you through political lobbying and misinformation campaigns. Though they say they're just trying to help gay people stop sinning or some crap like that."

Chris looked at him with new interest. Josh stayed informed.

"Travis told me his parents sent him to one of those ex-gay camps when he was in high school. He was there for three weeks or something and basically bailed. He said it was too hateful and that wasn't the true message of Jesus."

Huh. Chris pulled a photo of the crucifix that had been found in Travis's mouth out of the file. "Do you recognize this? It was found with him."

Josh took the photo and looked at it carefully before he shook his head. "No. Travis isn't—" he caught himself and choked back a sob. "*Wasn't* into necklaces."

"How about this?" She showed him the photo of the ring he'd been wearing.

"Yeah. He wore that all the time. That's his high school class ring."

Something occurred to Chris. "Did Travis attend church at all?"

"Almost every Sunday. Unless he was sick or something. I always thought that was weird. I mean, his mom uses religion to be hateful toward him and he goes to church anyway."

"Do you know where?"

Josh smiled. "You'd think he'd be all over MCC or something, but no. He went to Wellspring over on the West Side."

Chris let that thought bounce around for a bit. One of the big Protestant megachurches on Albuquerque's West Side, located at Central near Coors Boulevard. She pictured it. What would a young gay guy like Travis want with a megachurch, which more often than not tended toward literal interpretations of the Bible and expressed disapproval, at the very least, toward homosexuality? "Why did you report him missing?"

Josh looked at her, clearly perplexed at the question. "Because he was. Travis was really uptight about certain things, bless his heart. Other things, not so much. But church was one of those uptight things. On Sundays he always got up at seven thirty-five in the morning. He'd shower and put a suit on. For breakfast, he always had toast and fruit. He'd leave at eight forty-five so he could catch the nine-thirty service. After that, he'd come home and hang out. Maybe run errands or do laundry. He had to work at three at Pulse. He never missed work. He was never even late."

"What did he do there?"

"Bartending. He learned how in L.A. Plus we made extra money with the shows when we performed. We did that about once a month."

"Shows?" Harper interjected.

"Drag shows," Josh said, turning to look up at him.

Chris watched the exchange. To Harper's credit, his expression betrayed nothing.

"Why didn't you report him missing Saturday?" she continued.

"He told me Wednesday last week that he had a date for Saturday. He was really excited about it. He'd been kind of seeing a guy he'd met through church and I guess they were going out again."

"Did he say who it was?"

"No. Travis tended to be private about this guy." Josh paused and looked at the ground. He appeared to be thinking. He looked up at Chris again. "That's weird, too. He dated here and there and most of the time, he'd tell me who it was and where they'd be going. You can never be too careful. All it takes is some redneck with a homo problem to go Matthew Shepherd on somebody. But the guy from church — he didn't tell me who it was."

"Any ideas why not?" Chris pushed.

"I figured it was because the guy was closeted. I mean, you'd have to be to go to a church like that. Travis wasn't, but maybe he was at the church. I don't know. I asked him once why he went there and he said because it made him feel closer to his parents."

The guy might be a higher-up at Wellspring. Chris filed that thought for further exploration. "So he didn't come home on Saturday. Why didn't you report him missing then?" Chris asked again.

"I was in Santa Fe on Friday with my sister and I stayed the night. I work Saturday nights at Scalo, so I didn't expect to see him, since he had the date and all. I get home late and if he and this guy really hit it off — well, sometimes Travis did spend the night away. But he'd always call and leave a message on my cell if he was planning to do that. He didn't call that night and I kept checking. So I figured he'd be at home when I got off work. But he wasn't. I could tell, though, that he'd been home at some point. The clothes he'd been wearing to visit his mom were on his bed."

"So you don't know for sure whether he left those clothes there Friday or Saturday."

Josh drew a shaky breath. "No. All I know is he didn't show up Sunday morning and he didn't call. By two, I was about losing my religion over it. I must've called his cell twenty times but I think it was turned off because it kept bouncing me to voicemail after the first ring. Worse, his car was in the parking lot. That really scared me." Another tear coursed down his cheek. "Three o' clock rolled around and he didn't show. I called Pulse at three-thirty and they hadn't seen him, either. At five they called me asking where he was. That's when I called the police." He looked at her, anguished. "It's been the worst fucking week of my life." He dissolved into tears. "I'm sorry," he said between his sobs. "I can't believe he's gone."

Chris put a comforting hand on his shoulder. "Thank you for

your time. I'm really sorry for your loss." She squeezed his shoulder gently. "Do you have a ride?"

He nodded. "My friend Kathy will be here at three."

Chris looked at her watch. Two forty-five. "Do you think you could make a list of names for us? His closest friends and any other family you know about?"

He nodded assent and she pulled a form out of the folder and attached it to the clipboard. Harper handed Josh his personal pen. Josh murmured a thanks and began to write names down on the bottom half of the paper, the section delineated for that information.

He finished ten minutes later and he handed the clipboard to Chris and the pen back to Harper. "I sure hope you find whoever did this," he said.

Chris reached into the back pocket of her khakis for her wallet. She pulled one of her business cards out and handed it to him. "If you think of anything else, call me. My business cell is on there if you can't reach me at work."

"Thank you." He started to walk back toward the parking lot then stopped. "When do you think they'll be done with—" he glanced at the building.

"Another few days, probably," Chris said sympathetically. "Someone will call you. If you don't hear anything within the next two days, call me."

"Okay." He held onto her card as he waved and continued to the parking lot, where he got into a silver Lexus sedan.

Chris watched him then turned to Harper. "Let's check out the apartment and see if we can catch a few tenants. We'll also need the security camera film."

He nodded in agreement and followed her to the entrance. "Hey, Gucci," he said as she opened the front door.

She rolled her eyes but waited.

"What's MCC?"

"Metropolitan Community Church. It's a welcoming space for gay people." She waited for something further. Nothing came and he followed her into the building.

Chapter
Six

K.C. SPREAD THE autopsy photographs of Travis McCormick out on the table. Chris stood at her left shoulder, holding a cup of coffee. K.C. was wearing an Oregon Ducks baseball cap today that Chris assumed Megan had sent to her.

"And the crucifix was found in his mouth," K.C. said thoughtfully as she sorted through the images until she found the one that showed two gloved hands holding Travis's mouth open, presumably so another ME could take the picture. She absently pushed the sleeves of her plaid flannel shirt up to her elbows. She wore a pair of old jeans with holes in the knees.

"Under his tongue." Chris took a sip of coffee. K.C. and Sage liked decaf in the evenings, which Chris appreciated since caffeine kept her up.

"What about the ring?"

"High school class ring. I don't think it has much to do with anything."

K.C. nodded and stood back, hands on her hips, scanning the photos. She reached and picked up the image of the Bible verse number carved into his chest. "For God so loved the world that he gave his one and only son," she said softly, "that whoever believes in him shall not perish but have eternal life." She studied the photo.

Chris stared at her, feeling a prickle on her spine. "Kase, it kinda freaks me out to hear you quote scripture."

K.C. turned to catch her eye. She grinned wickedly. "Me, too. I know others—you wanna hear?"

"Hell, no. It's bad enough you study white supremacists. Knowing that you can spout Bible verses—damn. Next thing I know you'll start having bake sales and you'll be wearing dresses and heels on your way to church every week."

"No, *that* would be a sign of the apocalypse. Oh, and zombies. That's the *other* sign."

Chris laughed. "So what's the deal with John three-sixteen? I know why Catholics dig it. What about Protestants?"

"It's a popular verse, especially with younger Christians in

Protestant denominations. The teens and twenty-year-olds. Those big-ass youth gatherings and movements and all. You'll see it a lot there. It demonstrates that you're 'in with Jesus' and you're workin' your swerve for the Lord. It's supposed to be an affirming kind of statement, as it is for Catholics." She shook her head. "I've seen it lots of places, including tattoos and bathroom walls, but never carved into the chest of a dead man."

"Make that two dead men."

K.C. looked at her, waiting.

"The older case in Cruces I told you about. I'm going down tomorrow, hopefully, and I'll have copies made of stuff that might relate here."

"All right, let's think about this." K.C. picked up her cup of coffee and took a sip. "Two bodies, both young gay men. Both buried in similar circumstances, with similar M.O. Both with the same biblical verse on their chests, both with crucifixes under their tongues. Call me crazy," she said, "but I'm thinking we've got the same killer for both. Was there a lot of publicity around the Cruces case?"

"None that I can remember. I'll check while I'm down there."

"If there was, it could be a copycat."

"I doubt it. They're about five years apart."

"Good point." K.C. put her cup back on the table. "Oh, plus there's the *other* link. The ex-gay ministries." She picked up a pen and twirled it around her fingers. Chris smiled. It was a habit K.C. had when she was brainstorming.

"Out of Darkness for Travis," Chris reminded her. "I don't know yet about the Henderson case. I have a feeling, though, that it might be the same one."

"Out of Darkness formed in Dallas in..." K.C. narrowed her eyes slightly. "Nineteen ninety-three, I believe. Exodus International is the biggie. It formed in seventy-three as Love in Action. From that came a lot of offspring. Out of Darkness is one of them."

"So it makes sense that Travis's parents would send him to that one. It was right there."

"Yup. OD—love that acronym—offers a variety of programs, usually a minimum of two months. From what I found, they're all about 'freeing yourself from homosexuality through the power of Jesus Christ.' Here—" she picked up a stack of papers from the corner of the table. "I printed some stuff out for you. They really hammer on the Christ angle. They offer group therapy, mentoring programs, and summer camps." K.C. grimaced. "Yeah, wouldn't that be special. Spending summer with people who hate themselves. Like high school wasn't bad enough for that."

She handed the papers to Chris, who shook her head slowly.

"You know, when I was first coming out, I used to wonder what it would be like to suddenly wake up straight because it would be so much easier. But the reality is, I can't remember a day in my life when I didn't feel different. Hell, even as a little kid, I never felt like I could interact with guys the way other girls did. And then I realized that this is who I am, that it's intrinsic to my very essence and dammit, it's not me with the problem. It's the rest of the fucking world." She flipped through the papers, thinking about those lonely years struggling to understand why some girls made her feel tingly all over and no boys did.

"Amen to that," K.C. muttered as she took a sip from her cup. "The great tragedy is that people die to live that truth." She looked at the photos on the table and reached for one that showed Travis standing out in front of the Beach apartments.

Chris noticed her looking at it. "That's a more recent shot of him. The only one his mom had was taken when he was eighteen." *How a parent could do that to a child. Shut them out like that.*

K.C. made a disgusted noise in her throat.

"My feelings exactly. That one's from his apartment, which Harper and I checked out today after we talked to his roommate."

"How's the roomie doing?" K.C. set the photo gently back on the table and ran her fingers over it. The gesture touched Chris. K.C. had never worked on a murder case like this, though she was familiar with autopsy and law enforcement reports through her own research. "Not good," Chris answered. "He's a train wreck about this, but at least he knows he can talk to me." She knew K.C. would know what she meant.

Sure enough, K.C. shot her a look. "Speaking of which, how's working with Mr. Nickname going?"

"Don't know. The guy can be such a major ass one minute but then he'll surprise you. He was good today with Josh and also in the apartment. But he's made comments in the past that are typical cop homophobic." *Predictable straight guy cop shit.*

"Does he know about you?"

"Don't know that, either. I don't make it a secret around the department, but I don't broadcast. It's possible he doesn't. But the chances of that now seem low." She offered a dry laugh. "We'll see. But I fucking hate when he calls me Gucci."

K.C. raised her eyebrows. "What do you think he'd call me?"

"Probably something like Spacy. God, it drives me *loco*." She made an exasperated gesture with the papers she still held. "Just one of those guys who rubs you the wrong way."

"Lot of those around." K.C. set her coffee cup on the table. "I'm going to poke around some Web sites for you and see if I can find anything that might give us some insight about the crucifix and the verse. I'll also check in with some people in my secret network." She grinned. "I can't guarantee I'll find anything specific, since murderers like this have their own motivations as well, but at least we might be able to rule some stuff out."

"You're the best. I'll let you know what's up with the Cruces stuff, too." Chris slid the papers on Out of Darkness into one of the manila files sitting on the table. "And I'll read up on what it takes to un-gay yourself. Not that I'm looking forward to that." *It'd be like taking a chunk of your soul out.*

K.C. nodded absently and stood staring at the tabletop. Chris recognized the expression. She had entered research mode. "Josh said that Travis regularly attended Wellspring, right?" K.C. tugged on her lower lip, brow furrowed.

"Yeah. He apparently was dating someone he met there, though he went regularly anyway. Josh said Travis didn't talk about this one. Major closet case."

"Someone high up in the church, maybe?" K.C. looked at Chris.

"I'm thinking that, too." Chris picked up her cup.

"Wellspring. That rings a bell but I'm not sure why. I'll think on that for you. Are you going to talk to them?"

"Tomorrow. Harper got the names this afternoon and already called. We're supposed to meet one of the honchos at ten. Pastor Charles Mumford. Goes by 'Chaz' to his flock."

"Oh, really? Now that's interesting. He started in North Carolina," K.C. said. "Providence of Love in Raleigh."

"How the fuck do you know this stuff?" Chris looked at her in amazement.

"The long dry spells between serious relationships. Had to do *something.* Why not track fundamentalists?" K.C. smiled at her. "Anyway, watch out for this guy. If he's the same one, he's slick. Still reasonably young. I'd guess he's in his mid-forties by now and just hitting his stride. He's the kind of guy who could sell running shoes to paraplegics."

"What's his stance on gays?"

" 'Love the sinner, hate the sin.' Which, when you think about it, actually works for some people. This guy's been pretty open about his opinion that homosexuality is an abomination and that all you need is Jesus to leave the lifestyle. Let me do some poking around on him, too. I haven't followed his career since he left North Carolina in ninety-eight. Strange that he ended up here. New Mexico isn't exactly a haven for fundamentalist or evangelical Protestantism." She punched Chris playfully on the arm. "Thank God for all the Catholics here to keep those Protestants in line."

"*Por supuesto,*" Chris agreed. "So you're saying I shouldn't introduce myself as 'Chris, dyke detective' when we talk to him?"

She batted her eyelashes.

"Probably not the best approach," K.C. said, deadpan. She became more serious. "The guy's also got a problem with women. I heard a rumor, back when I was dissertating on neo-Nazis but still keeping an eye on the Christian right, that he smacked a few girlfriends around. Not corroborated, but..."

"I will for sure check that out. Is he married?" Chris lifted the cup to her lips.

"He was in the late nineties. But I don't know if that's changed. He probably wants to at least *appear* to be married, if nothing else than to look good with a conservative flock. So it's probably a good thing that Harper's going with you. The good pastor will probably spend most of his time talking to him. Which is fine. You'll get a chance to observe him, see what you think."

Chris nodded thoughtfully. "I have a feeling there's something about the ex-gay thing here. Something I'm not seeing yet. It's a tiny little itch on the back of my brain. I can't put my finger on it yet, but there it is."

K.C. started putting the photos back in the file. "You're an excellent cop, *amiga*. If that's what your gut says, then let's focus on that angle. See where it takes us."

"Thanks, *esa*." Chris helped with the re-organizing. They finished just as Sage opened the front door. Chris turned to look at her. Sage truly owned a room when she came in.

"My two favorite women in the world," Sage announced, beaming. She joined them at the table and slid out of her overcoat. "Hi, Chris. Have you convinced K.C. to try out for the police academy yet?"

"I'm too geeky," K.C. retorted, laughing, as Chris bent and pecked Sage on the cheek in greeting. K.C. took Sage's coat and placed it carefully over the back of one of the dining table chairs.

"Hi," Sage said softly to K.C. She ran her fingers along K.C.'s jaw.

"Back at 'cha. I missed you." K.C. slid her arms around Sage and pulled her into a quick kiss. "How was the benefactors' soiree?"

Sage rolled her eyes. "Typical. The next one's in Galisteo, though." She looked at K.C. hopefully.

"When?" K.C. retained her hold on Sage.

"The twenty-fourth. It's a Friday."

"I will so clear my calendar. I like going to these things with you, even though there's a lot of sucking up to do."

Sage grinned. "I like having you. Especially when you wear your cowboy boots. Yum." She pulled away. "Is there coffee left?"

"I'll get it," K.C. headed into the kitchen.

"And how are you?" Sage asked Chris.

"Fine and dandy. And I can't believe Kase lets you out of the house looking that good." Chris wiggled her eyebrows in exaggerated lechery. "On you, business attire could make grown men cry." The dark brown power suit brought out Sage's eyes. She also had her hair pulled back, which served to emphasize her cheekbones. The top three buttons of her off-white silk blouse were open, exposing a simple gold chain around her neck.

"Hell, it makes *everybody* cry." K.C. returned with a cup of coffee, which she handed to Sage. "It's true. Sage Crandall is not only the woman of my dreams, but also the hottest thing in the Southwest."

"You both are entirely full of shit. But I love you anyway. I'm going to change." Sage giggled and went to the bedroom, carrying her coffee.

"No, honey, don't. I like you just the way you are," K.C. called after her plaintively.

"Hold that thought," came Sage's voice from the bedroom, followed by the click of the door closing.

Chris smiled. "I love you guys. I love watching you. Please don't ever break up. My faith in the human condition is in your hands."

"Damn, that's a tall order," K.C. replied. "But I sure as hell am not planning anything as stupid as that. Getting shot at by neo-Nazis, okay. Infiltrating an ex-gay ministry, sure. Poking around in dead people's pasts, no problem. Breaking up with Sage? *Hell*, no."

"It warms my heart to hear you say that." Chris picked up her cup and went to the kitchen to refill it. When she returned, K.C. was sitting on one of the couches. Chris took a seat on the other. She set her cup on the coffee table, sliding a sandstone coaster underneath it as she did so. "Dayna's back," she said quietly.

"Oh?" K.C.'s tone revealed nothing but interest. "Did you see her?"

"I ran into her at the Nature Center." She remembered the jolt that raced down her spine when she realized the cyclist was Dayna.

K.C. remained quiet. Chris knew she was waiting for her to elaborate. "She asked me to dinner. And she apologized for not calling." Chris heard the bedroom door open and Sage returned to the living room, wearing baggy sweats and one of K.C.'s old UNM sweatshirts. Chris remembered when K.C. had bought it, the day after she had successfully defended her dissertation. Sage joined K.C. on the couch. She leaned against the arm closest to Chris and drew her legs up underneath her. She glanced at K.C., then at Chris.

"So Dayna's back," she repeated.

"How do you *do* that?" Chris asked. *Uncanny.*

"You were just saying that she apologized for not calling. I assumed you meant Dayna. So did she tell you why she didn't?"

Sage looked at Chris over the rim of her cup.

"She said 'shit came up' and that it was nothing I said or did."

"Ah." Sage took a sip. Chris waited, knowing she was assessing everything that was said and she'd offer an opinion when she was ready. And, usually, it got right to the heart of the matter.

"How'd dinner go?" K.C. picked up the conversation.

"Very well." Chris stifled an embarrassed cough.

Sage giggled. "Yeah, it sure as hell did. Damn, I don't think I've ever seen you blush like that."

"Jesus," Chris muttered. She reached for her coffee. "Yeah, yeah. It went extremely well."

"Dessert obviously did, too," K.C. teased.

Chris ignored the comment, though a wave of heat suffused her entire torso and spread down her legs. "I'm supposed to see her again on Friday."

"So—" K.C. started.

"I don't know." Chris held the cup with both hands and braced her elbows on her thighs. She stared at the coffee table.

"Holy shit." K.C. said softly. "You really like her."

Chris nodded. "It's not that I want to. I just do. Even though she didn't call for two months."

"Whoa. My best friend is having a major existential crisis right in front of my eyes."

Chris looked up at her. "Please, Kase. This isn't something I want to be teased about." Her tone sounded sharper than she intended and she saw surprise in K.C.'s eyes. "I'm sorry. That was harsh. I just don't know what I'm doing. Or even if I should be doing anything." She clenched and unclenched her teeth.

"What are your reservations?" Sage asked.

"The cop thing, mainly. Fucked-up hours. The horrible shit I have to deal with. It's not conducive to a long-term relationship." Chris had been repeating that mantra for so long now that it sounded trite.

"How so?"

Chris regarded Sage for a long moment before answering. "It's just not. The last two relationships I thought might be serious—they didn't like the cop stuff."

Sage leaned forward and set her cup on a magazine lying on the coffee table. "Why did you think those relationships were serious?"

Chris started, taken aback at the question.

Sage continued, sounding patient. "When you were with each woman, did you think about her all the time? Miss her when you were busy or out of town? Love hearing from her?"

Chris clenched her teeth. Sage had hit a nerve. She didn't respond at first. K.C. quietly stood up with her coffee cup and headed to the kitchen. "No," Chris said finally. She remembered Trish, especially, toward the end. Chris had dreaded her calls. They'd only end up arguing about some shit. It was a relief when Trish called her that day two-and-a-half years ago and told her it wasn't working out and could she come and get the CDs and clothes she'd left at Chris's. "Fuck," she said with resignation.

Sage reached for her coffee. "So maybe you used the cop stuff as an excuse to put a wedge in your relationships because you really didn't want to be in those relationships. What are you using the cop stuff for now?"

Chris rubbed her temples with her hands. "Fuck, I don't know."

"What do you like about Dayna?" Sage shifted focus, but Chris knew that no matter which direction Sage took the conversation, it was for a damn good reason.

Chris didn't hesitate. "She's funny. Smart. Athletic. We like to do some of the same things. She listens. More importantly, she hears. We share politics. We can be together and not say anything. And that feels good. When you don't *have* to talk or force things to happen."

K.C. returned to the couch with a fresh cup of coffee.

"So," Sage said, looking pointedly at Chris. "What are the red flags?"

"Besides mine?"

"We'll deal with those in a minute." Sage smiled sweetly.

Chris leaned back. "It bothers me that she didn't call for two months and then she shows up and it's like nothing happened. She picked up right where we left off. I don't understand that."

"What else?" Sage pressed.

"Her harem," Chris replied wryly.

K.C. suddenly became extremely interested in her coffee.

"How many other women is she seeing?" Sage asked. "Women, right? No men?"

"Yes. Women. She doesn't date guys. And I don't know how many. She said when we started dating that she wasn't really looking for long-term. She said she had just gotten out of a relationship a few months earlier and she just wanted to 'hang out,' as she put it. I was okay with that because of *my* baggage."

"And then?" Sage's voice was like honey. Smooth, sweet, irresistible. If she were a cop, there would be no unsolved crimes, because no matter who she talked to, they'd confess everything they'd ever done, whether it was illegal or not, since childhood.

Chris smiled thinly. "I found out I liked her. A lot." She felt disconcertingly warm and cold at the same.

Sage got up and joined Chris on the other couch. "Have you talked to her about this?" Sage asked before she took another sip of her coffee.

"No. I talked myself out of it. And then she left for San Diego. When she didn't call, I figured it was over." She glanced over at K.C., who sat watching her. K.C. smiled, encouraging.

"When you think about her," Sage continued, "what happens to the cop stuff?"

Chris laughed sheepishly. "It isn't really there. And then I'll remember. Like, 'oh, yeah. Can't go there. Cop stuff'."

"What did she say when you went to dinner recently?"

Damn. Sage is a force of nature. Chris looked at K.C., who shrugged helplessly with an "I told you so" expression. She turned her attention back to Sage. "She said there were some other things she had to take care of and they required a lot of her time and energy and she wasn't ready to talk about it yet. She said they had come up in California, as well." What was odd was that throughout dinner, Dayna had kept looking at Chris as if Chris knew what was going on.

"Well, that's honest, at least," K.C. offered.

"She cares about you," Sage said, with finality.

Both Chris and K.C. stared at her.

"How do you know?" Chris asked, feeling a weird hope at Sage's pronouncement.

"She's stalling for time because she knows you're commitment-phobic. She doesn't want to tell you what these other things are because she's afraid you'll bolt. And she doesn't want to allow herself to get too close to you, so she uses her other dates as cover. In the beginning, she probably *did* want to keep her options open." Sage sat back.

"But why didn't she call those two months? If you like somebody, don't you...oh, I don't know," Chris said petulantly, "contact them in some way?" She let herself express the frustration she'd felt at Dayna's protracted silence.

"What happened in her last relationship?" Sage asked.

"She's vague about it," Chris admitted. "And I don't push her."

"That never was your way," K.C. interjected quietly.

Sage nodded and squeezed Chris's thigh. "Something happened there. And she's not ready yet to deal with it. This isn't about you, though I know that doesn't make you feel better. And not calling you for two months wasn't about you, either. Wait—it was sort of about you because it was her way of trying to keep her personal baggage off of you."

Chris opened her mouth to say something but Sage cut her off. "No, maybe it wasn't the best way to handle things. But it was her way and it was the only way she knew at the time."

"What if you're wrong?" Chris asked, feeling a pang of misery that surprised her. *Shit. Maybe I like Dayna a bit too much.*

"She's a good person." Sage smiled. She could convince the Pope that he really didn't mean to be Catholic.

"You've never met her." Chris ran both hands through her hair, slightly exasperated.

"The way you talk about her and the way you feel about her project an aura." Sage moved closer and wrapped Chris in a gentle hug. "I can tell if a person's spreading bad energy through the people they come into contact with. She's not a bad person. She's got some stuff she needs to sort through and I hope she'll recognize that she can do that with you."

"There's an irony for you," K.C. added. "You found someone even more gun-shy than you."

"Maybe I did it on purpose. Maybe I was hoping she'd be unavailable." Chris pulled out of Sage's embrace.

"That is a pattern for you," K.C. said dryly.

Sage took Chris's hand. "I think you're drawn to Dayna because you know she can handle your shit. Those other relationships — Chris, they weren't for you. And you knew that. So you set yourself up for failure in order to move on. And then you took the blame on yourself for the relationships ending so you could use it as an excuse to protect yourself. There are usually two people in a relationship. Don't let your exes get away with no responsibility for what happened."

"But long-term stuff — and a cop's life — "

"Whatever," she snorted, but kindly. Her eyes seemed to sparkle. "You're more than capable of a solid, long-term relationship. Look at K.C." She arched an eyebrow playfully. "How long have you two been friends...and more, on occasion? Through all kinds of shit?"

"Damn," Chris said, chuckling. "You're my longest relationship, Kase."

"Well, yeah. I'm a total hottie."

Sage laughed and rolled her eyes.

K.C. stood and made her way between the couch and coffee table to plunk herself on Chris's other side. "We're long term, baby." She pulled Chris into a hug. "So go for it. Sweep Miss Thing right off her feet."

Sage hugged her from the other side. "I am so feeling the love right now," Chris said with another laugh.

"That's why you have us," K.C. teased.

Chris gently extricated herself and stood. "Y'know, my offer still stands to marry both of you. Weird polygamous shit notwithstanding."

"Hmmm. I think you need to check with Dayna on that." Sage stood as well and pulled Chris's face down so she could kiss her on the cheek. "Stop thinking. Let this unfold."

K.C. went to the table and picked up the files. She pulled Chris's leather jacket off the back of one of the chairs and handed it to Chris, waiting for her to put it on.

Chris took the files. "Thanks, Sage." No matter what the issue, Sage always had a new perspective.

"You're part of the family, Chris. Now relax."

"Easier said than done," Chris said, smiling.

K.C. followed Chris out the front door and down the steps to the curb. Chris placed the file on the roof of her car and looked up at the stars then back at K.C. "Sometimes I think about that day I met you. Remember that?" She thought back to that crazy party, during their college days.

"Sam Trujillo's place, over in the student ghetto. That house was party central. I didn't really know *him* all that well, but his roommate was in a class with me." She smiled at the memory. Chris could see her expression in the muted glow the nearby streetlight cast.

Chris nodded. "Yeah. Dave Johnson. That was his roommate. I knew his girlfriend, Tammy, and she invited me."

"By the time I got there, the place looked like Legends bar on New Year's Eve." K.C. chuckled. "Major fucking scene. I don't think I'd ever been to a party where you had to step over people passed out on the floor just to move around."

Chris laughed. "Damn, that's right. I stayed in the kitchen, pretty much. There I was, talking to—someone. I never did find out her name. And you came in and I don't know why, but I knew I had to talk to you, especially because you came in laughing and smiling. You seemed really *nice*. And smart. I could see that in your eyes. It wasn't like I wanted to get in your pants right then—I mean, I thought you were hot, of course." Chris grinned. *It's true.* K.C. was attractive. Athletic, nice body. Cute laugh. Quirky little smile and playful gray eyes that could shift to serious in a heartbeat. Her hair, a tousled dark chestnut mop, just begged for someone to run their fingers through it.

"Likewise," K.C. said, laughing.

"You only get better with age, *esa*. But as I was saying, there was something else about you that I wanted to tap into."

"I know. I felt it, too." K.C. spoke softly, almost reverently. She laughed again. "Plus, I thought you were beyond sexy."

"You never really told me that." Chris studied K.C.'s features.

"Yes I have. Shit, I do all the time. You just don't want to hear it. At least not from me." She punched Chris lightly on the arm. "So I know what Dayna sees in you. And I hope she realizes what she's getting if she decides to really go for it."

"I guess I'm scared." *Fuck, I don't know how to do this.*

K.C. stepped closer and hugged her again. "You won't know if you don't try. And you have me and Sage, if nothing else."

Chris held her tight, drawing strength from the familiar feel of K.C.'s body against hers. Eleven years, this woman had comforted her, provided a shoulder or a laugh, stuck by her even in Chris's darkest moods.

"Remember what you told me when I first met Sage?" K.C. pulled away but held onto Chris's hands. "You said that she might be good for me. And you told me not to let my relationship history determine my future." She squeezed Chris's fingers. "You were right. So have a little trust in yourself and in your friends. It's not like we just met you yesterday."

"I thank whatever god's listening every damn day for putting you in my life." Chris released K.C.'s hands and retrieved the file from the car's roof, staving off a tide of emotions.

"Likewise. Now take your cop ass on home and get some sleep. We've got work to do, *amiga*."

"Yeah. We do. Thanks."

"*De nada.*"

"You rock. Now get on into that house with that fine woman of yours. I'll talk to you later."

"Damn right." But she didn't go in right away. Not until the car had pulled away from the curb did K.C. go back inside. Chris watched her in the rearview then accelerated and turned her music on. Amos Lee, singing about how he'd give it up for someone, and settle down. *How appropriate.* Chris turned right onto Carlisle, headed for home and some down-time.

Chapter
Seven

CHRIS PARKED NEAR the main tower of Wellspring Church, which wasn't hard to do. This early on a weekday, there were empty spaces reasonably close to it, though the roundabout directly in front was a no parking zone. She grabbed her coffee cup from the holder near the gearshift and took a final swig, fortifying herself, then replaced it and opened her door. From here, she could see Harper's big frame standing in front of the main entrance. He looked like Colombo, with his rumpled tan trenchcoat. He liked lots of pockets, she had noticed, and he always had notebooks and pens buried in most of them. She wondered how he managed to keep them all organized.

Chris put her mid-weight jacket on as she stood in the parking lot. It was nondescript, navy. Department-issue. She'd decided her leather jacket would send way too many dyke signals. As if she didn't already look that way, with her black men's trousers, her light blue button-down men's shirt and her black Doc Martens. You'd have to have spent your life in a cave to not suspect that Chris Gutierrez was most likely a lesbian.

She bent to retrieve the manila file on the passenger seat, then locked up. A brisk early February wind ruffled her hair. That was one of the things she disliked about her home state. The damn spring winds that kicked up the high desert dust. Today promised to be the kind of day in which clouds of grit would blow across the mesas, driving dirt through the city, piling tumbleweeds and trash into forlorn corners and hanging plastic bags in leafless trees.

She hunched her shoulders slightly and studied the huge tower that loomed behind the large ovoid roof of what she presumed was the sanctuary. The tower's spire gleamed in the sun as she slowly approached the entrance. *How special. Gold.* Faux-dobe structures squatted next to it, providing space for classes, probably, as well as meeting rooms and a school. Chris had checked them out online and Wellspring was in the process of expanding its education programs to develop a school, K-8. Later on, they'd work on a high school. The place had just opened four years ago and already, it seemed, business was booming.

"Hey, Gucci," Harper said as she approached. His hands were sunk deep into two of his coat pockets.

She nodded at him. "I think you should handle most of this," she said simply.

He rocked forward on the balls of his feet. Harper tended to wear penny loafers, something incongruous, since nothing about him could be called preppy. He shrugged.

"I think the good pastor will relate better to a man," she explained.

A strange expression flickered through his eyes. He nodded. "Okay. You got a notebook?"

Chris patted her jacket pocket. She handed him the manila folder.

"All right." He turned and pulled one of the glass entrance doors open, motioning for her to precede him. She did so, stepping into the lobby and taking her shades off. She slid them into the breast pocket of her shirt.

"Nice," Harper muttered. The stone tiles of the floor resonated harmoniously with the smooth cream-colored walls. Colorful murals depicting biblical scenes decorated the walls, painted in such a way that they would appeal to children. Another room opened to their right through which Chris could see a reception counter. The French doors stood open, inviting them in. A book and gift store was to their left. In the center of the lobby, a hexagonal wooden table held a nice flower arrangement as well as assorted literature that churchgoers might find helpful. Chris glanced at the stacks and decided she would have a closer look on the way out.

"Hi," came a voice from what Chris presumed was the "welcome" office to the right. "Can I help you?" A heavyset white woman wearing a red skirt suit and black "sensible pumps" appraised them from the doorway. She looked to be in her mid-forties and she stood about six inches shorter than Chris. Her blond hair was pulled back from her face. Sort of plain, but pleasant. When she smiled, she was pretty.

"Yes, ma'am. We're with APD. I'm Detective Dale Harper and this is Detective Chris Gutierrez."

Chris winced inwardly. But at least he had tried to pronounce it correctly.

"Oh, of course. Pastor Chaz is expecting you." She stepped out of the doorway and moved to shake Harper's hand, then Chris's. A warm, firm clasp. "I'll let him know you're here."

"Thanks," Harper said as she headed toward what Chris assumed was the sanctuary underneath the big ovoid room she had seen from the outside. The entire reception area was designed like a theater, Chris observed. She saw what might have been a foyer beyond the big wooden doors that their greeter opened to get to the sanctuary. Chris assumed there were multiple entranceways into the sanctuary, and if it was anything like other megachurches, several tiers of seats probably led down to the pulpit, which was more a stage of sorts in one of these. Chris imagined it looked like a slick new Greek amphitheater, designed with an amazing sound system, good seating no matter where you were, but set up with intimacy in mind so that, wherever you sat, you felt a personal connection to Pastor Chaz.

The greeter reappeared, holding the wooden door open. "He'll see you now." She smiled, radiant, and beckoned them within, inviting them into the inner sanctum.

Chris smiled back, though her cult alert went off. She'd never cared much for churches like this, with their rock-star veneer and cult of personality that sometimes surrounded the ministers. She didn't care much for most organized religions, with their expectations both spoken and unspoken and the way they functioned to marginalize those considered different. *But who knows? Maybe this one's different.* She wasn't going to hold her breath, though.

She followed Harper into what did turn out to be a foyer, where a wide carpeted corridor surrounded the amphitheater. And, yes, several entrances led into the auditorium. "Through that door. Just go on down the steps. He's been rehearsing," the greeter said, to allay any suspicions that he would be doing anything untoward beneath the gaze of the sacred tower. What, Chris couldn't imagine. She doubted he'd murder young gay men right there on stage. *Though you never know, I guess.*

"Thank you," Harper said. He held the door open for Chris to precede him into the sanctuary.

She did so, then stopped, looking around. The place was huge. It reminded her of The Pit, where the UNM Lobos' basketball teams played. In fact, she was sure the Lobos could easily play a game here. All they'd have to do was remove the stage and a couple rows of seats.

The entrance she and Harper had used brought them in at an angle nearly front and center. Chris started down the steps, noting that everything here was carpeted. Like the inside of a theater, heavy drapes in maroons and golds hung over the walls and large cloth-covered panels had been situated at certain angles from the stage, probably for better acoustics. Two large video screens were suspended on either side of the stage. She threw a quick glance skyward at the curved ceiling, which reminded her of an observatory. Streaks of blue and green lights arched along the ceiling from lights in hidden recesses. Impressive. *I'll bet they do a hell of a light show.*

A white man appeared on the stage from somewhere behind the stage. Several instruments stood in one corner, including a drum set, four keyboards, a bass guitar, and two electric guitars. Chris supposed the place was riddled with cubbyholes and secret entrances for maximum effect, like a rock concert venue might have.

"Hi," he said in a pleasant male alto as they crossed the space between steps and stage. Chris assessed him. He wore grey slacks and a light blue button-down shirt that somehow hadn't wrinkled. His sleeves were rolled up to his elbows and his tie looked expensive. Silk, probably. Black loafers completed his business casual attire, their tassels peeking out from beneath the cuffs of his trousers. He was miked, but Chris figured he had turned the wireless off at the control clipped onto his belt.

"I'm Pastor Mumford. Chaz." He reached out and shook Harper's hand in what looked like a hearty man-grip. To Chris he just nodded quickly before turning back to Harper. Pastor Chaz stood an inch shorter than Chris and he carried himself like an athlete. Smooth. Confident, like he knew his body would do exactly what he needed it to do whether he was rocking out for Jesus or maybe running up a mountain. He looked trim and solid. Broad shoulders. His shirt was cut just right so Chris could see the outline of his biceps. He looked strong enough to carry Travis McCormick from a parking lot to a clearing in the bosque.

She continued to assess him while he addressed Harper. Pastor Chaz wore his hair—a nondescript brown—in a contemporary style. He was handsome in a boyish way and Chris could tell he used that to his advantage. Her gay-dar dinged. Pastor Chaz definitely tipped the scales in that direction. He wasn't as obvious as some, but she could visualize him cruising the occasional man. She checked his hands. He wore a wedding band. *Huh.* She'd run a check on him and find out if he was, in fact, married. Odd if he wasn't and still wore a band. She glanced at his neck, but if he wore a necklace, it was underneath his shirt and tie.

"So how can I help Albuquerque's finest?" he asked, gaze flicking in a cursory fashion over her to linger on Harper.

So there was something, then, to the rumors K.C. mentioned about Chaz's views of women. She took a small notebook from her jacket pocket along with a pen. She generally didn't interview this way, but with the pastor, she wanted to look busy.

Harper pulled the more recent photo of Travis from the manila folder and handed it to him. "Thanks for taking some time with us," Harper said. "Do you recognize this man?"

Pastor Chaz took the image and studied it. Chris, in turn, studied him, though it looked like she was merely waiting for his response. Was that a slight twitch at the corner of his mouth?

"He looks familiar..." the pastor started.

"We believe he was a member of your congregation," Harper said in his bland professional tone. "Could we check that against your formal list?"

The pastor smiled. "Of course." He handed the photo back to Harper. "I can't say for sure whether I know him or not. We have over two thousand official members."

"He was a regular," Harper pressed.

"Most of ours are," the pastor said, almost condescending but not quite.

"Sundays. Nine-thirty service." Harper slid the photo back into the file. The fingers of the pastor's left hand wandered to the wi-fi controls at his belt and started fiddling with them.

"His name was Travis McCormick. Ring any bells?" Harper's tone was friendly, though his demeanor remained implacable.

"Now that you mention it, yes," the pastor said smoothly. "He volunteered a few times for events that Wellspring Teens put on."

"Volunteered as what?" Harper asked, still friendly.

"Chaperone for dances. And, some Sundays, as a youth facilitator." Pastor Chaz folded his arms over his chest. "What's this about? What's happened?"

"He's dead, Pastor. We're trying to reconstruct his last movements." Harper stood looking down at him.

Chris watched him, too. Beyond his eyes widening slightly, nothing. Either he didn't know anything or he was damn good at hiding what he did know. Too soon to tell, yet. Chris made another notation in her notebook. She had her own shorthand for interviews.

"I'm terribly sorry to hear that. I haven't been contacted about services," he said, shaking his head. "Did he have family?" He sounded genuinely remorseful.

Harper shrugged. "Do you think you could tell us the last time you saw him?"

Pastor Chaz appeared to be thinking. "The last time he acted as a teen facilitator was the service after New Year's. I remember that because I stopped by the meeting room afterward to wish everyone a happy new year and he was there, cleaning up."

"Did you talk to him?" Harper asked, shifting his weight a bit.

"Nothing beyond a friendly hello and goodbye."

"You mean that particular time or in general?"

Good question.

"Both." The pastor smiled, a toothy, boyish grin.

"Would you mind if we spoke with some of the other church staff? Maybe someone here knows a bit more."

"Of course. Tell you what. Go check with Charlotte in the

greeter's office and she'll take you around. We're generally staffed most days of the week though hours vary, so I can't guarantee you'll find everybody. And she'll be able to check the membership rolls for you." He smiled again. "I hate to cut this short, but I have a service tomorrow evening and I need to prepare." He sounded almost apologetic.

"Sure thing. Thanks for your time," Harper said as the pastor turned abruptly and disappeared backstage. "And thanks for nothing," he muttered.

"What do you think?" Chris asked as she closed her notebook.

"He doesn't want to talk about this."

"But he just might not want the publicity for the church," she pointed out, though she didn't buy that.

"First he doesn't know Travis, then all of a sudden he remembers where he was before New Year's?" He sounded skeptical.

"Good point. Still, could be about publicity."

Harper pursed his lips and nodded once. "Maybe. Your turn. Let's go talk to Charlotte." He waited for Chris to precede him up the steps. She gratefully emerged from the auditorium into the foyer. Something about the vibe in the big room set her on edge, like the whole thing was designed for maximum spectacle and entertainment. It felt manufactured. An infomercial. Nothing at all like the warm intimacy of San Felipe de Neri. Chris had never really felt a connection with the Catholicism of her family, but she did find comfort in the rituals and she didn't mind taking *Abuelita* to mass now and again. This was something else entirely, seemingly designed specifically to showcase not a connection with God, but rather with the man on stage. *Or I could just be biased.*

She pushed through into the lobby and breathed an audible sigh of relief. She and Harper entered the greeter's office, but Charlotte wasn't in sight. Chris leaned casually on the high receptionist's counter and looked past it. A woman who might have been Barbie's younger Hispanic sister looked up at them from her desk in a far corner.

"Hi," Chris said with the slow smile that Dayna once told her could melt lipstick still in the packaging. According to her, it worked on straight women, too. "We're Detectives Harper and Gutierrez from APD. Pastor Mumford told us to check in with Charlotte about membership rolls for Wellspring. He also said that Charlotte could take us around."

"Oh, she'll be right back. But I can look something up in the rolls for you." She stood up from her desk and moved briskly to the desk positioned closest to the counter, which Chris presumed was Charlotte's. Chris shot a look at Harper. He seemed to be studying the other woman's movements. Chris couldn't blame him. Curves in all the right places and her slacks and blouse accentuated each one. The woman settled herself in Charlotte's chair and called something up on the computer.

"Thanks a bunch," Chris said. "We just need one name. Travis McCormick."

The woman's fingers hesitated and she turned to look at Chris. "He's a member," she said softly, eyes suddenly wide and worried. She pulled his name up on screen to show them. "What's going on?"

Chris straightened, preparing for the inevitable outpouring of emotion that her words would bring. "Would you print a copy of that out for me, please? Ms., uh—"

"Debbie Ruiz." She stood. "What happened?" She clicked on the command and a sheet of paper slid out of the desk printer.

"I'm sorry," Chris said gently. "We're investigating his death."

Her hands flew to her mouth and she gasped. "Oh, no. No."

Chris went around the counter to Charlotte's desk. "Please, Ms. Ruiz. Sit down."

Automatically, she did, a stunned expression on her face. Chris pulled a chair over from another nearby desk and sat down on Debbie's right. Harper remained at the counter, notebook ready.

"Ms. Ruiz, do you mind if we ask you a few questions about Travis?"

She shook her head, numb.

"Can you tell us when you last saw him?"

"Thursday the nineteenth. Oh, my God. I can't believe this." Tears welled in her eyes.

"Where?" Chris located a box of tissues on Charlotte's desk and placed it closer to Debbie.

"Here. He came by after lunch to talk to Kevin." She took a tissue and dabbed at her eyes. Her voice quavered.

"Kevin?" Chris asked.

"Stillman. The teen coordinator." She wiped her nose and took another tissue.

"Was there an event coming up that Travis was going to volunteer for?"

"I don't think so." She looked up at Chris. "Travis came by a lot because he helped Kevin with a couple of the other programs. He always stopped by here to say hi. He was so nice—" Her voice broke and she bit her lip.

"Do you know what those other programs were?" Chris handed her another tissue.

She hesitated, as if trying to remember. "There was the outreach program to get young people interested in coming. Then there was—" she lowered her voice a bit, "New Hope."

Chris leaned forward, cocking an eyebrow. "New Hope?"

Debbie glanced up, looking like a child with a hand in a cookie jar. Guilty and wary. She kept her voice low. "To help you if you don't like certain things about yourself."

A prickle danced down Chris's spine. She had a feeling she knew what Debbie Ruiz was talking about. "I'm sorry, Ms. Ruiz, can you explain a little better?"

She sighed and answered, voice still low. "Have you heard of Exodus International?"

Chris nodded.

"Like that." She looked extremely uncomfortable and she kept glancing toward the door. She clearly was worried about being seen talking to them about this topic.

Who is she afraid of? Chris stood, deciding to cut Debbie a break for now. Getting her into trouble with whomever freaked her out just wasn't good for that policework rapport. She returned the borrowed chair to its desk. "You've been very helpful, Ms. Ruiz." She pulled a business card out of her wallet and handed it to Debbie. "If you think of anything else that might help us find out what happened to Travis, call me."

Debbie nodded and reached for the piece of paper from the printer. She handed it to Chris and took her business card in return.

"Can I help you?" came Charlotte's voice from the doorway. "Oh, Debbie."

Chris looked from Charlotte to Debbie. Something beyond Travis's death had Debbie rattled. "My apologies," Chris said, coming around the counter. "Pastor Chaz said to see you about checking a name on the membership rolls and he hoped maybe you could show us around."

"Membership rolls?" Charlotte's matronly demeanor slipped off her face like a mask.

"Yes, ma'am," Harper stepped in, surprising Chris. But he had apparently read something in her because Charlotte relaxed. "We're investigating the death of someone who was a member of Wellspring."

"Oh, my," Charlotte said, one hand fluttering at her throat. "Who?"

Harper pulled the photo from the file and handed it to her.

"Oh, good Lord," she breathed.

"Did you know him?" Harper pressed carefully.

"Well, of course. Travis McCormick."

"Can you tell us the last time you saw him?" Harper had his notebook ready.

"Thursday the nineteenth. Such a nice young man. He always stopped by here to say hello when he was checking in about volunteering or he would come in on Sunday mornings. He was a regular at the nine-thirty service." She shook her head slowly, shocked.

"Ma'am —" Harper started as he returned the photo to the file. "Pastor Chaz said you would take some time with us. Show us around and maybe talk to some other staff members about Travis." He smiled at her. Chris watched the exchange, intrigued. Harper was good at this when he wanted to be.

"Of course," Charlotte said. "I don't know how helpful I can be. Travis worked mostly with Kevin, the teen coordinator, and he's not here today. But anything I can do to help, you just let me know, Detective..."

"Harper. Dale Harper."

She smiled back at him and motioned him toward the front entrance. Chris shot a glance at Debbie, who had retreated to her desk and was trying to look extremely busy typing something. She didn't look up. Maybe Charlotte had her scared. And Charlotte might be a direct line to Chaz, which was why Debbie was keeping her mouth shut. Chris turned and followed Harper out into the lobby, listening to Charlotte, now in her official tour guide mode. She droned on about the history of Wellspring and how it was such a blessing for Chaz to have taken the position as the senior pastor. Harper very subtly pumped her for information, much to Chris's surprise and appreciation. He was actually very good at insinuating himself into a subject's good graces. *Shit, why doesn't he do that more often? Save me some damn work.*

She kept notes as they worked their way through what Charlotte called "the education wing," mostly rooms used for Bible school and daycare, from the decorations. A few administrative offices and even fewer staff. Two vaguely remembered Travis because he helped with the youth programs, but they hadn't had much to do with him otherwise. Given the size of the congregation, Chris wasn't surprised.

The other building was full of rooms used for various meetings, Charlotte explained. Adult Bible study, religious classes, membership classes, AA, and Al-Anon. Nothing unusual there, either. They spoke briefly with three more staff members who remembered Travis as a nice young man who helped with the youth programs, but they didn't see him outside of that and didn't know anything about him otherwise.

Charlotte led them back to the lobby and looked discreetly at her watch. Harper took the hint. "Thank you so much for your time, Mrs. Doyle. If you think of anything else, just give me a call." He handed her a business card, which she took. Chris noticed that she allowed her fingers to brush his. So Harper had a way with certain ladies. Church-going, conservative types who liked to eat at Cracker Barrel and use words like "homemade" and "precious" in reference to children and collectibles. She cleared her throat to keep herself from laughing and availed herself of several of the information brochures lying on the hexagonal table while Charlotte chatted away with Harper. Chris took one from each of the twelve stacks.

"I sure will, Detective. And I do hope you find whoever did this. Such a shame. Such a nice young man." Charlotte shook her head and Harper echoed the motion. He glanced at Chris, a signal to leave.

"Thank you very much for taking all that time with us," Chris said as she moved to the front entrance. "Please do give Detective Harper a call if you think of anything else."

"Oh, I will." Charlotte smiled and offered a little wave at Harper as he waited for Chris to push the glass door open. He followed her outside but didn't say anything until they were nearly to her car.

"Something's funny there."

"Agreed." Chris stopped at the driver's side of her car and looked at him, waiting for more. She took her sunglasses from her pocket and put them on, and he handed her the manila folder.

"The pastor knows more than he's saying. Charlotte's covering for someone. Maybe the pastor. Maybe this Stillman guy." He flipped his notebook closed. "What'd you think of Ruiz?" He put the accent on the first syllable and made the second sound like "is." Chris stifled a sigh. The man was hopeless with Spanish.

"She's scared. Maybe of Charlotte. But Charlotte might just be covering for the church in general. She does seem to really like Chaz. Maybe she doesn't know anything, but is more concerned about appearances."

He nodded slowly then changed the subject. "So — Exodus International?"

"Big ex-gay organization." *And what do you think about that?*

"New Hope," he said thoughtfully. "So groups like that try to make people heterosexual." It wasn't a question and Chris didn't respond. She had figured out quickly that Harper tended to think aloud. He rocked forward on his toes and rocked back again then cleared his throat. "You think they work?"

"What do you mean?" She watched him behind her shades. He seemed uncomfortable.

"Groups like that. You think they can make people stop being queer?"

"Gay."

"What?"

"The term is gay, Harper. 'Queer' is still seen as offensive by a lot of gay people."

He shrugged and looked away for a moment, then looked back. "Gay, then. So do groups like that work?"

His discomfort grew. There was something personal here for him and she wanted to be careful. "There have been some studies done and basically, no, they don't work. What usually happens is that the person is still gay. They've just decided to deny that they're gay and not to act on it. In other words, they don't follow their true feelings. And a lot of them are more unhappy than they were before."

He fished his own sunglasses out of his left-hand inside breast pocket and put them on. "All right. Plan of action. How do you want to work this?"

Chris accepted the change of topic for what it was. His body language indicated he was clearly uncomfortable with the whole subject of homosexuality. But she did have to give him props for at least trying to be open-minded. "I'm going to swing by Pulse and talk to the guys there, see if the pastor or Stillman ever went." She held up one of the brochures. "Nice pics in here of both Mumford and Stillman. I got an extra for you." She handed it to him.

"Where's Pulse?" He opened the brochure.

"Central and Silver, east of Nob Hill. If you're headed toward the Sandias, it's on your right. You want to go?"

He cleared his throat. "Do you need me to?"

Clearly not. "I can cover this one. I went to high school with one of the owners."

Harper looked up from the brochure, seeming to consider that statement and what it might mean. "Okay, then. I want to have a look at the surveillance vids from The Beach. Maybe we'll get lucky." He held the brochure up meaningfully. "You going to Cruces today?"

She nodded. "I've got a hunch about this. You think you can follow up on Stillman? Oh, and can you check in with Sam at the ME's about trace? I want to know if there was anything we can use from Travis's body." She reached for her door handle, then stopped. "I'm not feeling Griggs or the father on this. You?"

"Nope. She's more the irritated type than the fly off the handle and strangle your own son with an electrical cord type. No matter what she thought of him. Plus, her alibi checks out."

Chris fought a smile at his description. "My thoughts exactly."

"And the dad's got the Atlanta alibi. Plus, he hadn't kept up with Travis for three years. Why would he start now? I'm thinkin' we chase these other angles."

"All right. What about Josh?"

"Nope. I'm not feeling that, either." Harper bounced on the balls of his feet.

"Same here. Okay. Let me know about the video from The Beach."

"Will do." He slid the brochure into one of his pockets and started to turn away. He hesitated, like he wanted to say something else. "I'll check in later," he announced in his flat, nasal accent.

"Same here." *And yes. I am. A big scary lesbian. Christ, just fucking ask already.* It was almost funny, how he danced around the issue. Well, it wasn't her problem. If he wanted to talk about it, all he had to do was bring it up. She wasn't going to hand it to him on a damn platter, though. "Catch you later," she said dismissively.

He grunted something in response and headed across the parking lot toward his Jeep Cherokee. Chris unlocked her car and slid into the driver's seat. She tossed the folder and the brochures onto the passenger seat and started the engine. The clock on her dash read 11:30. She'd have time to grab something to eat before going to Pulse. She turned left onto Coors Boulevard and headed south toward Montaño, which would take her across the Rio Grande, away from the West Side and Wellspring.

Chapter
Eight

PULSE NIGHTCLUB FACED busy Central Avenue, a main east-west route through Albuquerque, part of what had once been historic Route 66. This part of Central was maybe a mile east of Nob Hill, a funky artsy district. The farther east on Central, the seedier the area, though even here, west of San Mateo, one of the major north-south routes, glimmers of a better time lined the street, showing through the tired faux-dobe structures of 1940s- and 1950s-era motels that had since become havens for drug deals, prostitution, and desperation.

Chris turned right onto Silver Avenue and entered the alley behind Pulse so she could park in the back. She eased her car around a Budweiser truck. This early, the front door into the nightclub would not be open, so Chris would have to go through the back entrance, which led into Blu, the lounge that shared the same building. The structure itself was a blocky one-story, its cinderblock exterior painted black. A red jagged line like the reading off a heart monitor decorated the big sign that advertised it, though the building looked more like something from a warehouse district than a hospital. Sort of industrial, in a provincial imitation of big-city hip.

She pulled in next to a blue late-model Ford Ranger. Two other cars were parked near the back entrance, propped open so the Budweiser guy could come and go with his dolly. Blu offered plush velvet benches surrounded by ultra-cool neon and what Chris called "post-modern hippie shit" ambiance as patrons listened to a DJ spin chill and other electronica music. Entering through this door, customers walked through Blu to get into Pulse, which sported a nice dance floor and a stage in front of another DJ booth.

Pulse's interior tried to evoke a sort of smooth industrial feel without all the grease and grime of an actual factory, though the owners liked to change it up a bit and install different art or paint some of the walls different colors every now and again. The last time Chris had been here, which was maybe a year ago, the popular colors had been reds and soft yellows. She wasn't sure what she'd find this year.

She put her sunglasses into their case and put it in the glove compartment along with her personal cell phone, grabbed the manila folder and the brochure with Pastor Chaz's and youth coordinator Kevin Stillman's photographs, and locked up. At the back entrance, she waited for the beer guy to scoot through with his empty dolly. He smiled at her and she smiled back as she passed into the dark interior of Blu.

Like most clubs, it smelled of old, damp cigarettes and spilled beer. It didn't matter if nobody smoked in here for a month. It would always smell like a bar. Somebody had turned the radio on and a local hip-hop station was playing softly over the sound system. No one was hanging out in Blu, so Chris headed into the main bar. The color scheme for this year was black accented with slashes of teal and what Chris's gay male friends would call mauve. A darker shade of pink, Chris decided. Last year's colors were better.

"Hey! Look what the wind blew in!"

A voice from the DJ booth greeted her as she stood at the edge of the dance floor surveying the dim interior. A short man with black spiky hair emerged and bounded down the three steps to the floor just behind the stage. He wore loose blue jeans and an old Pulse T-shirt underneath a button-down black shirt that he had left open and untucked. She walked toward him, smiling, and he grabbed her in a huge embrace. Jason Alvarez—Alvie, as Chris called him—was one of Pulse's owners. He had graduated from Albuquerque High School the same year as Chris and though he had hung with the Goths during those years and Chris ran with the jock crowd—she had played varsity basketball—they had become friends their sophomore year when Chris faced down one of the football players who was harassing Jason for "acting like a fag." Jason never forgot that and ever since, he and Chris shared an "ol' school" tie, as he called it.

"What's up, *ese?*" Chris stepped back. "Let me look at you. It's been a while."

He struck a *Vogue* pose and swished across the dance floor.

"Work it," Chris said laughing. "Oh, yeah. You've still got it. Too bad I turned out a lesbian and not a nice gay boy like you."

He grinned. "You look good, girl. Still the hot butch I remember from back in the day. Bulldogs!" He growled and barked at the mention of the Albuquerque High mascot.

Chris grinned and shook her head. "Honey, stop. I was the jock, remember?"

"And for a damn good reason. You want a Coke or something?" He pulled her toward the bar.

"No, thanks. I'm good."

He motioned her to one of the barstools, taking the one on

Chris's left. "So what's up? I get the feeling you're not here to reminisce."

"You're right. At least not about us." Chris set the file on the bar and opened it. She removed the photo of Travis and placed it on the bar next to him.

He stared at it. "Oh, no. Shit."

"I'm sorry." She squeezed his shoulder. "I'm really sorry."

"Fuck. I heard that the guy they found in the bosque might be him. Damn. I was hoping he just hooked up with somebody and got caught up in a fuckfest. But it just wasn't like him to not show like that. And his roommate was completely freaked on Sunday. I had a bad feeling..." He muttered something in Spanish and picked up the photo, staring at it for a long time. "What happened?" He tugged on one of the myriad piercings in his right ear, a holdover from his Goth days. His voice held a slight tremor.

"I can't really say," Chris said quietly, hand still on his shoulder. "But we're following a lot of different leads. When was the last time you saw him?"

"He was here last Friday. What day was that?"

"The twentieth." She removed her hand.

"Yeah. He stopped by around noon to pick up his paycheck and then he came back that night around eleven."

"Was he with anyone?"

"I don't know if he came with anyone. I didn't see him until he was actually inside and everybody knew him because he bartended here. He was really, really nice. Damn." He cleared his throat.

"Weird question. What was he wearing?"

"Girl, please," he scoffed. "I'm a gay man. Of *course* I notice things like that. Distressed Lucky jeans—that pair looked good on him. Showed off his ass. White clubwear shirt, tucked in. He had a nice build and he wore those body-hugging shirts to show it off. Got him nice tips when he worked."

That wasn't what the crime scene team had found on Travis's bed at his apartment. So he had come home after the fight with his mother, changed, and gone out again. He was still alive for at least part of Friday night. "How long did he stay?"

"Honestly, I don't know. He generally didn't work Fridays but he did Saturdays. Except one of the other bartenders had picked up his shift for that Saturday. I asked him about it a few days before Friday and he said he had a date Saturday night."

"Did he say who the guy was?"

Jason was quiet for a moment. "No. He just said he'd met somebody and he seemed pretty excited about it." He shook his head. "I remember seeing him in Blu around one AM on Friday. He had a table in the corner. An older guy was sitting with him." He sighed heavily.

Chris opened the brochure she had picked up at Wellspring. Fortunately, the photos were arranged quite handily. Pastor Chaz was on the left, Kevin Stillman on the right. "Was it one of them?"

He took the brochure and studied it. "I don't think so."

Shit.

"Wait a sec." He got up and went around the bar and stooped, removing what looked like a shoebox from one of the cabinets underneath. He rummaged it in and pulled out a pen, then re-joined her. "Mind if I mark on this?" he asked, eyebrows raised.

"Go ahead." Chris pushed the brochure toward him and he took it and set to work on the photo of Pastor Chaz.

A few moments later, he finished what he was doing and handed it back to Chris, satisfied. "*That's* the guy who was sitting with Travis. And you know what? He's been in before."

Chris stared at the image. Jason had drawn a goatee and mustache on Pastor Chaz's face. "Are you sure?"

"Yep."

"Do you have surveillance cameras?"

"Oh, yeah. All the freaks around? You never know. We're mostly digital, so we stash the video on a hard drive for a while. I'll get Friday the twentieth ready for you. When do you need it?"

"Can I pick it up late tomorrow afternoon? It'll probably be close to say, four or five." She took a business card out of her wallet and handed it to him.

"I'll make sure it's ready." He sat back, regarding her as he put the card in his shirt pocket.

"So you've seen this guy before? A regular?"

"No, he's not. But I notice him when he's here because he's a bit older than the usual. And he's good-looking. He comes in probably two or three times a month. Always on Fridays. Oh, and he's a total closet-case. That's the other reason I notice him."

Chris looked at him. "What tells you that?"

Jason rolled his eyes. "You'd know if you saw. He comes in here and he always looks nervous, like he's afraid somebody who matters is going to recognize him. He'll hang out near the bar, usually. I've never seen him dance, but I *have* seen him check out the merchandise."

"Any action?"

"Not that I saw. But that doesn't mean it hasn't happened. We try to keep the bathrooms free of that shit, but sometimes somebody gets a quickie in the stalls. Or the parking lot." He looked at her and said dryly, "We've *all* done that."

She raised an eyebrow. "True. Can I talk to your other bartenders and barbacks?"

He snorted. "You need to ask? B-ball, it's *me* you're talking to. Alvie. We're homies, *esa*. Anything I can do for you, just ask." He grinned and punched her lightly on the arm, then checked his watch. "Adam should be here any minute. You wanna stick around a bit?"

"Sure. As long as it's not more than a half-hour or so." She smiled at him.

"Nah. Adam's good about that. You sure you don't want a Coke?"

"I *will* take you up on that. Diet."

He rolled his eyes and laughed. "Gotta keep that hot butch bod."

"Definitely," she retorted good-naturedly.

"Speaking of which," he said as he filled a pint glass with ice and then Diet Coke from the soda spigot behind the bar, "any nice *chiquita* in your life?"

"I date here and there," she said defensively as she took the glass from him.

He leaned on the cooler, watching her. "Just asking. Hell, if I was a dyke I'd be all over you like my cousins on a plate of empanadas. Damn. Remember how you had all the little *cholas* following you around? And they weren't even gay." He grinned as he picked up an empty glass and poured himself a Coke.

"So you say." Chris shrugged, embarrassed. "I never noticed."

" 'Cause you only had eyes for Maria Sanchez. Typical jock. Going after the head cheerleader." He chortled before he took a long drink from his glass.

Chris grinned. "She wasn't completely straight, you know." She took a drink.

He stared at her, eyes widening. "Shut up." His mouth dropped open. "No! You are shitting me."

She shook her head, still smiling over the rim of her glass.

"Oh, my God. Did her boyfriend — what's-his-name, the football player — find out?"

"Benny Johnson. She wasn't seeing him yet. I think she might have started dating him because she was worried she'd get stuck in gayville."

"She traded *you* for *Benny*? *Chica mas loca*. So what happened?" He took her glass and refilled it.

"I don't kiss and tell," she said, smiling wickedly as she took the glass back.

"Girl. You *have* to. I told you about Ricky Rodriguez."

"I didn't ask you to. But it was pretty funny that you got into the star baseball player's pants." She raised her eyebrows and laughed at the memories of Alvie's stories.

"What was funny was how fucking easy it was. He was *so* gay."

Jason refilled his own glass. "He ended up going to UCLA. His brother's still around, though." He swirled the drink with a straw. "So what happened with Maria?"

"It was a Friday, after a home game with Manzano. Our junior year. We totally kicked their asses and got into the tournament—"

"I so remember that! And you scored something like a thousand points. Everybody was talking about it on Monday."

Chris lowered her gaze, sheepish. "Well, maybe nine hundred."

He blew a trace of soda at her through his straw.

She laughed. "Anyway, the guys played after us and most of us stayed to watch. They got beat, but not badly. Maria was there and she kept coming over to talk to me when she wasn't out on the court bouncing around in that little skirt thing." Chris smiled as Jason laughed. "She was pretty hot."

"And?" he pressed.

"After the guys played, everybody headed home—you know how the crowds were at the games. That was what you did in the barrio, after all. Friday night high school sports. My brother Mike—"

"*Total* beefcake," Jason interrupted. "You have a beautiful family."

"God, Alvie. You cruised my brothers?"

"Just Mike and Pete. John wasn't old enough yet." He started to say something else, then thought better of it as Chris threw an ice cube at him. He caught it and tossed in the sink.

"Anyway," she continued, glaring at him in mock remonstration, "Mike let me borrow his car that night so I was going to the parking lot after everybody did their high fives and shit. I was pretty tired and just wanted to get home. I had just opened the door and I heard somebody shouting my name and there was Maria. She wanted a ride."

"Oh, of course. Because her perfectly good brand new car that her dad bought for her that year just didn't work at all."

"She wasn't driving it that night. She came with Lisa Romero and Lisa ditched her to go to a party and Maria had a curfew. So I said sure—*duh*—and we got to her house and—" Chris stopped and smiled. "Let's just say she didn't get out of the car right away."

"Holy fucking God. You made out with the head cheerleader. How long were you—"

"A couple of months. But I knew she was scared somebody would find out so I just...let her go." Chris remembered that, wondering at the little pang of sadness it brought.

"You haven't changed all that much, *esa*." Jason reached across the bar and squeezed her hand. "I don't know where you got that streak, but maybe you let go too easy sometimes. Maybe she wouldn't have ended up with Benny if you gave her something to hold on to."

"Listen to you. What are you? The Dear Abby of Albuquerque?" Chris stood and drained her glass as a man about Jason's height came in, dressed in tight black jeans and a turquoise T-shirt underneath a battered leather jacket. He glanced at Jason, then Chris, puzzled.

"Hey, Adam. This is Chris. She's with APD. She has some questions for you." Jason smiled. "See you tomorrow, B-ball. I'll go start working on those videos. Good to see you." He hugged her.

"Yeah. Good to see you, too. Thanks for the Coke."

He waved as he took the corridor back into Blu. Chris turned her attention to Adam, who was looking at her wide-eyed. He ran a hand nervously over his blond buzzcut.

"Don't worry," she said, "It's nothing you did. However—" She pulled Travis's photo from the manila file and handed it to him. He took it and sank onto a nearby barstool.

"Oh, fuck," he said softly. "So it *was* Travis they found. I heard rumors..." He shook his head and bit his lip.

Chris handed him a bar napkin. "I'm really sorry I have to tell you this. We're trying to figure some things out." She opened the brochure with the picture of Pastor Chaz that Jason had altered. "Do you recognize him?"

"Hell, yes," Adam said, wiping his eyes with the napkin. "He comes in usually on Fridays and I work this bar, which is where he hangs out." He handed the brochure back to Chris and she slipped it back into the file.

"Do you know his name?"

"No."

"How does he act?"

"Like he's scared somebody will see him. He tries to get that chair over near the wall and he orders a tall Jack and Coke, almost every time."

"Does he ever come in with anybody?"

"Not that I've seen." Adam stopped, thinking. "He does sometimes leave with guys, though. Nobody regular. I figured they're just quickies because he's probably married."

"Does he wear a ring?" Chris figured Chaz would probably remove his wedding band, whether he was married or not, when he came here.

"No," Adam said, confirming her guess. "But I assume he's closeted because he's married." He shrugged, a "you know what I mean" gesture. "I mean, when you get a closet-case like that in here, they generally act nervous because they're married to women. I've seen it a lot."

"Did you ever notice if he wore a necklace?"

Adam thought for a moment. "No, because he always wore a button-down shirt with a tie, so you couldn't see his neck. And that tie was never loose. It was like he came over right from an office job or something. I noticed that, because here, it's about club casual. He kind of stuck out in that respect because he looked like a lawyer or accountant or something."

"Did you ever see him physically engaged with anyone while he was here?"

"Not at the bar, though he cruised a lot. I did bust him in the parking lot once. I was taking a load of trash out and he was outside, up against the back wall tonsil-dancing with a guy. I don't know who it was."

"Do you remember when that was?" Chris leaned on the bar casually.

Adam visibly relaxed. "Around New Year's, actually. The Friday before." His brow furrowed. "You know, I just realized that when Travis came in on Fridays—he didn't usually work Fridays, but he liked to come in anyway—that guy would talk to him. I mean, not *every* Friday. But I noticed it really starting up around the beginning of December. He cruised Travis a lot, beginning around then."

"Did Travis ever talk about him?" Chris leaned forward a bit.

"Not really. He'd kind of joke with me a bit about how the guy was a total closet-case, but nothing mean. Travis wasn't like that. He was—" Adam stopped and cleared his throat, wiping his eyes again with the napkin Chris had provided. "He was really sweet. He said that he felt bad for the guy because he couldn't be himself, and Travis hoped some day that he'd be able to just be gay and be happy with himself."

So why, then, was Travis helping Kevin Stillman with an ex-gay program? What the hell? "Did Travis ever mention a church?"

"Oh, yeah. He went to Wellspring on the West Side." Adam looked troubled. "I don't know what his deal was with that. Sometimes if it was slow he'd ask me what I thought about Jesus and the Bible and I said I didn't, really. That I wasn't into anything that said people like me are going to burn in hell. And he would say that Jesus wasn't about that, that people got it all wrong. I think his family must've been religious or something and he never got over it."

"So when was the last time you saw Travis?"

"Friday the twentieth," he said without hesitation. "A friend of his roommate's dropped him off. He said his car's battery was acting up and sometimes it started and sometimes it didn't. I remember him saying that. He said he'd probably take a cab home. And that guy showed up around ten-thirty. He ordered his drink. About eleven

Travis came in and sat down next to him. He ordered his usual—a Michelob Light. Travis looked kind of surprised to see him here at first."

Maybe Travis wasn't expecting Chaz to show up Friday. Something changed. If Chaz was the man with whom Travis had the date scheduled for Saturday, then seeing him Friday might have surprised Travis. Otherwise, why wouldn't they just schedule a date for Friday, when Travis wasn't working? Something in Chaz's schedule must have shifted. *If Chaz is the guy Travis was dating.* And Chris had a strong feeling it was.

Adam continued, "They were acting pretty close. Intimate. They moved to Blu around twelve-thirty and I took trash out at one-thirty. They were still there, sitting at a table in the corner."

"Did they leave together?"

"I didn't see. I was cleaning up and when I went to check Blu, it was almost two and they were gone."

The surveillance tapes might show something. So Travis was still alive at one-thirty Saturday morning. Chris pushed off from the bar. "Adam, thank you. You've been really helpful." She pulled her wallet out of her back pocket and removed a business card. "If you think of anything else, give me a call."

He took the card and looked at it. "Gutierrez?" He looked at her closely then. "Are you related to John?"

"I have a brother named John. Do you know him?"

Adam looked at her, confused. "Um, he works here."

Chris stared at him. "Doing what?" *Holy shit. John's working at Pulse? When did that start?*

"He DJs in Blu on the weekends and does barbacking and bartending on Tuesdays and Thursdays." Adam shifted, clearly uncomfortable. He looked like he wanted to melt into the flooring. "Oh, my God. Did I just out him? Oh, shit."

Chris stifled a smile at his discomfiture. "Not entirely," she said after she recovered. "I just didn't realize he had taken a job here. It's all right. I already knew, though he hasn't officially told me. And it's not like I wouldn't understand," she said.

It didn't do anything to alleviate Adam's misery or embarrassment. "Fuck," he whispered. "Oh, my God. I can't believe this—"

As if on cue, a voice from the corridor called his name. "Hey, Adam! I can't find the invoice for—shit."

Chris's youngest brother froze in the corridor between Pulse and Blu. He stared at her, then at Adam, then her again. "Chris?" He said her name as if he was hoping that he'd wake up from a bad dream and he'd be in his bedroom, safe, and his older sister wouldn't be standing there staring at him in a gay bar.

"*Juanito,*" she said, addressing him with the pet diminutive she used with him. She smiled wryly. "Is there something you finally want to tell me? Even though we both know?"

"Uh—"

Adam groaned softly, looking like he'd accidentally run over somebody's mother. "I'm sorry," he whispered. "I didn't realize—"

"It's not your fault," John said, offering a chagrined smile. He ran a hand through his thick dark hair. He kept it shorter than Chris's. Hers fell just past her ears and his he kept trimmed above. Of all her brothers, John looked most like her. They took after their father in that regard except John didn't get as much height. He cleared his throat and waited for her to follow him back into Blu. He and Chris had always shared an unspoken deeper bond than what either had with their other brothers and they often didn't have to say anything to know what the other was thinking. So when John looked at her and turned away, Chris knew he wanted her to follow him. She grabbed the folder off the bar as she did so.

He sat down at one of the tables in Blu, broad shoulders slumped. He was built like the kind of gymnast who worked out on the rings. He remained quiet for a moment, then ran his hands nervously over the front of his Pulse T-shirt and then on his jeans, still staring at the tabletop. "I was totally going to tell you. Officially," he said quietly. "I know you knew, but I just—didn't want to talk about it much."

"It's okay. I've been waiting for you to tell me but I didn't want to push you. I figured you would when you were ready."

He looked at her, a younger male version of herself. They might have been twins. "So—how long?" he asked.

"Jesus, *Juanito*. All our fucking lives. Who did you think covered for you all those nights you ran late when Mom and Dad thought you were out with Ana?"

"That was you?" He stared at her. "I thought that was Mike. Except he really did think I was with her." He smiled at the memory.

She shook her head. "No, that was me, *hermano*. I know you covered for me, too. How come you've been scared to tell me?"

"I saw how Mom took it with you. I got scared, I guess, to tell anyone. Even you. And I guess I didn't want it to be true."

"Makes sense." She had come out to her parents when she was nearing her twenty-second birthday. Their father had lapsed into a strange silence and their mother burst into tears and kept saying the rosary and calling on *La Virgen* to deliver Chris from evil. It was a hot July day that felt worse than the coldest winter. And then *Abuelita* showed up suddenly, as if she had felt a tremor in The Force or something, and she sat her daughter—Chris's mother—down and told her in no uncertain terms that she was being *una madre horrible* to carry on like that. A terrible mother, putting her own daughter down like that. *Abuelita* tended to eschew English so the conversation went on in dramatic Spanish for a good hour and at the end of it, Chris's mother was crying all over Chris's shirt and her father had them both in a hug in his big arms and *Abuelita* had nodded sagely, dark eyes still flashing.

"Mom got over it, mostly," Chris said to him. "Well, maybe not entirely," she added ruefully. Their mother still hoped Chris would "snap out of it" and find a man.

"It's different for me," he responded. "I'm the baby boy."

He was right. Latino mothers, no matter their generation or how removed from their country of origin, often had different relationships with their youngest sons than with their other children. "You've got *Abuelita*, too," she pointed out.

"I know." He nervously ran his fingertips over the tabletop. "But it's hard. All that macho Hispanic bullshit. I'm no less a man than Mike or Pete. Or Dad."

"Being gay doesn't make you less of any kind of man. You've always been a guy. You were a great boy, you've grown into a wonderful man, and you're an awesome brother. I don't give a shit if you're screwing men or women. Or how you identify. Just play safe, be honest, and respect yourself." She saw in his demeanor the teenager he had been.

A softness entered his eyes. "Do you remember how you'd leave boxes of condoms in my shoes? I *did* figure out that was you."

Chris laughed. "It was the early nineties. I worried about you. And I knew if you asked Mike or Pete to get you some, they'd give you shit about who your girlfriend was. And I knew you were too embarrassed to ask me. Being a girl and all."

"I knew it was you, though. God, I really appreciated that." His voice was soft.

"Do you remember after I came out that day and *Abuelita* had gone home—"

"We went to get green chile burgers at The Owl Café. You and me." He smiled at the memory.

"You told me you didn't care that I was gay. You just wanted me to be happy and you asked if I had a girlfriend."

"And you said you did. That was Julie, from Chicago. I never liked her. She was a bitch."

Chris looked at him sharply, then started laughing. "Well, it didn't last long, did it?"

"No, thank God. Then you were with Laura. She was okay. But kind of weird. Then you dated Audra. She was pretty cute, but nervous. Then you whored around for a while."

Chris choked on another laugh. "Oh, you're one to talk. Are you seeing anyone?"

He shook his head. "No. Not really. Dating." He grinned then, the same grin that Chris had. "Then you tried to get serious, but you got all caught up in your cop show routine." He was teasing her now and Chris grinned back at him. They started laughing, then giggling like when they were younger, standing beneath the summer stars on the patio of the house where they grew up, roasting marshmallows over the dying coals of the barbecue grill that their Uncle Tomás used to cook and usually burn steaks.

"So how long have you been working here?" Chris finally asked. "And why didn't you tell me?"

"Since October. I'm saving up. I haven't really told many people that I'm moonlighting. I didn't feel like dealing with the questions."

"So you're moonlighting because...?"

He hesitated, then answered, shy. "I want to go to culinary school."

Chris stared at him. "Really? Where?"

"Los Angeles. I've been talking to *Abuelita*, getting her recipes and experimenting with them."

"I didn't know you liked to cook so much." *Damn. I need to hang out more with my brother.*

"I didn't either 'til about a year ago when I helped Dan Griswold with that catering thing. Remember that? I just took it to earn some extra money and I ended up — Chris, I loved it. It was like something clicked into place with me." He was animated, talking with excitement and reverence.

She leaned forward and squeezed his hand. "That sounds great. When are you going to tell Dad?"

He groaned softly. "I don't know. I don't think Dad'll be happy about it. You know how he is about his sons and the business. And Jesus Christ, there's the gay thing, too."

"He's got Mike and Pete to carry on with that. They both love it there. And now that Mike's married and about to be a father again, he's rooted. Gutierrez and Sons Construction will continue. As for the gay thing — *Abuelita* and I will run interference for you."

John sighed heavily. "I need to have a talk with everyone. I'm not sure yet. Soon. I'll call you, though."

"*Sí, hermanito.* You will." She used her stern cop voice with him and he sank lower in his seat. Their brother Mike said that Chris's cop mode could scare people shorter. And then he'd say that, obviously, Chris had used it on John most of their lives. John opened his mouth to say something else, but she put her hand up. "Wait. Whatever happens, you're my brother and I will always be there for you. If you need some help to go to school, let me know."

"It's a little more expensive than condoms in my shoes," he teased.

"And I'm making a bit more money now."

He smiled. "Thanks."

"*De nada.*" She regarded him for a moment, an older sister. "*Juanito,* in the future, please tell me these important things. I don't want to have to come to Pulse and ask Adam what's going on with you." She reached across the table and poked him playfully in the chest.

"I'm sorry," he said. "I really wanted to—I don't know. Make it formal between us. I know you've known and I don't know why I felt weird about telling you. I guess I wasn't ready to accept it completely. I guess on some level, maybe I hoped I wasn't. I mean, you already put Mom and Dad through it. I didn't want to do that again."

Not a bad point. "You can always come to me. But it's your responsibility to tell *la familia.* Let me know if and when you're ready and I'll help you any way I can."

He nodded and looked at her with an expression that said he would and that he loved her for it.

"Now. Time for other shit, I'm sorry to say." She opened the folder.

Chapter
Nine

CHRIS SAT IN her driver's seat writing up her notes. John had DJed at Blu on Friday the twentieth and he did remember seeing Travis with the man Chris suspected was Pastor Chaz. According to John, they left about 1:45 AM together. They did seem to be intimate, leaning toward each other and touching each other on the hands, arms, and shoulders. John claimed he didn't know much about Travis, though they did work together on occasion. He said Travis was always pleasant but, for whatever reasons, he and John didn't really talk much, though John was still upset when Chris told him why she had come to Pulse. She was extremely glad that John didn't know much more beyond what he told her. He didn't really pay attention to patrons, since he was mostly a barback and second bartender type and when he was DJing, he was focused on that throughout his shift.

Chris would have to notify her superiors that, yes, John Gutierrez was her brother, and if they requested a follow-up from Harper, she'd bring John to the station for that. She hoped they wouldn't because most likely, it would have to be during the day and John worked for their father at the construction business. Michael, Sr. would want to know why the police were questioning his son and John would be forced to either lie about it or come out before he was ready. She hoped the higher-ups would trust her judgment and not call him in for a statement.

Her personal cell beeped, indicating someone had called and left a message. She removed it from the glove compartment and checked the call log. K.C. had called an hour ago and Dayna about ten minutes ago. Chris's heart jumped a little. She dialed the number for her messages and entered her code. K.C.'s message was first: "Hey, Supercop. I've got some interesting info for you with regard to a certain pastor we talked about. You're probably on your way to Cruces, so just give me a buzz tonight if you have a chance. Drive carefully. Later."

Chris deleted it and waited for the second message. Dayna's voice oozed like warm honey into her skull. *Shit. How does she do this to me?*

"Hi, Chris. I've been thinking about you." Dayna laughed softly. "This might sound strange, but I miss you." She paused. Then, "God, I'm just not very good at this message stuff. Sorry. But I mean it." She cleared her throat. "I hope that doesn't freak you out." She paused again. "Um—Jesus, I suck at this." Laughing. "I really want to spend more time with you. I'm just putting that out there. And I want to try to make things right. Okay. Um...anyway. I hope you're doing well. Talk to you later. I'm *so* looking forward to Friday I can't even tell you. Bye."

Chris played the message again. Then she saved it and, before she could talk herself out of it, she dialed Dayna's cell. It was almost 2:00, so Chris doubted she would pick up, since she was usually pretty busy at work. Sure enough, Chris got bumped to voicemail: "Hi. You've reached five-oh-five, four-seven-oh, two-two-nine-seven. Or if you prefer, Dayna. I'm sorry I can't take your call, but please leave a message and I'll get back to you as soon as I can. Thanks."

Chris waited for the beep, nervously clearing her throat in the intervening seconds. "Hey. Thanks for the message. I'm actually about to drive to Las Cruces to follow up on something. I'll be back tomorrow afternoon some time. I've been thinking about you, too. Quite a bit, actually. And I'd definitely like to spend more time with you. If you can squeeze me in somewhere," she teased. "So, yes, talk to me later. I'd like that. Hope you have a good rest of the day. Bye."

She hung up and sat staring blankly at her phone. Had she sounded confident or nervous? She was pretty sure it was confident, but Dayna rattled her on so many levels. What did it mean, that Dayna wanted to spend more time with her? *Is she giving up her harem? And what's the deal with the two months' silence? K.C.'s right. I really do like her. Damn.*

Chris sighed and pulled her business cell from her pocket. She dialed Harper's number. He didn't pick up so she left him a message, briefing him on what she had learned at Pulse. She told him that when he watched the surveillance videos from The Beach he should watch for a man who looked like Pastor Chaz but with a mustache and goatee.

She hung up but thought of something and used the phone to take a picture of the alteration Jason had made to Pastor Chaz's photo in the brochure and sent that to Harper, as well, before placing the phone on the passenger seat. She buckled up and took the alley back to Silver so she could turn west onto Central and catch I-25 southbound. The drive from Albuquerque to Las Cruces was about 220 miles, roughly three and a half hours. She'd have plenty of time to sort through her day in the stretches of desert, grasslands, and arroyos that defined the topography between the two cities. Plenty of time to think about John, too.

CHRIS SANK INTO one of the plush chairs in her room at the Best Western Mission Inn. She positioned herself so that she could prop her feet on the king-sized bed. This hotel incorporated Spanish colonial/artsy New Mexico themes in its furnishings and room design, which Chris found tasteful. She'd stayed here in the past and enjoyed it for its location. Not too close to New Mexico State University, but located within the city proper.

Las Cruces was about a quarter the size of Albuquerque. It nestled in the Mesilla Valley, about forty-five miles north of the U.S.-Mexico border. It was a combination of old New Mexico agriculture, Latino and Hispano populations, college students, and conservative retirees. Mesilla, a much smaller community, was located just southwest. The Organ Mountains jutted east of Las Cruces, dark fangs that rose, almost other-worldly, from the floor of the Chihuahuan Desert, a stark reminder of New Mexico's volcanic past.

Culturally, Las Cruces straddled the boundary between Mexican and New Mexican, between Latino and old Spanish *conquistador* with Euro-American farmer mixed in for good measure. Blazing hot in the summer, relatively mild in the winter, it felt more like Tucson in some respects than New Mexico. Chris had almost gone to college at NMSU, but opted to stay in Albuquerque and attend UNM. She sometimes wondered how her life would have turned out had she moved to Cruces. At the very least, she probably would have had regular contact with the Mexican side of her family. She picked the bottle of iced tea up off the small hotel table and took a sip. No, her life was turning out pretty well, for the most part. If she could just get a few things figured out.

She reached for the hotel phone, opting for a more secure land line, and dialed K.C.'s home number, using an APD calling card. K.C. picked up on the second ring.

"Hello?" Her tone was tentative. Not a number she recognized on the caller ID, Chris realized.

"Hey, *chica. ¿Qué pasa?*"

"*Nada tostada, mi amiga.* Glad you made it okay. You have a few minutes?"

"I'm all yours." Chris smiled. She had her notebook and pen at the ready.

"Too tempting," K.C. said, laughing. "Okay, here's the deal. I first ran a couple of searches on our buddy over at Wellspring. Nothing too detailed at the outset. I just wanted to see what might be out there. Yes, he was at Providence of Love in Raleigh from

December, 1995 through summer, 1998."

"Is he from there?"

"Nope. I found some innocuous biographical info and I'm following up on it. Seems he's originally from Houston. He graduated from high school and went to Southern Methodist University in Dallas. Graduated, um, let me see..."

Chris heard K.C. rustling around.

"Here it is. 1983. B.A. in psychology. *That's* special," she said sarcastically. "Probably learned some psychological tricks before he went on to grad school at Oral Roberts University in Tulsa. Finished up in theology in 1986. Then he started doing the ministry thing."

"Where?"

"First locally, in Tulsa. Then—" she moved more paper around. "A Baptist congregation in Raleigh. He was an underling minister for a while, from what I gather, but worked his way to a more prominent position. He managed to get himself in the public eye with a charismatic fundamentalist approach."

Chris tapped her pen on the notebook, thinking. "What does that mean?"

"Major PR. He had his own radio spots and talk show on one of the local Christian stations there. He wrote an instructional booklet—ten things to bring yourself closer to God. I checked it out and it's fairly standard fundamentalist stuff, with incorporation of appropriate biblical stuff. Anyway, all that got him noticed when Providence of Love opened up and he was tapped for that."

"That's one of the megachurches, right?"

"Yep." K.C. rustled some more papers.

"So it'd be a job that every Christian minister worth his sacred satin boxers would covet." Chris wrote "Providence of Love" down.

"Definitely."

"So why—"

"—was he only there a couple of years?" K.C. finished. "That got me, too. I did a bit more digging, this time through some other sources that included church publications. In mid-1997, an anonymous rumor posted in a Raleigh Internet Christian chatroom started circulating that Pastor Chaz was a little light in the loafers."

"Holy shit."

"Definitely. Anyway, I can't verify that for sure because I can't find the posting. Which doesn't mean anything. Web sites and forums come and go, links die...you know how it is. So I checked with church gossip rags—which they archived online, bless 'em!— and found a little letter from June 1998 that someone in the congregation wrote anonymously accusing Mumford of taking advantage of young men. In the biblical sense," she added, bringing a chuckle from Chris. "Well, all hell broke loose, if you will, and in subsequent issues, people jumped this writer's shit about making such libelous claims. What's interesting is that the original letter got published in this thing at all. I have a feeling that the anonymous writer probably had some kind of 'in' with the rag editor to get that in there."

"Sounds like it. Any way to find out who it was?" Chris wrote "accusatory editorial, Providence of Love" in her notebook.

"I'm working that angle. But here's some more interesting stuff. In a few of the responses to that original rumor, people wrote in reminding everyone how involved Pastor Chaz was with ex-gay programs and 'spiritual treatment options' for homosexuals, so how could he possibly be one of *those*. And one of the programs he worked with was the Raleigh branch of Out of Darkness."

Chris chewed her lip. "Could be a coincidence."

"Or maybe not. I'm waiting to hear from a couple of contacts about it."

"Kase, you are my all-time favorite right-wing researcher."

"I'll bet you say that to all the girls," she said, laughing.

"No, that one's reserved for you," Chris said. "Okay. So what happened at Providence of Love in ninety-eight?"

"Hold on."

Chris heard K.C. set the phone down and what sounded like footsteps. Then she heard what might be papers again.

K.C. picked up the phone. "Okay, so I'm thinking the rumors were based on reality."

"You think?" Chris responded with a "well, *duh*" tone.

"Now, now. We can't just go jumping to conclusions. Well, we can, but let's not. I'll give you some more skinny and *then* we'll jump to conclusions."

"Perfect."

"All right. I'm waiting to hear from someone who's more in the know about what went down at the congregation about the time Chaz bailed. But I found the formal announcement of his leaving in one of the newsletters. I have a copy, for your viewing pleasure. Anyway, basically, the board announced that 'it is with great sadness that we are informing the congregation that Pastor Charles "Chaz" Mumford has decided to follow the path of God elsewhere. We wish him the best'."

"That's it?"

"No, there's more about all the good things he did and how wonderful he was and how dedicated to the word of God and blah blah blah. They didn't say where he'd be going, either. But—"

"You found out." Chris smiled. K.C. was dogged at research. More anal than most detectives.

"Well, of course. I wouldn't be able to keep my rep as your all-time fave wingnut researcher if I didn't. He went to—are you ready?"

"New Mexico," Chris breathed, daring to hope.

"Bingo."

"Fucking hell. What was he doing?"

"You're gonna love this. Grace Baptist in Las Cruces picked him up based on his rep in Tulsa."

"Even though he got basically canned in Raleigh?" Chris sounded skeptical. "What's the deal with that?"

"I'm checking on it. Chances are, they picked him up on a few conditions. And one of those was probably that he 'work on his issues.' That seems to be how congregations handle some of that. Come on, Chris. You've seen that with Catholics. Some priest gets found out for molesting altar boys and what do they do? They just ship him off to some other congregation or counseling program for him to 'figure it out.' Then he continues what he was doing. In both senses. Does it ever solve the problem? No."

She's right. "Okay, so Cruces picks him up. What did he do? Senior guy or not?"

"No. He was a junior minister until 2001, after which he went to Albuquerque, tapped by Wellspring for a senior job. I guess Cruces was his 'doing time' phase."

2001. The timing's good for Tyler Henderson. "My gut's telling me something here, *esa*. Did you find anything else during his Cruces time-out?"

"Well, funny you should ask," K.C. said. "The programs Grace lists include a 'spiritual salvation' for gay folks. I checked it and it's been around since ninety-seven. Could be Chaz agreed to help with that so he could go quietly from Raleigh."

"What's the name of it?"

"Hope Through Love."

Chris wrote it down. "Hey, can you do me a favor?"

"Anything for you, *mujer*," she teased.

"See if the name Kevin Stillman—" she spelled his last name "pops up with any of the places you found Chaz." Chris then told K.C. what she'd learned at Wellspring that morning and what she'd discovered at Pulse.

"Whoa. You had quite the busy day, girlfriend. All right, I'll do some more digging and I'll let you know what else comes up." She hesitated. "So, what's up with John?"

"I love that little shit to pieces," Chris said, sighing. "He's never been good, though, about talking about his stuff, so maybe it's okay that Adam outed him. Though he really didn't. Not like none of us knew. Anyway, it forced him to sit down with me and deal with it. I've had a feeling that he didn't want to come out because of how

Mom took it when I did. I mean, this is gonna blow her Catholic gasket for sure. Two of her kids. That's half her brood, *amiga*."

"But *Abuelita's* still around, so maybe that'll help when he does."

"I hope so." Chris leaned back in her chair, stretching her legs out. "But she's not getting any younger. And if she..." Chris's voice trailed off. She cleared her throat. "If he waits too long, she may not be around to help." The thought sat like a big stone in her gut and a vise wrapped around her throat. A world without *Abuelita* was not something she wanted to contemplate.

"Hey." K.C. interrupted Chris's morbid train of thought. "He officially came out to you. He told you his dream. He said he wanted to talk to *la familia* and he wanted to do it soon. He knows the stakes. And he knows he has you. And by extension, he thus has me. Since I'm practically your evil twin."

Chris smiled, forcing herself to relax. "True."

"Now go call Dayna." K.C. said it sternly, but Chris could hear the laughter behind the words.

"Ay-yay-yay. I swear Sage's psychic powers are rubbing off on you," Chris groaned.

"I hope so. I like that rubbing stuff." She laughed. "I'll keep on with my end and give you a buzz. I'm going to see who was around at Grace when Chazzie was there. You think maybe you should go talk to them now, since you're there?"

"I'll swing by tomorrow and see what turns up."

"Cool. Take care and drive carefully. Talk at you later."

"For sure. Hi to Sage. Bye."

Chris hung up and thought about what K.C. had told her. Good stuff, but still circumstantial. She wasn't positive that Chaz was disguising himself and going to Pulse. It could've been somebody who looked like him. A man who looked like Chaz had been seen in Travis's company before Travis was killed. But there was nothing concrete to suggest that Chaz had been that man. "Dammit," Chris muttered. They needed physical evidence. They couldn't bring Chaz in yet on what they had. Plus, he was the senior pastor at a church with at least two thousand registered members. Questioning him about his possible ties to a murder would bring all kinds of ugly publicity to the police department if they didn't have the shit to back up their smell. Chris picked her business cell up and used it to find Harper's number. She dialed it on the land line. He picked up on the second ring.

"Yeah. Dale Harper."

"Hey. It's Chris. I'm on a land line." She told him quickly what K.C. had found out and what she had learned at Pulse, excluding, of course, discussion about her brother's revelation. She'd chat with her superiors first about that, if necessary.

He was characteristically quiet before speaking. "Productive. Okay, here's what I've got. Stillman's out of town, visiting relatives in California. He'll be back Thursday. If he's in cahoots with Mumford, then he'll have a story ready. I'm thinking we should just bring him in. Get him off his home turf to talk to him."

"Good idea."

"Okay. I'll set that up. Went through the video for The Beach — got your picture. Yep, there's a guy who looks like that going in early Saturday morning. Like around two-fifteen. He's with McCormick. At three they both leave and head for the parking lot. I can't tell what car. The camera angle wasn't good for that. Since McCormick's was still in the lot, it wasn't his. I'll find out what Mumford drives and see if you get any hits for it off the Pulse video. Oh, and McCormick was looking a little shaky, like he'd been drinking. I went back through the autopsy and the ME didn't see anything that looked weird. I called and asked them to check again and told them what the video looked like. Sam said he'd swing by tomorrow to have a look."

"Good work, Harper. Thanks." He might be some kind of homophobic dickhead, but he was proving to be a good detective. "Did you ask about trace?"

"Oh, that's what it was. Yeah. They're still processing some stuff. Sam did find..." Harper trailed off for a minute, then coughed. "He did find what probably was semen on McCormick's sheets, but the samples are too degraded to determine anything. Body fluids like that only last a day or so. Sperm cells three days, max, he said. Plus, when Hopkins reported McCormick missing, the uniforms just checked for blood. So we're stuck there."

Shit.

"But he found some stuff under McCormick's fingernails. The ones that escaped animal activity. His left ring finger and a couple of the fingers on his right hand. Sam thinks it's spirit gum."

Adhesive. "Like what you use to stick a fake mustache on." Chris smiled grimly.

"Yeah. The theater crap. He thinks there might be some DNA in there we can use. I called Hopkins and asked if he'd be willing to give us a sample to rule him out and he said no problem. He's meeting me at the lab tomorrow to take care of that."

"Do you remember what Josh said Travis was wearing when he left the apartment that Saturday morning?" Chris was thinking about what Jason said he had worn that night.

"Um, jeans, I think. And a white shirt."

The same thing Jason had said. *Where did the perp ditch the clothes?* "Any other trace?"

"The perp definitely cleaned the body up. No fingerprints, but he could have been wearing gloves, too. They've got some fibers they're working on from McCormick's hair. Sam thinks they might be from a carpet."

From a car, maybe? "Okay, what do you think of this?" Chris asked. "The perp has a date with Travis. It's originally scheduled for Saturday but something happens, so the perp shows up at Pulse on Friday. They hang out, talk, and Travis brings the perp home. We don't know for sure if anything sexual happened. Remember Josh said that the clothes Travis was wearing when he went to visit his mom were on the bed. So the perp and Travis probably didn't have sex then. At least not on that bed."

Harper cleared his throat again. Chris decided it was a nervous tic. She continued. "The perp gives something to Travis that makes him a little woozy and he takes him somewhere. He might have driven him to the Nature Center where they did have sex and things got a little out of hand. However, I think that the perp took him somewhere he had planned because he had the time and the inclination to clean Travis up and get rid of his clothes. I don't necessarily think this was an accidental death during rough sex play. I think the perp set out to kill him." Chris sat back, waiting for Harper's response.

"Okay, but you're assuming that the guy McCormick went home with that night was the guy who was supposed to see him on Saturday. What if it wasn't?"

"True. But does it really matter? The man he ended up with on Friday was most likely his killer." She ran a hand through her hair. "Okay, let's just go there. Let's pretend Pastor Chaz is the man Travis was going to see on Saturday and the same guy who goes to Pulse on Fridays. So Chaz sets up the date for Saturday knowing Travis works that night. Why not just set it up for Friday? I'm thinking it's because Chaz has something he's already got scheduled for Friday but he really wants to spend some time with Travis. So he asks Travis if he can trade shifts for a Saturday night date. Then something changes in Chaz's schedule and he goes to Pulse on Friday. Maybe he hopes Travis will show up. Sure enough, he does."

"But why not just call him?" Harper asked in his flat upper Midwestern accent.

Good question. "Maybe Chaz is smart. He doesn't want anything traceable to him. And phone records are traceable. Maybe he never called Travis. Maybe they always just agreed to meet at Pulse. Speaking of which, have we found anything in his computer?"

"Not yet. They told me to check back tomorrow."

"Sounds good. I'll swing by Grace Baptist and see what there is to see. What else is on the agenda for tomorrow? "

When he replied, he sounded as if he had relaxed a bit. "I'll leave a message for Stillman, telling him to give me a call. We'll make it all official-like. Sam's gonna check out that video and maybe run another tox screen. See what he finds. The adhesive under the fingernails is a good angle, but I don't think it's enough for a warrant. Prosecutor'll put my nuts in a wringer if I ask to check a pastor's bathroom for spirit gum without anything concrete. We need more."

Chris wasn't sure if she should feel flattered or disgusted that Harper considered her enough of a guy to use that kind of metaphor with her. "Sounds good. Have a long talk with Sam about possible trace angles. And see what you can do about finding out what the good pastor drives. We need to link him to Pulse, make him sweat a bit. But we have to be careful. Especially since he's a pastor with a congregation that big."

"Yep. I'm on it. Okay, then."

And he hung up, as he always did after his signature sign-off. Still, in spite of whatever baggage Harper was lugging around, he seemed to be approaching the case as if it was any other, trying different angles, doggedly following leads, keeping her informed. She'd give him some props for that. She glanced at her watch. Almost eight. She took another drink from her iced tea and stood, stretching. Time to do some data entry. She pulled her laptop from its case and plugged it in so she could work at the table. Using the remote for the TV, she turned it on and found ESPN.

Chris typed up her notes from the day, putting them in a format that made it easy for her to cut and paste into department forms as necessary. She tried to do this ritual at the end of every work day, spending at least an hour dealing with notes and the findings of the day while everything was still fresh. Chris had taken some of K.C.'s methodologies and developed her own system.

She was just finishing up with what Harper had told her when her personal cell phone rang. Automatically, she glanced at her watch. Nine thirty-seven. She picked up her phone and checked the ID. Her heart skipped around inside her chest.

"Hey," Chris answered. "How are you?"

"Much better, now," Dayna responded.

Chris could hear that certain smile Dayna had in her voice. The way she sounded... *God.* She thought about the past Saturday night and pleasurable chills raced up and down her thighs.

"Chris?"

She snapped back to the present. "Sorry. Distracted."

"Oh, um, do you want me to call you back?"

Chris laughed, embarrassed. "No, no. I was thinking about *you* and got distracted." *Jesus. Why am I telling her that?*

"Well, thanks. Something good, I hope." Dayna sounded

uncertain. It was kind of sweet.

"Very. So—Friday. Do you drink rum?"

"Is that what we're having? Don't you think we should eat, too?" She was laughing.

"Hey, you'd be surprised what I can do with a good bottle of rum," Chris wisecracked.

"No, I don't think I would. Though I'd like you to show me anyway," Dayna teased, a come-hither tone in her voice.

"I just might take you up on that. So, rum?" *Will she notice if I totally pass out right here?*

"Yes. I do. Not a usual drink for me, but I can and do on occasion indulge."

"Excellent. Then the menu is now complete." Chris doodled on her notepad. Idle, swooping hearts.

"Can't wait," Dayna said, with a soft fervor that threatened to knock Chris onto the floor. She was quiet a moment before continuing. "I've been thinking."

"Oh?" Chris's pen stopped, hovered above the paper. "About?"

"You."

Chris felt a knot of anxiety in her stomach. *Fuck. Is she freaking out? And why does that freak me out?* "Anything in particular?" She hoped her voice didn't betray her unease.

"Everything. When I got your message today, I was so relieved. I was afraid you wouldn't call back, that maybe you decided not to— well, anyway. I was really glad you called."

"Same here. What's up?" Chris pushed a little, trying to find out how far she could go.

Dayna didn't hesitate. "I really like you. I realized how much when I was in California, and I think it scared me a little. But you knew that."

Chris exhaled softly. Her whole body had been holding its breath, it seemed. She pushed a little harder. "The feeling's mutual. Do you want to talk about California?"

"I do. But I'd prefer in person, if it's okay with you."

"That's more than okay with me. Are you all right?" *Good.* Chris hated to deal with intimate matters like this over the phone. She needed to see the other person, to gauge body language and assess responses. She knew it was part of being a cop, but she also just preferred dealing with people that way. Even if it was a painful situation. She went back to doodling, realized she was sketching a picture of Dayna from memory. Chris was actually a good artist, though few people knew about that talent. With quick, practiced strokes, Dayna's hair fell in waves past her ears, around her shoulders.

"Yes. You?" Dayna asked.

Chris's pen strokes slowed to a stop. A simple question, but one that went right to the heart of the matter. She clenched and unclenched her teeth before responding. "Very. I'm extremely glad I saw you on Saturday. Extremely. I'll be honest, though. I'm still not sure what's going on with you and I'm a little worried about that."

"That's fair," Dayna said softly.

Chris continued sketching, shading Dayna's cheeks and creating the sparkle in her eyes. "Okay, here's the deal. I like you. I like spending time with you. I'm attracted to you. I've enjoyed your messages these past couple of days. And I'm really excited to see you on Friday. I'd like to think that you'll trust me eventually and that you'll tell me more about California and what's going on now. So with that in mind, I'm going to keep calling you and I'm going to keep asking you out unless you say otherwise. The ball's in *your* court now. But you need to pass it back to keep this going."

Dayna was silent for a long while, but Chris could hear her breathing. She tried to sketch that certain smile Dayna had, but she wasn't sure she quite captured it. Instead, Chris quirked the corners of the sketch's mouth, which gave it a mischievous little grin. That, too, was an aspect of Dayna's personality.

"Thank you," Dayna finally said. She sounded relieved. "I can't wait to see you."

Chris's heart lurched into her throat. "Saying things like that— I'm not sure I'll be able to cook on Friday."

"Oh, you'll cook. Maybe not dinner, but you *will* cook."

Does she know how sexy she is? Chris felt a flush race up her neck. "Whoa. And on that note, I'm going to change the subject so I don't hurt myself here."

Dayna laughed, a rich warm spicy sound that poured over Chris's nerve endings and settled in her bones like lava.

"So, Ms. Carson," Chris said, flustered at the effect this conversation was having on her, "what's going on with you?"

An hour later, after they'd hung up, Chris was stretched out on the bed in her sweats and tee, grinning like a fool in the dark. She realized that the whole time she and Dayna had been talking, "cop stuff" hadn't been an issue. She liked how that felt, thinking that she didn't have to hide that part of herself. She listened to the hum of the heater in the corner and slid under the covers. Though Dayna was a little over two hundred miles away, Chris still fell asleep with her.

Chapter
Ten

CARL MAESTAS TOOK detailed, copious notes, Chris discovered. She was grateful, but a lot of it was overkill and he tended to state the same thing more than once, which made for slow reading. Consequently, she decided to start with the autopsy report and the crime lab findings and see how those coincided with Carl's notes.

Three hours later she sat back, tapping her pen on the edge of the table in the climate-controlled basement used to warehouse cold cases and accompanying evidence. It was sort of eerie, actually, because she was surrounded by shelves stacked high with plain boxes that held the remnants of people's lives. Most of these would probably never be solved, and eventually, even the memories would end up like these boxes. Warehoused and forgotten.

A couple of other people came in to use the battered file cabinets against the wall near the only entrance, but other than that Chris had the place to herself. She was using a legal pad, another research quirk she had picked up from K.C. On the top sheet she had written down the things about Travis's murder that might be part of the killer's signature: naked, position of the body, where he was found, ligature marks on his neck, bound hands, crucifix under his tongue, John 3:16 carved on his chest.

On the second sheet Chris wrote things about Tyler Henderson's murder that could be a signature. It was virtually the same list as Travis's page with the exception of spirit gum. Tyler's body had been exposed longer than Travis's and his fingertips weren't salvageable for trace because of animal activity. Fibers found in Tyler's hair proved inconclusive, but Chris checked and there were still three in storage that could be used as a comparison with the fibers found in Travis's hair. Still, the chance that Pastor Chaz had the same car now as then was pretty slim.

She flipped back to Travis's page and wrote "Out of Darkness." On Tyler's page she had written "Hope Through Love." It was possible that the pastor had met Travis in Dallas, when his parents forced him into Out of Darkness as a teen. But at that time, Chaz was already in New Mexico and as far as K.C could determine, he didn't take any side trips. Chaz might have come into contact with Travis when the pastor was still in Raleigh, working the local branch of OD there. Maybe a conference in Dallas? Possible. Probably not, though Chris would have K.C. check that angle out. It seemed more likely that Chaz met Travis either at Pulse or at Wellspring. With regard to Tyler, Chaz probably met him because of Hope Through Love. She didn't think there was any connection between Tyler and Travis. They just both ended up involved with the same man at different times.

She went through the lab and tox reports. *Ah.* She stopped and re-read a paragraph, then wrote "rohypnol" on Tyler's page. Commonly referred to as roofies, rohypnol was one of the date-rape drugs that got lots of attention in the late 1990s. The ME had run two screens on Tyler and a possible hit on roofies came back twice. It wasn't definitive, but it was better than conjecture. Carl had stapled a small piece of paper to the corner of the report, listing the symptoms of rohypnol in the blood: dizziness, drowsiness, sometimes excitability, and lowered inhibition. She'd call Sam at the crime lab and ask him about that possibility for Travis. That might explain why he looked the way he did on the video from The Beach.

Chris went back to the description of the crucifix found in Tyler's mouth. Plain gold, hanging on a chain with a clasp. Chris guessed "necklace" and the ME had categorized it as that, as well. The ME had found a hair in the necklace's strands but got no DNA hit in any database. Nonetheless, it was on file. If they could get a comparison with something off Pastor Chaz, they might be able to link him to Tyler and then, circumstantially, to Travis. A hit on Tyler could lead to a warrant to search Chaz's house for spirit gum. Chris would check the chain of evidence on Tyler's DNA test to make sure defense attorneys couldn't find fault with technique and get it thrown out as inadmissible. She'd also have Sam run another check on the crucifix from Travis's mouth.

She removed the photo of Robert Tyler Henderson from one of the folders she had placed on the table. It had been taken the year before he died. He was Caucasian, light brown hair, blue eyes. It was a posed shot, taken in a local studio. He had been wearing a black cowboy hat, black jeans, a white button-down western-cut shirt, and roper boots. He had been a rancher's kid, with a big open-air grin and a family agricultural heritage here in the Mesilla Valley.

Chris studied his eyes. All the hope in the world there. She imagined he felt an urge to be done with the bullshit in his hometown and just move on. According to Carl's notes, Tyler's closest friends said he wanted to move to Albuquerque, where he could be a cowboy but also the gay man he was learning to accept within himself. He had been a nice-looking guy, with a warm, friendly demeanor. A nice young man from a conservative, ranching, Baptist family. Sort of like Travis, who was born into a conservative, wealthy, Christian fundamentalist family.

Chris's thoughts went to John then, to how he, too, struggled with who he was. Their family was conservative and Catholic, steeped in the legacies of Latin American gender roles and weighty expectations for both sexes. There was no room for *jotos* in that tradition, no room for men who weren't automatically drawn to women. In Tyler's conservative ranching family, there was no room for a bunkhouse tryst between cowboys, between a rancher's son and a ranch-hand. Men weren't supposed to love men like that.

It was different, Chris thought, for men to come out. In families like hers or Tyler's or Travis's, the expectations placed on men — whether through culture or religion or a mixture of both — might be heavier. Passing on the surname in families like that fell on men. Taking over the family business fell on men. And no matter how much feminism had pushed on these doors, no matter how hard women and even some men worked to change culture and society, there was still no room for certain things within certain beliefs.

If Pastor Chaz was responsible for the deaths of these young men, he, too, was caught in a cycle of self-hatred and societal expectations that twisted his perceptions and left him uncomfortable in his own skin. Chris could almost understand the self-loathing within a man who preyed on men like himself, could almost understand a man like that projecting all the hatred he felt for who he was onto other men who seemed more at ease with themselves. Whoever killed Tyler Henderson and Travis McCormick hated what they represented but wanted it for himself. Chris's intuition kept poking at her. These weren't hate crimes. They were self-hate crimes.

She replaced Tyler's photograph and began packing up the materials. She would request an official evidence transfer from Las Cruces to Albuquerque. It needed to be done by the book, to keep defense attorneys from getting it thrown out. Putting the white file boxes in her private vehicle and driving them up to APD that day would screw whatever evidence they could use in the Henderson case against Pastor Chaz, if that's where Travis's case led them.

She went to the door and buzzed the front desk so someone could come and witness her signing off on the appropriate forms, always left with the materials. Plus, doing this would ensure that she had not left the evidence unattended. She returned to her table and stood waiting, watching the door. Once she was finished here, she would head over to Grace, then swing by the site where Tyler's body was found before she headed back to Albuquerque. She wanted to get a feel for the landscape, for where the killer might have parked, and why he might have chosen that location. The door swung open and Laura, the woman with whom Chris had made the original appointment, came in, dressed in a crisp uniform that echoed her manner.

"Thanks a bunch," Chris said, smiling. "Looks like I'll need to set up a formal transfer."

"Really?" Laura sounded interested. "Just let us know."

"I have a meeting tomorrow and then I'll probably be giving you a call." Chris signed the forms, initialed them, then dated them as well. Laura did the same, then re-sealed the boxes with special red tape that had been pre-printed with lines for dates and initials. Chris watched as she wrote the date and time on the tape in black sharpie. She initialed it and handed the sharpie to Chris, who initialed the line beneath Laura's. She, too, wrote the date and time next to her initials. She helped Laura return the two boxes to the appropriate shelves and then she followed her back to the receptionist's area so she could formally sign out there. Once she had completed the necessary paperwork and said her thank yous and goodbyes, it was nearly eleven. She had to get on the road soon to catch Jason at Pulse, but first, a quick trip to Mesilla and Grace Baptist.

"PRETTY CLOSE, HUH?"

Chris looked across the big table at Harper. They were sitting in an empty conference room at APD. It was almost 6:00 PM and she was tired. In her left hand she held a still image of a white man with a goatee and mustache that the lab had extracted from The Beach surveillance video. In her right she held the brochure from Wellspring, with the image of Pastor Chaz that Jason had altered.

She nodded. "I'm not sure it's enough, though. I mean, this guy —" she held up the image from The Beach, "might just happen to look like Chaz."

Harper leaned back and folded his arms over his chest. "Okay, yeah. But it is pretty close." He allowed the front legs of his chair to fall back to the carpet. "Oh, according to vehicle registration, the good pastor drives a late-model Lexus GX. He must be doing all right for himself over there."

An SUV. Easy to get a body in and out of something like that.

"It'd be pretty easy to stick a dead guy in one of those," Harper said, seeming to pick up on Chris's thought.

"We can't search it, though. Not yet. We have to find a link. Did you hear from Stillman yet?"

"I sure did. He'll be coming in tomorrow at two-thirty. Directly from the airport, actually. Maybe he'll be tired and we can put the screws to him." Harper picked up his big Styrofoam cup and took a sip of the nasty department coffee. "Sam called. He got your call about rohypnol after he watched the video with me and he thinks that's a good possibility, so he's running another panel. Good find on that." He bobbed his head at her.

"Surprising, actually. It's not street legal. I'd like to know how our guy got a hold of it. That's a good angle, too," Chris mused aloud. "You still have contacts in narc?"

Harper grinned at her, a surprising gesture since he rarely smiled. It made him look like a big, goofy teenager. "Gucci, I'm liking how you think. Why the hell I didn't think of that, I don't know. Yeah, I've still got some cred. I'll make some calls tomorrow and maybe we can come up with some weasel who pushes roofies. I mostly dealt with meth and heroin, but a lot of these creeps have full pharmacies to meet anybody's needs. Versatility, you know."

"Cool. Did Hopkins make it this morning?"

"Bright and early. Got the swab taken care of. Sam told him another couple of days on the apartment. He wanted to make sure nobody needed anything else from there. Should be cleared on Friday. Sam's processing the bedding now and the clothing he found in what looks like a hamper. Maybe we'll get some trace off that."

Chris told Harper about the hair that had been found entwined in the crucifix chain in Tyler's mouth. "If we can get something from Travis that matches the DNA found with that hair, we've got a link between the two. We still need something stronger to get Chaz in the circle. Got practically nothing at Grace. The staff in admin has only been there three years. None of them remember Chaz. The minister's out of town. They gave me a list of current board members, but I haven't had time to follow up. I want to see what K.C. finds on them, too. And then we'll go over the Pulse video." She rubbed her forehead in frustration. "Fuck."

"Hey, take a break." Harper said as he stood and began gathering the papers and photographs that he and Chris had been comparing. "Go home. Work on something else. We'll be talking about all this tomorrow with the boss-man, anyway."

"You sure?" She watched him, not used to this conciliatory side of him and not sure what to do with it.

"Yeah. No problem."

"Thanks. Catch you tomorrow."

"Okay, then." He gathered the files and exited, Chris behind him. Though she was tired and a bit hungry, she felt irritable, so she opted for a workout before she drove home. She retrieved the spare set of workout clothes she kept in her office and changed in the locker room. The main building here incorporated a gym and locker room on site. She busied herself with the free weights and did a hard mile on one of the treadmills, bantering with some of the male cops who were doing bench presses and squats. She chatted a bit with Erin Halstead, who had come in while Chris was cooling down on the treadmill. Erin told her she'd get a copy of her McCormick report to Chris the next day. Chris thanked her and headed back to the locker room.

By 7:30 she was at home, her legs stretched out onto her coffee table as she lounged on her couch, reveling in the candlelight from the mantel and the soft strains of Ravi Shankar's sitar emanating from her stereo. K.C. was a music fanatic and had turned Chris on to all kinds of artists from all over the world. Chris found that this little ritual she had in the evenings, in which she turned out all her lights, fired up her candles, and had some music going in the background, helped her detox from cop life. This case was pushing a lot of buttons. Tomorrow, she'd check in with her other cases, not only to get caught up, but also to clear her head a bit.

She'd already called K.C., who was following a couple of hits on Stillman and would know more the next day. Chris would be able to compare it to what Harper dug up on him. *Enough. Work shit, be gone.* She leaned her head back and closed her eyes, allowing her mind to wander all over Dayna Carson. Chris had breezed through her work and home e-mail accounts and discovered a brief message from Dayna on her home account:

Hi. Thanks for talking last night. I cannot believe how slow time seems to go when you're not around and how fast it flies when you are. I want to reverse that. Friday seems like a hell of a long way off, but I fill the space between now and then with thoughts of you. Hope to talk to you again before then, too. Dayna

Chris had typed a note back:

You're welcome. I've noticed that time thing, too. And though I do enjoy thinking about you, I prefer the real thing. So I'll see you Friday. Two days. I'm on countdown. Chris

Thinking about the e-mails caused Chris to reach for her personal cell, which rested on the couch next to her left thigh. Just as her fingers brushed its surface it rang. She picked it up and checked the ID. *God, I hope nobody sees this huge dorky smile on my face,* she thought as she answered. K.C. would tease the shit out of her at the sight.

"Hi there." Chris leaned back again.

"Less than two days now," Dayna said, an undercurrent of

laughter in her voice.

"Still too many. How are you?"

"Very well, thanks. And yourself? Are you back?"

"Yep. Enjoying some quiet time." Chris glanced at the candles on her mantel. "And no, you're not interrupting," she added before Dayna could say anything. "I think I like sharing some of my quiet time with you, actually."

"I'm glad," she said quietly. "That means a lot to me." Something unspoken hung in the spaces between her words.

"So what can I do for you?" Chris asked, following the cue.

Dayna giggled. It was a sweet, cute sound and Chris melted.

"That's a loaded question, Detective. And I'm not sure you're ready for an answer to it."

Damn. "And that's a loaded response, Counselor. Care to elaborate?"

"Sort of." Dayna's tone shifted from feisty to contemplative.

Chris remained quiet, letting Dayna guide the conversation.

"I was going to wait until Friday to talk a bit more about California," she started. "I prefer to deal with important matters face-to-face, but something came in the mail today and it explained quite a bit."

"Okay," Chris said, to let Dayna know she was listening.

"I sent you a Christmas card while I was there, with a letter. I debated e-mailing you, but I didn't like the way that felt."

"I didn't—"

"I know," Dayna gently interrupted. "That's what came in the mail. The post office fucked it up. It looked like somebody's pit bull chewed the hell out of it and it lay around for the last two months in some muddy back yard in the South Valley. It was almost torn in half." She started laughing, sounding relieved. "Before today, I couldn't figure out why you didn't mention anything I'd said in there. I mean, you left a message on Christmas and another on New Year's. Just nice holiday wishes and here I'd spilled my guts in that letter and not a word from you."

"Oh, my God," was all Chris could say. *She tried. She tried to tell me what was going on.*

"Exactly. And when we went out on Saturday, you seemed—well, you seemed really glad to see me but you were more reserved, like you kept waiting for me to tell you something. And I was thinking I already had. I couldn't figure out where you were coming from. It was rather freaky. But damn, it was so good to see you. And when you agreed to come over...well, I thought maybe you'd relax a bit more and we'd talk about it then. But we got kind of distracted." She laughed softly.

"Shit," Chris said finally. "I—well, hell. And here I kept

wondering what was going on with you and then there you are at the Nature Center and I'm thinking, 'well, maybe she'll tell me why she didn't call.' But no, it didn't come up, though it felt like it was there the whole time. And yes, I was *very* glad to see you." *Beyond glad. Approaching ecstatic.*

"Well, I was *very* glad to see you, too," Dayna said with equal emphasis. "So when I talked to you last night and you asked if I wanted to talk about California, I thought 'finally. She wants to talk about it.' But after I got the mail today, I realized you don't know *anything* about what was going on beyond what I said at Thanksgiving."

"That's true." Chris shifted her position to make herself more comfortable. "So..." she let her voice trail off, giving Dayna a chance to take the lead again.

"I'm sorry," she said. "Normally, I communicate much better than this. And I feel badly because you spent so much time not knowing what's been going on. And I handled this whole thing like a major ass. Is it okay with you to discuss it in person on Friday?"

"I'd prefer that." Chris hesitated. "What's the prognosis here?" *Please don't run. Please.* She caught herself. *Am I talking about her or me?*

Dayna didn't hesitate. "I really like you. And it scared me. I said all that in the letter. I also asked you for some time to think about things and get some of my past sorted out. What I really appreciated — and I appreciate it even more now — is that you called me, yes, but only to check in. You never pushed me, you never made any demands in those messages you left. You just said you were thinking about me and you hoped I was okay." She stopped.

Chris was holding her breath. She forced herself to exhale quietly.

"And you did that, not knowing what I had asked or what I had said, I now realize. Which makes you even more special than I originally thought." Dayna lapsed into silence and Chris listened to her breathe. She leaned forward, feet on the floor, and braced her elbows on her thighs, waiting.

"I have some shit I'm still dealing with," Dayna finally said. "I think you've probably already figured that out. And I'll tell you about it. *Again*, since I put it in the letter," she finished, laughing softly. "The bottom line is, I want to keep seeing you. So I hope you're okay with some unpacking."

"I'd appreciate that." Chris adjusted the phone against her ear. "And I'm glad you're willing to talk about it with me." A wave of relief rushed through her veins. "Thanks for letting me know about the letter. It does answer some questions," she added wryly.

"For both of us," Dayna agreed. "So, can you talk longer right now? Or do you need to be doing other things?"

"Well, there *are* a few other things I'd much rather be doing at the moment," Chris said, knowing she was grinning like a crushed-out teenager again.

"I'd ask you to tell me more about that, but I'm sure we'd wear out the batteries on our phones," Dayna laughed.

"Among other things we'd wear the batteries out on. And on *that* note, Counselor, how was your day?" She settled back against the couch, knowing that once again, after they'd chatted and said their good nights, Dayna Carson, Esquire, would be the last thing on Chris's mind before she fell asleep.

HARPER MOVED CLOSER, leaning over Tony's right shoulder. "There," he said. "Back it up a little. Slowly."

Tony did so, going frame by frame.

"Freeze it. Right there." Harper leaned in and stared at the screen for a long moment. "That looks like a Lexus SUV. What do you think?" He turned to Chris, who was watching the screen over his shoulder.

"What color is his?" she asked as she leaned in, bracing her right hand on the back of Tony's chair. He was hunkered over the keyboard, working the video from Pulse with practiced keystrokes.

"Silver." Harper frowned.

Chris drew her breath in through her teeth, making a tsking sound. It wasn't the best video and it was black-and-white, which limited what they could determine about color. But the SUV was light-colored. "Can you get a hit on the plate?" The driver had fortuitously parked the vehicle with the butt-end facing the alley and not Central Avenue. New Mexico did not require license plates on the front of a car, so had the driver parked it ass-end to Central, there'd be no way of knowing what the plate was.

Tony muttered something and typed a command, zooming in on the SUV's back bumper. "Looks like we can get a partial. I'll work on it and see what we've got."

"Thanks. Start it up again. What time is this?"

"Ten thirty-eight," Harper responded. He had his arms crossed over his chest and he was rocking forward onto the balls of his feet, then back. Chris wondered where he'd picked up that habit. She turned her attention back to the screen.

"And lookee here," Harper said triumphantly. "That looks like our guy."

They watched as a man emerged from the vehicle and walked to the back entrance, the one that took customers into Blu. He didn't look up and they couldn't really see his facial features.

"Fast forward to one-thirty," she instructed. "No, wait. One forty-five."

"All right. Hold on to your panties, folks." Tony's fingers typed away and the film sped up. He stopped it at precisely one forty-five and slowed it to normal time.

Chris pulled a nearby chair over from a desk and straddled it, resting her arms across the back.

"Looks like the usual shit that goes on outside a bar at night," Tony noted after a few minutes of watching men and a very few women come and go through the parking lot. Various cars left. The SUV remained. " 'Cept it's dudes and no chicks." He adjusted his glasses. "Kinda gross."

Chris shot a look at Harper, who remained impassive though his jaw clenched slightly. "Well, they probably think the same of you." She directed the comment at Tony.

"What?" He turned to look at her. "I'm freakin' *normal*."

"Oh, that's right. All normal people wear *Star Trek* outfits under their clothes," she retorted.

Tony's pudgy cheeks went from white to red in a manner of seconds. Harper's jaw was still clenched, Chris noticed, but he looked like he was trying not to laugh. Tony hunched even lower. "It's still gross," he muttered, nervously tugging on his ponytail.

"So's screwing a Klingon. Not my thing. Doesn't mean I'll insult you if you decide to hook up with one." Chris gave him one of her cop glares and he immediately shrank another two inches. Harper cleared his throat and hid his mouth with his hand. He was definitely trying not to laugh. *Huh.*

"Hey, check it out," Harper said abruptly.

She turned back to the screen and checked the digital time display in the upper left corner. 1:47 AM. "That's Travis," she said softly. The video wasn't great, but he was wearing what Jason had said. Jeans and tight white shirt. He was carrying a jacket that he put on in the parking lot. He turned back to the entrance of Blu, waiting, it seemed, and saying something. Another man emerged then, head slightly down. The same man they'd seen leave the SUV three hours earlier.

"He knows," she said, grim. "He knows about the cameras. He didn't look up going in, either."

They watched as the man slid his arm around Travis's waist and walked with him to the SUV. The two stopped for a long, lingering kiss at the driver's side, the man's back to the camera.

Tony shifted uncomfortably in his seat. Chris saw him trying not to watch, but he kept sneaking a look at the screen. *Uh-huh. Klingon, my ass.* Tony would probably take it from Captain Kirk if he could.

Travis broke the kiss first and went around the front of the SUV.

The other man opened the doors with his key fob. The SUV's back lights blinked as he did so. Chris could barely see the top of Travis's head as he waited for the passenger door to open. Then his head dipped as he got in and the vehicle shifted with Travis's and his date's weight. The man backed out of the parking space, the SUV's rear away from the cameras.

"He backed out that way on purpose," Chris said. "It would have been easier for him to back out the other way. I'll bet money he didn't want the plate facing the camera."

"He's slick," Harper said in agreement.

Chris nodded. K.C. had said the same thing about Pastor Chaz. This had to be the same guy. Had to be. She forced herself not to go there completely. *Follow the evidence,* she repeated to herself. The front bumper was devoid of any kind of decorative plate. The SUV drove past the camera's field of vision.

"There you go." Harper rocked forward on his feet again. "See if you can get a read on that plate. That's our best bet right now. You heard the boss-man this morning. We don't have enough for a warrant on this guy yet. We have to make better links." He caught Chris's eye and she nodded.

"Okay." Tony's fingers flew over the keyboard again. "I'll let you know in a few."

"Thanks," Chris said, though she was still irritated with him. She checked her watch. Nearly one. Kevin Stillman was scheduled to arrive. She had just enough time for a workout.

Chapter
Eleven

CHRIS WAS PREPARING the interview room at 1:55 PM when her business cell rang. She answered it.

"Hey, Kase. Whatcha got?"

"Hey, girlfriend. You're gonna *love* this. I got some stuff back on your guy Stillman about an hour ago, while I was teaching."

"Hold on. Let me get something to write with." Chris sat down at the table and picked up a pen, then pulled her legal pad closer. "Okay. Hit me."

"Stillman and Mumford were in the same graduating class at Oral Roberts. Now, Stillman grew up in California, so I don't think he knew Chazster before Tulsa. At any rate, they created a men's bible study group together at OR and it became one of the most popular groups on campus. They called it 'Free Through Faith.' It was frequented mostly by young, attractive guys trying not to be gay."

"Fuck," Chris whispered.

"No doubt. Here's the obvious part. A lot of the guys in this group were constantly hooking up with each other, according to one of my sources, who tracks the effectiveness of ex-gay groups in the country. He got interested in what was going on at Oral Roberts because he lived in Tulsa and spent a lot of time poking around the university. Anyway, my source — he's at the U of Oklahoma now — is also gay and he found a network of OR guys cruising around the Tulsa bars during the time Chaz and Kevin were there. All these guys seemed to belong to one particular Bible study group at the university. *Voila.* Chaz and Kevin, Inc."

"So is Stillman gay?" Chris was scribbling notes in her shorthand.

"You'll have to tell me when you meet him. He was married twice to different women, but I'm thinking that shit's probably a cover."

Chris frowned. "So what happened to him when they graduated?"

"Well, *duh*. Chaz got him a job at the Tulsa ministry as the youth coordinator. Imagine that." K.C. injected an innocent tone into her voice.

"Did he go to Raleigh?"

"No. Stillman stayed in Tulsa when Chaz left. At that point, it looks like he was in his first marriage and the ministry in Tulsa wanted to keep him on. But I assume he stayed in contact with the good pastor."

"So when did Stillman come to New Mexico?" Chris tapped on her legal pad with her pen.

"He took a job in Albuquerque in 1996, *before* Chaz arrived. He hung out at Calvary Baptist for a while doing volunteer coordinator stuff and youth education. And—here's a nice gem—he helped coordinate Hope Through Love with Chaz when Chazster got himself exiled from Raleigh. When Chaz came to Albuquerque, he of course immediately hired Kevin at Wellspring."

"That's *very* interesting. You find out anything about Hope Through Love?"

K.C. laughed. "Of course. It was modeled along the lines of the group they had going in Tulsa. Primarily young men, trying not to be gay. I've got the stuff at the house, next time I see you."

"This is starting to sound like some kind of fucked-up dating service for ultra-closeted gay fundamentalist Christians." Chris wrote "dating service" on her legal pad with a question mark.

"Yes and no." K.C. was thoughtful. "I mean, I suspect that Chaz really does struggle with being gay, if that's the case. I can't find anything on whether something happened to him in his past. He might just come from a super-conservative family and it fucked him all up. Expectations versus reality. You know how that can go. He may have started these groups really hoping that he could scare himself straight, as it were, but temptation kept knocking on his door and every time he gave in, it created more guilt and self-loathing and maybe it wound him too tight until he finally snapped."

"Or somebody threatened to reveal his secret. That's always a good motive for murder." Chris wrote that down as well.

"Same coin, different sides," K.C. said. "The closet is a scary place for some and if you believe you have a lot to lose, it pushes you farther into it but your demons get bigger. You lose perspective. Could be that's what happened. Or, alternatively, maybe Chaz really felt something for Travis and that scared the shit out of him and he couldn't break it off, because Travis went to Wellspring. Maybe he thought Travis would get weird and tell people there and he'd have another Raleigh on his hands."

Chris could totally see that happening. "Anything else?"

"Not on Stillman. I should have some more about Mumford, though. I'm waiting for another contact who tracks southern fundamentalist churches to send me stuff on Providence of Love. Networking, girlfriend. It's all about networking."

"Kase, you're the best. I'll take you and Sage out as soon as we all have some breathing space."

"No worries. Let me know when you wanna stop by and see this stuff. I've gotta run. Another freakin' meeting. Catch you later. Bye."

"*Claro*. Bye." Chris's thoughts went briefly to her brother. John felt trapped sometimes, but he had come to a point of acceptance about himself and he was willing to live as he felt himself to be. Still, he could be so vulnerable on so many levels because he was always trying to live up to the macho standards of Latino manhood. Mike, Pete, and their dad presented as typical Latino men. They saw themselves as protectors of women and children and the primary breadwinners in their own families.

When Chris and her brothers were growing up, it wasn't okay for boys to cry or show much emotion and Mike and Pete whaled on John quite a bit because he was the baby of the family and also because he clearly wasn't as into the manly-man games his brothers played. Now that John was a bit more comfortable with who he was, maybe he'd settle into himself and he'd make healthy relationship decisions. The thought of John involved with someone like Chaz Mumford made her stomach turn. *Fucking predators.* If anyone messed with John — well, there was no place on the planet he could hide.

Mike and Pete would help her, too, if something like that happened to John. They might freak out when John finally came out to them, but he was their brother and she knew she could count on them to protect him. They had freaked out a bit with her, but they were always there for her and now, in the years since her initial coming out, it wasn't much of an issue anymore. Mike even tried to set her up on dates on occasion, though the women he thought Chris might like were more along the lines of women *he* would like.

She went to find Harper so she could tell him what K.C. had found out about Stillman. They had about fifteen minutes before he was scheduled to arrive and she wanted to make sure they were both on the same page. Ten minutes later, she settled herself into a chair in the interview room and went through her notes one more time, looking up from the table when Harper brought Kevin Stillman in. It wasn't the room they had used for Travis's mother, but it was comfortable, lack of windows notwithstanding. The lighting here was softer than in traditional interview rooms and the chairs were well-cushioned. Chris preferred this room because it helped her "good cop" demeanor, and she found she was able to extract more information from people once they relaxed a bit.

"Mr. Stillman," she said, standing and acknowledging him.

"Thanks for coming in to talk with us. I'm Detective Gutierrez and you've already met Detective Harper. I know you've had a long day of travel and we really appreciate this." She smiled and motioned at the chair across from her. The nervousness in his eyes dissipated at Chris's words and he sank into the proffered seat and removed his brown leather jacket, which he arranged on the chair back.

He looked to be roughly Chaz's age, maybe a bit younger. He wore his hair — a few shades darker than platinum blond — in a hip style, trimmed above his ears and neckline, wavy across the top. Sort of a windblown look. He had blue eyes set just a tad too close together, giving him a suspicious appearance. He offered a warm, disarming smile, which lent him an "aw, shucks" air. Sort of cute, in a geeky way, Chris decided. Kevin was slender where Chaz was more athletically built, though he wasn't nearly as thin as Travis's roommate. He was wearing tan Dockers-style trousers and a red polo shirt that he unconsciously smoothed with one hand. Chris's gay-dar alerted her immediately. *Yep. Another one.*

"Coffee?" Harper asked.

"Please," Stillman responded. Harper flicked a glance at Chris, and it dawned on her that Harper allowed her the extra "private time" with the subject to build a rapport without him present. Harper quietly let himself out of the room and Chris made a show of opening one of the manila folders on the table, observing Stillman the whole while.

"Do you know this man?" Chris removed the more recent photo of Travis and slid it toward him.

Stillman only briefly looked at it before nodding.

He expected this. He's talked to Chaz. "Can you tell me his name?"

"Travis McCormick. He attended Wellspring," Kevin said softly. "Terrible, what happened."

"I'm sorry," Chris offered. "I understand that he was known at the church."

"He was very helpful, especially with some of the youth programs. He volunteered quite a bit." Stillman glanced up at her, a wan smile on his face. She could read exhaustion in his eyes, but behind that was something else. Fear?

Harper entered and shut the door. He put the large Styrofoam cup on the table to Stillman's right, along with a pile of sugar and packets of fake creamer. Across the brim of the cup he balanced a stir stick. He took the chair on Stillman's right and removed a small notebook from his shirt pocket along with a pen. Practiced, smooth, unobtrusive. Stillman began doctoring the coffee.

"I know this is probably hard for you," Chris said gently, "but can you tell me when you last saw him?"

"Thursday afternoon. Not last, but the one before."

The nineteenth. "Where?" Chris leaned forward slightly, still relaxed, keeping her tone conversational. She had the feeling that Stillman could spook.

"Wellspring. He came by because he's been helping me organize a couple of our outreach programs."

"Which ones?"

"We're doing one that we hope will bring more young people into the church, plus we're working on a new educational curriculum for teens."

Chris watched him closely. No mention of New Hope. "How long had Travis been doing that with you?"

Stillman took a sip of his coffee before he answered. "Maybe a year. A bit less."

"Do you know how long he'd been attending the church?" Chris opened another folder as she talked.

"Almost two years. He went right into membership classes and finished within two months." He set the coffee back on the table but kept his hand around the cup. No wedding ring.

Chris placed a brochure on the table in front of him. It was printed on pale blue paper. "Was Travis involved with helping you with this program?" She watched him carefully. His jaw clenched and his nostrils flared slightly.

"Maybe a little."

Harper watched him, too. He wrote something in his notebook.

Chris opened the New Hope brochure and with the tip of her pen, pointed to Travis's name, which was printed right underneath Kevin Stillman's at the bottom of the right-hand fold. "For more information, contact Kevin Stillman or see Travis McCormick after early Sunday service," she read. Stillman licked his lips nervously before hunching his shoulders.

"Okay. Okay, yes. He did help with that program."

"What did he do?" Chris left the brochure open though she leaned back slightly, taking her pen off the paper. She had built the rapport, now she was carefully pinning him. Harper continued to write.

"He would return calls for me and set up group meetings."

"And how often would those happen?"

Stillman shrugged. "Twice a month." He avoided her gaze.

"Did he attend these meetings?"

"Not usually, though he'd set up for them and then re-arrange the room when it was over. Make coffee and that sort of thing." Stillman's fingers nervously tapped on his coffee cup.

Chris allowed a pause to hang in the air for a bit, increasing the tension he was clearly feeling, exhibited in the stiff way he was sitting. "Mr. Stillman," she said, leaning forward again so she could place her elbows on the table and interlace her fingers, "could you explain why Travis McCormick, who identified as an openly gay man, would be helping you with an ex-gay outreach program?"

A flicker of disbelief entered his eyes. "What do you mean?"

Harper glanced at Chris, a slightly bemused expression in his eyes. He shifted his attention back to Stillman.

"He was a bartender at a local gay bar here in town, he performed every once in a while in drag shows, and he dated men." The edges of her tone suggested that she would not be taking bullshit.

"I —" Stillman began. He ran both hands through his hair. "He said he didn't want to be gay anymore."

Is this guy for real? "Explain."

"He — well, he said he'd help because he was tired of the pain of being gay. He even went out a few times with Debbie Ruiz, one of our administrative assistants."

Ruiz? He couldn't have been *dating* her. Time for a follow-up with her, as well. Something occurred to Chris. "How often did *you* ever make calls to interested people for New Hope?"

"Never," he said earnestly. "Travis said he would do that because he didn't mind and I hate talking on the phone..." His voice trailed off, eyes getting wider as something occurred to *him*, as well. "Oh, Lord. When I started the program eight months ago, twenty people expressed an interest and started coming to meetings. But it seemed people kept leaving so by the time we had the last meeting in December, only three showed up."

Holy shit. Travis was talking people out of New Hope. From the look on Stillman's face, he might have been thinking the same thing. Chris switched tacks.

"Who schedules events for the church?"

Stillman relaxed, more comfortable with this line of questioning. "It depends on the events. Charlotte Doyle handles most of that, but each staff member puts in a request at least a month in advance, especially if the event isn't one of our usual."

"Usual — meaning what?" Chris had leaned back, relaxing a bit to see if she could keep him on board.

"Like AA or Bible study. Those groups generally always have the same rooms, same times, same days each week. But they still have to file their reminders because sometimes, they might have a special event that means the meeting or class could go over its allotted time." He was forthcoming with this information, which didn't hit any sore spots.

"So what meetings or events are generally scheduled for Friday nights?"

He looked at her, uncertain. "I don't know exactly. I think

there's an AA meeting. Charlotte would have that information."

"How about Saturday nights?"

"I know about a seniors' meeting. I know there are others but I'm not sure. Just the usual church stuff." He took another sip of coffee, maybe to give his hands something to do.

"So presumably, you also attend events at the church depending on what you have going on with the work that you do. What about Pastor Mumford? Is he ever there for night-time events?" She kept her tone even but curious, with a hint of friendliness. Harper scratched his nose but didn't look up from his notebook.

Stillman slowly set the cup on the table. Chris could tell he was trying to buy time, trying to figure out how to phrase his answer. "There's the Wednesday night service, of course. If we have special events, like concerts or speakers, he attends." He stopped.

"What about Saturday, January twenty-first?" Chris took another sheet of paper from one of the folders.

"We did have something scheduled then. A last-minute thing," Stillman said cautiously. "A popular speaker from Phoenix was able to schedule us in. We'd been hoping he could but it didn't look like it was going to happen. But then we got the call the Monday before and we really scrambled to get the word out. We didn't need to worry, though, since he had posted it on his website. It sold out by Wednesday."

"Reverend Jack Springer," Chris said thoughtfully, setting the flyer she had pulled from the file onto the table. "Did you attend?"

"Of course. Reverend Springer is extremely important. Just about the entire staff was there."

"Pastor Mumford?" Chris asked, as he began tapping on his coffee cup again.

"He was there. He introduced the reverend and warmed up the crowd." Stillman's tone was almost rapturous.

Chris wasn't sure if he was having warm and fuzzy feelings for Springer or Mumford. She put her money on Mumford and took the opportunity to segue. "How well do you know Pastor Mumford?"

The question took him aback at first. "Okay, I guess. I was grateful he hired me at Wellspring."

"Would you consider yourselves friends?"

His fingers quickened their rhythm on his coffee cup. "I suppose. I've worked at Wellspring for about four years and we do have to go on church retreats together and deal with church business. So in that respect, we're friendly."

Chris sighed heavily, making a show of it. She sat up straighter and Harper looked up. He had stopped writing. "Mr. Stillman," she said, weighing her words with disappointment, "I'm going to ask you again. How well do you know Pastor Mumford?"

Stillman licked his lips again and glanced at Harper. Finding no help there, he looked at Chris again and wilted further in his seat. She waited him out.

"Pretty well," he finally said, eyes on the table. "We went to college together."

"Oral Roberts," Chris stated flatly. "Graduated in 1986 with an advanced degree in theology, just like the pastor. Is Wellspring the first job he offered you?" she asked, testing him more.

"No," Stillman whispered. "The first was in Tulsa."

"Where did he go after Tulsa?" Chris had hooked him. She started reeling him in.

"Raleigh. Providence of Love." He sounded miserable.

"Did you stay in touch?"

"Yes." Both his hands now cradled his coffee cup.

"And how long was he in Raleigh?" Chris wanted to see how far she could push him, how much control Mumford had over him.

"Um..."

"Simple math," she said crisply. "December, 1995 to summer, 1998. Where did he go after that?"

The expression on his face was bleak. "Las Cruces."

"Where were you when he was in Las Cruces?"

"Here in Albuquerque. I had just gotten married and I was working at Calvary Baptist."

"And you arrived in Albuquerque when?" Chris leaned back, crossing her arms over her chest.

"Uh, 1996."

Chris switched tacks again. "Why did Pastor Mumford go to Las Cruces?"

"He was offered a really good job."

"Better than Providence of Love? With a ten thousand-member congregation?"

"He wanted a change." Stillman looked like he was hoping he'd disappear, that the earth would just rip open and swallow him up.

"Why?"

"I don't think that's my question to answer," he retorted softly. He had reached his threshold.

Chris allowed her gaze to blow right through him. It was a look, Jerry Torrez told her once, that could freeze Death Valley in July. He told her to use it sparingly, since she didn't want to lose her "good cop" edge. Stillman's hands trembled slightly, even though they gripped the coffee cup.

"Can you tell me where you were on the night of Friday, January twentieth?" she asked, keeping him off guard.

"I had a Bible study group at my house until nine." His body relaxed from relief as he provided his alibi. "Some of the group stayed after and we watched a movie — *The Bourne Identity*. After the movie, a couple of the guys helped me clean up and they left around midnight." He shifted nervously. He wasn't telling her something.

"We'll need some names of people who were there to verify that." She waited before continuing, letting the silence wind him tighter. "What happened after everyone left?"

"I went to bed."

"So no one else can back that up?"

"No. I'm divorced. No kids. Look, everybody left around midnight and I went right to bed. I had to be up early to help get things ready for Reverend Springer." A flash of anger marked his response.

My ass. Somebody stayed the night with him. Wasn't Mumford. At least not until after two or three. "All right. If you could write down the names of some of the people who were at your home the night of January twentieth, we can take care of that right away. Detective Harper —" She looked at Harper, who nodded and pulled a file toward himself.

"Just a couple of forms," he said to Stillman, a friendly note in his voice. He slid them to Stillman and handed him his own pen.

Chris gathered her own files and stood. "Thank you again for your time, Mr. Stillman. We may yet be in touch. And if you think of anything else that might help us, please let us know." She caught Harper's eye and Harper pulled a business card out of the inner pocket of his blazer and set it on the table next to Stillman. Chris left the room and headed toward her office space to wait for Harper. She also needed to check her phone messages. By the time Harper's big shoulders appeared over the top of her cubicle walls, she was working on her notes.

He crossed the space to her desk in two steps and took a seat opposite her. "Squirrelly," he said, running a hand over his brushcut. He tossed the file onto her desk but kept the forms that Stillman had filled out. "He's covering for Mumford about something. Not sure what. I'll see what I can get out of the five names he gave up."

"I think he's lying about Friday night."

"Same here. You think he's in on the McCormick thing?"

"No. He doesn't have it in him." Chris rubbed her face briefly.

"I'm with you there."

Chris continued analyzing out loud. Harper was actually pretty easy to bounce things off of, once you got used to his impassive, unreadable surface. "But someone stayed the night with him, and most likely it was someone in that Bible group."

Harper leaned back and nodded his head thoughtfully. "So why not just tell us?"

"Because it's probably a man and the guy's probably married to a woman." She looked at him to see what his body language would tell her.

"Jesus," he said. He sighed and shook his head. "I don't get that. Why the hell get married if you're just gonna screw around on the side?"

Interesting. He didn't make any kind of comment about screwing around with people of the same sex on the side. "Maybe he got married hoping it would keep him straight," she said. "People get married for the wrong reasons all the time. In this case, I'm guessing the guy's gay and can't deal with it so he hooks up with a woman. Might even have kids. But it's not who he really is. He feels trapped and he's desperate for the kind of love and affection he really should be getting. But because he's surrounded himself with all these beliefs about how evil he is or how wrong his feelings are, he gets stuck in the closet."

Harper ran his hand through his hair and cleared his throat.

Uh oh. Double nervous tic. Chris waited.

"So what's on next?" he finally asked. It wasn't what he'd intended to say, but it wasn't Chris's job to pull it out of him.

"Got a call from the aunt in Dallas, finally. She left a message." She looked at the piece of paper on which she'd scribbled notes. "I'll call her back in a few. She didn't say much except that there was a short memorial service on Wednesday and could I call her." Chris shrugged. "This is the aunt Travis lived with after he ran away from Out of Darkness. I suspect she wants to vent a little bit. But she might know something. I'll check it out."

He nodded. "Still waiting on the rest of Travis's e-mails. Most are just checking in with what's needed at the church. A few to friends. Nothing that jumps out, though. What about that Ruiz woman at the church?" He almost pronounced her name correctly.

"I think that's an angle we need to follow up." Chris leaned back in her chair and regarded him. "I got the feeling that maybe Travis was sabotaging New Hope. And I think Ruiz was in on it somehow, which is why she seemed a bit scared on Tuesday. I'm going to stop by tomorrow morning."

Harper almost smiled. "Good idea. Keep 'em wondering what we know and give 'em a little police presence."

"Cool. Will you find out what Stillman drives?"

"Yep." He pushed himself up using the chair's armrests. "Let's see what we can come up with. I'll check in with Sam at the lab, too. Boss-man won't let us go much further with this if we can't get something concrete. Okay, then." And he left, headed for his own office space across the hall. Chris finished with her notes from the Stillman interview, then reached for the piece of paper with Travis's aunt's number on it. She sighed, not looking forward to dealing with more grief. Still, you never knew what kind of information you could get. She dialed the number and settled herself more comfortably in her chair.

Chapter
Twelve

K.C. HAD SPREAD papers out all over Chris's dining room table. She found what she was looking for and handed it to Chris. "Check this out. One of my sources actually had a copy of the church rag from Providence of Love—the one with that anonymous letter. He copied it and faxed it to me."

"Shit," Chris muttered as she read through it. "Nice. 'This writer wonders how a man who purports to spread the Word of God could sink to such depths of perversion. Mothers, lock up your young men and be wary of a snake in the grass.' That's almost poetic." She glanced at K.C. "I didn't think you could be mean and poetic at the same time. But here it is."

K.C. nodded. "I had a thought about that letter. What if it was written by somebody who had the hots for Chazster but got dumped? I'm thinking a man wrote that. I don't know why, but it feels like something a tweedy guy with a tight-assed walk would write."

Chris laughed and placed the paper back on the table. "How do you want your burger?"

"Cooked," K.C. said innocently.

Chris smacked her playfully on the arm with the spatula. "¿Queso? Chile? What's your mood tonight?"

K.C. did a little dance. "Wild. Hook me up with all of the above."

"Will do." She left K.C. in the dining room and went to doctor the hamburgers on the grill, thinking about the anonymous letter. When she came back into the house, K.C. had organized the papers on the table, leaving half of it cleared so they could eat. Chris set the plate with the burgers on a counter in the kitchen. K.C. already had individual plates ready, with lettuce, tomato, onion, and three dill pickle chips on Chris's and lettuce and tomato on K.C.'s. She had put a serving of potato salad on each plate. Chris's had extra paprika sprinkled on it.

"God, Kase. I'm not sure if it's creepy or cute that you know me so well." She placed a bun from the grill onto K.C.'s plate and graced it with a burger loaded with green chile strips and cheddar cheese. She did the same with her own plate.

"Whatever," K.C. said, as she took the two plates to the dining room. "Grab me something to drink," she called from the other room. Chris took two bottles of Tazo tea from her fridge and joined K.C. in the dining room. She put one in front of K.C.'s plate and then sat down to her right.

"Uh huh. You should talk," K.C. said. "You of course gave me the bottle with the shit I'm drinking most these days." She smiled and shook up the bottle before she unscrewed the top. "So what's the deal with our fave fundie pastor?"

Chris filled her in on what she'd learned in Las Cruces and how the interview with Kevin Stillman had gone. They talked while they ate, bouncing ideas off each other.

"So basically," K.C. said after she took the last bite of her hamburger and swallowed, "we've got a hell of a lot of circumstantial shit but nothing good enough to get the prosecutor to push for a warrant for Chazster's house. And I need to see what my contact has on Grace Baptist."

Chris half-smiled at K.C.'s nickname for the pastor. "Oh, I talked to the aunt today. The one who took Travis in after he bailed from OD."

"And?"

"She wanted me to know that neither of Travis's parents showed up for the memorial service and how could they call themselves Christian if they rejected their own son that way." Chris pushed a bit of potato salad around on her plate. "How the fuck do you do that? Your only child?" She thought briefly of John.

"I don't know, *amiga*. That's some serious issue build-up there. Did the aunt have any ideas?"

"Ellen. Aunt Ellen. She heard from Travis two to three times a month and she sent him a bit of money now and again when she could. Which explains the deposit here and there into his checking account over the past two years. A couple hundred dollars every few weeks. She said he never asked for it but she knew he never would and she figured he could use it."

"That's nice," K.C. said softly. "How long did he live with her?"

"A good two years before he tried his luck in L.A. She said he worked as a waiter while he was living with her and took a few business classes through El Centro, the downtown community college there in Dallas. He paid her four hundred dollars a month for rent after he got a job and get this—she took that money and opened a separate account and when he left for L.A., she gave that to him. He had no idea she'd been doing that, apparently."

Chris picked up her bottle of tea and stared at it thoughtfully.

"She was more a parent than anyone else in Travis's life. She had no idea he was dead until her 'tightwad brother,' as she referred to him, called her to let her know. She hadn't spoken with Paul since he and Angela put Travis in the OD program because she was so angry about what had happened and she wasn't sure even her true Christian faith would allow her to forgive them."

"How is she?" K.C. asked quietly.

"She's a wreck but she's also pissed as hell, convinced that if Paul and Angela had been better parents, this would never have happened." She shrugged. "She might be right." *A chain of events.* "But then again, she was a pretty good contact for him, it seems."

"There are lots of players here," K.C. offered. "In the big, existential picture, that might be true. But in the small, pragmatic picture, I'm leaning toward the good pastor." She stood and picked up the plates. Chris watched as she took them into the kitchen. She heard K.C. scraping them into the trash and then putting them into the dishwasher. The fridge opened and closed and K.C. reappeared with a fresh bottle of tea for Chris.

"Living room time," Chris announced. She stood as well and took the bottle into the living room, where she plopped onto the couch, feet on her coffee table. K.C. took the big matching chair to Chris's left, set at a right angle to the couch. The chair faced the fireplace.

"So you think Travis was messing with the ex-gay outreach program at Wellspring." K.C. smiled. "That's sort of appropriate somehow. But why make the effort to do that?"

"Not sure." Chris shook her bottle and opened it. "I'm going to see what the good Ms. Ruiz has to tell me about it. She knows something and she's scared about it." Chris leaned over and picked up her stereo remote from the coffee table. She turned on some music. A bit of ambient chill tonight. She turned the volume down slightly and set the remote on the couch next to her.

"How about this," K.C. said. "Travis is pissed at somebody at Wellspring. Chaz? Kevin? Somebody else? We don't know. Let's just say he's pissed. So he decides to 'get even.' Maybe he's pissed about the hypocrisy. He's at Pulse one night and recognizes Chaz from Wellspring and he decides he's going to sabotage their ex-gay program over there." She stretched her legs out and regarded Chris.

"Possibly. I mean, sabotage is the intent. But why? Maybe he did have an ax to grind about fundamentalist hypocrisy, but he still seemed to be into his Christian faith. Maybe there's something more personal here. I'm thinking Ruiz is the key to that mystery."

"What about Henderson? Did you get a sense of what went on prior to his death from the case notes?"

"And then some. If Tyler so much as scratched his ass in the days leading up to his death, Maestas recorded it in those notes." She was quiet for a bit. "I read through the notes again and here's what's kind of weird. Tyler didn't have much contact with his family, so this comes from the friends. Apparently, he had been seeing someone but he wouldn't name names. Now for him, that wasn't unusual, according to his friends. He was a more private guy, apparently, than Travis was. But two days before he disappeared, according to his closest friend, he was upset about something."

"Upset? Or angry? There's a difference," K.C. interjected.

"True. The notes say 'upset.' The friend, Theresa Johnson, kind of pushed him a little bit about it and he apparently got really upset and also a bit angry at that point." Chris threw a glance at K.C. "And he kept saying something about how people who love each other shouldn't fuck around and he, Tyler, had had enough of 'half-assed promises' and he intended to make sure that a certain someone couldn't 'take advantage' of anyone ever again."

"Huh." K.C. said. "So maybe this guy he was seeing was Chazzie and maybe he kept telling Tyler that he was going to run away from the church and join the gay life but as time went on, it became more and more apparent to Tyler that Chaz was just feeding him lines. And who knows? Maybe Chaz had started to replace Tyler, too. Maybe Tyler confronted him, threatened to out him. And Chaz snapped. If, in fact, Chaz is our guy."

"I'm thinking that, too." Chris took a drink of tea, then continued. "It's going to take a hell of a lot of digging to uncover proof of that angle here. Which is why I'm hoping we can link Tyler to Travis through the trace evidence. If not, maybe we can get somebody indicted for Travis's murder, at the very least. Whoever did this, though, is careful. And because we're dealing with a major congregation, we can't go running around putting too many screws to people without good reason. The press loves to go after cops who mess with God-fearing people, whether there's justification or not."

K.C. nodded, staring at the fireplace, in research mode. Chris studied the label on her bottle. *What are we not seeing? Everybody makes mistakes. What are Chaz's?*

"At this point," K.C. said, "it looks like the guy who left The Beach with Travis that night is Travis's killer. But even if you get Chaz to admit that yes, that's his car in Pulse's parking lot and yes, he was gettin' a little somethin'-somethin' from Travis, it doesn't necessarily mean he's the same guy at The Beach."

"See what I mean?" Chris's question was rhetorical. "This guy is slick, like you said. The clothing on the man at the Beach matches the clothing on the man who left Pulse with Travis. So we can say they're probably the same guy. What we cannot yet say is that the guy is definitively Chaz. Nor can we say that the man on both videos is

Travis's killer. We have to find a physical link to Chaz and so far, that hasn't happened." Chris made a disgusted sound. "Fuck. Round and round I go with this shit. Down time, *esa*," she said, meaning she wanted to stop talking about work.

K.C. grinned mischievously. "Okay. How about Dayna? What's up with Miss Thing?"

Chris laughed. "You need to get right to the point, Kase. I don't know half the time what you want to talk about." She took a drink of tea and filled K.C. in on some of the conversations that she and Dayna had been having.

"How trippy is that?" K.C. mused when Chris had finished. "A card that never made it. That happened to me once. A bill came back to me, the envelope sliced completely in half. The postal service has this 'we're sorry' rubber stamp that they put on the outside of the fucked-up mail. I wish I had one of those for every time I screw up. Just stamp a piece of paper and send it out."

"Mistakes were made," Chris intoned sarcastically.

"So," K.C. started. "How do you feel?"

Chris smiled. "I'm relieved. I mean, I don't know yet what the deal was with her while she was in California, but it makes me feel better that she told me about the card and that she hasn't been sure where I've been coming from, either. It felt genuine."

"And?" K.C. prodded.

Chris didn't answer for a bit. *And I think I like her more than I should.* "I really like her," she finally said.

K.C. raised an eyebrow. "What's the unspoken part?"

Chris looked at her, slightly surprised. She sighed, relenting. "More than I should."

K.C. stared at her for a long moment. She leaned forward, intent. "Chris, I've seen some women come and go out of your life. I know that some of them you liked more than others. I also know that you keep things in your life fairly compartmentalized. There's your personal file, your professional file, your family file, your friend file. Sometimes, that's a sign of really good boundaries. But other times, it's a sign that you're maybe afraid that someone could get into more than one file. Now, I know that over the years, you've let me into some of your other files besides the 'friend'. "

Chris opened her mouth to say something but K.C. put her hand up. "There's always a risk when you let people access more and more of your files. I know you're a very private person in many respects, but I also know that you're capable of being transparent when it comes to your feelings and thoughts about things. My point is, yeah, it's scary to let people see your files. But it can also be extremely lonely and maybe not entirely healthy if you don't."

Chris nodded slowly, feeling a bit chastised and knowing that she couldn't really use the "cop stuff" excuse after what Sage had said to her on Monday. *Dammit.*

"Now, I haven't had the opportunity to hang out with Dayna much beyond a couple of barbecues here and there. And I know how you are about introducing girlfriends to me. You generally wait until you're sure it might get serious. So I figured you and Dayna were keeping it light."

Chris started to say something, but K.C. headed her off. "And I'm not always the best judge of character, but the way you talk about her and the way you look when you talk about her makes me think that she's different than your usual."

"How I look? What does *that* mean?" Chris realized she must have sounded petulant because K.C. gave her a "whatever" look and rolled her eyes.

"You are so busted with this. Come *on*. Your whole face lights up when you talk about her. And—I don't know how to explain this, actually. It's—it's like you have this *glow* when she's on your mind."

"*Glow?*"

K.C. laughed at Chris's mock indignation. "Yeah, you big ol' detective. *Glow.* Like a *girl.*"

Chris threw one of the couch pillows at K.C. She deflected it and it flew across the room to bounce off the front door.

"Good shot," she said, laughing. "Listen to me. A glow. And it's really nice to see. You're relaxed and excited at the same time. I've never seen you like that with anyone and I've gotta tell you, I like this look on you. I like this side of you and I think you should take the leap."

"I'm not sure I know how," Chris admitted. *I don't know if I've ever just let myself go there.*

"Who does? I mean, nobody writes a manual for this shit. How could you? Everybody's different. But how will you know if you don't just freakin' do it?" K.C. leaned forward again, using her hands for emphasis. "And once you get past the initial parts—you know, where every day you're learning something new about who she is and it's so fucking exciting—a whole *other* level opens up and then you're learning more about what makes her tick. It's really cool and it's really interesting and exciting in different ways. And yeah, sometimes annoying because you find out the not-so-good stuff or the baggage that doesn't match yours and the shit that you realize you need to figure out to move to even more levels."

Levels. It made Chris giddy, thinking about uncovering the things that made Dayna Carson who she was. *Shit. I might be in some trouble here.*

"It's the scariest thing I've ever done, in some ways, to hook up with Sage," K.C. continued. "I don't always know what I'm doing and neither does she. But I made a rule with myself—especially after thinking about what happened with Melissa—that I would never avoid things with Sage, that I'd talk shit out. It's hard sometimes. And yeah, she can drive me completely crazy." K.C. smiled softly. "But I love her more than I can possibly say and I know—not just in my head but in my heart—that what we're building will stand up to anything." She regarded Chris. "I want that for you. I want you to have that feeling with someone." K.C. stood then. "But," she said, "if you don't unlock the door, Dayna can't come in."

Chris stood as well and pulled K.C. into a hug. "And how much for this session, Doctor Fontero?"

"A six-pack of chilled Fat Tire and a pan of that green chile lasagna you make."

"Damn, you're the cheapest therapist ever."

K.C. released her. "That could either be really good or really bad." She grinned. "All right, I'm leaving that shit for you because I have my own copies. Still checking on some Pastor Chazzy stuff. Still waiting on Hope Through Love info. I'll let you know as soon as I hear something." She moved to the front door and took her fleece jacket off the coat rack. "Thanks for feeding me, *amiga*."

"Part of my therapy payments," Chris said.

"Oh, hey—" K.C. paused while putting her jacket on. "Tomorrow's the big date, huh?"

Chris flushed. Heat raced up her neck. "I'm kinda nervous about it, actually. Excited to see her. A little worried about what she might have to say. Worried I won't do or say the right thing."

"It'll be fine. *More* than fine," K.C. assured her. "Have a great time and call if you need to decompress." She grinned wickedly before turning and opening the door.

"Thanks, *esa*. Drive carefully and hi to Sage."

"Always. Talk at you later." K.C. headed down the walk to her car, parked on the street.

Chris stood at the open front door, waiting until K.C. was in her car and pulling away from the curb. She watched until K.C. turned left. Chris closed and locked the door and lit the candles on the mantel. She stood staring into the flame of the candle whose container was decorated with an image of *La Virgen*. Her personal cell phone rang. Chris crossed the floor to the coffee table and picked her phone up. Her heart backflipped as she answered. "And a good evening to you, Counselor. How was your day?"

CHRIS ARRIVED AT Wellspring at 8:03 AM the next morning. This time, she took her cup of Starbucks coffee in with her. Props like this humanized her in the eyes of people she talked with, she had discovered. And this time, Chris wore her black leather jacket. It could make her feel, oddly, a bit more approachable. More a person than a cop. She pulled the door open and stood once again in the foyer. She took her shades off and slid them into the inside pocket of her jacket. Charlotte wouldn't be in until 9:00, which gave Chris nearly an hour with Debbie Ruiz. The more seniority, Chris guessed, the later you could come in.

She entered the administrative office and stood at the counter. Debbie's back was to her. "Hi, Ms. Ruiz," Chris announced. Debbie started and turned from her monitor. She looked nervous when she realized who it was. "Chris Gutierrez, APD. I was hoping you had a few minutes to talk a little more."

"Um..." Debbie started, glancing around furtively. An automatic reaction. Maybe Charlotte was some kind of psycho boss who freaked out if paperclips weren't lined up properly on her desk. "Sure." Debbie stood, looking entirely unhappy about the decision.

"Grab your coat," Chris said amiably. "You can show me the grounds."

This seemed to sit very well with Debbie and she relaxed a bit as she shrugged into a long black overcoat. She locked the office door and followed Chris outside, into the chill February breeze. Beautiful blue sky again, but the New Mexico wind hadn't started up yet. Debbie pulled a pack of Marlboro Lights from her coat pocket. She glanced at Chris questioningly.

"Go ahead," Chris said. She waited for Debbie to light up and then the two of them began to walk through the parking lot, toward the site that would become an academy in the future. Contractors had already marked its dimensions with wooden stakes and orange plastic flags. The Sandia Mountains loomed to the east. The future school would block the view of them from the parking lot. *Too bad.*

"Ms. Ruiz," Chris said carefully as they walked, "what was Travis's involvement with New Hope?"

Debbie visibly stiffened and said nothing. She took a long drag off her cigarette.

Chris stopped and looked down at Debbie's eyes. Debbie dropped her gaze.

"I know Travis was gay," Chris said quietly. "What I'm trying to understand is why he might have been involved with a program like New Hope. It could help us find out who killed him."

Debbie drew a shaky breath. The hand that held her cigarette trembled slightly. "We got to be friends," she said softly. "He was so sweet. I was going through a break-up and Travis—he just knew when people were going through things." She brusquely wiped at her eyes with her free hand. "He was really into the message of Jesus. Moreso than a lot of people who go here, I'll tell you that," she said cryptically. "And he'd get upset some days when he heard people talking about how evil it is for people to be gay."

"Why did he come to church here, if that kind of message upset him?"

"He said it was familiar to him, that he had grown up in a fundamentalist household. But he wanted to change things. He didn't like some of the exclusion he said he felt here."

Chris took a sip of her coffee as Debbie smoked.

"One day," Debbie said finally, "he took me to lunch. This was about a year ago. April last year, I think." She sniffed and pulled a Kleenex from her coat pocket so she could wipe her nose. "He saw something that he wasn't supposed to see and at first, he wouldn't tell me. Finally, he did." She stared off across the empty lot that would one day hold a Wellspring school.

"What did he see?"

"Kevin Stillman and another member of the congregation being extremely physical with each other in the sanctuary. Backstage."

"And was this other member a man?"

Debbie nodded. "Married. With children." Debbie laughed suddenly, a harsh sound. "I already knew. I had known for a couple of months."

"How did you know?" Chris took another sip.

"I have to be all over this church all the time, all day. I see things. I hear things. I'd seen Kevin kissing this guy. They were over in the meeting room building. It was almost six and hardly anyone was around. The door was partially open but I saw enough to know what was going on. They didn't see me, though."

"Why was Travis upset about that?" The breeze had picked up a bit and blew Debbie's hair into her face. She turned so her back was to the wind.

"Because Kevin was already working on New Hope and Travis thought that was so hypocritical. He—I don't know. When Travis set his mind to something, he crusaded."

Interesting choice of words. "So he decided to help with New Hope because...?"

"He wanted to shut it down. He knew Kevin wasn't very good with PR so he volunteered to help with that bit of it. Everybody who had any interest in it, Travis would contact them. He didn't tell me exactly what he said, but slowly, people stopped coming to the meetings and no new people signed up. I guess he was pretty good at getting the word out." She laughed, but the sound held no humor.

"What's your role in this?"

Debbie stubbed her cigarette out on the ground and lit another after glancing back toward the main building.

"I gave him Kevin's schedule and a membership call list. Most of the people who were interested in New Hope were already members. And I'd direct people who were interested in the program to Travis rather than Kevin. Other than that, I was just his friend."

"But he could get that contact information from the people themselves," Chris said. "Why was that important?"

Debbie smiled grimly around her cigarette. "He said he could use the list for leverage. With one mass e-mail, Travis could out Kevin and anybody else he wanted to the entire congregation." She shrugged. "Seriously, I don't think he would ever do that. He could get pissed, but he wasn't sneaky like that. Still, he said it could be an option if things got ugly. That's what he said. Ugly."

Ugly in what way? "Did Kevin know that Travis had found out about that relationship?"

"I don't know. Maybe. Around December, it seemed that things were tense between Kevin and Travis. But since I didn't hear anything, I wasn't sure what it was. It was between them, because rumors fly around here and nothing got out about that." She stopped then, and glanced back toward the main entrance. Chris waited, deciding that Debbie wanted to say something more but she was debating whether she should or not. She took another pull on the cigarette and exhaled slowly.

"Okay, maybe that's not entirely true. I found out that Travis was seeing someone in the congregation."

"Who?" Chris kept her tone relaxed, though she had a feeling she knew what Debbie was going to say.

"Don't be too shocked," she said, half-sarcastically. "Pastor Chaz."

She shoots, she scores. "How do you know?"

"Travis told me. I think he really liked Chaz."

"How did they manage to see each other?"

"Travis said that Chaz *never* called him and *never* e-mailed him. They'd talk briefly after Sunday service and Fridays Chaz went to Pulse. They'd 'make appointments for counseling,' is what Travis said they called it. That was the only way, he said, that Chaz would see him. If they used a professional-sounding code like that."

"Did Travis ever say anything about issues between Kevin and Chaz?" Chris asked before taking another sip of coffee.

Debbie thought for a bit. "Not really. I can tell you, though, that Chaz is the top in *that* relationship."

Chris gaped at her, surprised that Debbie would use that term. Debbie noticed and managed a smile. "Travis wasn't my only gay friend," she said. "I've been around. Besides—" she gave Chris a quick up-and-down, "*you* know exactly what I'm talking about. And no, I don't think Chaz and Kevin were sleeping together regularly but it wouldn't surprise me if Chaz used Kevin every once in a while for sex."

Chris arched an eyebrow. *Very informative morning.* She glanced at her watch. 8:45. Debbie noticed.

"I have to get back. Certain *people,*" she emphasized, "like to know everybody's business."

"Ms. Ruiz—"

"Debbie."

Chris nodded and offered a smile. "Debbie. Thank you so much for your time. Could you come to the station on Second and Montaño and give us a formal statement?"

She looked at Chris thoughtfully before replying. "You know, a couple of days ago I probably would've said no. But I'm tired of the bullshit at this place. And I really liked Travis and no one deserves what happened to him." She sighed heavily. "I'll come down on my lunch hour." She stubbed out her cigarette.

"Thank you. Ask for me or Detective Harper."

Debbie nodded and started walking back toward Wellspring. Chris returned to her car and sat in the driver's seat for a bit, writing out some notes. A red Buick LeSabre cruised into the parking lot at exactly 9:00 AM. The driver parked in a slot marked "reserved" and Charlotte Doyle got out. She shot a glance at Chris's car but she had sunglasses on and Chris couldn't tell what specifically she was looking at. Chris decided to pretend that she had just arrived, too, and she'd throw a few questions at Charlotte. That might take heat off Debbie, given what Chris suspected was Charlotte's extremely suspicious nature. She locked up and followed Charlotte into Wellspring.

CHRIS FINISHED GOING through the three complaints against Charles Mumford. The pastor had been married once, and that was the last complaint against him. It was dated June, 1999, Las Cruces. By September they were divorced and according to public records, Chaz hadn't remarried. *So why does he still wear a ring?* It's not easy to fool a big congregation like Wellspring. Did he have a "cover date" for official functions? Or maybe he just made up some story about how his poor wife died and he couldn't ever remarry. *Shit. Maybe he killed his poor wife. God knows. That's a whole other investigation.*

She read through the first two complaints. Similar circumstances. An argument that escalated. In the first, dated November, 1988, the victim alleged that Chaz had shoved her against the kitchen stove, which left a big bruise. Then he allegedly slapped her. The second incident occurred in May, 1993. The victim in this case alleged that Chaz had punched her twice and shoved her against a wall. Her head slammed the wall so hard, the victim contended, that her skull had put a dent in the drywall.

The first two complainants indicated that they were engaged to Chaz. None of the three pressed formal charges. There might be more, Chris thought, or maybe Chaz took out his frustrations on his boyfriends after a while. She looked up from her desk at Harper, who had just appeared in the doorway.

"So our guy has a history of slapping women around, huh?" he said sardonically, acknowledging Chris's earlier call to him. He came in and eased into the chair facing Chris's desk. "Got Ruiz's statement. Good work on that. I called the boss-man to see if maybe we've got enough with this statement to bring our man in for a nice talking-to in a formal interrogation room." He scratched his arm. "Sam called from ME. He should have something back about that stuff under the vic's nails next week. Might be some skin cells in there. And he'll have the fibers analyzed probably by Monday. Oh, and more good news. He did find traces of rohypnol this time but not much. He ran another test and it came back positive but not conclusive. Still, it's something." He looked down at his hands. "Coroner's releasing the body today. It's going back to Dallas."

Chris nodded. Aunt Ellen wouldn't have to wonder where Travis was anymore, if he was okay. If he was unhappy or tired. If he was seeing someone who made him happy. Sadness flooded her chest.

"But," Harper said as he looked at her again, "Sam went back over the body in his usual careful way. He does at least two checks, maybe more if something bugs him."

"And?" Familiar anticipation raced through her gut.

"He got something else. McCormick apparently used a lot of hair gel. And sometimes, if you don't rub the stuff in all the way, it sticks to your skin. Sam found some at the hairline above the forehead. The perp missed it. So did Sam, for that matter, the first time. It's about as big as a dime."

"And?" She had never seen Harper this animated.

"He's got a partial print," he said triumphantly, leaning back.

"Fuck," Chris breathed.

"He'll be running it through CODIS for shits and giggles. *And,*" he continued, "I had a little chat with a drug rat named Chuy Hernandez down in the South Valley."

At least he almost pronounced Chuy's last name correctly. "Rohypnol?"

Harper nodded. "He said that he sold a couple of roofies to a white guy in January, after New Year's. He was worried the guy was a cop but he decided the guy wasn't because he was driving a silver Lexus SUV and no cop would be able to afford one of those," Harper said dryly. "I cut those pictures of the pastor and Stillman out of the brochure and put 'em on a plain sheet of paper next to each other and Hernandez fingered the pastor."

Chris's office phone rang. She looked at Harper and he motioned for her to answer.

"Hi. Chris Gutierrez."

"It's Tony. I was able to get a partial plate on that SUV. You ready?"

"That's great. What've you got?" Chris picked up her pen and prepared to write.

"It's local. M-R-N dash six and what might be an eight or a nine. That's it."

"Shit, that's actually better than what I thought you'd get. Thanks, Tony."

"Yep." He hung up.

Chris did, as well. She looked through her notes until she found the plate number for Chaz's vehicle but she already knew that she had a match of sorts. "M-R-N dash six nine two. That's his plate. Tony got M-R-N dash six and either an eight or a nine, he said. Let's call the boss-man and see if we have enough to apply for a warrant to search Chaz's car and maybe even his garage. I'd say we have enough to bring the good pastor in for another little chat, too. He's already lied about how well he knew Travis."

Harper looked downright happy. "Curiouser and curiouser," he said.

Chris looked at him, surprised. "I never took you for an *Alice in Wonderland* fan."

He smiled sheepishly. "My daughter used to say that a lot when she was growing up. That was one of her favorite books."

"Daughter?" *I'll be damned.*

Harper looked down at his hands again then back at her. "Yeah. She'll be twenty-two this year."

Chris leaned back. "Where is she?"

"School. The University of Wisconsin."

"Geez, Harper, I never figured you for a dad. You have any other kids?"

"No. Just her. Terri." He suddenly looked uncomfortable.

"Well, hell. Has she been to visit yet?"

"No," he said softly. "We don't talk much." He cleared his throat.

"Oh." Chris carefully eased off the topic. "Sorry." She hesitated for a moment, then changed the subject. "All right, next step. Sam'll update us early next week. We might have enough for a warrant, but I don't want to alert Chaz to that. Let's check in with the boss and see if we can just bring Chaz in for a chat first. If he knows we're working on warrants, he might do extra cleaning, which might screw us." She stood up. "Let's go see The Man," she said lightly.

Chapter
Thirteen

CHRIS STOOD AT the island in the center of her kitchen and cast a critical gaze across the counters. She tended to clean while she cooked, so at the end of the meal, there wasn't much to do. She had made a Cuban-style salad, which sat in a large Mexican bowl, pale orange and deep blue triangles painted over the white body.

Chris loved Mexican pottery. She had driven *Abuelita* to Chihuahua to visit family four years ago and she had bought her set of dishes there, in Cuauhtémoc. Mexican dishes were thick and sturdy and Chris liked how the simple geometric shapes painted around the edge of the plates and the rims of the bowls evoked a clean elegance. Mexican blue, terracotta oranges and reds, and splashes of goldenrod. The interesting thing about Mexican color combinations was how bright, primary colors could end up being so soothing. And with the right lighting, they could also be joyful.

Jesus. I'm doing Mexican feng shui *or something.* She checked the timer, clicking away on the counter by the stove. Dinner would be ready in an hour, at six-thirty. She inhaled slowly, then exhaled, slamming her day into a back closet. Tonight was about other matters and Chris wanted to be sure she was present.

She went into the living room and lit the candles on the mantel. She also turned on the fireplace. John and Pete had converted it to natural gas two years ago, which meant it was mostly for mood, but it did provide a bit of heat for the living room. *Abuelita* loved to sit near it when she visited, watching the flames on the fire log. Chris selected some music and loaded it into her CD player. She put it on "random" and then inspected the dining room table. It was more intimate to set a place at the end opposite the window and set the other to that person's right, rather than across from each other. Silverware, cloth napkins, placemats, water glasses. She lit the three medium-sized pillar candles at the end of the table that sat closest to the window that looked out into her back yard. *Martha Stewart, here I come.*

Back in the kitchen, Chris squeezed a bit more lime over the salad. She took the plate of eggplant slices out of the fridge and set it on the counter next to the stove, near the timer. A large, cast-iron skillet waited on the front burner for her to begin cooking the eggplant in olive oil, basil, and arugula. Chris went light on the garlic and added a touch of New Mexico red chile powder to the oil mixture she'd brush on. She glanced at her watch. In fifteen minutes, Dayna would be here. Chris smiled. Dayna was always on time.

She took another deep breath and rubbed her hands together. She had everything prepped for mojitos. It was just a matter of timing. A mojito tasted better freshly made, so Chris would wait until Dayna arrived to prepare them. She exited the kitchen and walked down the hallway to the master bedroom. She opened her closet door and inspected herself in the full-length mirror, making sure everything was in place.

She had chosen light blue Levi's and a black button-down silk shirt whose sleeves she had rolled up to her elbows. She had unbuttoned the top two buttons on the shirt so that her necklace was visible, a silver chain from which hung a small teardrop-shaped pendant inlaid with turquoise and onyx. Chris had bought it at Santo Domingo Pueblo, north of Albuquerque. She checked her shoes, a pair of men's black Kenneth Coles on which she had splurged over Christmas. Dayna had commented once how she liked Chris's simple, practical style of dress, how it suited her. Dayna said it made Chris even sexier.

God, I'm like a teenager in lust. She smoothed the front of her shirt and glanced at her watch for the hundredth time, at least. Ten minutes. Dayna had left a voicemail on Chris's personal cell around lunch, saying she was beyond excited to see her that night. Chris returned the call and left a similar message. She had managed to duck out of work at four so she could get things ready.

I'm so damn nervous. She ran her hands through her hair and returned to the kitchen. Already, the main dish was sending tantalizing wafts of chicken and mojo New Mexican style into the dining room. She checked the timer, knowing that it would tell her another thirty minutes to go. She inspected the eggplant strips and the marinade yet again and decided she needed a touch more red chile powder before she cooked them. As she was reaching for the small glass jar on the counter, she heard a car door slam. More specifically, the door of a Toyota truck. The front doorbell rang a few seconds later. *Forget the chile.* Chris went to answer the door.

"Hi," Dayna said, smiling when Chris opened the door.

Oh, my God. She looks so good. Shit. "*Bienvenidos,*" she said softly, motioning for Dayna to come in.

"I was feeling rather French today," Dayna said, holding up a bottle of red wine in one hand and a bouquet of flowers in the other as she took the one step and entered the house. "I know we're having rum, but I was hoping maybe another time, we could try the wine."

"Absolutely." *I think I want many, many other times. But I'm not quite sure how to do it.* She took the wine and flowers in one hand and helped Dayna remove her coat, which she hung on one of the empty pegs of her coat rack. "I hope you parked in the driveway," she said, looking down into Dayna's eyes. She wore glasses with stylish artsy frames that matched the blue of both her exquisitely cut shirt and her eyes. Chris hoped her body would remember to automatically breathe for her.

"I did. Thanks." Dayna carefully took the flowers out of Chris's hand. "I'll take care of these." She didn't move, though, and instead just continued to regard Chris. "I missed you," she added quietly.

Chris leaned in, meeting Dayna's lips with her own. She wrapped her free right arm around her and pulled her close, gently exploring Dayna's mouth with her lips and the tip of her tongue. A white-hot jolt bounced from her head to her feet and back again, lingering between her thighs and in the pit of her stomach. Dayna responded immediately, her amazing lips guiding and teasing Chris's tongue. Chris's heart jackhammered against her ribs. The sensation was almost painful but she ignored it as Dayna pulled her closer, melding her breasts to Chris's, moving against her in a way that was both familiar and new. Chris groaned and pulled away.

Dayna laughed softly. "I know how you are when you're cooking. You'd better check on whatever smells so damn good."

Chris took Dayna's free hand in her own and pulled her to the kitchen.

"Oh, my God. What *is* that?" Dayna inhaled deeply.

"Chicken mojo. Sort of. I have different recipes." Chris set the bottle of wine on the island and glanced at the timer. Just right. She squeezed lime juice into the two tall glasses she had left on the island next to the mojito ingredients. She sprinkled powdered sugar into the juice then dropped a few mint leaves in both. With a wooden muddle, she deftly crushed the mint.

Dayna was watching her, still holding the flowers. "I'm not sure why, but what you're doing right now is really turning me on."

Chris glanced up and smiled. "You're one to talk. There's a vase—"

"In the cabinet by the back door," Dayna finished. She opened the requisite cabinet and removed a tall clear vase with a blue rim. Dayna filled it halfway with warm water and dissolved a teaspoon of sugar in it, stirring with a long wooden spoon. Chris took both glasses and filled them with ice at the fridge. As she did so, Dayna opened one of the kitchen drawers and retrieved a pair of scissors. She remembered where things were in Chris's kitchen and it brought a strange little lump to Chris's throat. Dayna deftly cut the ends of the flowers with her right hand.

"There's a lefty pair in there," Chris said as she poured rum into the glasses.

Dayna turned to look at her, grinning. "When did that happen?"

Chris shrugged, sheepish. She concentrated on the glasses as she splashed club soda over the ice and rum and garnished each with fresh mint. "November."

"Wow," Dayna said. "I'm — that's really nice." She held Chris's gaze a bit longer before she returned to her flower arranging. Chris watched her ass as she did so. Dayna wore a pair of low-slung hip-hugger jeans with a wide brown leather belt. The jeans fit her ass and thighs beautifully. Chris was sure they were the same jeans Dayna had been wearing that Thursday evening in Santa Fe last June when Chris first saw her. They were at the opening reception for a conference at La Posada Hotel and Dayna was chatting up some lawyer-types, animated. Chris decided she was intriguing and she liked the vibe Dayna gave off. She was wearing her hair pulled back that evening, which gave her a sort of natural, sporty appearance. Dayna Carson was beyond hot, Chris thought that night. And it only got worse because when Dayna left her group and walked to the bar for her first drink, Chris had nearly swallowed her teeth at the sight.

"You were wearing those jeans the night I first saw you," Chris said as she handed Dayna a glass.

"Well, aren't you the romantic one. Remembering my jeans." Dayna clinked her glass gently against Chris's. She had finished with the vase.

"Among other things." Chris watched her.

Dayna took a sip of her drink. "Jesus. This has to be the sexiest thing I've ever had in a glass," she said, surprised. "I've had mojitos, but this — no, this is a 'Chrisito.' " She sipped again. "Good fucking God. Unbelievable."

Chris smiled, flattered and strangely shy. She turned her attention to the eggplant.

"And *you* were wearing black pants and an olive-colored shirt." Dayna moved to stand beside Chris, watching her cook. "It really brought out the tones of your skin. You had your sleeves rolled up like now. You were wearing that watch you have with the silver and turquoise band and you were drinking Santa Fe Pale Ale."

Chris looked at her, not sure what to say, and turned her attention back to the skillet, where the eggplant crackled in the marinade. "You know, there're always spots in the police academy for a strong woman with excellent powers of observation." She turned the eggplant over.

"I'll leave the cop stuff to you," Dayna said, laughing. She leaned her back against the counter to Chris's left, head turned toward her. "I watched you for an hour at least. I liked your smile and the way you moved."

"Oh?" Chris kept her eyes on the skillet. Cooking over such high heat, she had to observe food closely to make sure it didn't burn. "How's that?"

"Your body language. Secure, confident. I liked how it made me feel, to watch you. Safe. And I hadn't felt that way for a very long time." Dayna reached over and brushed a lock of Chris's hair off her forehead. She leaned back against the counter. "I had this incredible urge to do that to you even then. I just wanted to touch you, to see if you were real. Because I'd never felt anything like it."

Chris turned her head to look at Dayna. "You were wearing those jeans and a plain white button-down shirt. You kept your sleeves down. Your hair was pulled back and you were drinking Sam Adams. You were wearing the glasses that you have on now and small gold hoop earrings." Chris returned her gaze to the skillet, trying to ignore the electric thrill the memories brought. Almost done. She returned to the memory. "I liked your vibe. And your laugh. The first time I heard it, I was on my way to the bar and I passed within ten feet of you and you laughed and it sounded like spicy molé. So on my way back to my group, I walked slower, within a few feet so I could hear your voice." With a practiced motion, Chris used the spatula to scoop the eggplant out of the frying pan and put it on the plate. She turned the burner off and placed the skillet on one that was unused, leaving the spatula on the plate of eggplant.

Chris moved then, and braced her hands on the counter's edge, one on either side of Dayna. She could smell Dayna's cologne, light with floral and citrus notes. She'd know that cologne anywhere, because on Dayna, it created its own signature. "You drink beer slowly," Chris said. "It was almost forty-five minutes before you went to get another one." Chris watched a smile tug at the corners of Dayna's mouth, stared into her impossibly blue eyes, the color of a Mexican sea at sunrise, of a splash of weathered cobalt against the creamy surface of village pottery.

"And I went back to the bar," Dayna continued softly, sliding her hands up Chris's arms to her shoulders.

"You were waiting for the bartender. It was pretty crowded." Chris moved closer, pressing against her, needing to feel her.

"It was," Dayna breathed. "And hot." She arched an eyebrow playfully. "Oh, and loud. But I heard this voice to my left and I knew it was yours. It was exactly how I imagined you would sound. Warm, like your smile, and secure, like the way you move."

"I said—" Chris began, watching Dayna's face. *She's so beautiful. So amazing. I am such a goner.*

"'Excuse me'," Dayna said, giggling. "You said, 'excuse me. Did you drop this'? " And you handed me a fresh bottle of Sam Adams and you smiled. And the first thing I thought after you said that was 'oh, my God. She has the best smile.' And then I thought 'who *is* this woman'? " Dayna's fingers brushed Chris's neck and chills threw themselves down her back.

"You took the beer and you said, 'Wow. Thanks. I'm Dayna Carson'. " And you reached over to shake my hand. I remember I took your hand and you had the best handshake. Then I said, 'I'm Chris.' And you said, 'Just Chris? Is this a Prince or Madonna thing?' "

Dayna's fingers brushed Chris's jaw. "You laughed and handed me one of your business cards."

Chris pulled Dayna closer against her and leaned down, her lips hovering over Dayna's. "It was a test," she said mischievously.

"And how'd I do?" Dayna's lips barely brushed Chris's. It sent more chills rocketing through Chris's abdomen.

"You pronounced it perfectly." Chris ran her lower lip along Dayna's, hoping she wouldn't pass out at the sensation, hoping she could keep this moment close for a long, long time.

"Gutierrez," Dayna said against Chris's mouth, affecting a fake Marine Corps growl, "shut the hell up and kiss me."

Chris did just that and it was like coming home and the first step of a new journey, the feel of Dayna's mouth and tongue on her own. Their kisses deepened and Dayna's fingers were in Chris's hair, holding on as if it had been years since they'd seen each other, and the space between them echoed of time well spent and shared smiles. Chris couldn't remember where or when she was, couldn't recall who she might have been before that moment, didn't ever want to be anywhere else as the present beneath her lips bumped a future of maybe's and definitely's.

An insistent beeping worked its way around the edges of her consciousness. Chris was only vaguely cognizant of it and she dismissed it automatically. Nothing mattered beyond what was happening here, nothing beyond the connection between her and Dayna, unbelievable Dayna. The beeping increased in decibels, poking at her hearing. Dayna started laughing. "Um, I think that means dinner's ready," she said, lips moving with her words against Chris's mouth.

Chris sighed, disappointed as the room settled into place again. "I think I might prefer dessert, actually," she said, almost oblivious again to the timer. The expression in Dayna's eyes lodged itself in Chris's heart, whispering promises of something even deeper. And it was both the most incredible and yet scariest invitation ever.

"I'm thinking we might need to keep our strength up for tonight," Dayna finally said, a smile joining the look in her eyes.

"In that case—" Chris released her, albeit reluctantly. "Dinner is served." She handed Dayna her drink. "Please. Go sit down."

Dayna shot a smoldering look over her shoulder as she exited the kitchen and Chris inhaled, then exhaled deeply before she took the clay pot out of the oven. The state she was in was an accident waiting to happen. *Christ. How would I explain* that *at the emergency room?* She imagined the headline: "Hot and bothered lesbian spills entire pot of chicken mojo down shirt in sexual fantasy accident." Carefully, she put the clay pot on the stovetop and with a thick pair of oven mitts, she removed the cover and set it aside. A few minutes later, she brought it to the table in a separate dish, over rice. She also brought the salad and eggplant.

"You are a woman of many talents," Dayna said as she served Chris and then herself from the main dish. "Some of which I want all to myself."

Chris's breath caught in her throat at the comment and she focused on serving eggplant and salad before she returned to the kitchen for the pitcher of water in the fridge. At the table, she filled both their empty water glasses and set the pitcher aside. She glanced at Dana's mojito. Still over half a glass. She sat down and Dayna picked up her mojito.

"To dinner," she said.

Chris raised her own drink.

"And to what tomorrow brings." Dayna touched glasses with Chris, took a sip, and turned her attention to the food. She took a bite of the chicken mojo. "Oh, my fucking God," she said in reverent tones. "Don't they eat this on Mount Olympus?"

"Glad you like it." A warmth spread through Chris's limbs. Dayna affected her that way. Since the beginning, there'd always been a little thrill when Dayna was around. As they continued to see each other, though, the tingle gathered strength into a full-on electrical blast that heated Chris's blood and left her perpetually warm, wrapped in both comfort and a deep, slow-burning passion she'd never experienced. *I'm going crazy. Completely.*

They laughed and chatted through dinner, talking a bit about work but mostly about things they'd done, places they'd been, and past events in their lives. Chris loved these moments with Dayna, because the rapport between them was easy and safe, a meeting of mind and spirit, whether the topic was mundane, goofy, or serious. Dayna could be at once irreverent and professional, each facet equally sexy. *God, what she does to me. Does she even know?* Chris watched her and grinned as Dayna mimicked one of her colleagues, a big bull of a man prone to pissing most sentient beings off. Conversation drifted to other matters, including family and, of course, sports. Chris loved that she could talk sports with Dayna.

At just the right time, Chris began clearing the table. Dayna

helped and Chris watched her surreptitiously as she cleared plates
and put leftovers — of which there weren't many — into containers
that she then placed in the fridge. Chris liked how Dayna looked in
her kitchen, liked how it felt to have her in the house, sharing space
and time. She set to work making two fresh mojitos, reveling in the
moment, enjoying the company, and trying hard not to freak out
about possibility.

As she was crushing mint in the glasses, Dayna finished with the
last of the salad and opened the fridge again, looking for a place for
it. Chris kept her fridge and cabinets well-organized, which saved
time when she cooked. Dayna said something under her breath and
Chris looked up. Dayna had found the bowl of fresh strawberries on
the second shelf. "You are too much," she said softly.

"Pre-dessert," Chris said, raising her eyebrows up and down in
an imitation of Groucho Marx. She brought the glasses to the fridge
and filled them with ice then poured in the rum and seltzer. This
time, she added a cinnamon stick to each as garnish.

Dayna took the bowl of strawberries and her mojito and headed
for the living room. Chris knew she'd take the end of the couch that
was closest to the fireplace. Then she'd set the strawberries on the
coffee table and eat a few. Throughout the conversation, she might
eat a few more. She liked to pace herself with strawberries. Chris
threw a glance around the kitchen and, satisfied, she turned out the
light and joined Dayna on the couch.

"Where did you find these?" Dayna asked, licking her fingers.

The gesture short-circuited Chris's brain momentarily.
"Cruces," she finally managed. "Local hothouse."

Dayna ate another one, then kicked her shoes off and drew her
legs up underneath her on the couch, expression contemplative but
wary.

Time for more serious things. Chris settled in on the opposite
end, positioning herself so she could face Dayna, one foot folded
under her on the couch, the other on the floor. "Thanks for joining
me for dinner," she said, opening a door for Dayna to proceed.

Dayna smiled. "I can't believe how lucky I am to have met you.
And I want to talk more about that, but there's another matter I need
to clear up."

Chris sipped her mojito, waiting. Dayna wasn't one to dance
around a topic.

"My ex," Dayna began, "had some problems. I haven't really
told you much about her."

"No. You haven't. But I figured you would at some point."

Dayna's jaw tightened slightly as she regarded Chris. "I met
Anne through colleagues when I was still working and living in L.A.
She did entertainment law while I was involved in criminal law. Still,

we had things in common and we started seeing each other about four years ago. It progressed quickly. Maybe too quickly. But—" she paused. "You can never know if you don't take a chance, I guess." She shot a meaningful glance at Chris before continuing.

"I knew Anne had some problems. She was bipolar and very open about that with me from the beginning. She managed it well with medication and she did have a psychiatrist she saw twice a month. So after about a year, when it seemed that she was doing well and we were pretty stable, we bought a house together. Things were going very well at both our jobs, and we had the down payment." Dayna took a sip of her drink. "We settled in and I thought that this was it, that we'd play house and have a future. And that's how it went for about a year." She rubbed her forehead lightly for a moment.

"What happened?"

Dayna chuckled, a dry sound. "What *didn't* happen? Basically, Anne had gone off her meds when we bought the house. But it took about a year for things to really get out of hand. All these overdue notices for bills started arriving in the mail. She said she just forgot to send the check in, no big deal, she'd take care of it—I wanted to believe her."

"Of course. She was your partner, after all." Chris's gut clenched. *What a mess.*

As if reading her thoughts, Dayna said, "It was a total clusterfuck. And then the phone calls from collection agencies started. Anne and I had always maintained separate accounts except for one, which was for household bills. The mortgage, phone, utilities. That kind of thing. I had a bad feeling so I checked the joint account after about a month of the notices and phone calls. Anne had cleaned it out. I went through her credit card statements—God, I hated to do that. I felt so badly about it. But a couple of my checks had bounced for household bills and I needed to see how bad the damage was." A current of underlying guilt marked her voice.

"You did what you thought the circumstances warranted," Chris offered.

"I suppose. It still doesn't sit right with me." Dayna took another drink before continuing. "Anne had maxed out all her credit cards. Thousands of dollars. She had been on spending sprees all over L.A. and online, buying insane things like diamond-encrusted cufflinks and Japanese weavings. All that stuff ended up in a storage unit and the contents got auctioned off because she hadn't paid the rent for it. And she had no money coming in. I went to her office the day I found out about the joint account and—" she shook her head. "Anne wasn't working there anymore. She hadn't been to work in two months. Her boss—*former* boss who was one of the firm's partners — took pity on me and said, colleague to colleague, that Anne had been behaving erratically at work and wasn't showing up and when she did come in, she would be dressed inappropriately and her behavior was over the damn moon."

"Jesus," Chris said softly. "And you seriously had no idea?" Too late, she realized how that sounded.

Dayna looked at her and her response was tinged with sarcasm. "No, I didn't. No, I don't know why I didn't see it. I should have, but there you go. I didn't. I suppose I wanted to give my partner the benefit of the doubt."

"Hey," Chris backpedaled. "That's not—" *Shit.* "I'm not questioning your judgment. It's just—"

"Just what? Yes, I should have been more cognizant, noticed the signs. But give me the benefit of the doubt, would you? One or the other of us was always on some business thing or working late or whatever. I have no idea what she was doing those two months she wasn't working. Yeah, that shows you how much attention I was paying. Yeah, I really fucked up there. But then again, we actually didn't see each other much. Thinking about it now, I don't think we went to bed at the same time for weeks." Dayna picked at something on the knee of her jeans. "I hadn't been out of law school that long and I was working my ass off, trying to make that big impression and land that sweet job." She looked up. "It's not unusual for new lawyers to work sixty to eighty hours a week. Maybe more. That was me. And I didn't see the signs of trouble with Anne. Or maybe I avoided them. So yes, I fucked up."

Chris waited a bit before saying anything. "Any of us could. I work too much, too. Sometimes I use it as an excuse, maybe. Anybody could avoid dealing with some things by putting in more hours at work," she finished awkwardly.

Dayna stared at her for a moment then smiled. "Chris, sometimes you need to just shut up."

"Uh—"

"You're trying to make up for an insensitive comment, but you're just adding to it." She leaned over and squeezed Chris's hand.

"I'm sorry." Chris smiled back.

"Accepted. So are you interested in this story or is it making you uncomfortable that I might have really bad judgment?" Dayna injected humor into the question, but Chris sensed a challenge as well.

"Yes, I am interested. And no, I'm not uncomfortable." *Just kind of an idiot.*

Dayna studied her for moment, then continued. "I found out that Anne had been going off and on her meds for a couple of years before we met. Maybe testing herself, to see how long she could go.

But the problem is, when you're bipolar, sometimes you're not always a good judge of your own character when you're off your meds." Dayna's lips tightened into a thin line. "Then right after we bought the house, she apparently just stopped taking them altogether. Some bipolar people are able to maintain a veneer of stability for long periods of time without medication. But when they're in manic phases, they can be financially, emotionally, and socially out of control. Depends on the severity. Anne's was obviously on the more severe side."

Chris rubbed her hand on her thigh a few times, filling the silence.

Dayna let out a long breath. "After I went to Anne's office that day, I went right home and she had left. Most of her stuff was gone. Some she had thrown out onto the driveway. Other stuff was either at the bottom of the pool or just lying around the house. I called her mom, who I didn't have a very good relationship with, but she at least said that Anne was there in San Jose with her. She started to blame me for Anne's condition and on some levels, I still wonder if she's right. If I had paid attention, gotten her some help..."

Dayna sighed and carefully swung her legs off the couch, putting her feet on the floor. She pulled her glasses off and put them carefully on the coffee table with one hand while she rubbed her eyes with the other. "Anne's family is extremely homophobic and they figured that Anne's relationships with women were part of her overall condition." Dayna gave a harsh little laugh. "Can you imagine? 'Why no, I'm not gay. I'm bipolar.' Oh, well, *that* explains it. Carry on."

Chris stifled a smile. "Did Anne come back?"

"No. Clearly, it was over. And I had to get things figured out, how much she owed, and what I could and could not do about that, since we had legally combined parts of our lives. I sold the house—I went to San Jose, and fortunately she was fairly lucid and signed all the proper forms. Most of what I got for the house I used to pay off Anne's debt. I also undid everything we had done together, legally. Power of attorney, wills, that kind of thing. I had to work with her family so that they saw that I wasn't trying to fuck them over. They hired an attorney, fortunately, and he was pretty sympathetic about the whole thing."

"Did you get the financial side resolved?" Chris kept her tone level, though she imagined the stress that Dayna had gone through and she just wanted to reach out and hold her in the wake of her own screw-up, tell Dayna that she was sorry for what happened with Anne and thanks for explaining but please don't let it affect what could be developing here and now. And then she caught herself. What *was* developing? She focused again on Dayna.

"Mostly. I spent so many hours on the phone explaining what had happened. Credit cards, banks, credit report agencies. It was a goddamn fiasco." She took a sip of her drink, as if trying to calm herself. "A few actually forgave some of the debt. Some worked out different payment plans. I used whatever assets of Anne's were still in my control to pay that off, too. And I paid off a few myself. I mean, Anne wasn't malicious. She was sick."

Dayna sat staring at the bowl of strawberries. She turned her head then to look at Chris and offered her a wan smile. "So after months of dealing with shit, I began to think about maybe starting over somewhere else. I had met an attorney at a conference in San Francisco. That was maybe two years ago, right before everything blew up. He was from Albuquerque and he asked if I'd ever tried the prosecuting side of things. I hadn't and he said that I should, that I had a real knack for it and there might be a job opening at the Albuquerque office." She laughed and rolled her eyes. "I'd been to Albuquerque a couple of times, but, I mean, I'm from San Diego and I was living in L.A. Why the *hell* would I want to go to Albuquerque?"

"There are a few good things about it," Chris teased.

Dayna looked at her, eyes catching the reflection of candlelight. "One amazing thing in particular," she said simply.

Damn. Chris reached for her drink, using the motion as something to help her both deflect and absorb Dayna's comment.

"I didn't think too much about it," Dayna continued. "But then I got this call about four months later and it was that attorney and he said there was an opening here and he thought I should apply. Well, you know, I was so tired all the time, after working so much and dealing with Anne's shit that I thought, 'what the hell?' and applied. They flew me out for an interview and what do you know? I really liked it here. It felt right. I remember flying back to L.A. and thinking that I was ready to pack up and leave. Three days later they called with an offer. And here I am."

"Lucky for me." Chris took a sip of her mojito, savoring the little kick the cinnamon gave it.

"And me." Dayna flashed the smile that could melt the polar ice caps.

Dayna took a sip of her drink as well and ate another strawberry. "This has been a long, convoluted story. But there's a point to it," she said wryly. "I got the call before Thanksgiving from Marnie that Mom had broken her leg and because she's not in the best health anyway and she had nobody living with her, she needed some help. The three of us talked about hiring a nurse, but that was really expensive and we decided that we needed to spend more time with Mom anyway, so I'd take the first shift and then Tory would take the second. Marnie still lives in San Diego, so she ran errands for us and did shopping and shit. I stayed at the house with Mom, getting her to do the exercises the doctor recommended and trying to keep her from getting depressed." She stopped suddenly. "Fuck, I'm completely off track. Okay. Remember when I told you I had to go to San Diego?"

"I do. The end of November." *The same day I bought the lefty scissors.*

"I got to San Diego that evening and I had a weird message on my phone. The lawyer Anne's family had hired said to call him, that it was extremely urgent. So I did, that night." She rubbed her temples. "And here's where I maybe freaked out."

Chris adjusted her position. She exhaled slowly, realizing that she had been holding her breath.

"Anne had been in a car accident a week earlier. I didn't know. I mean, I wasn't part of her life anymore. Hadn't really been for nearly two years, because she'd gone to San Jose. He told me she was in a coma at a San Jose hospital. Vegetative state. No brain activity whatsoever." Dayna swallowed hard. "I felt sad when he told me. I mean, there was some love there. And we had some good times. But why the hell was he calling me about it? I asked him and he said — he said that the family had been going through her stuff."

Preparation for the worst, Chris thought.

"And they found this life insurance policy." Dayna stared at Chris with a perplexed expression. "Anne had put me down as the sole beneficiary on this policy and somehow, she had managed to keep it current. The one thing she managed to stay focused on." Dayna took another sip of her drink. "It's worth a hundred and fifty thousand dollars."

Oh, shit. Which meant Anne's family probably freaked, too.

"I didn't want the money," Dayna said softly. "I didn't even know Anne had done that. The family, of course, was raising holy hell about it and immediately contested Anne's 'sound mind and body,' and on and on. I told the attorney I didn't want it and could we please get my name off it. He said that this would leave no beneficiaries, as Anne hadn't stipulated another, and the family most likely wanted the money. He was telling me that the family was dug in for a long legal battle. I told him I didn't care. I didn't want the money if she died. So he said he'd take care of it and he'd call me back."

Uh-oh.

Dayna sighed heavily. "Four days later I get another call from him. She had died..." Her voice trailed off and Chris could hear tears. She automatically moved and pulled Dayna against her.

"It hurt, to hear that." Dayna drew a shaky breath and leaned into Chris. "Of course, they didn't tell me where the memorial service was, but the attorney told me where she was buried. I needed closure so I went up to San Jose the day Tory got to San Diego to hang with Mom." She tightened her grip on Chris. "It was a nice cemetery. Nice view. I'm glad I went and saw her name on the headstone. It closed at least one chapter."

Chris stroked Dayna's hair, a touch of sadness whispering through her bones.

"But there was still the fucking policy."

Dayna's grip on Chris's shirt tightened.

"The family had been arguing about whether to take her off life support before she died and the attorney had to go out of town for a couple of days and then Anne went and died without help, leaving me as the sole beneficiary of this fucking thing. I had to go to San Jose in the middle of December and put on record that I didn't want this damn money — as soon as I found out about it, I didn't want it or the baggage that came with it — but of course, Anne didn't name anyone else and the family, rather than letting it all go, immediately contested Anne's intent because she was 'mentally ill' and on and on. I had written a formal letter and had it notarized, going on record that I wanted nothing to do with this money. Last I heard, the family was still contesting the whole thing. Their attorney said I might have to go back to San Jose to give a deposition."

Chris shook her head, commiserating, but her years in law enforcement had taught her that no matter the amount, people did insane things for money.

Dayna pulled away slightly and looked at her. Chris kissed her lightly on the forehead and Dayna leaned into it, sighing. "I wonder," Dayna said, "if this wasn't Anne's way of trying to apologize to me somehow."

"Seems like it." Chris hugged her tighter and Dayna relaxed against her. They were quiet for a while, sitting there on the couch, watching the fireplace. Chris let all the information Dayna had revealed settle for a bit before she spoke again. "Besides my insensitive comment tonight, why didn't you think you could talk to me about this?"

Dayna pulled away again so she could look at Chris's face. "Please, Chris," she said with gentle patience. "I hadn't told you much about what had happened between Anne and me because I didn't want you to think that I made a habit of somehow getting involved in shitty financial and emotional situations like that. Besides, you were pretty up-front with me about not wanting anything serious."

Chris nodded slowly, acknowledging Dayna's observation.

"After we first met, you talked about being a detective, and about how it was hard for some people to understand where you're coming from because of what you have to see and deal with. You said you didn't think a serious relationship was a good idea for you." Dayna's mouth quirked in a wry smile. "You basically said the same things I was saying to you those first few weeks."

"Okay. I see your point," Chris relented. "We hadn't really talked about what we were doing or where we were going and I just assumed, given the other people you were dating and that you had told me you didn't want to be serious, that I'd keep it that way, too. But I guess I just figured you'd tell me if things were bothering you." She squeezed Dayna's hands gently and released them. "I guess I should have asked. Or been more clear. Or something. I'm not very good at communication when it deals with my own emotional involvement." She stopped, surprised at her admission.

"I've noticed that," Dayna said, not unkindly. "But you've been honest and you've given me space. And you didn't blow me off."

"I can be kind of an asshole sometimes, but I do like to hear things directly from the people involved. And I wanted to hear directly from you what was going on."

Dayna pulled completely away from Chris and folded her arms over her chest. "So do you think you're able to talk a little bit now about us?"

"Us?" Something like panic shot through Chris's chest but she fought to control it, trying to focus on the here and now. What happened in the past didn't have to color what was happening now. "Sure," she said, hoping she sounded steady.

Dayna arched an eyebrow, clearly aware of Chris's discomfiture. "Do you remember our first kiss?"

Chris relaxed and smiled. *There is no way in hell I could ever forget that.* "A month after the conference. I had asked you out formally the week before and you had asked me out for that night." Chris paused, wondering how much she should say. She took a chance. "It was—" she shook her head, at a loss. "There are no words."

Dayna held Chris's gaze, steady. "I didn't see anyone else after that."

"Wha—why didn't you say something?"

"I was afraid you'd think I was getting too serious and you'd back off. And I was afraid that maybe my judgment was fucked up and that—"

"I'd turn out to be unstable. Or shitty. Or an asshole." She held her hand out and Dayna took it.

"Maybe. After all, it was two years before I realized that Anne— well, anyway. But here's the deal, Chris. I really started to like you when we were dating last summer and I guess I wanted to see what it was like, to allow myself to get to know one person again. Then

California — and shit came up again. I didn't feel like I had the right to call you and dump all this heavy crap on you when you had no point of reference for it. So I wrote the letter and sent it. In that letter, I told you a bit about my past with Anne and the latest developments."

She paused and then her words came in a rush. "And I told you that I hadn't been seeing anyone else since our first kiss, and that I really wanted you to know that. I told you that I had to deal with my past again and I needed some time for closure and that I really wanted to see you when the dust settled. I told you that I would leave that up to you, because I knew what a major data-dump this was and if I had too much shit going on for you, I'd understand if you wanted to end it.

"And then I spent a lot of the first part of January dealing with Anne's family and this stupid money shit again." She paused. "You didn't say in your phone messages that you wanted to see me again, but you didn't say you *didn't* want to, either, and I was assuming you'd gotten the letter. Since I hadn't really heard from you either way, I was going to bite the bullet and call you to see where you were with this. Thank God for nice January days in the bosque," she finished, gripping Chris's hand tightly.

"Definitely," Chris agreed.

"All right. So we've been sort of testing each other's boundaries all week. I still really like you and I enjoy your company. I know we both have some things to work out — you've told me a little bit about your past relationships, and you've made it pretty clear that you're not sure you're good relationship material." She stopped and took a breath. "I'm not sure what I'm ready for, either, but I like how I feel when I'm around you and I hope that you might be willing to keep dating me, no pressure, no expectations, to see what happens here, if anything. Maybe we'll just be perpetual dates," she finished with a smile.

Chris waited a few moments, making sure Dayna had finished speaking before she said anything. She thought about the conversations she'd had with Sage and K.C. that week, and about how a part of her felt strangely empty when Dayna left and she didn't hear anything from her. "I'd like that," she said slowly. "I'm not sure what I'm ready for, either, and I don't want to make any promises, but I like you, too, and I really enjoy the time we spend together." The confession dispersed her anxiety, rather than increasing it, and that surprised her.

"Okay. So basically, with regard to you and me — here's what happened," Dayna said. "Girl meets girl. Girl A has a law background and baggage with an ex. Girl B has a cop background and lots of baggage with that. Girl B doesn't think she'll ever find anyone who can put up with the cop shit, so she keeps people at arm's length—"

"And Girl A is questioning her judgment after the ex and decides that no way in hell is she going to try to deal with a relationship until—oh, I don't know. Ninety-seven years of therapy. Or something." Chris rolled her eyes, playing along.

Dayna snorted and pushed her playfully back against the couch. "Nice," she said with mock sarcasm.

Grinning, Chris sat up. "Girl B—" she stopped. "I think I want to say something here. But I'm not sure how," she admitted.

Dayna regarded her quizzically for a moment. "You don't have to if you're not ready. We'll just go back to eating strawberries and drinking Chrisitos," she said lightly.

Chris didn't respond right away. The silence lengthened until Dayna broke it.

"Hey, it's okay. We don't have to talk any more about *us*." She stroked Chris's arm.

"I know. But I think I want to."

Dayna repositioned herself on the couch, putting some space between them, giving Chris some room. "When you're ready," she said quietly.

Chris nodded and studied her knee for a long while. "This is hard for me," she finally said.

"It's all right. I don't want you to feel like there's pressure to say anything. So how about we just—"

"Girl B really missed Girl A," Chris blurted and she immediately wanted to grab the words and stuff them right back down her throat. Until she saw Dayna's expression.

Dayna moved closer and touched Chris's cheek. "Girl A really missed you, too. And Girl A didn't handle some things very well and she should have called you. I should've done a lot of things that I didn't. I'm sorry about that."

Chris leaned into Dayna's touch. "Thanks. I wish I had left more detailed messages."

Dayna smiled and Antarctica thawed and sea levels rose instantaneously. Chris pulled Dayna against her and lay back on the couch, wanting to feel as much of Dayna as she could, along with the jolt she knew would zip through her heart. Chris smiled, wondering if Dayna could see the sparks flying out of her head.

"I'm so sorry," Dayna said, her face very close to Chris's now. The look in her eyes told Chris she meant it, that she wanted to put things right. And Chris knew that she needed to suit up for the game, as well. Not entirely sure what that might mean, she opted to start slow.

"Can we make a rule, maybe?" Chris asked, all too aware of

Dayna's breath on her face and every curve, every muscle of her body conforming itself to hers.

Dayna pursed her lips, uncertain. "What kind?"

"Maybe talk about shit as it comes up?" Chris let her hands slide down Dayna's back.

"Good rule. Seconded." Dayna brushed her lips lightly over Chris's. "Do you plan on using that rule, too?"

"I can't guarantee I'll be very good at it, but I'm pretty sure I want to try."

"That's half the battle. Thanks for listening tonight."

"I'm glad you told me. And I'm sorry for being an ass." Chris exhaled, the sound a half-breath and half-moan as Dayna's lips traced her jaw, then lingered on the spot where her jaw met her neck. *I might die here.*

"You owned it." Dayna kissed Chris's neck. "So let's talk about food, Detective."

Chris closed her eyes. "You want some recipes?"

"That's not what I had in mind."

"Uh..."

"I was wondering," Dayna whispered against Chris's ear, "if I could make you breakfast in the morning." She gently nipped Chris's neck, then ran her tongue along her earlobe.

"I was hoping you'd ask that," Chris gasped, knowing it would probably only take one touch from Dayna to send her through the roof, the way she was feeling at that moment.

Dayna sat up suddenly, straddling Chris again.

"Hey —" Chris groaned plaintively.

"Shhh." She placed her fingers over Chris's lips then reached for a few strawberries and held them in her right hand as she deftly unbuttoned Chris's shirt with her left and pulled the front of it out of Chris's jeans. "God, I love looking at you," Dayna breathed, running her left index finger lightly down Chris's chest, between her breasts, to her waistband.

Chris rested her hands on Dayna's thighs, lost in the moment and savoring the energy between them. Dayna's left hand pushed Chris's shirt open. She rested the strawberries on Chris's abdomen, shooting Chris a saucy grin, and quickly unhooked Chris's bra, using both hands to push it aside.

Chris released a breath — a jagged exhale — as Dayna's fingertips lightly brushed her nipples in slow, circular patterns. "Tease," Chris growled, barely able to contain the tremors that danced through her torso.

"You don't know the half of it." Dayna laughed softly as she unbuttoned her own shirt and shrugged out of it. She leaned down slightly so Chris could undo her bra — carefully, so as not to dislodge the strawberries. Dayna allowed the straps to slip down her shoulders then her arms, watching Chris's eyes, an unspoken invitation in her expression.

Chris took it, let Dayna's breasts fill her hands and her nipples harden against her palms. Dayna moaned, a long low sound edged with promise. She covered Chris's hands with her own and closed her eyes. All Chris could think to do was sink farther into the heat between them, letting her hands track lines down Dayna's sides to come to rest at her hips, Dayna's hands still hitchhiking on her own. Chris ached at the sight, inhaled sharply as Dayna released her hold on Chris's fingers. She picked up the strawberries again and bit the tip off of one as she held Chris's gaze. Chris's breath lodged behind her sternum as Dayna squeezed strawberry juice over each of Chris's nipples, then gently dragged the moist fruit down Chris's abdomen.

"Jesus," Chris breathed, watching as Dayna bit the tip off another strawberry and dripped its juices over her own nipples. She tightened her hands on Dayna's hips, meeting the rhythm of Dayna's slow grind with her own. "You're completely amazing," she said softly.

Dayna smiled impishly and bit into a third strawberry, drizzling its juice over Chris's lips. She leaned down and kissed her long and hard and Chris responded, the feel of Dayna's naked torso against her own setting off incendiary devices beneath her skin that blazed across her bones, etching both desire and hope into her marrow. "Dayna—" The exclamation slipped past Chris's teeth and rode the breath they shared, easing itself between their lips.

Dayna stopped, her mouth hovering barely a feather's touch from Chris's. The expression in her eyes spoke of dreams and truths, of a long common road, and of a welcome at the end of a lengthy trek.

Chris's heart threw itself into her throat as Dayna brushed Chris's hair away from her forehead, rested her fingers on Chris's cheek. "I want you," she whispered and her words were warm on Chris's lips.

"I'm yours," Chris breathed, every cell ablaze.

Dayna responded with a deliciously torrid smile and a long, lingering kiss that accompanied them down the hallway to the bedroom.

Chapter
Fourteen

CHRIS STIRRED AND rolled over, wondering vaguely what had disturbed the delightful morning haze that enveloped her. There it was again. She opened her eyes, reluctantly allowing the day to claim her. The noise again — her phone. The business cell. She groaned and reached for the bedside stand. She clumsily grabbed the phone and flipped it open, putting it to her ear.

"Yeah. Gutierrez," she croaked. She cleared her throat.

"Morning, sunshine," Harper intoned.

Christ. She sat up and checked her alarm clock, also on the bedside stand. 8:58. "Yeah, yeah. What's up?" She ran a hand through her hair and rubbed her eyes, trying to clear the vestiges of sleep from them. She heard music playing in the other room and the smell of chorizo and eggs cooking sent a flush down her thighs. She quickly tabled that thought and focused on the matter at hand.

"Thought you'd like to know that our good buddy Stillman got the crap kicked out of him Thursday night."

"What the hell? Where is he?" Chris was wide awake now.

"UNM hospital. Busted ribs, assorted bruises, and a broken jaw. They've got him wired up, so he can't really talk too much."

"Fucking shit," Chris muttered.

"You kiss your mother with that mouth?" Harper was in rare form.

"You this fucking annoying every morning?" she shot back.

"Yep. All right, here's what we know, based on what information he gave at the hospital. Stillman claimed he was assaulted outside his house around eleven-thirty PM."

Oh, sure. "Who called nine-one-one?"

"Nobody. He drove himself to the hospital."

"After an assault in his driveway? Bullshit."

"Yep. Pretty flimsy, I think. The attending doc contacted a couple of uniforms to come over and take a statement, which is just as vague. I had a thought, so I drove over to his place this morning and they're condos. Somebody would've heard *something*. So I checked in with the closest neighbors, got some statements."

"Jesus, Harper." Chris was impressed. He was productive.

"And nope, they sure as hell didn't see anything outside. However, here's a tidbit for you. The neighbor on the right—one of those nosy old ladies—said that Stillman had been home since about nine-thirty that night and that at ten, he had company." Harper paused. "I asked her, you know, did she happen to notice what the company was driving. And she tells me a silver SUV. She says she knows the car because it's over at Stillman's place a few times a month so she didn't think anything of it."

Chris thought for a moment. "Did she hear anything unusual?"

"I asked her. And she said a couple times she thought she heard yelling—these units share a wall—and then a couple of thumps. About ten-thirty, she hears the SUV start up and drive away, in no hurry. She likes to stay up for Leno, she says, so that's how she knows. Leno was just starting his monologue." Harper's tone was dry.

Chris got the feeling he was actually pretty good at talking to nosy old ladies. "So what's the game plan?"

"I called our boy Chaz and left a message asking him to call me as soon as possible, that we have some new information we need to discuss with him. Nothing specific, but enough to make him sweat."

"Have you heard back?"

"Not yet. I'd like to get him in on Monday, see whether he looks like he's been beating on anybody."

"I've got a better idea. Let's catch a service tomorrow."

"I was afraid you'd say that." He sighed. "Early? Or later?"

"It'll have to be later," Chris said. "I'm taking my grandmother to church tomorrow." It was actually Pete's turn, but he was down with the flu and had left a message with Chris Friday morning.

"Well, hell, Gucci. You're just gonna be gettin' right with the Lord in all kinds of ways. I'll meet you there and I'll let you know if anything else comes up before then."

"Thanks. Take it easy." She rolled her eyes at the nickname but for whatever reasons, it wasn't bothering her as much anymore.

"Okay, then." He hung up.

Chris closed the phone and returned it to her bedside table before she surveyed the tangled mass of sheets and bedding. There were no words, she decided, to describe the previous night. Sex with Dayna was always incredible, but last night was different somehow. Deeper. More intense, if that was possible. And definitely the most passionate night she'd ever spent with anybody. She shut her eyes at the memories, allowing them to wash over her like a tide. *I'm in trouble,* she thought, remembering the taste of Dayna on her lips, how it felt to be inside her, and the need she had to just hold on to every moment with her as long as time allowed. *But God, it feels so good.*

"Mmm. That's a nice view."

Chris opened her eyes. Dayna stood at the foot of the bed holding a cup of what Chris surmised was coffee. She was wearing her glasses, Chris's shirt from the night before, and a smile. Her nutmeg-brown hair fell to her shoulders in delightful waves, mussed from last night's activities. Chris felt her mouth drop open though she recovered admirably. "I'm not sure about *that*, but the one I have is unreal." She knew she was grinning like an idiot.

Dayna moved to the bedside and sat down. She handed Chris the cup. "Good morning," she said as she leaned in and kissed her.

"No," Chris breathed as Dayna slowly pulled away. "It's an *excellent* morning."

Dayna ran her fingertips along Chris's jaw, over her lips. Chills erupted on every part of Chris's skin and she tightened her grip on the cup, willing the coffee not to spill.

"Do you have to work?" Dayna asked softly.

"I always have to work," she said, smiling. "I'll probably check in with a couple of people today, but we're in a waiting pattern for a bit and I got caught up on my other stuff already."

"Did you have any plans?" Dayna's lips ran lightly across Chris's chin and she delicately nipped Chris's lower lip. Her fingers tracked down Chris's neck to her chest and hovered at her breast.

"Uh—I honestly don't know because I can't really think when you do that."

"Such power I have." Dayna laughed as her fingertips grazed Chris's nipple and danced down her abdomen.

"You have no idea," Chris said between her teeth.

Dayna kissed her again. "It's mutual." She pulled the sheet away from Chris's thigh. "Hungry?"

Chris swallowed hard. "Yes. In all senses."

"First things first." Dayna's lips grazed Chris's cheek. "Have breakfast with me."

"HI, CHRIS," SAGE answered.

"Hi, Sage. How's your Saturday been?" Chris stood at her stove, heating the leftover chicken mojo for dinner.

"I had K.C. out back doing some cleaning. She's in the shower. I'll have her give you a buzz when she's done." Sage's voice held a note of laughter.

"About time somebody put her to work," Chris said, smiling. She stirred the pot.

"I completely agree." Then in typical Sage fashion, she abruptly changed the topic. "So how'd it go?"

Chris laughed and she knew it sounded sort of embarrassed but also giddy.

"It went well, then. Have your questions been answered?" Sage's tone was gentle and held a smile.

"Yes and yes. We spent today in Santa Fe." Chris leaned against the counter, absently staring at the flowers Dayna had brought the night before.

"That sounds like it went *more* than okay. How do you feel?"

Chris thought for a moment, trying to put her emotions into words. "My world is rocked," she finally said. "Right off its axis."

Sage started giggling. "And it's rolling down Central right now?"

"Yeah. Something like that. I feel sort of out-of-control but—it's amazing." Chris sighed. "I don't know what the fuck I'm doing." She picked up the wooden spoon to continue stirring.

"You're letting her in. That's a huge step for you, so yes, it feels scary. But you're doing exactly what you should be doing. I can hear it in your voice."

"I hope so. I'm so out of my element here." Chris turned the burner off. *So completely outta control.*

"Relax. And let things happen."

"Thanks for the pep talk." Chris removed a plate from her cabinet.

Sage laughed. "Of course," she said in a "well, *yeah*" tone. "What's a good day this week to have dinner with us?"

"I'm not sure. Maybe Wednesday? I'll have to check my schedule and I'll call you back." Chris emptied the contents of the pot onto the plate.

"Um, you'll need to check with Dayna, too," Sage corrected.

Oh, my God. "Shit. This is like bringing her to meet my parents."

"No, it's far worse than that," Sage responded, laughing. "And K.C.'s already met her briefly a couple times."

"But *you* haven't. And this is a little different context—" Chris started.

"No, it's a *lot* different context," Sage said, still laughing. "Does she like Greek? How about Yanni's? Check with her and let me know so I can coordinate."

"I think I might be more nervous about this than I was about Friday," Chris grumbled good-naturedly.

"Whatever. It's just me and K.C."

"Exactly." *And that is way scarier than the parents.*

Sage giggled. "It'll be a total blast. All right, I'll have K.C. call you back. Take care."

"You, too. Bye." Chris hung up and set the phone on the table before she took a bite of her dinner. It reminded her of Dayna and the night before. She chewed, thinking about the conversation they'd had and how it made her feel. Yes, it scared her. Dayna scared her. She set her fork down. What about this was scary? What was she afraid of, exactly? She thought about how she and Dayna had met, and how they'd had two lunch dates in the two weeks after the conference. Neither Chris nor Dayna had called them dates, but that's what it felt like. And then they did a dinner. That was *definitely* a date.

Chris picked up her fork and took another bite. Why was this so scary? When it was so damn easy to be around Dayna? Okay, so if things didn't work out between her and Dayna, so what? *Shit happens. Been there, done that.* Break-ups weren't a problem for Chris. No, the problems arose before that, in the growing discontent from whichever woman Chris had tried a long-term relationship with, and from Chris's subsequent withdrawal. She set her fork down again. Or had she, Chris, withdrawn *first*? Sure, like Sage had said, there were two people in a relationship and her exes bore some responsibility for what happened before and after the break-ups. But maybe Chris had helped things along.

Why? Why do I do that? Was it about trying not to be vulnerable? Not letting people in to see some of the really horrible things she had to deal with as a cop? Was she afraid she'd bring some of that home? Maybe lose control and end up like those other cops who smacked their partners around? Was that it?

Chris stared at her plate. No, she decided. That wasn't it. Not completely. She did worry about bringing her job home with her, but she'd never worried about some kind of crazy temper tantrum against a family member or girlfriend. It had never happened and she'd been a cop for several years. Wouldn't violent tendencies have shown up already? So what was it, then, that freaked her out about relationships? Was it something as simple as just not sure she was ready for anything serious? Or just choosing the wrong women with whom to try a serious relationship?

She finished her meal and took her plate into the kitchen where she cleaned up and brewed a quarter of a pot of decaf coffee, thinking again about the initial weeks with Dayna, and about their second dinner date in particular. She and Dayna had gone for coffee after eating. They'd ended up at the Flying Star, a local hipster café with unbelievable desserts, and then wandered down Central together afterward, chatting. Dayna had taken a chance with that date, Chris knew. She had asked Chris to pick her up so they could go in one vehicle, which meant that Chris found out where she lived.

Chris poured herself a cup of coffee and on the way into the living room she picked the phone up off the table. Once settled on the couch, she sipped from her cup, recalling the rest of that second date with Dayna. Chris had driven Dayna back to her condo, located in a complex tucked away in the North Valley off Rio Grande Boulevard. Chris walked Dayna to her front door and waited for her to open it. "Thanks," Chris said. "Can we do this again?" Dayna gave her that damn smile and took Chris's hand. "Definitely," she said. And they stood looking at each other, the smell of honeysuckle and wisteria in the cool air.

Chris smiled, remembering how fucking nervous she felt. She wanted to kiss Dayna so badly that it was a physical pain against her ribs but she could only stand there, frozen, until she finally managed to say something. "So what works for you?" she had asked and before she could register what was happening, Dayna slid her other hand around the back of Chris's neck. Gently she pulled Chris's head toward hers. "You do," she had said, and she kissed her, introducing her to the mind-boggling and wholly incredible lips of Dayna Carson, Esquire. It went on and on, and Dayna tasted faintly of coffee and mint and her tongue felt like satin and Chris just knew she'd be needing to call 911 for a defibrillator. They had pulled apart after what could have been a few minutes or a few hours—Chris had no idea—and Dayna said, sounding breathless, "Damn. Can we do *that* again?"

And it felt like that still, with Dayna. *So what is so scary?*

Chris's home phone rang, interrupting her thoughts. She checked the ID before answering.

"*Esa*," she said in greeting to K.C. as she stood and walked back into the kitchen to pour another cup of coffee and get focused.

"Hey, homegirl. Sage tells me *somebody's* date extended into today." She was laughing.

"Yeah. And I don't really know how to talk about it yet because I'm—"

"Off your fucking axis. You *go*, girl!"

Chris grinned. "That could be a new hip expression we should spread around, *chica*. 'Are you off your fucking axis?' "

"Totally. I am *so* using that in my classes. Maybe without the 'fucking' part, though."

"So, *¿qué pasa?*"

"Damn. I wanted gossip. *Oh*, well. I'll pry it out of Dayna at dinner," she said innocently.

"And what makes you think I'm bringing Dayna to dinner?" Chris retorted.

"Whatever. Sage'll send out some freaky vibe signal and Dayna will just know to show up at Yanni's on whatever night we come up with."

Chris groaned. "True. Okay. Gossip later. How's that?"

"*Perfecto.* And now, shop talk. Ready?"

"*Sí. Dame, mujer.*" Chris leaned on the island in her kitchen, pen and notepad at hand.

"I have a contact based in Phoenix who used to live in Las Cruces," K.C. began. "She's at ASU now. She was in Cruces from 1995 through about 2000. She's a political scientist who got all interested in how Protestant churches fared in the Mesilla Valley so she ended up hanging out at Grace Baptist and she remembers when Chazzy got there."

Chris smirked at K.C.'s latest nickname for him. "Did she meet him?"

"Yep. She attended a few services here and there and talked to members of the congregation, interested in whether they had moved to Cruces recently or historically had been there. She said Chaz started dinking around with Hope Through Love within the first year he was there, but we knew that, too, because it was already in existence."

"Did he say anything about his former job?"

"He mentioned he was from Tulsa, she said, but he apparently never mentioned North Carolina. She found out he had been there when she was doing some research on megachurches." K.C. paused. "Hold on a minute—let me grab this paper—okay. So she thought that was kinda weird. I mean, Providence in Raleigh was one of the biggest megas around. If you're a pastor in that circuit, it's ultra-awesome if you're at a place with a huge congregation and rep like that. But Chazster never breathed a word about it. So my contact decided to follow up on that."

Chris sipped her coffee and moved to the dining room table, cup in one hand and pen and paper in the other. "So what'd she find out?" she asked as she positioned herself at the table.

"She also discovered the ex-gay thing and that Chazzy was in trouble for getting a little too friendly with guys—I was gonna say male members, but we already knew that," she finished with a sly tone.

Chris almost spit her coffee out.

"*Anyway.*" K.C. was laughing. "My contact knew a few folks in Raleigh and what do you know, but she found the guy who wrote that letter."

"No shit?"

"For real. As we suspected, he was the editor of the church bulletin and after he published that, he resigned as editor within a few days, it looks like, apparently telling the board to kiss his ass, basically. His name is James F. Bates. Good thing his first name isn't Norman, I guess."

Chris grinned. K.C. was on a roll tonight. She wrote the name down. "Did your contact know what happened to him?"

"No, sadly. He dropped off the radar."

"I'll see if we can get a fix on him. So how about Hope Through Love? Anything more about that?"

"From what she gathered, it was a lot like the group Chazzy and Kev put together at Oral Roberts. Lots of nice-looking young men. My contact got kind of suspicious about that so she asked one of her female friends to call for information about the group and she was told that it was 'too full' and 'please check back later.' Apparently, there weren't any women in this group. Or in the Oral Roberts group, either. So maybe your idea about a dating service was right on."

Chris's gut clenched. *Or maybe it was a trap, set by a predator with a self-loathing problem.* She'd check with Kevin or Debbie to see if she could get a member list of New Hope, find out if it was all men. Chris wrote that down as a reminder.

"Oh," K.C. continued, "I got the info on the Out of Darkness angle. Remember Chazster was at Providence of Love and involved in the local branch of OD? Well, the branches rarely interacted and rarely do now, with each other. Each one takes direction from the mother ship, if you will, but they don't really chill with each other."

Chris tapped her pen on the table. "So Chaz probably didn't meet Travis 'til his Albuquerque days. Coincidence on the OD thing."

"Yeah, that's what it looks like. And *voila*—I'm going to e-mail you a list of the church administration that was on board at Grace Baptist in Cruces about the time Chazzy arrived. Maybe they'll tell you what the conditions were for his position there. Because you can be *damn* sure they're not going to release that kind of skinny to a lowly researcher or consultant such as myself. This requires the heat-packin', no-fuckin'-around approach that officially licensed law enforcement personnel are so good at employing. You in particular."

"Aw, you flatter me so," Chris teased.

"No way, *hermana*. See what they'll cough up for you. So what's up now with our buddies Chaz and Kev?"

Chris briefly filled her in.

K.C. let out a long exhalation when Chris finished. "No shit? Chaz might've smacked Kevin around?"

"There's something freaky about that situation. When I talked to Debbie Ruiz on Friday, she seemed to think that Chaz and Kevin hooked up every so often for a little action but that Chaz was the top in that relationship."

"'Top'? Did she actually use that term?"

"Yep. And she said she had other gay friends besides Travis. She pegged me, too," Chris added wryly. "Oh, and I checked Chaz's record with women. No formal charges ever filed, but he did have some complaints against him. Two fiancées and his first and only wife. I did a search of public records and found no reference to any other marriages, but he still wears a wedding ring."

"Huh. Maybe he wears it for show. And Chaz and Kevin are in some kind of weird relationship together," K.C. mused.

"At the very least," Chris confirmed. "I don't think I'd call it 'lovers' because it seems Chaz probably just uses Kevin when he wants to get off and demonstrate his continued dominance. However, something got to Chaz Thursday and whatever Kevin told him that night, Chaz didn't like it and Kevin paid a price. I don't think it's a coincidence that Chaz was over at Kevin's house the same day we talked to Kevin." Chris wrote some more notes. "And I don't think it's a coincidence that Kevin showed up at the hospital after Chaz — if it was Chaz — left his place."

"Nope, doesn't seem coincidental. So what's the deal?"

"We've still got a whole lot of circumstantial evidence but nothing really concrete. Chaz clearly lied about knowing Travis and we'll confront him on that, see what shakes loose. I haven't connected him yet to Tyler. I'm going to call the detective back who worked that case and have another chat with him. I don't recall seeing Chaz's name in the notes, but I could've missed it."

"Doubtful," K.C. said. "You don't miss stuff."

"Thanks, *chica*. At any rate, we're waiting on some trace and DNA results to come back, but if Chaz isn't in the system, it doesn't mean a whole lot. If we don't have anything really to pin on him, we can't get a DNA sample from him voluntarily and I doubt the DA'll grant a warrant for it. We need a better link either from Tyler or Travis to Chaz. Once we get that, we might then be able to link all three. Given that it seems he's smacking Kevin around now, I have a feeling he's wound a little tighter than usual."

"Sounds that way," K.C. agreed. "He's got you and Harper up his ass with a major police probe and if Kevin told him what you asked him during *his* interview, then Chazzy knows that you've got some dirt on his past. He's got a lot at stake here, given his public versus his private situations and frankly, I'd be surprised if he *wasn't* sweating."

"True. But it only makes him that much more dangerous. Desperation has a funny way of doing that." Chris's tone was grim because she'd seen people snap for less.

"All right," K.C. said. "I'm going to do some more poking on the Hope Through Love angle. If we can place Tyler in that group or within the congregation, then we can build that link from him to Chaz and you can use it to tighten the screws. Somebody always knows something. It's just a matter of finding the network."

"You should've been a cop."

"I don't think I have the emotional resilience for it," K.C. said quietly. "I about lost my shit in that whole fucked-up skinhead crap with Megan."

"No, you didn't. I was there, *esa*. I saw it all go down and you managed to hold a lot together. You're more than resilient. *Estás una piedra en tormentas fuertas*."

"A rock in storms, huh? That could be a song. There's your new career if you ever get tired of the one you've got. You could be the next Selena. A hot dyke Selena."

"I'm being serious, Kase," Chris pushed gently. K.C. was generally uncomfortable about compliments so Chris made sure to give them to her liberally.

"I know," she relented. "Thanks. But I think I'll just be your back-up researcher, okay? Just promise me you'll always be careful out there."

Chris took a sip of her coffee before answering. "Always."

"I'm serious, *mujer*. I would so kick your ass if anything happened to you."

"That's a thought too frightening to think about. You kicking my ass." Chris smiled.

"It could happen," K.C. teased. "And now—how about some gossip?"

Chris laughed. "Damn, I was so hoping you'd forget about that."

"Never. For real. How'd it go with Dayna?"

Chris set her cup down. "I was actually thinking about that before you called. For the most part it went really well." Chris told K.C. the story of Dayna's ex and about some of the conversation they'd had afterward.

"Okay, so you fucked up a little bit when she was telling you about her ex, but you cleared the air. So did you tell her how much you missed her while she was gone?" K.C. asked, teasing.

"I did, actually," Chris said.

"Are you serious?"

"Yeah. It was hard. But I did it."

"Oh. My. God." K.C. sounded stunned. "You're not shitting me, right?"

"Not about this."

"Whoa. So how did that feel?"

Chris picked up her cup again. "Scary at first. But then it was like a relief."

"That's—Chris, that's really great. So what do you think?"

"I'm not really clear on that yet. We both agreed that we like each other and we want to continue seeing each other, but even she admitted she wasn't sure what she was ready for, so for now, we're just sort of taking it as it comes."

"I'm really proud of you," K.C. said. "So tell me what you were thinking about before I called."

"*Ay dios mío*," Chris muttered, but she smiled. "I was wondering why shit like this scares me."

"And what conclusions did you reach?"

"None yet. But I can tell you that I haven't found a rational reason for my fear."

K.C. was quiet for a moment before she addressed Chris's comment. "All right, do you remember when you sat me down and we had that chat about Melissa when I came back from Texas and I was all freaked about whether to try to come to some kind of closure about what happened between us?"

"Yes..." Chris said, hesitatingly.

"My turn."

Chris groaned.

"You're scared because it's a perfectly natural thing to feel, when dealing with emotional intimacy. Nobody wants to basically put their soul on a plate then hand it to someone else and say, 'here. Hope you don't lose this, break it, or fuck it up.' But when you think about it, do you *really* lose your soul if that other person doesn't treat it right? No." K.C. answered her own question before Chris could. "You have a choice, if someone fucks you over like that. You take your soul back and get on with it and share it with someone else who's going to treat you with respect and kindness, or you let that other person have all this power over you by letting them keep your soul and, for good measure, you let them hand you a suitcase that you lug around as baggage for the rest of your life. Or, alternatively, you hoard your soul and end up a crazy old woman with a hundred and thirty-two cats."

"Are you saying that I need to own my shit, Doctor Fontero?" Chris asked, smiling.

"You do own it, for the most part. What you need to do is make sure you're ready for someone who's going to treat you right and who seems willing to hand you *her* soul, as well. Good relationships are two-way streets, Chris. It's one thing to suit up for the game. It's another to play it."

Chris started laughing. She'd had that same metaphor on her mind the night before. "Okay, Coach."

"So are you ready for the big game? Or do I need to bench your ass? There's no shame in either, as long as you're completely honest about your decision."

"Shit. I think maybe you *could* kick my ass."

"Told you." And there was a smile in K.C.'s voice. "Just make sure you keep that communication going between you and Dayna. Okay, lecture done. Let me know about dinner on Friday at Yanni's."

"Will do. All right, I need to call *Abuelita* and check in with *mis padres*. Thanks for everything, *esa*. Including the lecture."

"*De nada*. And you know I only tell you these things because I care."

"I must be *muy especial*.

"Completely," K.C. said, laughing. "I'll give you a buzz probably tomorrow."

"Excellent. Hi to Sage and I'll catch you later."

They said their goodbyes and hung up. Chris checked her watch. Nearly 7:00. She dialed *Abuelita*'s number.

Chapter
Fifteen

CHRIS FOUND A parking space at the far end of the Wellspring lot, near the parcel of land designated for the new academy. She nosed in, admiring the stark western faces of the Sandias out her windshield. Fifteen minutes before the second service started and she was not looking forward to it. *Me and church don't get along too well.* She finished her coffee — she had swung by the Flying Star on Central before she headed north and crossed the river at Montaño — and left the cup in her cupholder. She wanted to go back by *Abuelita's* at some point this afternoon to check on her plumbing repair from last week and make sure nothing else needed doing. One of the good things about growing up a contractor's kid, she knew how to do things around the house.

She steeled herself and got out of her car, locking up before she headed for the entrance. Most of the people she passed were white — men in suits and ties, women in dresses or pant suits. Even the children and teens looked well-scrubbed and well-mannered. *Like Stepford*, Chris thought darkly as she passed a few of the families. She knew her jeans and leather jacket stuck out like an evening gown at a nudist beach, but she didn't care. She wasn't trying to impress anyone here. For once, the wind wasn't blowing enough to kick up any damn dust. The air hung still and cool and the sky radiated a crystalline blue. A perfect February day, slowly leaving winter behind and sniffing around the boundaries of spring.

"Hey," Harper said in greeting. He was standing to the left of the main entrance, hands shoved into his trenchcoat pockets. He wore faded grey slacks, his scuffed loafers, and a button-down light blue shirt with a black tie.

"You look like a G-Man," Chris said dryly.

"And you look like you're about to jack a Harley," he said blandly.

She fought the grin but then decided to let him have it. He smiled back.

"Ready for your second dose of our Lord and Savior?" Harper pulled his shades off and stashed them in an inner pocket of his coat.

Chris thought she heard an undercurrent of sarcasm, but she couldn't be sure. He'd make a great poker player. Maybe she'd take him out on the circuit for extra money.

"Hell, yeah," she muttered.

He nodded once and held the door for her.

Once inside, they passed to the left, away from the greeters' office and Charlotte's prying eyes. Chris figured Charlotte would give Chazzy a heads-up if she saw them in the lobby and Chris didn't want to chance that. She wanted to keep him off-guard. She had called Debbie that morning before she picked up *Abuelita* and asked her if she could put a list together of New Hope members. Debbie said she'd try and she told Chris to stop by after the service.

Chris didn't see her as they passed the office. She and Harper ended up amidst a huge family, which offered them more cover from Charlotte, and they entered the massive sanctuary unnoticed. The place was nearly full and the dull roar of hundreds of different conversations accompanied them down the stairs. Harper pointed to a couple of empty seats next to each other — one on the aisle — about a third of the way up from the stage.

Harper went in first and removed his coat, folding it carefully over his lap. He wasn't carrying his gun in his usual holster. He was probably wearing a concealment holster — a "belly-band" — that showed no clips. Wouldn't want to freak out the congregation, after all. Chris slipped out of her leather jacket and did the same as Harper, arranging it across her lap. Chris generally packed a SIG-Sauer P225 and today was no exception. She, too, had worn a belly band. Not the easiest way to access her pistol should she need to, since she'd have to unbutton her shirt, but the band ensured that her weapon would remain concealed. She tended to wear men's button-down shirts, and she tucked loosely when wearing a belly band to provide a little extra coverage. The holster rested under her trousers above her left hip, gun butt facing forward.

She had opted to wear a dark blue denim shirt today and a pair of dressy khakis with her black Doc Martens. Harper handed her a program and she skimmed through it, noting that Chaz's name was on it. So he hadn't rescheduled. Today's sermon, she read, was titled "When the Truth Hurts." She grimaced at the irony. The lights suddenly dimmed and a hush fell over the congregation. Chris settled into her thickly padded seat and waited for the show. And what a show it was. It began with total darkness in the sanctuary for a good ten seconds, finally broken by blue and red lights that lasered across the domed ceiling from one side of the room to the other, accompanied by a throbbing bassline and techno beat. *He's been spending way too much time at Pulse,* Chris thought as the pastor's voice suddenly cut through the music.

Light flooded the stage and there stood Chaz, dressed in black trousers and pale yellow shirt. His tie incorporated darker shades of yellow and splashes of blue and black. Natty. He wore his black tasseled loafers and he was wired for sound. He looked like a frat boy, but ten minutes into his spiel, it was very clear how he managed to draw guys like Travis and Tyler to him. Along with hundreds of others. He was performing, but he had an almost animal charisma and charm and he used the cadence of his voice and carefully articulated repetition of select phrases about love and hope to entice listeners into his circle. He sounded warm and supportive, explaining that yes, the world was cold and ugly and yes, even he had succumbed to temptations, but all would be redeemed. Just allow Jesus into your heart and the Lord into your life. Chris shifted in her seat, wondering if Chaz thought about what he was spouting, if he thought about smacking the shit out of at least three different women and a coworker, if he even made it a point to recognize the hypocrisy of his nights at Pulse and the brutal irony of his attractions to men as he stood up there and sighed about "temptations of the flesh."

Chaz also used his body language to remarkable effect. He emphasized his points with a quick stride, then coaxed viewers closer with a tentative step. A few times he left the stage to enter the audience, touching people, comforting them, offering hope. Chris looked around the sanctuary, at the hundreds of faces enraptured, caught up in the glory that was Pastor Chaz, the man who would show them the path to righteousness. *Yep. He's got an assload at stake.*

She dug in the pocket of her leather jacket and removed a small pair of binoculars that she used on stakeouts. She waited until the band on stage began to play a rousing rockish tune about finding hope in the house of the Lord. Chaz was standing still, beaming, hands clasped in a prayer-like gesture in front of his chest. Perfect. Chris zeroed in with the binoculars. *Oh, yeah.* Two big band-aids covered the knuckles of his right hand and she thought she detected discolorations on his left. She quickly scanned his face. Was that a cut on his lower lip? She handed the binoculars to Harper and gestured at her own knuckles and lip. He acknowledged her observations with a nod and did his own scan. When he handed the binoculars back, he nodded again. She slid them back into her jacket pocket.

Fifteen minutes later, the service came to an end with another spectacular light show. The throbbing, thumping music swelled into a final crescendo, then faded, and the house lights came up, perfectly synchronized. Quite a crew behind the scenes, Chris thought, as she and Harper stood up and put their coats on. All around them, people were engaged in doing the same thing, talking excitedly about what they'd just seen. Harper glanced at his program.

"Looks like our guy holds court in a half-hour in the reception area. Probably snacks and drinks." He shoved the program into his pocket. "Let's see if we can find his dressing room." Chris moved into the aisle and let Harper precede her down the steps to the main floor. They dodged tight knots of people who were on their way up and out, no doubt to see if they could catch a glimpse of Pastor Rock Star. Chris muttered "excuse me" several times as she bumped into a few of the faithful. She fell in behind Harper, whose linebacker frame caused people to move around either side of him, like water around a boulder in a stream.

They finally reached the stage and ascended the steps. The musicians were busy unhooking mic wires and turning amps and pedals off. The drummer looked up as Chris and Harper passed him. "Can I help you?"

Chris ignored him and went right to the back of the stage, where she pulled the edge of one of the heavy red velvet curtains away from the other so she and Harper could go backstage.

"Excuse me—" came the drummer's tentative voice.

"It's all right," Harper said, not unkindly. "We're with the band."

Chris shot him a "what the hell?" look. *So he's got a humor seed in there somewhere.* The curtain fell into place behind them and they stood in a forest of technical equipment, lighting scaffolding and control boards, and assorted boxes. They worked their way around extra amps, massive speakers, and various instruments. Several people milled around doing backstage-looking activities. Others were saying things into walkie-talkies. Chris glanced around, looking for Chaz. Harper tapped her arm and gestured with his chin at a small group to the right. Three techs and Chaz, who was berating one about something. The tech on the receiving end of Chaz's wrath looked positively miserable, and the other two shifted uncomfortably, looking anywhere but at what was transpiring.

They approached, and Chris felt a grim little pleasure knowing that catching Chaz in a scene like this would serve to keep him off guard about what APD was up to and what they might have on him. She kept her expression neutral as Chaz's gaze flicked from the hapless tech to Harper, then Chris. Whatever other insults he was prepared to sling died on his lips when he recognized them.

"Pastor," Harper said evenly. "Wonderful sermon." He glanced at the young men looking at him, all three puzzled but relieved that someone had interrupted Chaz's diatribe.

"We'll continue this later," Chaz said to the techs. It was an obvious dismissal and they hurriedly dispersed, the one who had taken the brunt of Chaz's wrath slinking toward the farthest end of stage right. "Can I help you, Detectives?" Chaz's hands were resting on his hips and he put an insolent inflection on the last word.

"I sure hope so." Harper smiled but the expression in his eyes was hard and flat. "We have some new information that's come to light, as well as some photographs that we'd like you to have a look at."

Chaz opened his mouth to say something, but Harper interrupted and Chris heard a low, dangerous undercurrent in his words. "At the station, Pastor. Monday. I've checked your schedule with Mrs. Doyle and you have Monday afternoon free. Three o' clock works for us." He hooked his thumbs on his belt and took a relaxed but vigilant stance.

"I...ah, that is —" Chaz fumbled for words, visibly unnerved.

"Problem?" Harper interrupted. "We're located at Second and Montaño. Now if you decide that you just can't do your civic duty in this case and you don't show up, the DA might not take too kindly to that. Cooperation is extremely important in criminal investigations, and I'm thinking it might not look too good if a man of God such as yourself decides that he's just got no time to help the community police department solve the murder of one of the members of his congregation." Harper shifted, putting himself closer to Chaz, keeping his thumbs hooked on his belt.

Chaz's nostrils flared and his jaw muscles clenched. Harper was pushing him, trying to get a rise out of him. This was a new side to how he worked.

"I'd hate to see that little tidbit come out at the next department press conference," Harper continued.

Chaz's face reddened slightly. *Short fuse.* Or maybe he'd just been feeling a bit pressured lately.

"Three o'clock," Chaz said softly, keeping his hands on his hips.

Chris observed his stance and how he held himself. *This guy is a trained fighter.* "Pastor, we'd like to follow up with Mr. Stillman while we're here. Is he around today?"

He slowly turned his gaze to hers and Chris saw a gleam of contempt in his eyes as he looked at her. She felt vindicated that he had to look up at her face. She didn't bother going into cop mode with him because it wouldn't have much effect, she knew. Women didn't register as anything to be concerned about in his world. So she just regarded him impassively, as she might look at a microscope slide.

"I haven't seen him, but he might be up at the reception area," Chaz said smoothly.

Slick. "I couldn't help but notice you seem to have been involved in some sort of altercation," she pressed.

His eyes narrowed. "I box." His tone was cold, daring her to continue.

"Really," Harper broke in. "I boxed in college. Can't say I was much for bare-knuckle fighting, though. Why do you spar without gloves and head protection? Not a good image to present to the young children of the congregation, I would think," he finished with a "golly-gee-whiz" sort of emphasis.

Chaz shifted his attention back to Harper and he regarded him for a long moment. *Male assessment time.* Chris watched, fascinated by this almost primal display of masculine prowess. An entirely silent pissing match. Chaz blinked first.

"Thank you so much for taking the time to stop by." The pastor's expression softened. "I'm glad you enjoyed the service and I'll see you tomorrow afternoon. If you'll excuse me, I have to attend to other duties." He flashed them both a disarming grin and turned quickly away, with an almost military clip. He stopped and chatted with a few techs, then disappeared behind a stack of boxes as he headed for some secret exit, no doubt.

"Huh." Harper sucked air through his teeth. "That was *some* mood swing."

"You get the feeling that he's barely holding shit together?" Chris mused aloud, attracting a disapproving look from an older guy with a headset as he brushed past. She smiled at him. *Yeah, I cuss. And?*

"Yep. He's got a lot going on, after all." Harper grimaced and headed out the way they had come, through the thick curtains. The musicians were done on the stage and a couple of teenaged boys were going row to row picking up discarded church programs as Harper and Chris climbed the steps out of the sanctuary.

Wellspring devotees filled the lobby, laughing and talking. There was a line out the bookstore door, presumably of the faithful buying copies of the pastor's sermon. Chris stopped off in the greeters' office, scanning quickly to be sure that Charlotte wasn't around. Debbie was chatting amiably with an older Hispanic couple. She smiled when she noticed Chris. "Excuse me a minute," Debbie said to the couple. She went to her desk and picked up an unsealed white envelope which she handed to Chris.

"Thanks." Chris took it, offering a smile and a wave as she left. Debbie nodded and returned to her conversation. Harper stood waiting outside, rocking back and forth slowly on the balls of his feet. She pulled the sheet of paper out of the envelope and read it quickly before handing it to Harper. "A list of New Hope members before Travis talked them out of it."

Harper handed it back to her and she slid it into the envelope. "All men," she said. "Just like Hope Through Love in Cruces and the ex-gay group he and Kevin started at Oral Roberts." She started walking across the parking lot, toward Harper's white Jeep

Cherokee. He followed and Chris continued talking. "Which means Chaz might not have been *all* about bringing people out of a life of sin. If he really wanted to do that, then there'd be women in the groups. I think he uses these groups to lure men to him."

Harper didn't say anything at first, but he cleared his throat. Chris stopped at the Jeep and waited. He had his sunglasses on so she couldn't discern the expression in his eyes. "Are all these groups like that?" His hands were shoved deep into his coat pockets.

"No. The leaders of some of them think they really are helping people avoid sin. They really do think they're doing conflicted people a favor. And maybe some of the people who go into the groups feel like at last they've got the help and support they need to not be gay. I haven't met any yet, but I'm not discounting that there are some." She put her hands in her jacket pocket. "But I've also heard stories and met some people who hooked up with each other in same-sex relationships through ex-gay groups."

"What's your take on Mumford?"

Chris pursed her lips. "I think he's a predator who happens to be attracted to men. He has issues with women and whether that stems from growing up in a conservative or fundamentalist household, I don't know. He's a narcissist and enjoys the power that comes with his position at Wellspring and other congregations. He's also smart and covers his ass well. I expect him to show up with a lawyer tomorrow."

Harper absently rubbed the back of his neck with one hand. "Yep. But we had him goin' there, didn't we?" He smiled conspiratorially. "All right. What's the plan?"

"Is Kevin taking visitors?"

"I'll check on that." He pulled his notebook out of his inside pocket.

"I'm following a few things up on the Henderson case. I'd like to make a link from Tyler to Chaz, but I'm not sure we can. What's the story with Sam and trace?"

"He said he'd call tomorrow and let us know what, if anything, he got from Travis's fingernails and what's up with that partial print."

Chris stood thinking for a moment, then told Harper what K.C. had discovered about the man named James Bates in North Carolina. "I'm going to run a check on him today and see if I can maybe contact him. Find out what happened at Providence. That could be good ammo tomorrow."

Harper finished writing in his notebook and tucked it back into his pocket. "Sounds good. Okay, then." He pulled his keys out and opened the driver's side door. "I'll catch up later."

Chris tossed him a wave and headed toward her own car,

smacking the envelope lightly against her thigh. She'd run the check on Bates, pick up a couple of files for other cases, and swing by *Abuelita's*. But first, maybe another cup of coffee for the road before she got to the station. Chris waited her turn in the line of cars leaving the parking lot before pulling into traffic on Coors.

IT TOOK CHRIS the better part of an hour to narrow down a list of possible James Bateses. On the plus side, only six shared the correct middle initial. Three of those lived in the greater Raleigh area. One was forty-four and the other thirty-seven. The third was eighty-six so Chris ruled him out. On her desk phone, she dialed the number that public records showed for James Frederick Bates, thirty-seven.

A woman answered, puzzlement in her tone. Probably had caller ID. Chris identified herself and explained briefly that she was trying to track down a James F. Bates who had attended Providence of Love in the mid-nineties. After about five minutes, when it became clear that this James Bates was not the right one, she apologized for bothering her and thanked her for her time. Chris hung up and glanced at her list.

James Frederick Bates, you're the next contestant. She dialed the number for the forty-four-year-old. Voicemail picked up and a soft-spoken man instructed her to leave a message either for Jim or Michael. This sounded promising — could be a gay couple — so Chris left her contact info and explained who she was and that she was working on a case in Albuquerque that seemed to have a connection to Providence of Love. She hung up and glanced at her list. Well, might as well rule some others out. She phoned the last three in North Carolina and did just that. If this Jim guy didn't pan out, she'd have to expand her search and she was not looking forward to that. Her business cell rang.

"Chris Gutierrez," she answered.

"All right, got some news." Harper never wasted much breath on salutations unless he was being sarcastic. "Stillman will be released from the hospital tomorrow. I'm thinking I'll swing by there today and see if I can pry anything out of him. I think you scared him on Thursday," he added, a hint of humor in his voice.

"That's me. Scary cop. I'm working on the Bates angle and I'm about to see if I can contact a few people formerly of Grace Baptist in Cruces. Let me know if you want me to show up at the hospital and look menacing."

"Will do. Okay, then." And he hung up.

Chris closed her phone and looked at the list of names she'd printed out that K.C. had e-mailed her. Grace Baptist Board of

Trustees, 1992-2000. *Shit*, Chris thought as she stared at the nearly thirty names. She checked the dates. Ah. Eight names for 1996-1998 and four of those names carried over from 1998-2000. Maybe she could get some contact info for the trustees who served from 1998-2000. Chris accessed the appropriate databases and sat back in her chair, sipping her now cold coffee as the system churned through reams and reams of data. She glanced at her watch. Nearly two. She needed to finish up here so she could stop by *Abuelita*'s again as she had promised she would.

Thirty minutes later, she had addresses and phone numbers for the board members who served from 1996 to 1998 and the four newcomers who served from 1998 to 2000. One hadn't turned up and Chris did another kind of search on a hunch and found out that he had died in 2002. She put a line through his name and wrote the letter "D" next to it. Checking in with the Grace Baptist Board would be tomorrow's first project. She gathered up some files for other cases she needed to close out and shut down her computer. "Hey, Al, I'm outta here," she called across the labyrinth of cubicles.

"All right. Take it easy," he shouted back.

In the parking lot, Chris opened the back of her car and unlocked one of the hidden storage compartments underneath the rear mat. She put the files in it next to her pistol, which she never wore into *Abuelita*'s house. She removed her portable toolbox from the compartment and reorganized some things before driving toward Old Town. Chris turned left onto Second and headed south to Lomas, which would merge near Old Town with Central.

Abuelita—Carmen Garza de Montero—still lived in the neighborhood in which she had settled over sixty years ago with her husband, Luis Montero Ramos. They had left Chihuahua in 1943, following the promise of work and prosperity in an American wartime economy. Luis opened a Mexican grocery store on west Central, just before it crossed the Rio Grande, and for years it stayed in the family until the mid-1970s, when Luis finally sold it to another Latino family.

Chris remembered *Abuelo* Luis as a strong, dynamic man with an odd sense of humor and sparkling eyes. He died of a heart attack just before Chris turned ten and *Abuelita* Carmen never remarried. She had given birth, like clockwork, to four children starting in 1945 with Marisól, the oldest, followed two years later by Tomás, and two years after that Luis Jr., and after another two years, Rosa, the youngest, who was Chris's mother. Of her maternal aunts and uncles, Chris was closest to Tomás. Luis Jr. died in Vietnam when Chris was barely a year old and Marisól lived in Santa Fe with her second husband. She ran in different circles and Chris rarely saw her except at family gatherings.

Chris's mother Rosa and her siblings grew up in the house Luis and Carmen bought so many years ago. When Rosa was eighteen, she married Michael Gutierrez, a tall, brash New Mexican with family roots that went back to the Spanish explorers. *Abuelita* was pleased but also disappointed that Rosa hadn't gone to college. Chris knew that was a dream *Abuelita* had always harbored and when Chris graduated from UNM, *Abuelita* cried like a baby, seeing her dream finally achieved by her granddaughter.

Like her own mother, Rosa gave birth to four children like clockwork and all four spent nearly as much time with *Abuelita* as they did with their own parents. Chris, especially, bonded with her grandmother. It was *Abuelita* who first asked Chris about her feelings for women when Chris was still in high school and it was *Abuelita* who told her that no matter what, she would always love her *nieta*. And then she had smiled, a sly look in her twinkling dark eyes, and said, "*Comprendo, mi'ja. Los hombres no tienen siempre, que las mujeres quieren.*"

Chris still laughed at that. "Men don't always have what women want." She pulled up in front of *Abuelita*'s house, noticing that the wooden picket fence out front needed painting again. Maybe a turquoise blue this time. *Abuelo* Luis had added on to the original two-bedroom structure, making an extra bedroom and sitting room off the master bedroom, but the house was still small, like many of the homes in this quiet residential area tucked between the Rio Grande bosque and Old Town. Most of the houses were adobe and faux-dobe, cheerful little bungalow-style *casas* with flat roofs and weather-stripped vigas still protruding from the original walls above the windows. Spanish flowed freely here still, and it wasn't unusual to see kids running from yard to yard, screaming and laughing while teenagers loitered on front porches, watching each other hungrily, some trying to stay out of gangs.

Here in the North Valley, older neighborhoods were originally zoned as rural, so it wasn't strange to see chickens wandering around in front yards and rabbit hutches hunkered against side walls. Big cottonwoods and Chinese elms shaded some yards and sidewalks buckled from the roots, making it a hell of a lot of fun to ride a bike or skateboard down them. A harmonious mixture of Mexican and New Mexican, where roots south of the border intertwined with the centuries-old culture of Spanish *conquistadores* and Native peoples. It was all of these and something else and the only way to describe it to outsiders was to shrug and say "*es nuevomexico.*" It's New Mexico. And somehow, that explained it better than anything else could.

Chris removed her tool box from the front seat and locked the car. She reached down to open the gate — it and the fence stood about

thigh-high—and entered *Abuelita's* front yard, with its perfect
squares of lawn on either side of the walk and ceramic flowerpots on
her porch. Out back and in her kitchen she grew a plethora of herbs.
Abuelita brought a *curandismo* tradition with her from her village in
Mexico and she herself learned the art of healing from her
grandmother. In this neighborhood, *Abuelita* was a respected
curandera and old neighbors and new immigrants would come to her
for remedies from aching muscles to strep throat. On several
occasions, *Abuelita* had delivered neighborhood babies.

Chris took the three steps onto *Abuelita's* tiny, immaculate porch
and knocked on the door. *Abuelita* hated the doorbell so Chris had
disconnected it years ago. She heard perky footsteps on the wood
floors within and the skittering of tiny canine claws. *Abuelita*
appeared in the window next to the door, checking. Her entire face
lit up with her smile and she quickly unlocked and opened the front
door.

"¡*Mi'ja!* I lost track of time!" she announced in Spanish.

Chris held the security door open and leaned in to kiss her on
the cheek. *Abuelita* spoke English well enough, but she rarely did so
unless interacting primarily with English-speakers.

Chris switched to Spanish. "Creating your medicines, I'm sure."
She smiled and entered, careful of Rudolfo, *Abuelita's* little terrier
mutt who wiggled in paroxysms of delight when he recognized her.
Rudolfo had shown up on *Abuelita's* doorstep nearly eight years ago,
shivering and practically starved to death. *Abuelita* took him in and
nursed him back to health "*con secretos Mexicanos*" and the two had
been inseparable ever since.

"How's the sink?" Chris asked.

"Better than new. If it wishes to break again, I will call you.
Come, come. Have something to drink with your old grandmother."

Chris set her toolbox down by the door and picked Rudolfo up,
petting him and crooning in Spanish. He whined and cried, glad to
see Chris. It had been hours since that morning, after all. Chris set
him down with a final scratch behind his ears and followed *Abuelita*
into the kitchen, Rudolfo close behind. The house mimicked
Abuelita's childhood home in Chihuahua. Low beamed ceilings,
smooth adobe walls, and comfortably worn wooden floors decorated
with colorful thick rugs. The living room held a gas fireplace—
courtesy of Chris's father and brother Mike—and two worn,
overstuffed chairs. A new couch sat against the wall at right angles
to the two chairs and a heavy Mexican-style coffee table crouched
between them. A cabinet next to the front window held a television.
Abuelita didn't watch it much, though it was on at the moment,
turned to one of her *telenovelas*. Several jar candles burned on the
mantel while smaller candles flickered in the nichos set into each of

the walls.

Chris entered the kitchen, her favorite room in *Abuelita*'s house. The largest room, it provided extra counter space and cabinets. *Abuelo* Luis had created a walk-in pantry for his wife's herbs, with wonderful shelving that incorporated cubbies and tiny drawers. A window over the sink looked out into the small, walled back yard where Chris and her brothers had installed a flagstone patio and ramada. A large picture window on the wall near the table provided most of the light.

Here at the 1950s table edged in chrome Chris had learned how to remove the insides of an egg through a pinhole and the finer points of poker, a game *Abuelita* picked up when she immigrated. She had spent endless hours drawing and painting at this table while *Abuelita* cooked or created herbal tinctures for friends and neighbors. And she had learned to cook, listening to *Abuelita* describe how something was supposed to taste and how to adjust a recipe through "feel." She learned the best cuts of meat and how to make empanadas that melt in the mouth. And through it all, *Abuelita* patiently taught Chris the finer points of living, the importance of kindness and humor, and the necessity of taking time for oneself in the midst of a day.

Chris took off her jacket and placed it over the back of the chair on her left. She sat down in the chair closest to the window. It was the chair she always took, and she could remember sitting here on her knees because she wasn't yet tall enough to reach the table without doing so. She smiled, watching *Abuelita*'s petite frame move purposefully around the kitchen. She was barely five feet tall, but her spirit made her seem larger.

Chris couldn't remember a time *Abuelita* had not worn a dress or skirt. Today she wore a light blue one-piece cotton dress drawn in slightly at the waist, beneath her perpetual apron. She wore her long grey hair pulled tightly back from her face, knotted in a graceful braid that fell down her back. The old radio on the shelf over the sink was tuned to a Spanish-language station, playing a ranchera. Chris relaxed as she always did here, the day receding beneath the onslaught of *Abuelita*'s generous spirit. As if concurring, Rudolfo plopped himself onto the small rug near the back door, issuing a contented sigh.

"Ah, *Chrisita*. I am so glad you came back." *Abuelita* placed a large steaming mug of tea and a spoon in front of her. Chris sniffed it, recognizing chamomile and a bit of mint. Peace tea, *Abuelita* called it. She slid the honey pot closer to Chris, then went back to the nearest counter where she was working on some kind of herbal concoction. "Has *Juanito* talked to you?"

Chris finished stirring honey into her mug and looked up,

cautious. "I saw him on Tuesday and he called Thursday and left a message. Why?"

"I think he has much in common with you," *Abuelita* said, studiously concentrating on the powders she was combining in a ceramic bowl.

Chris regarded her before responding. "In what sense?" *Abuelita* was preparing to announce something.

Abuelita stopped her ministrations and turned her head to focus on Chris. "He told me something that he has not told your parents." She shrugged and a wicked smile danced on her mouth. "I see he has told you as well. Though you and I, we knew."

Chris looked down at the table, guilty. "He said he would let everyone know soon."

Abuelita went back to her work, hands moving surely from jar to jar. "My love, I have known these things about you and him since you were children. Your mother has, as well, though she prefers to avoid matters of the soul. You know he wants to go to Los Angeles, yes?"

"He told me." Chris took a sip of her tea. It was rich and pungent, like the way the desert air felt after a heavy rain.

"He is very happy about this," *Abuelita* continued. "He wants to come back when he is finished and open a restaurant of his own."

Chris looked up at her, surprised. "When did he tell you that?"

Abuelita shrugged, something she did to deflect a question. "He will let us all know when he is ready." She finished with the herbs and began putting the lids back on the jars. "And your news?"

Abuelita always knew things. Chris took another sip and waited, expectant.

"*Mi'ja,*" she said softly, stopping what she was doing abruptly to regard Chris. "*Mi'ja,*" she repeated, dark eyebrows lifting as she wiped her hands on a dish towel that she returned to the counter before coming to the table and sliding primly into the chair on Chris's right. "What news?" she asked, wonder in her tone. She covered Chris's right hand with her left. "Who is she? Who has won my granddaughter's heart?" Her eyes softened and she placed her own right hand over her breast.

Chris laughed softly and shook her head in a "why do I even try to keep things from her" motion. "I don't know about *that*. But there seems to be someone, yes."

"Dayna," *Abuelita* announced after another long moment of charged silence. "She came back to you." She gently squeezed Chris's hand, then nodded once, an acknowledgment of something. "I knew she would. She is special and she cares about you very much."

Chris sighed and grinned. "First Sage and now you. How do you know these things?"

Abuelita snorted and threw her hand in the air in a dismissive gesture. "It is only a matter of opening oneself. Sage knows that secret, as well. And I suspect she has been telling you similar things, yes?"

"She has."

Abuelita laughed, a soft, rich sound. "As she should." She stopped laughing suddenly and withdrew her hand from Chris's and leaned forward, a puzzled expression on her face. "Why do you fight her?"

"Fight her?" *What?*

"Dayna. Why are you fighting her?"

Chris frowned, uncertain what *Abuelita* meant.

"You are afraid," *Abuelita* said softly, gazing into Chris's eyes, appraising. "You think it will be like the other times, yes?" She sat back. "No," she continued gently. "Change your way of thinking. I know you have felt, all these years, that the work you do would prevent you from finding a match."

Chris squirmed, sixteen again, feeling almost like when *Abuelita* asked her if she perhaps liked girls more than boys.

"Dayna has entered your life to show you that your way of thinking does not have to be the future you live." She smiled tenderly and brushed her fingers across Chris's cheek. "Allow yourself to love her."

Chris's heart lodged in her throat and she had no answer. *Love?* Panic wrapped around her guts but *Abuelita*'s cool, strong hand covered her own again.

"Your heart," she said quietly, "is here." She reached with her free hand and touched Chris gently on the chest. "Not here." Her fingertips grazed Chris's forehead. "*Oye, mi'ja. ¿Qué dice tu corazón?* That is where your answers lie. Your heart."

Chris had an almost overwhelming urge to cry with relief but she didn't know why. *Abuelita* stroked her face, smiling. "She has been waiting for *you*, as well."

Chris sighed. "It's hard," she muttered. Rudolfo bumped against her leg, whining in sympathy, and she reached down and petted him to reassure him that she was fine.

"It is always hard to trust. Allow yourself." *Abuelita* stood then and leaned over to kiss Chris gently on the forehead. "Dayna trusts you with her heart. She waits to see what you will do with it." She picked up Chris's empty mug. "The girls are coming over this evening for cards. Do you want to stay?"

Chris chuckled. "As much as I would love to, no. Thanks, though. Another time." The girls were a group of neighborhood women who ranged in age from forty to eighty-five. Every Sunday evening, one of them hosted a card game at her house. This week, it was *Abuelita's* turn. Chris sat in every now and again and always ended up laughing so hard she would be sore the next day, but tonight she needed to get some work done. And call Dayna. She hadn't talked to her since last night and today, Dayna had gone mountain biking with friends near Santa Fe. *It's like I'm having withdrawals.*

"But I'll set up the extra table and chairs for you," Chris said as she stood and gave *Abuelita* a quick squeeze. "*Gracias. Te amo.*" She kissed the top of her head before she went to the second bedroom to fetch the card table.

Fifteen minutes later, Chris gave Rudolfo a few extra pets at the front door before she collected her toolbox. "I'll see you soon. My love to all the girls."

Abuelita smiled impishly. "There are a couple who would gladly accept it."

"¡*'Lita!*" Chris gulped. "I did *not* need to hear that." She stepped out onto the porch, knowing she was blushing.

"It's true." *Abuelita* shrugged, still smiling slyly. "*Te amo, mi'ja.*" She blew Chris a kiss from the doorway as Chris headed down the walk to the gate. Chris stood looking at her for a few moments before air-kissing her and letting herself out, making sure the gate latched behind her. When she had gotten her toolbox locked away and settled into the driver's seat, *Abuelita* waved again. Chris waved back and pulled away from the curb as *Abuelita* shut the front door and turned on the porch light.

Chapter
Sixteen

CHRIS'S PERSONAL CELL phone rang as she was nearing downtown. She glanced at her car clock. Nearly five and early February's long shadows stretched across Lomas. Chris picked the phone up off the passenger seat and smiled when she saw Dayna's name in the cell's ID window.

"Hey," she answered. "I've been thinking about you." She adjusted the phone against her left ear, steering her car with her right hand.

"Awww..." Dayna teased. "I really miss you," she added in a more serious tone.

"I miss you, too," Chris responded and it was easy to say it this time. *Christ.* "How was your ride?" She shifted the topic, deciding that she'd probably better focus on driving.

"A complete blast. Where are you?"

"Driving east on Lomas. You?" Chris maneuvered into the right-hand lane. She heard traffic noises and voices in Dayna's background.

"Il Vicino. We're having beer and pizza and yes, I'm trying to bribe you into stopping by." Dayna laughed and Chris slowed down, knowing that if she didn't, she'd probably end up on somebody's front lawn. Especially with Dayna's laugh in her ear.

"Hmmm. Beer and pizza." Chris kept her tone thoughtful. "I don't know...what else is in that deal?"

"Me running my hand up your thigh under the table."

"I'm in." Chris grinned. "Ten minutes."

"I love it when you get all cop-like," Dayna said, giggling. "See you in a few. Bye."

"Bye." Chris hung up and turned right onto Carlisle. In six minutes she had managed to park down the block from Il Vicino, a post-retro Euro-style Italian bistro that brewed its own beer. It was part of the funky and hipster Nob Hill area that Central Avenue bisected. As Chris walked toward the restaurant, she saw Dayna standing out front, wearing loose navy sweats and a baggy grey UCLA hoodie sweatshirt. A battered red baseball cap graced her head. She looked cute as hell.

"Not bad," Dayna said as Chris approached. "You're early."

Before Chris could say anything, Dayna was hugging her, holding on tightly. Chris closed her eyes momentarily and responded in kind. "Wow. What's up?" A few pedestrians eased past them, trying to avoid them, the newspaper machines near the curb, and the steel bistro tables out in front.

"I really, really missed you," Dayna said against Chris's chest. "And I have to talk to you about something."

"Uh-oh." A knot tightened in her chest.

Dayna pulled away slightly, smiling mysteriously. "No, nothing scary. But we made that rule Friday night. Where we talk about stuff as it comes up. So, here's me playing by the rule." She took Chris's hand and moved toward the restaurant's entrance. "Eat first. Talk later."

Chris grinned, relaxing slightly. "Sounds good."

Dinner turned out to be a lively affair. They sat at a back table, which was actually a half-booth. Three people could sit in the booth part and three others could crowd across from them in chairs. Chris recognized the other two women from the Nature Center the weekend before. Jan, the spiky-haired brunette with the silver SUV, was a manager at REI, an outdoor gear store, and Leah, a short-haired blonde, was a tax attorney. It was obvious they were a couple, from how they interacted with each other. Dayna had already ordered a pizza and it arrived within ten minutes. Chris indulged in a beer, opting for the Slow Down Brown ale. Conversation went from politics to sports to local issues.

About an hour after Chris's arrival, Jan and Leah got up to leave. After exchanging goodbyes, Chris and Dayna were left alone.

"Nice people," Chris said, running her fingertips over Dayna's knuckles.

"Very. They've been trying to hook me up for months." Dayna interlaced her fingers with Chris's.

"Oh? And how's that going?" Chris raised her eyebrows quizzically.

"I did a much better job on my own." She smiled. "They've wanted to meet you for a while."

"I hope I passed." Chris brought Dayna's hand to her lips. What was this weird little rush she felt, knowing that Dayna wanted her to meet her friends?

"With flying colors. Jan gets this look on her face if she doesn't approve of something, though she denies it. It didn't show up at all and I think she might actually have a crush on you now," Dayna added, laughing.

Chris blushed and cleared her throat nervously. A young man

came by and picked up the empty pizza tray and plates. "Another beer?" he asked Chris.

"No, thanks. I'm good."

He smiled and moved away. Chris turned her attention back to Dayna. "So what's up?" The tables nearest them were empty, offering a bit of privacy.

Dayna continued holding Chris's hand. "I really like you," she said softly. "And I know we talked about our jobs last summer a little bit."

Chris waited, torn between how it felt to hold her hand and concern about what she might have to say.

"But neither of us really seemed in a place then to think about possibility." Dayna looked up then. "I talked to Joey Trujillo today."

Chris's brow furrowed, puzzled. "On Sunday? Doesn't the DA even get a day off?"

"She'd been out of town and I left a message on her cell."

Chris must have looked even more confused, because Dayna continued, patient. "I told her I was seeing someone who works for APD and that I needed her to know — full disclosure and all that — so I could recuse myself from cases that you work on."

Chris stared at her, thoughts running riot through her head. She slowly pulled her hand out of Dayna's and ran her fingers through her hair. *Fuck.* "I —" she started.

The smile on Dayna's face faded.

"I can't ask you to do that," Chris finally managed.

"You didn't."

Chris rubbed her temple. "Shit. I mean — this isn't coming out right. What I'm trying to say is that I don't want to be the cause of you losing opportunities in your job." She stopped and clenched her teeth. *Too late.* She kicked herself mentally. She had known this would come up. Dayna was a prosecutor, after all. It was bound to come up. So why did it freak her out? And why did she feel like she was suffocating all of a sudden?

"What are you saying?" Dayna had distanced herself physically as well as emotionally, sitting a bit farther away in the booth.

"Fuck. I don't know. Can we get out of here?"

Dayna silently complied and slid out the opposite end. Chris grabbed her jacket and left a five-dollar bill on the table along with the five Jan had left. She followed Dayna out onto the sidewalk, into the night chill. Dayna headed east on Central, her body language broadcasting hurt and anger.

"Dayna —" Chris hurried to catch up with her. Though Dayna was a good four inches shorter, her current stride was impressive. "Let me sort this out."

"What's to sort out?" she asked, voice clipped. "What the fuck is there to sort out?" She stopped suddenly. "Dammit, you knew this would come up. We talked about it a little before I left for California." She threw her hands in the air, frustrated. "It was a matter of time — we both said that — before this would come up." She kept her voice even, but the edge beneath it cut. Chris would hate to face her in a courtroom.

"You're right. We did. And I guess I hoped that it wouldn't come up." Chris shrugged into her jacket, needing something to do with her hands.

"Why would you even think that it wouldn't? Does what I do mean so little to you that it wasn't even on your mind?" She turned and continued walking.

"No — Dayna, please. Will you wait?"

Dayna stopped again and folded her arms over her chest protectively. She looked like she was going to cry but her eyes registered that she was pissed, too.

"I'm not making myself clear."

"No, you're not."

Chris tried again. "Okay. Yes, I guess I knew this would come up. But I guess I wanted to believe that it wouldn't, that I wouldn't have to make a choice between you and your job."

It was Dayna's turn to look confused. "I don't understand."

Fuck. Fuck fuck fuck. "Okay, look. In the past, my cop stuff generally dictated whether I got involved with someone and how long that relationship would last. But I never acknowledged that. I always figured if I didn't think about it, things would work out. Or not." She stopped then. *I avoided it. Hoping it would go away.*

"I'm still not getting it. What do you mean, choosing between me and my job?" Dayna shifted her stance, wary.

"I don't want you to compromise your profession for me," Chris blurted.

"Excuse me?" Dayna's tone suggested that Chris had just told her she wanted to hire her as a call girl.

"You haven't been with the prosecutor's office that long. And already you're going to be recusing yourself from cases because of me. I don't want to ruin your new beginning." She got the words out in a rush and realized she wasn't really sure what she was trying to say. Was she trying to stop seeing Dayna? That thought hurt too much to contemplate. So what exactly was she doing? *What the fuck is wrong with me?*

Dayna stared at her for a long time, standing on the darkened corner of Central and Tulane. When she spoke, it was with resignation and affection. "You can be such a dork sometimes."

Chris started to say something but Dayna interrupted. "*You*, Chris. *You* are part of my new beginning. I talked to Joey because I *wanted* to. I talked to her because I'm really into you and because I want to continue seeing you—even if it's just dating— without damaging my work with the prosecutor's office or their rep, for that matter. It was *my* decision." She softened her tone. "I know you're, like, Super Cop and all that, but you really need to stop using that angle for every little thing that happens in your relationships. If you want to push me away, you'd better come up with a better reason than protecting me from my job."

Ouch. Chris winced inwardly. *"Change the way you think."* *Abuelita's* words, just a few hours old. Sage would call this a cosmic moment, in which angst and joy were two sides of the same coin. "You're right," Chris relented quietly. "You're absolutely right. I'm sorry."

"For?"

"Making myself cop of the world. And I'm sorry for not discussing this earlier with you. Maybe we should have on Friday."

"Yeah, maybe we should have. I'll own part of that."

"It's my fault, too," Chris said. "But I was trying to give you a safe space to say what you needed to say and I guess I didn't really think beyond that. I managed to wrap my head around telling you I wanted to keep dating you and I didn't take the next logical step."

"And I appreciate all of that," Dayna responded. "I managed to admit that I wanted to keep seeing you, as well, and it occurred to me today that I should probably talk to Joey. I think maybe I should have talked to you first about that."

"No," Chris said slowly.

"No, what?" Dayna's eyebrows raised in surprise and Chris smiled.

"I think it's a good thing that you actually just called Joey. That way, I have to deal with it and I have to deal with my feelings."

"I see. So you're saying that if I *had* talked to you first, you might have used that as an excuse to...what?"

Chris knew that Dayna was fully cognizant of what the answer was. But she wanted Chris to voice it herself. She did. "Back off."

"Would you really have done that?"

"I don't know. Given my pattern, probably. But I think, too, that I would have then realized what a fucking stupid thing that was to do and I would have realized that it was just old stuff making me react that way and I'd—"

"Beg for my forgiveness?" Dayna smiled.

"Would I have to?"

"No. But I *would* ask you to explain yourself."

"And I'd try. But I'm not very good at doing that," Chris said. "Doesn't mean I don't want to try," she added. "And yeah, talking to Joey has sort of been in the back of my mind but I guess I've been avoiding the topic for a variety of reasons."

"Such as?" Dayna pressed, and Chris was glad she did, as difficult as this conversation was.

"I wasn't sure where things were between us when you went to California. So I wasn't even sure we were still seeing each other then. And yes, I didn't really say what I wanted or what I expected before that. I guess I maybe didn't want to get my hopes up. Or something." She stopped then, giving Dayna a chance to respond.

"You use the cop stuff to avoid bigger issues. Why?" Dayna jammed her hands into the front pocket of her hoodie.

"I—" And then it hit her. Again. "Fuck, Dayna. I'm scared," Chris announced. She thought about what K.C. had said about the different files of Chris's life, about not letting people in or taking chances.

Dayna relaxed. "So am I." She regarded Chris with a mixture of optimism and caution. "And I knew the first month we were dating that you had a little baggage with relationships. You've been pretty honest about that. But you seem to enjoy hanging out with me—"

"I do." *More than I thought I ever would with anyone.*

"And even when I had my California weird-out, you didn't break it off." Dayna stopped and cocked her head, crossing her arms over her chest. "Correct me if I'm wrong, but it seems to me that you're the type who would tell a woman that you didn't want to see her anymore."

"Yeah—"

"So what exactly are you doing here?"

"Being a complete and total idiot. I'm sorry."

"Well, now that we've got *that* cleared up, you want to tell me what's *really* going on?"

Chris nodded and headed down Tulane, away from Central. It was sometimes easier for her to talk while walking. "There is an element of cop stuff here," Chris said quietly. "I'm not closeted at work, but I am private."

"You're private anyway," Dayna pointed out. "But I understand." Within a half-block of Central they entered a residential part of Nob Hill, not too far from where K.C. and Sage lived. They walked along Monte Vista, a broad avenue that paralleled Central, linking the UNM campus to Carlisle.

"I think it freaked me out," Chris said after a while, "that you talked to Joey, because it means that you're thinking about something more permanent with me. Even if we just call what we're doing 'dating,' it still requires that Joey know about it. And my initial reaction to things like that is generally knee-jerk."

Dayna stopped at the next street, which would take them back to Central and Il Vicino. "Was I being presumptuous?" she asked. Chris could almost feel her withdraw, though there was a challenge in her voice. Tempered, fortunately, by the look in her eyes.

"For someone who's dealt with relationships in the past in a more mature and healthy fashion, no. You weren't. For me, it's old stuff. And I realize that. I just don't always know what to do with it." She gently extricated Dayna's hands from her hoodie pocket and pulled her into a hug. "I'm sorry," Chris said softly. "I'm so sorry. I made you feel bad. That is not at *all* what I wanted to do." She rested her cheek against Dayna's head and held on to her, to the warmth and safety she felt there, and to a growing realization that hovered unspoken between them. "I really like you, too," Chris said softly, marveling at how easy it actually was to say those words. "And I really want to keep seeing you."

"So are you okay with my talking to Joey?"

Chris kissed her lightly. "I am, actually. I forgot for a minute that you're in the *now* and that doesn't have to be like the past. But I'm not very good at letting people in sometimes."

"Neither am I. So I guess we're in the same boat."

"You think you can be patient with me?" Chris asked hopefully.

Dayna moved a bit so she could look at her. "I can. But I have another condition." She was half-teasing.

"Shit. Medical?" Chris looked at her innocently.

Dayna smiled. "Sort of. A heart condition, you could call it. I want to get to know you better and I would really appreciate it if you not see other people. Unless, of course, you decide this isn't for you. In which case, I'd appreciate it if you'd let me know." The professionalism of her words was tinged with a bit of uncertainty.

Wow. Chris looked down into Dayna's eyes, and the ramification of her words should have made her bolt, should have triggered whatever demons had a stake in that kind of reaction. But the reality of the last few months was, Chris realized, a break in her pattern anyway. "That won't be hard," she said, "considering I haven't been with anyone *but* you since I first saw you."

Dayna stared at her. "Are you serious?"

"Yep."

"Why didn't you tell me on Friday?"

"I got distracted?" Chris phrased it as a question and shrugged helplessly. "You have that effect on me."

Dayna pulled away and smacked Chris lightly on the arm. "You didn't see anyone else while I was in California?"

"No."

"Why not?"

Chris smiled sheepishly. "I admitted to myself that I liked you too much. And I wanted to hear from you directly. If you didn't want to continue, well, I'd deal with it. If you did — well, I'd have to figure out how to deal with *that*, too. And clearly, I'm not exactly doing that very well—"

Dayna put her finger over Chris's lips then slid her arms around her neck. Before Chris could say anything else, Dayna kissed her and it didn't matter, what she was going to say. She forgot what it was, anyway, beneath Dayna's lips.

"Do me a favor," Dayna murmured against Chris's mouth after a few long, delicious minutes.

"Name it."

"Talk to me *before* you freak out."

Chris grinned. "That's new and different for me." She leaned in and brushed her lips along Dayna's jaw.

"I'm serious," Dayna said.

"Same here." Chris stopped and looked at her. "I'm completely serious when it comes to you." *And that, too, is new and different.*

Dayna kissed her again and Chris didn't care that they were making out on a street corner, not thirty feet from someone's front door. She didn't care that she was broadcasting what she felt to whomever drove by. All she cared about was how this moment washed over her, and that Dayna wanted to build something more with her and, more importantly, that she, Chris, was okay with that. Chris broke first after a few more minutes and buried her head against Dayna's neck, holding her tightly for a while. Dayna responded, fingers of one hand in Chris's hair.

Chris reluctantly released her. "I have some work to do at home tonight." She added a soft groan for emphasis.

"Want some company?" Dayna smiled up at her. "I have some cases I need to read through." She stroked Chris's cheek. "No pressure. No demands. I just want to be near you."

Chris smiled. "I'd really, really like that."

"Then it's settled." Dayna linked her fingers with Chris's and pulled her up the street, back toward the restaurant.

CHRIS SAT AT her desk Monday morning rubbing her eyes with one hand, holding on to her *mas grande* Starbucks coffee cup with the other. She'd spent two hours on the phone already talking to former board members of Grace Baptist Church in Las Cruces. After seven phone calls only two former members were willing to talk about Chaz Mumford and both told the same story, in very different ways. Olive Baxter and Clyde Marshall served on the Grace board of trustees from 1996 to 2000. They'd been re-elected to an extra term following the expiration of their first.

Chaz arrived in late summer 1998, Olive had said. And right off, she didn't think something was quite right about him. Chris pressed

her on that and Olive said that she thought he was "too smooth."
Like a used car salesman, she'd said. Olive had a light, whispery
voice with traces of an East Texas accent. Despite her wavering
tones, she sounded chipper. Chris figured she was a nice elderly
white lady who spent a lot of time with her grandchildren and
church friends. But Olive also had an ear to the ground at Grace. She
had been against bringing Chaz to Cruces because of what had
happened at Providence.

"Can you explain a bit?" Chris had asked.

"Oh, now, honey, it was quite scandalous," Olive said, dropping
her voice conspiratorially. "He's one of those types who likes the
menfolk a little too much, you know. Now, I don't believe in judging,
mind you, but it's one thing to fall into sin and stay there like a pig in
bits and it's another to try to get yourself out of it."

"So you don't think Pastor Mumford was interested in getting
himself out of it, as you say?" Chris tapped her pen on the edge of
her desk. She was trying to be offended, but Olive's turns of phrase
and down-home manner made it damn hard.

"Oh, no." She tsked. "Seems he picked up right where he left off,
acting the fancypants and chasing after the menfolk."

Chris cleared her throat, trying not to laugh. "Was the pastor
involved with a group called Hope Through Love?"

"Well, of course." Olive sighed. "Sometimes I think the entire
church system carries on like a horse's patootie. Pastor Renfield — he
was the senior pastor then — decided that it was somehow a good
idea to bring Pastor Mumford here. Now I'm not wishing ill on the
dead, but if I had my druthers, I wish I had told Pastor Renfield that
his idea made about as much sense as bringing a bull to a baby
shower."

Chris wrote that one down. It was priceless. "Pastor Renfield is
dead, then?"

"Why, yes he is, poor man. Dropped clear dead from a heart
attack in April three years ago. But where was I?" She clicked her
tongue on her teeth. Chris imagined Olive sitting in a big overstuffed
chair in her living room — she probably called it a parlor — sipping tea
and watching for the mailman. "Yes, well. Pastor Renfield agreed to
bring Pastor Mumford on board if he did some kind of church
penance. Oh, my Lord, honey. That was Hope Through Love. Might
as well have tossed a hungry fox into a chicken coop. Seems to me if
you want to stop indulging in the sins of the flesh, you might want to
stay away from the flesh."

And on that note... "Mrs. Baxter, do you remember a young man
named Tyler Henderson?" Chris took a sip of coffee while she waited
for Olive's response.

"Oh, yes. Little Robbie. The Hendersons are good people. It

broke his daddy's heart when he — well, I shouldn't gossip so."

"When he found out his son was gay?" Chris asked carefully.

"Why, yes. I mean, everybody knew it. Robbie never made any secret of it." She paused. "He didn't seem *that* way, if you know what I mean. He was such a handsome young man. And so polite. With the most wonderful deep voice, like his daddy. Oh, he was a looker. All the girls always wanted to go with him to dances when he was in high school..." her voice trailed off as she reminisced. "I thought he might be interested in that lovely Theresa Johnson. They were always together. But I suppose not. He didn't *seem* that way, you know."

Theresa Johnson. The best friend. Chris wrote her name down. "Do you happen to know whether Ms. Johnson is still in Las Cruces?"

"Oh, yes, honey. She's now Theresa Willington. She married Ernest's boy — what was his name? — Toby. Two children, last I heard. Boy and a girl."

Chris interrupted her reverie. "Mrs. Baxter, do you know whether Tyler — Robbie — was involved in Hope Through Love?"

Olive clicked her teeth again. "That was a sad story. When Robbie's daddy found out about — well, *you* know, he packed him up and sent him to one of those programs to help break you of feeling lustful toward your own kind. Now, I'm not one to judge, but I think that just ended up turning Robbie more against his family. As soon as he came home, he wouldn't have anything to do with his daddy, especially. Broke his mama's heart. Where was I? Oh, yes. The year before Robbie passed, he did attend a few meetings with Hope Through Love. And then, if my memory serves, he stopped coming to church not long before..." she trailed off. "Terrible. Just terrible."

Chris tried to bring her back to the conversation. "Do you have any idea why he might have stopped attending Grace?"

"No, honey, I don't. Well, wait. Now, I don't like to gossip, but it seems to me that Pastor Mumford spent quite a lot of time around Robbie, actually. Come to think of it, Robbie did a bit of work around the church — he was good with his hands — and I know there were times in the evenings and weekends when not many other people were around. I heard a rumor that Robbie and the pastor might have — well, *you* know." She tsked again, this time more emphatically. "You want my opinion, that Pastor led Robbie astray. And him calling himself a man of God. Well, it just gets my dander up. Pastor Renfield should never have agreed to let that man come to Grace."

Chris gently interrupted. "Mrs. Baxter, you've been very helpful. Would you mind talking to us in the future if we think of anything else?"

"Oh, honey, you just call anytime. Except not after seven in the evening. That's my television time. And my meeting time on Tuesdays and Thursdays. Oh, and every other week Wednesday is bridge night."

Chris smiled. "Yes, ma'am. I'll be sure to call you during the day. Thanks again. Take care."

"You, too, honey. You're a nice young lady. You take care. Bye, now."

Clyde Marshall had corroborated Olive's story about disapproval with regard to bringing Chaz in from Providence. Clyde, however, did make it a point to note that Chaz was a great speaker and quite motivational. Chris asked if Clyde knew why Chaz had to leave Providence and he had said darkly that it had to do with sins of the flesh and that's why Chaz was required to lead Hope Through Love though Clyde, like Olive, felt that was a big mistake. Clyde also remembered Tyler Henderson, but he didn't know much beyond how sad it was, what had happened. He was less tactful than Olive and said that homosexuals had no business leading anybody's congregation and that Pastor Chaz clearly wasn't much interested in changing his ways and the rumors began flying within a year of his arrival.

Chris asked if Clyde thought that Chaz was blatant about his proclivities and Clyde grudgingly admitted that no, he wasn't, and he did seem like a nice enough man. Still, Clyde said, given what had happened at Providence, it made no sense to bring him to Grace and put him in charge of a group like Hope Through Love, which needed strong, normal men leading it. Chris had thanked him for his time and hung up.

She checked her watch. Nearly ten. Harper had already checked in with Kevin at the hospital and got mostly sullen silence, he reported. When he tried to push the Mumford angle, Stillman had clammed up. Harper told Chris he thought Kevin was scared pissless, as he put it, and decided to see where today's chat with Chaz would take them before dealing with the pastor's "busted-up pool boy" again. Chris actually laughed out loud at the remark. Harper was still an enigma, but he seemed to have his heart in the right place.

Chris had just started to run a search on Theresa Willington when her desk phone rang.

"Chris Gutierrez," she answered.

"This is Jim Bates. In Raleigh. You called yesterday," he said in a soft North Carolina drawl with an indefinable inflection that sent Chris's gay-dar rocketing past "six" on the Kinsey Scale.

"Mr. Bates. Thank you so much for calling back. Unfortunately, I can't tell you too much about our investigation at this point, but I can tell you that it involves a member of a church here. Charles Mumford is the senior pastor at this church and we're following up as many angles as we can. My understanding is that you were a member of Providence of Love when Pastor Mumford was there."

"I was a member then. I'm not now."

"Did you leave before he did?"

"Yes."

Chris waited for him to offer more but he didn't, so she continued. "Okay, Mr. Bates, here's what we're trying to ascertain. We've uncovered an anonymous letter that appeared in the Providence church bulletin in June, 1998. The letter accused Pastor Mumford of sexual acts with men."

"And?"

Was that just a touch of hostility? "Our sources have suggested that you were the writer of that letter."

"Excuse me, but so what? It's not a crime to write a letter to a publication." He'd gone from hostile to defensive.

So he probably was *the writer.* "No, sir, it most certainly is not. If you were the author, would you be willing to tell me a bit more about what might have caused you to write it?"

A long pause descended between them. Chris could almost see him, licking his lips, trying to figure out how to best address the situation. Please, just talk, she thought. *Get it out of your system. And please don't make me have to come up with reasons to subpoena you.*

"Why?" he finally asked. "You're not even in the state. What is this about?"

Chris switched to a more conciliatory tone. "Well, as I've said, I can't reveal too much, but we are investigating some things here with regard to the pastor and that letter does have bearing on some allegations that have come up here, in New Mexico."

"Which parts of the letter?" He was cautious now. Chris would have to handle this delicately.

"We're trying to verify that Pastor Mumford has had sexual affairs with men in the past—"

"Because it establishes a pattern of behavior," Bates said. "I know a bit about investigations," he said cryptically.

"Can you—"

"All right, Detective," Bates said. "I'll provide what information I can, in the interest of doing my civic duty."

"I appreciate that, Mr. Bates. I'd like to make it clear that you're not the one under investigation."

He chuckled, but not out of humor. "You still have to open *all* the coffins after a flood."

Chris made a noncommittal noise, uncertain what that meant.

He must have sensed her confusion and he offered an explanation. "In these parts, when it floods, sometimes the water moves enough dirt to bring buried coffins to the surface. So during the clean-up, you have to open all of them to try to figure out who's inside for reburial with the correct headstones. And you never know what—or who—you might find when you do that." He laughed softly. "The dead do still rise. At least here in the South."

"Mr. Bates, if you're concerned about violations of your privacy, or about your safety—"

"Yes to the former, not really to the latter, since the good pastor seems to be a couple thousand miles away. But I would appreciate it if you could keep as much of this conversation anonymous as you can. People like me can lose their jobs around here if certain parties find out about their *proclivities*."

"I understand. I'll do what I can, but I can't completely guarantee that, because if this investigation results in legal charges and a trial, we may need to contact you again." Which meant that Bates might not want to help them after all, but Chris was always forthright when dealing with potential witnesses.

"Refreshing," he drawled, tone a little warmer. "I appreciate your honesty, Detective."

"So you think maybe you'd like to check a few coffins with me?" She tried to lighten the mood a bit.

He laughed at her remark, and this time he sounded genuinely amused. "Why not? Yes, I was at Providence when *Chaz*—" he almost spat the name, "was ministering to the congregation. And yes, I wrote the letter."

Score. "How were you able to get the letter into the bulletin?" she asked, verifying what K.C.'s source had uncovered.

"I was the editor at the time."

Bingo. Chris hesitated then, trying to figure out how to keep the delicate rapport between them. "My apologies, Mr. Bates, but I need to ask you a few personal questions. If you're uncomfortable with any of them, please let me know."

"Fire away," he said, with something like resigned bravado in his voice. "But here's your disclaimer. The subject matter might offend some listeners," he finished, with what might have been wry humor. He sounded like he was relaxing a bit. Maybe he *did* want to get this off his chest.

"I don't think you need to worry about me," she responded, equally wry. "All right," she said. "Given the subject of the letter, were you ever involved in an intimate relationship with Mumford?"

"I'm not sure I'd call it a relationship," he said tightly. "We were intimate a couple of times, yes." He paused, perhaps waiting for her reaction, to see whether she was one of the homophobic kinds of police detectives.

"Would you say that the two of you dated, then?" Chris kept her tone conversational, as if they were just two people hanging out talking about work or other mundane matters.

"I'm not sure it was even *that*." He sounded more relaxed. "No dinner or dancing or spending quality time together, if that's what you're asking. It was all very closeted and the two times we were physical, we met at my house and he made it a point to park a couple blocks away and come in through the alley." He made an impatient noise in his throat.

"How did you and Chaz meet? Just through interacting at the church?"

"Yes. Because I edited the bulletin, he came by quite a bit to provide news and whatnot for it. I was already editor when he was hired on as pastor, so we did have a lot of interaction before anything happened between us."

Chris made a note on her legal pad. "Do you recall if Chaz was married then? Or involved with women?"

"No. He never mentioned women—at least not in the sense of 'girlfriend'— and he didn't wear a wedding ring."

So after the 1993 assault report, Chaz didn't hook up with another woman until Cruces. Chris made a note of that, too. "Can you tell me a little bit about the ex-gay group Chaz was involved with at Providence?"

Bates didn't respond right away and Chris winced inwardly, thinking she might have pushed him a little too hard. Finally, he spoke. "Chaz was pretty into that, so I figured he was just your typical 'love the sinner, hate the sin' Christian. I felt pretty comfortable at Providence, because for the most part, nobody overtly bashed gays. The Southern thing to do is whisper behind your hand over lunch about other people's personal lives. So I knew that some people knew about me though I wasn't formally out, and I knew that they didn't approve, but they were courteous and as long as I didn't make any big 'do about it, neither did they. Typical Southern stand-off about skeletons in the closet. Don't ask, but tell in low voices around the kitchen table."

"So when did you think that Chaz might actually be gay?"

"Honestly, my gay-dar blipped the first time I met him, so I thought maybe he'd had *experiences*, if you will, in the past but it hadn't worked for him. Then when he came to the bulletin's office to get me to post the announcement for the ex-gay group, I decided he was working something out personally, too."

Chris wrote that down. "Do you recall the name of the group?"

"It was a chapter of Out of Darkness."

"How many members were in it?"

He hesitated, probably thinking. "Oh, I don't know. They met in the evenings twice a month. I'd guess maybe thirty. But I don't know for sure. It wasn't something members talked about."

"Were there women involved in the group?"

Bates laughed. "Hell, no. Within about two months, I noticed it was all men and a few rumors started up that it was more a gay dating scene than anything else. But at first, I just assumed Chaz was more comfortable working with men than women. If women wanted an ex-gay group, there were people on staff who could have facilitated."

"Did Chaz ever try to explain why it was men-only?"

"He called it a 'men's Bible study group' as well as a 'way to find relief from sinful urges.' Once he started with that 'men's Bible study,' the rumors sort of went underground, but they didn't entirely go away."

Chris took a swallow of coffee. "About how long did you know Chaz before you started seeing him?"

"Oh, let's see..." he paused then continued. "It was actually around the beginning of 1998, the year he left. February, I think. I've tried to forget it, I suppose," he finished dryly.

"Did he approach you?"

"I'd say it was more a mutual thing, as much as I'd like to blame *him* for the entire thing. One night, I was working late alone, finishing up the bulletin, and he stopped by the office. I didn't realize he was still at the church, and he startled me. He laughed and said something about how dedicated I was and—" he cleared his throat. "One thing led to another and I wasn't seeing anyone at the time and he said all the right things and yes, I was younger and dumber and believed it all. And I somehow managed to excuse his work with Out of Darkness." Rueful embarrassment tinged his words. "Denial, Detective. Not just a river in Egypt."

Chris waited a few moments before responding, so as not to come across as impatient. "And how long were you intimately involved?"

"Up until I wrote the letter. I wanted more, he led me on, and everything became abundantly clear when I discovered him banging a member of Out of Darkness backstage in the sanctuary. So the rumors about that group as a dating scene were more than just rumors."

So much for Chaz keeping personal and professional separate. "After hours, I assume?"

"Technically. There're usually meetings and whatnot at churches in the evenings, as you probably know, but the sanctuary is actually the most private room that time of day because everybody uses the classrooms. By ten or so, most people are gone. I had been working late again, trying to put the latest issue together—the two volunteers who usually helped me were on vacation—and on my

way out, I heard a bit of Bible-thumping, if you will. Matt McGuire
was a screamer, too," he finished, his tone lightening a bit.

Chris fought a smile. "Did either see you?"

"Oh, good gravy, no. I remember it was around eleven and I
heard what sounded like groaning. Now, rest assured, I know the
difference between good groans—the kind people make when
they're involved in a little mattress dancing—and bad. That is, the
kind you make when someone's opening a can of whup-ass on you.
These groans were the good kind. So, curious and prone to that
Southern snooping thing, I wanted to find out who was getting it on
backstage. They weren't in the pews, Detective. They had the good
sense to take care of business backstage, but the bad sense to leave
the door open a bit. All I had to do was listen for a bit and I knew
right away it was Chaz and another boy-toy."

"So you didn't confront him then?"

"Of course not. Or afterward. I may have been younger and
dumber but I knew that dropping the bomb there or waiting 'til later
wouldn't accomplish anything. Matt McGuire wouldn't admit to
anything and it was my word against the great Pastor Chaz's and I'm
a bit on the femme side, in case you haven't figured that out yet," he
said slyly. "So who are the congregation and the church board going
to believe? A swish like me or manly-man Chaz who runs an ex-gay
group?"

Bates was probably right about that prediction. "So instead, you
wrote the letter pointing out that Pastor Chaz was a hypocrite."

"He pissed off the wrong queen," Bates said with a shrug in his
voice. "Never, ever cross a queen with access to media," he added
with a wicked undercurrent of laughter.

Chris smiled. She'd achieved a stronger rapport with him.
"What did you think would happen after the letter hit the public?"

Bates was quiet for a moment before answering. When he did,
contrition underlay his explanation. "Honestly, I was originally
furious about getting played. But I didn't write the letter right away.
My mama always told me to cool my heels before jumping the ditch.
So I waited a couple of days to see how I felt. And then I got to
thinking about it and I realized that this couldn't be any kind of new
thing for Chaz. He'd probably been doing this for some time. So it
became a mission—not to say I'm proud of my obsessive destructive
streak—to enlighten the congregation about the hypocrisies
occurring right there in the house of the Lord. I guess I thought there
would be a bit of gossip, Southern style, and the rumors might make
things a little hot for Chaz. And then it would eventually fade away
but he'd stop pursuing the men of the congregation. I seriously
thought that's what would happen."

"And what *was* the actual fallout from your letter and the

ensuing discussion?" Chris asked before she took another sip of coffee.

He sighed heavily. "Oh, honey. The proverbial shit hit the fan. Lord have mercy, I had no idea it would cause the uproar it did. I guess I should have, but I didn't. Make no mistake—I expected some kind of come-to-Jesus moment, but this was nuclear. Anyway, other men in my position, if you will, came forward and said they'd had carnal relationships with the good pastor, too. They confessed this to me and also to a couple of the junior ministers. Some of those I doubted, but a few were credible. Within three days of the letter's release, the board was trying to put a lock on the situation. Including on me. They asked me to resign and I told them they'd better have a good reason for asking, besides publishing an anonymous letter in the bulletin. They demanded to know who had written it and I told them I had verified the writer's identity and I wasn't going to tell them. So they instead asked me to 'take a few days off' while they investigated. Which was basically their way of firing me. But they also put Chaz 'on vacation' while they dealt with it all. The congregation blew a gasket and a couple of stories did appear in the local gay papers, but the mainstream media wouldn't touch it. In the South, honey, you do not call attention to church matters that might make Christians look bad. It's all about God, guns, and faded glory here."

Chris nodded to herself. "Did Chaz know it was you who wrote the letter?"

He was quiet for a very long time before responding. Chris heard him breathing, so she knew he hadn't hung up. "He figured it out," he finally said, bitterness lacing the words.

"Did he say anything about it?"

He laughed, a harsh guttural bark. "He beat the living hell out of me, Detective."

Holy shit. Chris set her coffee cup back on the desk without taking a drink.

"Make no mistake, I put up a good fight," Bates continued. "June twenty-first, 1998. I may be a queen but I'm not a shrinking violet. Bastard came to my house after the bulletin with the letter was mailed. I had actually unplugged my phone, because as the editor, I was fielding some pretty angry calls myself. I decided to stay away from Providence for a little bit, until the heat died down. Anyway, about four days after the bulletin went out, there was Chaz standing on my porch looking like he had just dragged a cross up a hill himself. So I opened the door, thinking he wanted to talk."

"What happened then?" Chris was writing furiously.

"He forced his way in. I knew he was strong. But he was pissed, too, and that made him extra strong. He gave me two black eyes, a split lip, and two cracked ribs. Plus, I was bruised from here to Richmond. He told me if I said anything else, if I went to the police, if I told anyone what had happened, he'd out me to my family and at work. And here, unfortunately, that carries weight. And he also said that if I pushed him too far, he'd come back and finish the job."

"Finish the job?" She knew what he meant but she wanted to hear it from him.

"Kill me, I guessed." He was somber.

"Did he do or say anything else that night that stands out for any reason?"

He was quiet again. Chris thought she heard a television in the background. When he spoke again, his voice was strained. "After he finished beating me nine ways to Sunday, I remember I was lying there on the floor, looking up at him. I couldn't see very well because my eyes were swelling up." He cleared his throat softly. "Here's a weird thing. He was crying."

The tip of Chris's pen hovered over the paper. *Crying?*

"I couldn't really see, but I heard him. Not big drama queen sobs. Sniffles, like a little kid. That was scarier in some ways than him kicking my ass, because he was whispering stuff I couldn't make out, which made him sound crazy, like he was talking to himself before he finished me off. I honestly thought it was my last day on earth." Bates lapsed into silence, remnants of the fear he felt that day years ago lingering on the phone line.

"Did he leave then?"

"I wish. No. He pulled my shirt up—I was wearing a T-shirt— and he wrote something on my chest with a ball-point pen. It felt like a tattoo gun. Worse, actually, because of my broken ribs."

A familiar prickle raced up Chris's spine. "What did he write?"

He laughed softly, sadly. "It took some doing, with a ball point pen. Thank Jesus it didn't scar. Otherwise it'd look like somebody branded me with John three-sixteen."

Fuck.

"Any other time I'd be okay having that on me somewhere. It's a nice verse. But since what happened—" He tried to laugh, but the sound was forced, couched in layers of the past.

"So you didn't go to the police."

"No. I had too much at stake. He knew that. He's very good at finding your weak spots and exploiting them. Plus, the police here aren't that understanding, shall we say, of gay people."

"Did you tell anyone else?"

"I went to the emergency room over at Raleigh General. I told them I'd gotten into a fight at a bar and I didn't want to file any kind of report and that I wasn't sure who it was, since several people I didn't know were involved. They patched me up and sent me on my way and didn't ask many questions even with that verse on my chest."

Chris frowned. "Generally, hospitals are required to file a report with the police when a possible assault occurs. Did the staff tell you that?"

"Yes. And maybe they did anyway, but I didn't hear anything from the police or the hospital after they checked me over. The emergency room doctor told me to follow up with my regular doctor in a few days."

"Okay, Mr. Bates," Chris said, choosing her words carefully. "We may need to contact the hospital and your doctor to verify your injuries. Not because I don't believe you, but because if this investigation, as I've said, ends up in a trial—"

"It'll be evidence," he finished quietly. "I understand. He attacked me June twenty-first, 1998." He repeated the date. "I don't remember the name of the doctor who checked me over at the hospital, but I still have the same GP. Greg Bloomfield, here in Raleigh."

"Thank you." Chris wrote the name down next to the date of the attack, which she'd noted at his first mention. "Did you tell anyone else what happened?"

"Yes, in spite of what Chaz threatened. I told a couple of my close friends and my roommate, who was also a friend. She needed to know, since I wasn't sure whether Chaz would come back. Maybe we were all in denial, but we ended up treating it as a gay-bashing, which happens all too often in these parts, and hardly anyone reports those. That's the story we told to people who asked what happened to me. We said I got jumped outside a restaurant in D.C. We figured that'd keep people from trying to follow up."

"So no one said anything to the Raleigh police and as far as you know, the three people you told didn't repeat the true story?"

"As far as I know. And the community here can be rather tight, so if one of them had told, it would have gotten back to me."

"When did you leave Providence?"

"Soon after that. I actually didn't go back after the attack. I called three days later and said I had an emergency in the family and I had to leave town and didn't know when I'd be back and I was resigning from the bulletin." He made a derisive noise in his throat. "Much to the board's relief, I'm sure. And I found out what people thought of me. Not one person from the congregation contacted me. So much for Christian kindness."

Ouch. "Did you see Chaz after the attack?"

"No. I stayed far away from Providence. I thought about getting a lawyer and going to the cops, but my mama didn't raise no fool, either. Pick your battles and all that. Besides, the next month—July—

Chaz left Providence. I guessed they gave him a choice. Leave on his own or go after being fired. I didn't know where he went, but I breathed a little easier."

Chris scanned her notes for a moment, making sure she had the information she needed. Almost. "Mr. Bates, do you recall whether Chaz wore any jewelry?"

"Um..." He thought aloud. "No rings or bracelets. He tended to wear shirts and ties, always buttoned to the top. And even in the humidity here, he always looked pressed. Wait—he did wear a necklace. And he didn't take it off the two times we were at my house engaged in—ah—intimate matters."

"Do you remember what the necklace looked like?"

"It was just a gold chain with a small gold cross."

Another score, maybe? "Mr. Bates, thanks so much for returning my call. And thank you for being so forthcoming. I know this wasn't easy for you and I greatly appreciate your cooperation."

He laughed. "Well, honestly, I've wondered if anything Chaz did would catch up with him. Maybe it finally has..." he paused, and when he spoke again, it was with regret and a warning. "I know you can't tell me exactly what's going on, but you want my advice, find something for sure and pin it on him as soon as possible. Because he's slippery and he covers his tracks. He's an angry, angry man, Detective. And smart. After he finished with me that night and left, I knew that he really *could* kill me. If you want my opinion, it was just a matter of time before he killed someone and I sure as hell didn't want to be the first. So I hope you wrap him up before it comes to that."

Too late. Chris's instincts were screaming Pastor Chaz's guilt, no matter how circumstantial the evidence at this point. "Thanks again, Mr. Bates. If you think of anything else, please call either this number or my business cell. And I'll do my best to protect your identity, but I don't think you need to worry about Chaz showing up in Raleigh again."

"I actually have worried about that off and on, but when he left in ninety-eight and didn't reappear, I did breathe a bit easier. Still, I do appreciate it if you'd try to keep my name out of this. Unless it's absolutely necessary."

"I'll let you know what happens. Thanks again." She provided the number of her business cell, and said a quiet goodbye before hanging up and pushing back from her desk. Time to find Harper and compare notes before the good pastor joined them that afternoon. She stood, taking her coffee, now cold, with her.

Chapter
Seventeen

LIEUTENANT JERRY TORREZ leaned back in his chair, which squeaked softly in protest at the change in position. He laced his fingers behind his head and regarded first Chris, then Harper, his dark eyes unreadable. Jerry was pushing fifty-five, though he still comported himself with the energy and athleticism of a man twenty years his junior. The only obvious signs of his age were the speckles of grey at each temple and deep crows' feet in the corners of his eyes. He had shaved his mustache off last year and that, too, took the years off him.

"You've got a lot of pieces here," he said in his *nuevomexicano* drawl. Jerry was originally from Española, twenty miles north of Santa Fe. Chris sometimes thought that the northern New Mexico accent mimicked the slow crawl of lowriders down a city street, punctuated with various exclamations that sounded like the hiss and pump of hydraulics as the drivers jacked the vehicles up high above the asphalt only to lower them just as quickly to mere inches over the pavement.

"And some connections, but nothing strong enough for a warrant on his house." He sucked air in through his teeth thoughtfully. "This is good shit, *amigos*. But we've got to connect the dots." He leaned forward so suddenly that the chair didn't have a chance to protest. "This Mumford sounds like a real *cabrón*. But he's smart, and that makes him dangerous. Still, the smart ones get careless. They think they know everything. They get comfortable and they feel superior. Like Superman. But there's always a weakness."

"What about the fibers? Consistent with a late-model SUV. Can we get a warrant for his car?" Harper's elbows were braced on the armrests of his chair and he was leaning back, the front legs a couple inches off the floor.

"I've already called Joey on that," Jerry said. "I think we might be able to at least search his car. Was McCormick a bleeder?"

Chris shook her head. "No open wounds on his body. Autopsy confirmed that. He died of asphyxiation as a result of strangulation." *Probably no blood in the car, either.* She wished she knew where

Mumford had killed Travis, wished again that they had the clothing
Travis had been wearing. Chaz didn't seem like the trophy type, but
stranger things had happened. He might've kept some of Travis's
personal effects.

Jerry reached for the file on his desk. "What was the TOD?"

"ME estimated he'd been dead at least five days, probably a
week. Which is consistent with the video from Pulse and The Beach.
That was probably the last few hours of his life." Captured on grainy
video. The last movements of a vibrant young man.

"So we have a history of violence directed at both men and
women," Jerry mused aloud. "We've got a biblical verse reference on
three different men. We've got similar MO with two dead men. And
all three we can connect to Mumford. Circumstantially, this is all
pretty damning. But the burden of proof is on us and a good defense
attorney will take this shit apart, chew it up, and spit it back out. A
jury might buy it, but there's no guarantee. Especially with the
pastor angle. We've got to have more physical evidence."

Harper nodded slowly. "We've got witnesses who'll probably
testify. Stillman might not, but Ruiz will. Maybe some Cruces
connections. And the guy in North Carolina might help us out."

Jerry reached for his can of Diet Sprite. He had been trying to cut
back on his caffeine for weeks, after his doctor told him he needed to
be careful with his heart. "What about the goop under the vic's
fingernails?"

Harper shook his head. "Haven't heard yet. Sam thought he
might know this morning, but we're still waiting."

"I'd say that's your best bet to link Mumford to McCormick.
And if we do have viable DNA there, we might be able to link it to
what's on file for Henderson. Speaking of which, they delivered the
evidence in the Henderson case." He looked at Chris then. "We've
got it in lock-up. I signed for it."

"We need to get into his house," she said abruptly.

Jerry shrugged. *"Pues...¿y qué entonces?* So you find roofies.
That'll get him some attention but it's a first offense, no biggie. He'll
get probation. So you find this spirit gum. So what? That shit's not
illegal."

"But the chemical composition of spirit gum varies brand to
brand. If what's in his house matches what's under Travis's
fingernails—"

"True," Jerry concurred. "But again, you might be able to find
that brand in twenty other houses in the neighborhood."

"I think he killed Travis at his house," Chris said flatly. Harper
swiveled his head to look at her.

A tiny smile tugged at the corners of Jerry's mouth. "Why do
you think that, *esa?*"

"It makes sense for the profile we're getting on this guy. He's neat, clean, and meticulous. Watching that service yesterday, for example. He plans and makes sure everything's in place so that nothing goes wrong. Chaz probably figured out that Travis was sabotaging New Hope. Chaz and Travis clearly had a consensual sexual relationship. Maybe Travis threatened to out him. So Chaz decides it's time to get rid of Travis. Beating the crap out of him, he figures, isn't going to work because Travis is in with too many people at Wellspring and because maybe Travis isn't like Bates. Maybe Travis had a big mouth and Chaz knew that. Unlike Bates. Chaz knew he could intimidate Bates. He knew just a beating would make him back off."

Jerry nodded, watching her and smiling. "Go on."

"So Chaz makes a special date with Travis. Saturday night. Maybe he tells Travis what he wants to hear. Undying love and devotion. Stuff he told Tyler, but Tyler pegged Chaz as a liar, too, and he was like Travis in that he wouldn't just shut up. Chaz wants to get rid of Travis and he figures, 'who's going to link some dead queer to me'?"

Harper looked thoughtful. "Yeah, that makes sense. He sets up the date for Saturday but that Springer guy decided to come through on Saturday. So that throws a bit of a monkey wrench into Mumford's plans. Maybe he decides, 'well, hell. I'll cancel Saturday with him and off him another time.' But he decides to go to Pulse Friday, on the off chance that he'll see McCormick. He does. He's prepared. He talks McCormick into his SUV and off they go to the vic's place because Travis tells him that his roommate is gone for the night."

Chris picked up the conjecture. "Chaz slips roofies to Travis at the apartment, making it easier to walk him out the door to his vehicle. Then he takes Travis to his own place and does the deed. My bet's on the bathtub, so he can clean up afterward. It's a hell of a lot easier to clean piss and shit out of a bathtub than a rug," she said grimly.

Jerry sat looking at her, nodding. "I like it. Now prove it."

SAM PADILLA CALLED Chris's business cell from the Medical Examiner's office at 1:43 PM.

"Hey, *amigo. ¿Qué tienes?*"

"I've got epithelials under McCormick's nails, preserved in the spirit gum. We do have preliminary results back on DNA but there's no match in the database."

Fuck.

"But I took the liberty of running it against what they've got from the Henderson case—I called down there a couple days ago and had them fax me the results."

"And?" Chris's stomach knotted.

"We've got enough of a match to say it's probably the same guy." He sounded a bit triumphant, even though he concluded with, "The only problem is, we don't have anything to compare it to Mumford's."

"Shit. But Tyler and Travis are linked. That's huge, Sam. *Mil gracias*. Did you get anything out of McCormick's vehicle, by any chance?"

"Almost done. We have no body fluids, if that's what you're asking, and nothing except a few Wellspring bulletins, some empty pop cans, empty water bottles, hair gel—what any one of us would probably fling around in our vehicles. Nothing, though, to say who killed him."

"Does the vehicle run?"

"Nope. Alternator's dead."

So it *was* just simple car trouble. Chaz probably didn't have anything to do with that. "This is great. We're talking to Mumford today and we'll see if we can get a swab off him. If he says no, Joey might grant us a warrant based on all of the evidence. Thanks again."

"No problem. We're getting the chemical composition of the spirit gum, too. I'll be in touch."

"Take it easy." Chris hung up and sat staring at her computer screen. Now would probably be a good time to go get a swab kit from the crime lab, which was right across the parking lot from the police department. *Chazzy might be amenable today*, she thought as she stood. But she wasn't counting on it.

She took her notes and files into the interview room and Harper joined her twenty minutes later so they could make sure they were on the same track. At 2:55, Harper's cell rang. He glanced at it, then at Chris.

"Show time," he said sardonically before he answered. "All right," he said. "Be right out." He hung up and stood. "Back in a few."

Chris nodded and organized the files. Within a minute, Harper opened the door and held it, waiting for the men who accompanied him to precede him.

Chaz entered the interview room with a lawyer in tow, as Chris suspected he would. She didn't recognize the attorney, but that didn't matter. Chaz moved stiffly, like he was sore from a rough night. He lowered himself carefully into a chair at the conference table and the lawyer took the one on Chaz's right, smoothing the front of his dark grey suit coat as he did so. He looked like the type of guy who might have spent his college days rowing at Yale when he wasn't hazing younger versions of himself into his fraternity. Chris briefly caught Harper's eye but her colleague's expression remained inscrutable.

"Can I get you some coffee?" Harper asked. Both Chaz and the attorney declined. Harper shrugged and took the chair opposite Chaz, to Chris's right. The attorney sat across from her. Harper spoke first. "I'm Detective Dale Harper." He paused just long enough that Chris knew he wanted her to introduce herself.

"And I'm Detective Chris Gutierrez. Thank you for coming in," she said blandly, watching as Chaz's upper lip twitched slightly. His gaze cruised over the stack of files set neatly to her left and lingered on the swab kit, which consisted of a small test tube and a long-handled buccal swab, both sealed in plastic. She had positioned this in plain view next to the files along with a sheet of fingerprint tape. He then glanced at the microphone set up in the center of the table.

The lawyer nodded his perfectly coiffed head. "I'm Thomas Parks, legal counsel for Wellspring interests."

And that would include Chazzy, Chris thought. Parks wore a class ring on his right hand and a wedding band on his left. He looked about Chaz's age and he was obviously making a boatload of money, from the cut of his suit. Chaz was dressed in black trousers and a light blue shirt. His tie was black silk, with a colorful abstract design that ran from about midway down to the tip.

Harper launched right into it. "Mr. Parks, we are recording the proceedings here. Do you have any objection to that?"

"None at all."

"Pastor?" Harper turned to look at Chaz, who shook his head.

Harper nodded and leaned forward, resting his elbows on the table and clasping his hands in front of him. "Pastor, we've requested your presence here because we've uncovered some things that indicate that you haven't been entirely forthcoming with us in this investigation, and we'd just like to make sure you understand that this conversation is going on record and it is in your best interests to cooperate with us."

Chris hadn't seen this side of Harper. He'd never really commandeered an interview with her prior to this. She watched, interested to see where he'd take it. Parks moved in his chair, smoothing his suit coat with his right hand.

"Specifically, Pastor, my colleague here and I approached you at Wellspring last Tuesday the thirty-first at ten AM. It was an appointment that you agreed to. I asked you if you knew Travis McCormick, who was a formal member of the Wellspring congregation. You informed us that you knew him in passing and that the last time you had seen him was right after New Year's.

Would you like to amend that statement?"

The muscles in Chaz's jaw clenched but he said nothing.

Chris handed the file on the top of her stack to Harper. He opened it and pulled out a still image derived from the Pulse video. In it, Chaz and Travis were lip-locked, standing next to the SUV. Harper placed it on the table in front of Chaz. "This is from video taken at Pulse nightclub on Central Avenue. The date and time, as you can see there in the corner, is Saturday, January twenty-first, one forty-nine AM. Travis was reported missing Sunday the twenty-second."

"What's this?" Parks asked. "That could be anyone."

Harper placed another image next to it, showing the license plate on the back of the SUV. "MRN dash six and possibly a nine there. Your plate number is MRN dash six nine two. The make and model of your vehicle is a Lexus GX."

Parks waved his right hand dismissively. "Coincidence on the plate. It's somebody else's vehicle."

Harper then removed a sheet of paper with a list of plate numbers and the makes and models of the vehicles. "I took the liberty, Mr. Parks, of running all the combinations of numbers that we could possibly derive from this image. MRN dash six nine and dash six eight show up on these nineteen vehicles. The third number for each is everything except two, which is what appears on the pastor's vehicle registration. None of these vehicles listed here, you can see, is an SUV. Which leaves two possibilities. That is Pastor Mumford's vehicle in the parking lot of Pulse nightclub and that is Pastor Mumford with Travis McCormick or —" he paused for effect, "that's Pastor Mumford's vehicle and someone else was using it. Which is it, Pastor?"

"This is crap," Parks said quietly with a hint of bombast in his voice.

Harper removed another image from the file. This one showed the man from Pulse walking Travis into The Beach. He placed it next to the others. "This is from security cameras at Travis's residence. Saturday, January twenty-first, two-sixteen AM." He then placed another next to it, showing the man from Pulse leaving with Travis, half-supporting him. "This was taken at three-oh-one AM. This is probably the last time anyone — except you — saw Travis McCormick alive. So. Is that your vehicle in the parking lot of Pulse? And if so, who's that with McCormick?"

"Well, it's clearly not the pastor. This man has a goatee," Parks stated smugly.

"True," Harper responded, unruffled. "However, the Medical Examiner has determined that the man who was last with Travis McCormick seems to have affixed a goatee to his face with spirit gum, residue of which was found underneath McCormick's fingernails. Last time I checked, Mr. Parks, spirit gum is generally not a good substitute for sexual lube. Unless one is looking for a bit of trouble extricating. The only reason anyone uses spirit gum is for theatrical performances, generally those that involve sticking facial hair onto one's skin."

Chaz seemed to pale slightly and Parks pursed his lips with distaste. Chris tried not to stare too hard at Harper. He had actually implied a sexual relationship between Chaz and Travis. And without batting an eye. *Holy fuck, he used the word "extricate."*

Harper continued, his tone flat but with a don't-fuck-with-me undercurrent. "In addition, the pastor is known as a fairly regular patron of Pulse. Bartenders and managerial staff have identified him, with the use of this image." Harper then took the color brochure out of the file and opened it to the picture of Chaz onto which Jason had drawn the goatee.

"That's a leading image," Parks said tightly. "If you present that to people, of course they'll finger whoever this is in the video."

Chris handed another file to Harper. He pulled a statement out of it and slid it across the table to Parks. "This is the statement of one of the owners of Pulse. He added the goatee to the image when my colleague asked whether the pastor had ever frequented his establishment." He then pushed the file toward Parks. "You'll find other witness statements in there. All of which will tell you that a man matching the pastor's description frequented Pulse, generally on Friday nights. Now, Pastor, you haven't yet answered the original question. Is that you in the parking lot of Pulse? If not, who is it and why did you loan him your vehicle?"

"Don't answer that," Parks interjected.

Harper leaned forward. "Mr. Parks, do I have to remind you that this is a homicide investigation? A man is dead. The pastor's vehicle is associated with someone who most likely was the last person on this earth to see that young man alive. I think it's fairly clear why your client needs to answer the question." He turned his gaze back to Chaz. "Is that you? Or did you loan your vehicle to someone?"

Chaz shifted. Chris watched his eyes, watched a flicker of something come and go within them. "It's me," Chaz said quietly. Parks glared at him. Chaz ignored him. "I'm sure you understand why I didn't say anything last week. I—I've had some problems with unnatural urges and I'm sorry to say I succumbed to Travis's advances." He sighed heavily. "A man in my position—well, you understand why I couldn't—" he stopped and looked pleadingly at Harper.

Parks picked up the ball. "Surely APD understands the sensitive nature of what Pastor Mumford is implying here. Wellspring, as you know, is a large congregation, and the pastor is an extremely popular man. Accusations like this could bring a lot of publicity — not only to Wellspring, but to APD as well." He snapped that pronouncement like a whip.

Don't buy this shit, Chris thought as she watched the exchange. *Don't do it, Harper.*

"According to the Medical Examiner," Harper pointed out, "McCormick was dead no later than the morning of Monday the twenty-third. Chances are, Pastor, that you're the last one to have contact with him before his death. That puts you in a difficult position. I understand that."

Good. He's not getting sucked in.

"All the more reason not to tell you," Chaz said contritely. "I know how this looks. Please."

Piece of shit. Chris pulled another file from the stack and passed it to Harper. He opened it and glanced at the contents before directing his attention back to Chaz.

"Pastor, we were fortunate enough to get a fingerprint off McCormick's body as well as a bit of skin that wasn't his. From that, we have a DNA profile. I'm sure that in the interests of cooperating with this investigation, you'll do the right thing and provide us with a sample of *your* DNA as well as your fingerprints to help us rule you out as a suspect."

Chaz's eyes narrowed slightly. He glanced at Parks. Chris could almost see the wheels turning in his brain. He was probably thinking they were bluffing, since he had washed Travis's body oh, so carefully.

"Get a warrant," Parks said tightly. "All you have is some shitty video images and a quick feel and make-out session in a dark parking lot of some irreputable homo bar. Pastor Mumford is a man of some stature in this community, whose selfless acts override any kind of one-night weakness he indulged in with some kid who just happens to wind up dead soon after. He was asking for it anyway, hanging out in places like that."

Chris checked the lock on her temper. She knew Parks was trying to push buttons, trying to make either her or Harper say or do something that would reflect badly on APD. "So it's about reputation, then," she said quietly, turning her full cop gaze onto the attorney. He blanched.

"Reputation. Of course." Her tone was cold and her voice felt like ice as it exited her throat. "A man of God who hides his proclivities with lies versus a young, idealistic, gay man who believed that Jesus loved everybody."

She could feel Harper's eyes on her, knew that maybe she should shut up. But her youngest brother John floated in her mind's eye and what the hell would she do if that was *him* lying face-down in a bosque grave, a cross shoved under his tongue and a Bible verse tattooed with a razor into his chest? She pulled another file out of the stack and removed several sheets of paper. "Your reputation, *Pastor*," she said sarcastically, "precedes you." She pushed the sheets of paper toward him, holding his gaze, in full-on cop mode. "You were engaged to be married three times. Care to tell Mr. Parks here what happened to those women?"

Chaz's eyes narrowed slightly. Parks addressed Chris. "What the hell does this have to do with anything?"

Chris turned her cop glare back to him. "So you know, Mr. Parks? All three of Pastor Mumford's fiancées reported that he physically attacked and beat them. One of those women became your wife, Pastor, as you might recall. But marrying you didn't stop your temper. She left, too. Sadly, none of those women filed formal charges because they were afraid for their lives."

"This has nothing to do with anything." Parks tried to airily dismiss Chris and she recognized his tone. A hyperactive, aggressive bitch. Just ignore her. She saw his opinion on his face, as clear as if he had reached over and smacked her with it.

"It has everything to do with Travis McCormick," Chris said tightly. "Perhaps the pastor would like to explain to you why he left North Carolina." She shifted her attention to Chaz, who was glaring at her with pure malice. "Or did you not know?"

Parks remained impassive, though he flicked a glance at Chaz.

"Remember this, Pastor?" She removed a copy of the letter to the Providence Bulletin that K.C. had managed to acquire and slid it toward him. He ignored it and instead held her gaze, his flat and empty, sizing her up. Chris pushed him. "Seems you've had your 'unnatural urges' for a hell of a lot longer than you're willing to admit. And right now, I'm waiting for a report from Raleigh General Hospital. It'll tell me the extent of the injuries to one James Bates, sustained when you attacked him in June, 1998. A neighbor saw you push your way into his house. And that same neighbor watched you leave, with blood on your shirt and your hands." Chris hedged on that last bit, trying to make it seem as if Bates hadn't talked and that there was another witness he needed to worry about.

Here Chaz looked at Parks. He kept his hands clasped on the table in front of him but his knuckles were turning white.

Chris leaned forward then, pressing her advantage, however small. "You want to talk about your tenure in Las Cruces? Maybe chat a little bit about Tyler Henderson?" She kept her voice low, dangerous. She wanted to see him flinch. He did nothing except return her stare. It was the look, Chris knew, of a predator. In this case, the imperturbable, expressionless stare of a reptile. A snake, perhaps. Or an alligator. He was looking for her weaknesses and if she wasn't careful, he'd find them. If he hadn't already. She held his gaze and he slowly lowered his first, letting her know that she had this round. But not to count on that the next time. The thought chilled her.

"This interview is over," Parks announced. He stood up and Chaz followed suit, a bit paler than when he came in, but in his eyes Chris detected something else, something shrewd. Deadly. Parks motioned for Chaz to precede him out of the room. He turned to address them again. "You'll be hearing from me. In the meantime, if you don't want a big PR stink, I'd suggest you refrain from visiting Wellspring or Pastor Mumford again."

"On what grounds?" Harper asked mildly as he, too, stood. He was taller and broader than Parks.

Jesus. Another pissing match. Chris remained seated, watching.

"We're trying to solve a homicide." Harper folded his arms over his chest. "Pastor Mumford was one of the last people—if not *the* last—to see Travis McCormick alive. I'd say that gives us a good reason to come sniffing around his place of employment or chat with him a bit more. Especially when the warrant comes through."

Parks blinked first. Without a word, he strode out of the room. Neither he nor Chaz looked back.

Harper looked down at Chris, a grim smile on his lips. "Busted."

"Nice work, Harper," Chris said as she stood up and helped him gather their material together. "Maybe tomorrow we'll have the warrant. If Chaz doesn't bail on us and we get the sample, we can maybe get a rush on his profile." *But that still gives him a few days to either leave or snap.* She kept that to herself, figuring Harper was thinking the same thing.

He nodded slowly. "That was some tough talk there," he said quietly. "Rattled 'em both. What do you think about a media drop, let Mumford know that we're gonna tie the perp's—his—ass to Henderson without letting much out?"

"Hell, yes. Let's talk to Jerry and see what the DA has to say."

"Yep." He followed her down the corridor back to the sergeant's office.

Chapter
Eighteen

"WHOA," K.C. SAID softly, regarding Chris from her position on the couch. "Chazzy's our guy."

"Looks like it." Chris was sitting on the other sofa at K.C. and Sage's, unwinding after the day. She heard Sage in the kitchen. Dayna was having dinner with some attorneys from Chicago, so Chris wouldn't be seeing her tonight. *Unfortunately.* "That's where the evidence is leading us. Plus, today during the interview—" She took a sip of coffee before continuing. "He's clearly hiding *something.* Watch the evening news tomorrow for the media announcement. I called Carl Maestas down in El Paso and told him that we had a link from Travis to Tyler. Then I called the Henderson family."

"How'd that go?" K.C. leaned forward and picked up her cup from the coffee table.

"Not good. I talked to Tyler's mom, which was probably the best thing under the circumstances. His dad apparently wasn't exactly Mister Understanding when Tyler came out. I explained who I was and that while investigating this other murder we'd found a possible link to the death of her son and that the media would be releasing a story probably tomorrow." Chris sighed. "She told me in no uncertain terms that she wanted nothing to do with any more investigations, that we had no right to go dredging up the past. I told her that it was my job to do this and as long as Tyler's death remained unsolved, his killer was out there, maybe doing the same things to others. She hung up on me. I'm sure she'll be hearing from the Las Cruces media outlets soon enough. That sucks. I hate that part of my job."

Sage appeared in the doorway to the kitchen. "Damn, I have these extra empanadas. Whatever shall I *do* with them?" She rolled her eyes innocently.

Chris grinned. "Well, ma'am, as an officer of the law, I can assure you that I and my friend here can take them off your hands so they'll quit bothering you."

Sage leaned against the wall, fanning herself with a hand. She affected a fake southern accent. "Why, Officer, I can't begin to tell you how grateful I am for your kind offer. You just sit tight, Sugar, and I'll be back before you can say 'Scarlett O'Hara was a big ol' hussy'." And she disappeared back into the kitchen.

K.C. chuckled. She glanced at Chris. "So—" she raised her eyebrows in a question, a cute little smile on her lips.

"I'm still off my fucking axis, *chica*." Chris grinned. "She had the talk with the DA yesterday."

Sage reappeared with a plate piled with empanadas in one hand and two smaller plates and napkins in the other. She set the empanadas—half-moon-shaped pastries—in the center of the coffee table and handed plates to K.C. and Chris. "Peach-pineapple." She plopped down on the couch next to K.C. and pecked her on the cheek before focusing on Chris. "So Dayna's recusing herself from cases you work on."

Chris stared at her, the pastry halfway to her mouth.

Sage continued as if nothing had happened. "And you probably freaked out, nearly hyperventilated, and then realized that there's something about this Dayna that you just can't stand to be without." She batted her eyes at Chris. "How'm I doing?"

"Fucking hell." Chris pretended to check her clothing. "Where'd you put the tracking device?"

"It's just a matter of learning how to read people." Her eyes twinkled. "And it's sewn into the lining of your jacket. Per Dayna's request." Sage arched an eyebrow and reached for an empanada. "I'm trying a new recipe. What do you think?" She took a bite and chewed thoughtfully.

Chris bit into the light warm dough and flavor exploded in her mouth. "Mmm," she managed while chewing. "Wow. Sage, these are unbelievable. Where did you get the recipe?"

"For real, honey. These fucking *rock*." K.C. took another bite. "Damn. I cannot believe my girlfriend is a cross between Martha Stewart and Angelina Jolie. Shit. Who knew?"

Sage giggled and snuggled against K.C. "It's *Abuelita*'s recipe. I'm taking some to her tomorrow for her opinion."

Chris finished chewing and swallowed. "So do you, *Abuelita*, and John hang out together now, cooking and creating all day?" She knew Sage and K.C. swung by on occasion and ran errands for *Abuelita* or just visited with her, but this sort of surprised her.

Sage's face lit up. "That's right. John wants to go to chef school. I'll call him and see if he wants to practice over here." Sage turned to K.C. "Is that okay with you?"

"Sweetie, you can have the entire UNM men's rugby club over here if you want to share recipes with them and turn our kitchen into a fine dining experience."

"Chris, can I please borrow your brother for culinary

excursions?" Sage lifted her eyebrows, teasing.

"Shit, there's no one on the planet who can resist you," Chris said, laughing before she took another bite. "Kase, you never had a chance."

"I know. Lucky me." K.C. smiled and planted a kiss on Sage's cheek.

"You can use my brother for whatever you want," Chris said between bites. The empanada tasted slightly different than *Abuelita*'s. Sage used a bit more cinnamon, which created an intriguing blend with the pineapple.

"So Dayna had a chat with the DA." K.C. glanced over at Chris. "Are you okay with that? Or do you not want to talk about it?" She took the last bite of her pastry and sat watching Chris.

"No, it's okay. I'm starting to figure out that talking is a good thing."

"Shut *up!*" K.C. stared at her in mock horror. "I mean, *don't* shut up!"

Chris tossed one of the sofa pillows at her, which Sage caught.

"Hmmm." Sage placed the pillow against the opposite arm of the couch. "She wants to get serious with you."

"Yes. And yes, I did freak out. But I recognized it for what it was — baggage — and yes, there's something about this Dayna that I can't stand to be without." Chris held Sage's gaze.

"Whoa," K.C. whispered. "Could it be...the 'L' word? And I'm not talking the TV show."

Sage had a certain smile that made her look as if she knew something you didn't but it was okay, her knowing, because whatever it was, Sage would hold it close and protect it for you until you figured out what it was. That was the smile that pulled the corners of her mouth up and sparked in her eyes in the aftermath of K.C.'s comment. Chris furrowed her brow. *Love?* The thought darted through her head, churning up all kinds of anxiety and little demons with spiked claws. But underneath that, she felt a deep warmth, maybe bottomless, that spread across her nerve endings like warm honey. Like Dayna's laugh and the expression in her eyes when Chris caught her looking her way. *Love?*

"I don't know," Chris said softly. "I'm scared shitless."

"Trust this process," Sage said simply. "She's making room for you in her life and she's not the kind of woman who does that lightly. She knows a damn good thing when she finds it."

"And if she doesn't, I'll talk to her," K.C. added, grinning.

Chris's personal cell phone rang.

"Ask her if she can have dinner with us this week." Sage smiled impishly and reached for K.C.'s cup.

Chris checked the number on the ID screen. She laughed.

"Damn, Kase, I don't know how the hell you and Sage keep any mystery in your lives." She held the phone up. "I'll take it in the kitchen."

K.C. pulled Sage against her. "Don't mind us. We'll see if we can discover uncharted territory while you're busy." Sage giggled and Chris blew them both a kiss as she answered her phone on the way into the kitchen, a cheery, retro room with original counters from the 1940s.

"Hey," Chris said. "We were just talking about you."

Dayna laughed. "I wondered. My ears are burning. How are you?"

"Missing you." It got easier to say that every time she did. Chris stood at the back window, looking into the mud/laundry room. Beyond that was a back porch. She could just see the small mother-in-law cottage through the mud room window. Jeff wasn't home tonight, but he had left the light on over his front door. "How was dinner?"

"Over, thankfully. How are K.C. and Sage?"

"Great. Sage is trying to set up dinner this week, probably at Yanni's. Any chance of that happening?" Chris heard Dayna rustling. Probably looking for her appointment book, a brown leather-bound affair.

"What about—" Dayna paused. "Hell, it'll have to be Friday. Does that work?"

"I think it's fine for me. Let me check with—"

On cue, Sage entered the kitchen with K.C.'s cup. She refilled it at the coffee pot. "I'll talk to her," she said, a mischievous glint in her eyes. She held her hand out for the phone.

"Oh, *hell*, no," Chris retorted, half-laughing.

"It's okay," Dayna said, a smile in her voice. "I'd love to talk to...Sage? Or K.C.?"

Chris groaned. "Sage." She handed the phone to her and Sage grinned triumphantly.

"Hi, Dayna. You and I haven't formally met. How are you?"

Shit. Chris watched the exchange, wondering what Dayna was saying. Sage suddenly laughed.

Chris ran a hand through her hair just as K.C. appeared in the doorway. "Yikes," K.C. said, reading the situation correctly. "C'mon, stud," she said to Chris. "Let's leave the womenfolk to their chatting."

Sage shot her a mock glare that K.C. answered with a slow sexy air-kiss before she grabbed Chris by the arm and pulled her back into the living room.

"I'm really fucking nervous about this dinner thing," Chris admitted as she sank onto the couch again.

K.C. stood looking at her. "Girlfriend, it'll be fine."

"I'm more nervous about this than taking her to meet *Abuelita* or *mi familia.*"

K.C. smiled. "I think that might be a compliment. Or not."

Chris ran both hands through her hair and glanced toward the kitchen. She heard Sage talking and laughing. "It is. Your opinion means a hell of a lot to me, *esa.* Sage's, too. I know *you've* met her a couple of times, but that wasn't really in-depth."

"Y'know, I don't pretend to have Sage's gift with people," K.C. responded, "but I ain't no dumb-ass, either. And I've got a good feeling about this, *amiga.* Dayna's really good for you. She's willing to take chances even though she knows how freaky you can get."

Chris shot her a mock cop grimace.

"Whatever." K.C. rolled her eyes at Chris's attempt to look scary. "Dayna deals with her shit and she tries to make things right. But she doesn't seem the type to take bullshit. You need that. You need someone who reminds you that there's more to life than your job."

"Seems I told you something like that not so long ago."

K.C. grinned. "And you were right. So I'm passing your advice back to you."

"Ms. Carson would like to speak with you, Detective," Sage announced from the kitchen doorway, holding the phone up.

Chris looked pleadingly at K.C., who just shrugged with a "women!" expression. Chris stood and crossed the room. Sage handed her the phone and flashed her a mysterious smile.

"Hey again," Chris said as she entered the kitchen.

"I didn't get a chance to tell you that I miss you, too," Dayna said. "And Friday's good all around. Seven at Yanni's." She sounded excited. "I'm really looking forward to it."

"Really?" Chris relaxed.

"Well, *duh.* K.C. and Sage are important to you. I want to know you better and I want your friends to see that. Plus, they seem like really cool people."

"Damn. Thanks."

"Oh, my God," Dayna said, realization in her voice. "You're nervous."

Chris cleared her throat.

"You are. You're nervous. Hon, don't worry about it. It'll be a complete blast."

"Hon." She called me "hon." Oh, my God. Chris's heart sprouted wings, the tips of which fluttered against her ribs. *And it makes me feel really good.* "Um — okay, then." *Shit. I sound like Harper.*

Dayna was laughing. "Now that's pretty damn cute, you all flustered up like that. I'd sure like to be there with you right now," she said, adding a little Texas twang.

"Shit," Chris muttered. The grin on her face threatened to split her head open.

"Damn cute," she repeated softly. "Okay, I'm still here at the restaurant and about to head on home. Any chance you might be in my neck of the woods tomorrow? Lunch? Coffee?"

"I don't know yet." Chris regained her composure. "We've had some new developments and I might need to hang out around the office. I also have to close out a couple of other things. Not that I wouldn't drop any of that for five minutes with you."

"That's sweet. Well, if anything changes, you know where to find me. Damn, I haven't seen you in — what? Twelve hours? That's too long."

"I agree. I'll call you regardless, how's that?" Chris felt another face-splitting smile building.

"Hell, yes. All right. Be safe and I'll talk to you later. Bye."

"Bye." Chris slowly closed her phone. She stared out the kitchen window through the mud room toward the ramada. *She called me "hon."* Did she know it? Did she do it on purpose? Did it just slip out? She heard footsteps behind her.

"I think what we have here is an obvious case of brain freeze, brought on by the voice of an attractive woman," K.C. stated matter-of-factly. "Chris Gutierrez, you are clearly off your fucking axis."

Chris started laughing. She turned around. "Yep. Completely. I have no clue where I left the damn thing. Hell, I doubt I could find it with both hands and a laser sight right now." She shook her head, smiling. "I might be going insane."

Sage appeared, carrying empty plates. She placed them in the sink. "Going *sane* feels a hell of a lot like going *in*sane." She glanced at Chris. "You're on the right road this time."

"Sure looks like it," K.C. agreed. "So. Friday at seven. Cool."

Chris slid her phone into her pocket. "I love you both. Thanks."

"K.C.'s escort-a-cop at your service." K.C. snapped a salute at Chris, then looked at Sage, who was about to start washing dishes. "Sweets, leave those. I'll get 'em."

"That's my girl. Still romantic after all this time." Sage grinned and hugged Chris. "You have done well, Grasshopper," she said. "Trust the process. Have a good night." To K.C., she said, "Don't be too long," and the tone in her voice coaxed a flush up K.C.'s neck. Sage's heated glance swept from K.C.'s eyes down to her waist then back again. She arched an eyebrow and with a devilish smile sashayed out of the kitchen.

"Damn," K.C. muttered as she followed Chris to the door.

Chris bit her lip to keep from laughing. "I think I can make it to my car okay. Thanks, *esa*. I'll talk to you later. Don't want to keep

Sage waiting, after all." She was out the door before K.C. could retort.

CHRIS AND HARPER stood in the hallway of the fourth floor of the downtown Albuquerque courthouse. The building had been completed in 2001, but it seemed it was still undergoing renovation because of flaws in the design. Typical New Mexico. What worked elsewhere was not a guarantee in this state. Part of the state's quirky heritage. Still, strategically placed windows kept these inner corridors from feeling like mausoleums. Chris glanced at her watch again. Joey Trujillo had been in chambers with Judge Arthur Torrington for a good thirty minutes. The story about "possible links" between Travis McCormick and Tyler Henderson might actually make the noon newscast, which was in thirty minutes.

"You think we can score a television around here?" Chris asked Harper. He was rocking forward on the balls of his feet. Maybe it was a meditative thing, that habit of his.

"I was just thinking that. Somebody in this place should have one. Let me check this floor."

Chris nodded as he moved down the corridor, trenchcoat hung over his left arm. She could smell somebody's microwave lunch, wafting from down the hall somewhere with the passage of busy-looking people. A compact man in crisp new Wranglers, black cowboy boots, and a starched denim shirt stood on the opposite side of the hallway, waiting outside a different courtroom. Puebloan, Chris guessed, by his physique and clothing. He looked to be about her age, with hair the color of a raven's wing. He wore it just above his ears. He was leaning against the wall, his fingers half in his pockets.

A woman laughed in one of the clerk's offices nearby and Chris felt a little jolt. It sounded like Dayna. She allowed herself a quick reminiscence. She had called Dayna again last night when she got home and they had talked for another thirty minutes. The conversation had been easy, arousing, and secure. Harper reappeared, interrupting her thoughts.

"Got one. Torrington's clerk." He looked at his watch. "We've got some time yet."

"Sounds good," she said, noticing how neither of them chose to sit on the benches. The Puebloan man opted not to, as well. The sounds of an office building floated around her. The distant clicking of keyboards. Talking. The hum of a copy machine. Another burst of laughter from the clerk's office to her right. Chris turned to look at the doorway. That sounded too much like Dayna. She heard the woman who had just laughed say something.

"I'm gonna grab some lunch. Back in a few." And Dayna emerged from the clerk's office. Seeing her was a punch in the gut but in a really good way. Dayna had a certain casual artsy flair to her professional wardrobe and she was exhibiting it with today's outfit, which consisted of a long flowing black linen skirt, a pearl-white blouse, and a loose black linen jacket. She had her hair loosely tied behind her head, which allowed it to frame her face nicely but kept it off her shoulders. She was not wearing her glasses so Chris got the full effect of Dayna's gaze when it landed on her.

"Wow. Now *there's* a tall drink of water," she said, laughing with pleasure and surprise. She approached and stopped inches from Chris. "Hi. Fancy meeting you here." She carried a briefcase in her left hand.

"We must run in similar circles," Chris said. She lowered her voice and leaned closer. "Do you think anyone would notice if I pushed you up against the wall and kissed you until you couldn't breathe?" She was rewarded with a slight flush on Dayna's cheeks.

"Tempting. Very." She looked past Chris, over her left shoulder. "Hi. I'm Dayna Carson, with the prosecutor's office." She stuck her right hand out as Chris moved aside so Dayna could shake Harper's hand.

"Dale Harper. Gucci's lapdog." He actually smiled.

"Gucci?" Dayna lifted an eyebrow and shot Chris an innocent look. "I think she's more the L.L. Bean type. Though I see your point."

Chris rolled her eyes. "Harper and I are working the bosque case. Joey's trying to get us a warrant." Chris motioned with her head at Torrington's closed chamber doors.

"Damn. I guess that means you can't join me for lunch."

"Sorry." Chris shrugged helplessly.

"How about a quick cup of coffee downstairs?"

Chris checked her watch then glanced at Torrington's door again.

"Go ahead," Harper interjected. I'll call you if —" he motioned with his chin at the judge's door.

"Thanks. You want one?"

"Yeah, actually. Black." He folded his arms over his chest and pushed forward onto the balls of his feet.

Chris nodded once and turned to accompany Dayna down the corridor to the elevator. Three other people were on board. Otherwise, Chris would have availed herself of the few seconds of privacy to take another ride on Dayna's lips. Instead, they chatted amiably on the ride down to the atrium, where a coffee cart stood near the front entrance, just out of the wind from the doors.

"This place feels like a bank," Chris said as they walked

together. Dayna wore black cowboy boots with her skirt and the heels made a comforting sound on the marble floor. *Jesus, I want her. Not just now. Not just tomorrow. Every day I can possibly get.* She ignored the old fear that percolated in her depths and it stilled. Not feeding it seemed to make a difference.

"But there is good coffee." Dayna approached the vendor and ordered an Americano. Chris ordered two more. Dayna started to open her briefcase but Chris put a hand on her arm.

"I've got it." Chris paid and waited for her change. Dayna doctored hers a bit at the cream and sugar station that took up the far end of the cart. A splash of half-and-half. Chris did the same with hers. She left Harper's untouched and took lids from the stack, putting them on both her cup and his. She then followed Dayna to a small table nearby that looked out the massive glass windows toward Lomas. Across the street was the monolithic Aztec-looking new Federal courthouse.

"What a great surprise," Dayna said, watching Chris's face. She leaned forward slightly. "You are so fucking hot. I think it's the badge. I love how you wear it on your belt."

Chris smiled, embarrassed.

"Or the gun. Who am I kidding? It's everything. Good God, I could go on all day about how hot you are. And about all the things I'm attracted to about you." She took a sip of coffee. "And I have, actually."

"Oh?"

"My sisters are now entirely tired of hearing about you. But all my San Diego friends want me to bring you out there so they can meet you. I hope you don't mind."

Chris shook her head. "No. No, I don't. When?"

Dayna looked at her sharply. "When what?"

"When are we going to San Diego?" Chris watched Dayna's eyes, allowed herself to sink into them.

"Seriously?"

"Completely."

Dayna was about to respond when Chris's business cell buzzed with a text message. She pulled it off her belt. "Shit. Joey's done."

Dayna laughed softly. "A woman's work—I'll call you later. I want to finish this conversation. And start some other things." She gave Chris one of her charged smiles as she stood and picked her briefcase up from the neighboring chair. "Have a good rest of the day."

"You, too." Chris retrieved the two cups of coffee and stood looking at Dayna. She knew she was grinning.

"I feel the same way." Dayna reached out and squeezed Chris's arm before she grabbed her coffee and turned and walked toward the entrance. Chris watched her leave then headed back upstairs. She emerged from the elevator and went down the hall to where District Attorney Joey Trujillo stood talking to Harper, her petite frame dwarfed by his. She wore a crisp purple power suit and she kept her perfectly coiffed dark hair short.

"Hey, Joey," Chris said as she handed Harper his cup of coffee. "What's the word?"

"Good news. Torrington agrees there's probable cause. Car, garage, and house." She then smiled. "And DNA. I suggest you call and set it up through Parks if you can't get Mumford to respond." She switched the files she was holding to her other arm. "I need you to be careful on this. We don't need any bad press right now, especially in the wake of the other problem last year. So far, you've both been exemplary. Do I need to spell this out any further?"

"No." Chris glanced at Harper. He nodded at Joey.

She looked at Chris again. "Can you stick around for a few minutes after?" The tone of her voice did not suggest room for compromise though she sounded pleasant enough.

"Will do," Chris assented, suspecting Joey wanted to talk with her about Dayna.

"Excellent," Joey said as she handed the warrant to Chris. "Let's go watch the news."

Chapter
Nineteen

CHAZ MUMFORD'S HOUSE occupied a spot in one of the newer West Side developments. Typical faux-dobe with a hefty dose of California ranch-style, it sat on a bluff whose soil nearly matched the shade of stucco on the house's exterior. Chris noted that each home in this subdivision had lots of space around it. She paced off a good ten yards from the bottom of Chaz's concrete driveway to the house on the left and fifteen to the house on the right. His driveway ended at his attached garage, whose plain putty-colored door faced the street.

Two unmarked police cars sat in front of Chaz's house. Harper's Jeep Cherokee was parked down the street. Chris had come with him. Jerry Torrez was the supervisor on this little jaunt, which put Chris's mind at ease. If anyone could handle Chaz and Parks, it was Jerry. He had driven one of the unmarked vehicles. Sam Padilla from the ME's office had ridden with him and the two sat in the vehicle, chatting. The other police car, whose doors were open, held two experienced cops: Jason Martino, whom Chris had worked with when she was a beat cop, and Tracy Valdez, who'd been on the force nearly as long as Chris. Tracy loved being a beat cop and she was damn good at it. Tracy and Jason lounged in the front seat of their car, also talking.

"Not a bad view," Harper observed from his vantage point at the foot of the driveway, looking out toward the western mesas. "If desert's your thing." The space between houses here allowed a sense of privacy, if residents sat on their back patios watching the sun set over the five extinct cinder cone volcanoes.

"It's not yours?" Chris asked, sweeping the cul-de-sac with her gaze.

He shrugged. "I've seen worse."

Chris turned to study the exterior of Chaz's home. It mimicked New Mexican style with its big, wide porch, roof supported with three large wooden columns. A large picture window overlooked the front porch. Chaz had installed plantation shutters over the window and those were closed. No peeking, Chris thought. *Somebody might see his secrets.* A chile ristra hung against the wall next to the front door and a wrought iron bench sat beneath the window. Somebody had xeriscaped the front yard with native plants. Chris recognized lavender, yucca, sage, and desert willow. Honeysuckle vines clung to a trellis near the front of the house. In a month or so, the flowers would start to bloom. She loved the smell of honeysuckle. At least Chaz had good taste in vegetation.

Harper's cell phone rang. He answered. "Yeah. Dale Harper."

Chris checked her watch. Nearly three. She looked at the other houses nearby. No grass. All xeriscaping. A tricycle and a Tonka dump truck sat on the porch of Chaz's immediate neighbor to the left. Working neighborhood, Chris surmised, as the only signs of movement came from tumbleweeds that the wind lodged in the corners between houses and in the larger bushes that dotted front yards. This time of year, the West Side palette was made up of dingy grays, yellows, and browns punctuated by the seemingly ubiquitous plastic grocery bags that floated past on breezes or hung in the spindly trees that people tried to plant. In twenty years, they might have some shade over their porches.

"Okay, then." Harper hung up and turned toward Chris. "That was Parks."

Chris kept her face expressionless with an effort.

"He's pissed." Harper slipped his phone back into his coat pocket. "Who the hell do we think we are, harassing the good pastor like this."

Chris couldn't see his eyes behind his shades. "So where's Chaz?"

"Apparently on his way. Wellspring's only a couple of miles from here." He gestured vaguely southeast, though Chris was well aware of its location in relation to Chaz's house.

"Is Parks joining us for the festivities?"

"Of course. He wants to see the warrant." Harper rocked forward on his feet, arms folded over his chest.

"Fuck him. We're not waiting for his ass."

Harper sucked air through his teeth. "Not sure how you really feel. Can you elaborate?"

Chris shot him a look, but his expression remained bland.

"What'd Joey have to say to you?" he asked suddenly.

"Clarification about something," Chris said. "Nothing to do with this case."

Harper made a noncommittal noise and looked to his left, down the street toward a main road. "She must be worth it," he said, not really looking at her.

Chris frowned. "Who?"

"Carson. That's her name, right?" He glanced at her but his

shades helped him maintain his impassive G-man persona.

Chris stared at him, glad she had her own sunglasses on. "Yes, that is her name. Dayna Carson." She watched him, but nothing in his demeanor changed so she continued. "And, yes, she's worth it."

His upper lip twitched, almost imperceptibly. He nodded once, more to himself than for anything else. "How'd you meet?"

Chris could read nothing in his tone. *Well, he asked.* "At a law conference in Santa Fe last summer." She looked past him down the street, affecting an air of unconcern, like she talked about her lesbian love life all the time with every big straight male cop on the force.

A silver Lexus SUV rounded the corner, tires squealing a bit on the asphalt.

"Here's our guy," Harper announced, Chaz's arrival changing the topic. Jerry emerged from his vehicle, carrying himself with his usual bearing, a mixture of military precision and casual alertness as Chaz tore past the parked vehicles in front of his house and made a big show of turning quickly into his driveway. Chris and Harper watched as he slammed on his brakes in front of his garage door and rammed the vehicle into Park.

"That can't be good for his transmission," Harper muttered.

Jerry exchanged a look with Chris as Chaz climbed out of his vehicle, moving stiffly. If he had been a dog, all the hair on his back would be standing up. Jason and Tracy stood next to their vehicle, hands resting on their police-issue belts. From the corner of her eye, Chris saw Sam gathering his crime scene box from the trunk of the car.

"Pastor," Harper said in greeting. Chris didn't say anything. She just studied Chaz. He still wore band-aids on the knuckles of his right hand and the bruises on his left knuckles still showed reddish-purple. His shirt was buttoned to his neck and his tie maintained its neat knot. If he had a necklace on, she'd never know it unless he took his shirt off.

"I'm Sergeant Jerry Torrez." He handed the warrant to Chaz. "Your vehicle, garage, and house. Including your household trash. And a DNA sample. We do appreciate your cooperation, sir." He offered a thin smile. Jerry was very good about sounding approachable, but people learned quickly that they should not mess with him. Chaz took the warrant but didn't look at it. Instead, he glared at Harper and Chris in turn, not saying anything.

"How long will this take?" he finally asked.

"I'm sorry, Pastor, but I simply don't know how long. We'll try to complete our work as quickly as we can with as little inconvenience to you as possible. So, the sooner you let us in, the sooner we can begin."

Chaz looked uncertain for a moment, like he wanted to wait for

Parks, but then he must've thought about how it looked, having police personnel hanging out in front of his house. He handed the warrant back and, without another word, went to the front door and unlocked it, throwing it open and gesturing at the interior with an arrogant flourish. Sam stood next to Chris. "And so it goes," he said under his breath as they headed up the walk to the porch.

Chris muttered an affirmative and entered the house just as Chaz's lawyer pulled up in front. She turned and watched him through the open door.

"Looks a little pissed," Harper said.

"You think?" Sam asked as Parks strode up the walk and through the open door.

"Who's in charge here?" Parks demanded.

"Mr. Parks? I'm Sergeant Jerry Torrez." He handed the warrant to the lawyer and addressed the others. "Let's go, people. Look lively."

Sam handed Chris a pair of latex gloves. She thanked him and followed Harper into the living room, glad to leave Parks with Jerry. Parks argued loudly and vehemently with him. Or rather, he blustered and berated. He might as well have told the Sandias to crumble. Jerry was simply not one to be ruffled. Two tours in Vietnam and twenty years on the force made Jerry Torrez an immovable man. He pretty much ignored Parks but offered a polite comment now and again to him as Sam directed the two teams going through the house. Chaz stayed with Parks throughout, but Chris knew he watched everything they did.

Chaz's house was largely devoid of personality. It might have been an ad in a magazine. Every wall was a pristine white, with no artwork hanging anywhere. His furniture was low-slung Euro-industrial style in blacks and grays, with lots of stainless steel. Very minimalist. Like a German gay man obsessed with Bauhaus might be. No photographs of anyone. Not even in the room he used as an office. No computer in evidence, either. Chaz must be a laptop man.

"It's like he lives in the business suite of a hotel," Harper said as he looked through Chaz's closet. They had started in the master bedroom, snapping their latex gloves on before they entered. Their feet sank into plush gray carpet. The color reminded Chris of a tabby cat a friend of hers had adopted. White plantation shutters covered the window here, as well. The king-sized bed's headboard almost, but not quite, touched one wall and Chris had a feeling that if she took out a tape measure she'd discover that the center of the headboard was placed at the exact center of the wall. Like the living room, his bedroom furniture was sleek Euro-modern.

"Even his clothes are color-coded," Harper added. "He's got all his jeans hanging up, too."

Sam took a photo of the closet. "This could be an ad for California Closets."

Chris finished with the dresser. "I'll trade you. Make sure I didn't miss anything here."

Harper grunted something in reply and moved to the dresser. Chris stood looking at the clothes hanging in the closet. "You notice he has all the same hangers? Wooden. Same color, same size. And all hanging the same direction." *Major OCD. And that might play in our favor.* She started with his shirts. Chaz organized them by color, as Harper said. All solid. No patterns. No white. Reds, oranges, yellows, greens, blues, purples, and blacks. From lightest shade to darkest, which made it easy to distinguish where one color ended and another began. They were all the same brand and same size. JoS. A. Bank Clothiers. *Fancy.*

She finished with his shirts, checking sleeves for blood or unusual stains, and moved to his dress trousers, the same brand as his shirts, also arranged by color. From khaki this time to light grey to dark grey to navy to black. Perfectly creased, all hanging uniformly. Chris noted the size of each. Thirty-two waist, thirty length. The pockets were empty. All his clothing looked pristine.

She moved the shirts aside and examined his ties, hanging on a rack on the back wall of the closet. He liked blacks, grays, and navies for his ties, sorted by color and design. The same brand as his shirts and pants. She moved next to his jeans, surprised that he had any. Eleven pairs. On a hunch, she counted his pairs of trousers. Ten. Two of each shade. She counted his shirts. Twenty. Each shade had an even number. Four red, four blue, and the rest two each. She counted the sweaters. Ten. She counted his ties. Twenty. Four in the black category, Four navy, four light grey, four dark grey, and four a sort of charcoal color.

"Harper, how many T-shirts do you count in his dresser?" Chris asked over her shoulder.

"Um—hold on. Twenty-two."

"Give me a rough color break-down."

"Four red, four blue—the rest are two each."

"Any white?" she asked.

"Yep. Two."

"Pull the white ones." Chris stopped what she was doing and wrote the numbers and colors down in her notebook. She slid it back into the pocket of her leather jacket.

Harper put the two white tees on Chaz's bed. "One of these is consistent with the rest. American Eagle." He pointed to the second. "This one's odd man out." He checked the tag for the brand. "Never heard of it."

Chris took a look at the tag. "Some kind of clubwear place,

probably." From the material, it was designed to be worn tight. She looked up at Harper. His expression told her that they were both thinking the same thing. "Let me check something in the closet," she said. *Eleven pairs of jeans.* She checked the tags on each. All were American Eagle brand except one. She checked the tag. Lucky. She checked the size on the other ten pairs. Thirty-two waist, thirty length. She checked the size on the Lucky brand. Thirty-three waist, thirty-four length. "Sam, could you come here?" Chris called out the door down the corridor toward the kitchen.

He obliged and Chris showed him the discrepancy. "One of our witnesses at Pulse says Travis was wearing Lucky jeans the last night he saw him there. And a tight white shirt."

"Huh." Sam took a few photos and stepped back from the closet then looked at the clothing on the bed. "Why the hell would he keep it, if that's whose it is?"

Chris shook her head. "Trophies? But that seems so out of character for him."

"Hold on. I'm going to get a couple of evidence bags."

While Sam was gone, she checked the rest of Chaz's closet. Shoes also by JoS. A. Bank, organized by color. Two browns, two blacks. A couple of pairs of running shoes, Nike. Matching in color and design. Two pairs of black flip-flops. All consistent in size. He hadn't kept Travis's shoes.

"Hey," Harper said.

Chris looked up. He had pulled the dresser away from the wall slightly and his penlight was on.

"You never know what you might find," he said. "Have a look."

She peered into the two-inch gap he'd created. A matchbook lay on the floor, open. They waited for Jeff to photograph it and remove it with forceps.

"Uh-huh," Jeff said. "Pulse. There's a phone number."

Harper looked at it. "It's familiar to me. Hold on." He opened his pocket notebook. "Yep. It's McCormick's cell phone."

"But Chaz never used it. We've got Travis's cell phone records to confirm that."

Harper shrugged. "Just more ammo."

Sam reappeared with paper evidence bags. He dropped the matchbook into one and sealed it, then wrote time, date, and place on the outside.

They finished in the bedroom with no further discoveries and moved to the master bathroom. Chris marveled at its almost blinding white walls, the monotony broken by chrome accents and fixtures. Two dark blue towels hung on the rack closest to the shower stall. They looked like they had never been used. The shower stall was tiled in a shade of blue that seemed to perfectly match the towels.

"It's like a hospital," Harper said. "Only with a little more upscale class."

Jeff went over it with luminol and found no traces of blood or body fluids. He then took a screwdriver out of his crime kit and pried the drain cover up in the shower stall. "Sometimes you get lucky," he said, as he extricated a few strands of hair from the drain, which had gotten wrapped around the crossbars of the drain. Chris fought an urge to gag. For some reason, those nasty clumps of hair in a drain made her queasier than any homicide scene. She swallowed and looked away as Jeff put the hairs in another evidence bag.

Harper went through the medicine cabinet. "Mumford's a healthy guy," he muttered. "No 'scrips." He opened a bottle of Tylenol. "Hello. Got something else in here. Looks like—" He carefully shook the bottle a bit to arrange the contents. "Ecstasy and a couple of garden-variety roofies. That's special. I'll see if the roofies match my man Chuy's stash. We've got him on possession if nothing else."

Jeff took a few photos and bagged the bottle.

Harper opened the top of the toilet tank. "You never know," he said. "People put things in the weirdest places. Found a hand in one once, in a Ziploc."

"You mean people put weird shit in the weirdest places." Chris inspected the shower stall and the doors. No water stains or build-up. *Does he even live here?*

They finished in the master bathroom and checked the second bathroom, which also looked like it had never been used. This one was a more traditional set-up, with a tub and a chrome shower curtain rod screwed into the walls. The cabinets were empty. *No toilet paper.* Anywhere. Or shower curtain, which didn't necessarily mean anything, but it sure would make it easier to drag a body through a house on a shower curtain liner. Especially if that body was wet. Steel shower curtain clips remained on the rod. She inspected them. "Huh."

Harper looked over at her.

"What do you make of this?" She pointed out a couple of small pieces of jagged plastic still attached to the clips.

Harper moved closer and with his flashlight inspected one of the clips. He then pulled a magnifying glass out of the pocket of his coat.

"Damn, what *don't* you have in there?" Chris asked as he trained the glass on one of the clips.

"Supper," he shot back. "Looks like somebody pulled a plastic liner off the hooks. Ripped it." He glanced at her. "In a hurry to get the damn thing off." He returned the magnifying glass to his pocket. "Plastic like that sure makes a nice sliding surface across carpet for something big and heavy. Like, say, a dead guy." He went to the doorway and called Sam in to take photos and confiscate the hooks.

They moved to the kitchen, easily a master chef's dream. Maybe some day John could have a kitchen like this, Chris thought, looking around. Big, stainless steel appliances, plenty of cabinets and counter space. Everything designed for ease of access. And all pretty much empty. Chris opened the refrigerator, knowing Chaz was watching. A glass bottle shaped like a cylinder that contained some high-end water, two bottles of organic salad dressing in the top shelf of the door, a carton of orange juice, and a bottle of cranberry juice. Nothing in the crispers, nothing in the butter shelf. It was the cleanest fridge she'd ever seen. She opened the freezer. The icemaker tray was full but the freezer itself was empty. She had Sam take some photos of the contents.

She checked the cabinets. One contained ten highball glasses, all positioned symmetrically in relation to each other. The next cabinet over held ten plates, plain white with a black edging. Stainless steel pots and pans hung over the island in the center of the room, a combination countertop and two-burner cookery. The pots looked brand new, hung in descending order of size. She found the silverware drawer. Ten each of forks, knives, spoons, and soup spoons. Cooking implements—stainless steel—hung on a rack fastened to the side of the island. She went through the rest of the cabinets and found nothing. No food. No crumbs. A bit of dust, but that was typical New Mexico. Nobody lived here for any amount of time without a dust build-up in unexpected places. Sam snapped more photos of the cabinets' contents.

Parks muttered something to Chaz, who said nothing. Chris knew Chaz was studying her. And Chaz knew that she was aware of what he was doing. She opened the drawers of the kitchen island. *Get a good look,* she silently told him. *Because if you try anything, mine will be the last face you see.* She straightened. Nothing in the island, either.

The door off the laundry room took them into the garage. Sam looked to his right and found the light switch and the push pad for the main door. He flicked the first and pressed the second and the door to the driveway opened with clicks and creaks.

"I'll have a look at the vehicle," Sam said, hefting his crime scene toolbox and crossing the concrete floor to the outside.

"Jesus," Harper said, looking around. "This guy is a freakin' robot. This is the cleanest garage I've ever seen."

Chris waited for a comment about gay men and garages but it didn't come.

"I don't think he even parks in here," Harper continued. "I don't see any tire marks on the floor." He paced the length of the garage, looking down. "Ah-ha. Dirt in the corner. He might be human."

Neatly arranged plastic bottles of oil, transmission fluid, and windshield washer fluid occupied the shelves. On the wall the garage shared with the kitchen hung a variety of tools but upon closer inspection, Chris doubted they'd ever been used. No sporting equipment, no boxes, no piles of stuff that most people would put in their garages until one day, they'd look at it and say: "Okay, time to get rid of this shit." Nothing like that.

"What's your take?" she asked Harper.

He shrugged, still scanning the walls. "Our guy's got a few hang-ups. OCD to an extreme. He'll probably have to bleach the whole place once we're gone." He tossed her a glance. "I'm gonna borrow Sam's luminol."

Harper approached the SUV where Sam was working and returned with a spray bottle. He picked a few places on the shelves and sprayed. He also sprayed the step up into the kitchen. Finally, he sprayed a path from the kitchen to the middle of the garage floor and then closer to the door. They waited a few minutes. Nothing.

"Damn," Harper grunted.

"I have a thought," Chris said quietly.

Harper looked at her. They were standing half-in, half-out of the garage in the lengthening evening shadows.

"I'm pretty sure those are Travis's clothes that Sam bagged. What bothers me is that Chaz didn't get rid of 'em. He knew yesterday we were up his ass. Why would he take that chance?"

Harper rocked forward on his feet, absently watching Sam at the Lexus. Chris decided the quirk was, indeed, a meditative thing for him.

"Plus," Chris continued, "Chaz doesn't wear white. No white socks, no white underwear. But he went out and bought a brand new white tee. And he had to buy it as a single, which means an odd number. He bought it so he would have *two* white tees. Including Travis's. That had to be hard. He probably buys his clothes in even numbers. And he bought in a color that stresses him out. Then he put it in his dresser."

Harper nodded, still watching Jeff. "So he wanted to keep Travis's clothes. That's kind of trophy behavior."

"Maybe. Maybe not," Chris said. "Think about Travis. He'd been cleaned off. Death is not pretty. Whatever you ate and drank before you catch that final ride comes out. Chaz is smart, yeah, but maybe his motivation for doing the clean-off and preparation with the Bible verse on Travis's chest and the cross under the tongue isn't just about hiding his tracks. Maybe it's about guilt."

Harper swiveled his gaze back to her. "Damn, Gucci. You might be on to something."

Chris gestured for him to follow her down the driveway, out of earshot of the house. "And think about white. It's a color of purity in a lot of cultures. Like a wedding gown. Chaz doesn't do white. I don't think that's just about fashion or OCD. He doesn't feel pure enough to do it."

Harper stared at her, a strange expression on his face. "Goddamn," he said softly. "He kept McCormick's clothes to remind himself of what he did. And not in a good way."

Chris shrugged again. "It's possible. I don't know whether he actually consciously recognizes that he does these things partially out of a sense of guilt. As far as I'm concerned, he's sociopathic on lots of levels and still a predator prone to violent outbursts. But there's always a calculation behind the violence. He knows how far to take it to get the results he's looking for. With Travis and Tyler, he had to take it over the line because they weren't the kind to shut up."

Harper was nodding more emphatically. "And Stillman's kind of a pussy." He stopped suddenly and cleared his throat, realizing what he had said. Chris motioned him to go on. She'd heard it and worse before. Harper continued. "Stillman's easy to push around. So our guy beats him up a little, tells him to shut the hell up, and Stillman does it."

Chris smiled grimly. "Shit, he's been doing it for years. He's been Chaz's little pool boy, as you said, since college, at least. He covers for Chaz, too." Chris's voice trailed off. *Covers for him.* "Oh, my God."

"What?" Harper looked at her.

"Stillman covers for Chaz. What if Chaz never brought Travis to *this* house? Why would he? I mean, look at it. What if he didn't kill him here after all?"

Harper jumped onto her thought, eyes widening slightly. "Stillman's. He killed McCormick at Stillman's."

Chris stared at him. "Chaz was the guy Kevin had over that night. But it was after the fact, after the movie party. And Travis was with him."

They both turned at the sound of a car door closing. Sam was done with the Lexus. He joined them with his kit. "Not much," Jeff said. "No surprise, given the inside of the house. I got some fibers for comparison purposes. If McCormick was in that vehicle dead, there might be epithelials in the back. I took samples from several areas and we'll check 'em, but I'm betting Mumford used some kind of liner back there. Probably plastic."

Chris and Harper exchanged glances.

"All right." Sam smiled. "Now for the fun part. DNA swab. I'm expecting him to bite the tip off and swallow it."

"But not to cover his tracks," Harper said blandly. "He'll want you to dig through his shit for it later. To make a point."

Sam's expression said *eeww*. "Jesus, Harper. That is beyond wrong."

"This from a guy who studies stomach contents under a microscope." Harper shook his head and looked at Chris before he headed up the driveway. She followed him back toward the front door so they could wrap a few things up with Chaz and Parks, including the discovery of illicit drugs in the house. It wasn't much, but it would have to do for now. They probably couldn't bring him in on that yet, but it was a bargaining point. They also needed to pay a visit to Kevin Stillman because if there was a crack in Chaz's carefully orchestrated façade, Stillman was it.

HARPER PARKED IN such a way that he blocked Kevin Stillman's driveway. He and Chris got out of the vehicle and headed up the short driveway to an even shorter walk that took them to the front door. The units were nondescript faux-dobe townhouse style, bunched in threes. Each one claimed a small patch of lawn out front. This time of year, the grass was a yellowish-brown. Raised stoops served as porches. Harper stepped up and pressed the doorbell, then looked up to his right. It was nearly dark but Chris followed his line of vision and saw an elderly white woman in the upstairs window of the neighboring unit. Harper stepped back slightly so she could see him. He waved and she waved back, smiling a bit. Kevin's "nosy neighbor."

"You've got quite a way with the ladies," Chris said, stifling a laugh.

He grunted softly and flashed a half-smile. "You'd know."

Chris stared at him, not sure how to address this comment. Joke? Sarcasm? Kevin's door opened before she could. When he recognized them, he started to close it, but Harper's big left hand stopped the motion.

"Mr. Stillman," he said quietly. "Could we have a word with you?"

"Leave me alone," Kevin said between his teeth, around his wired jaw. He had to talk with his teeth clenched together. Chris inspected him in the pale yellow glow from the porch light. He looked like a pissed-off raccoon, with his black eyes and bruised jaw. But he also appeared extremely tired, and the haunted expression in his eyes told Chris that Kevin might be ready to talk.

"Please," Harper said in his most patient tone.

Kevin looked past him to the street, suspicious and wary. With pronounced resignation, he opened the door and moved aside so they could enter. He shut the door behind them and looked sullenly from one to the other. He wore baggy grey sweats and sweatshirt.

Chris appraised the interior. Unlike Chaz, Kevin clearly lived in his place. Big, comfortable-looking furniture, a television droning in the background. A staircase to the right led to the second floor. Photographs of people Chris surmised were relatives and friends hung at intervals on the stairwell walls. A pair of battered muddy tennis shoes had been tossed near the bottom steps. Chaz would've had a cow at that. Kevin didn't lead them into the interior and Chris didn't push it.

Chris caught Harper's eye and he nodded. She looked at Kevin.

"Why won't you press charges against Chaz?" she asked. Sometimes getting right to the heart of a matter kept people off-balance and they ended up revealing more than they intended. In this case, her words had that effect.

Kevin's eyes widened slightly and he shook his head. "I can't."

So it was Chaz who beat the shit out of him. "Kevin," Chris said, using his given name to encourage intimacy, "we can help you. What Chaz did was wrong. It's assault."

Kevin shook his head sadly. "He doesn't mean it," he said, trying to articulate his words around the wire in his jaw. He looked at her then, with an "oh, shit" expression when he realized what he had just revealed.

Gotcha. "I understand," Chris said, calling on her counseling background. "You've been friends with him for a long time. So you know him pretty well."

Kevin stared at her, fearful.

"But friends don't beat each other up," she continued. "Chaz is sick. He needs some help. He needs help to stop hurting people he cares about. Like you." She let a pause settle over them. "And Travis." Another pause. "And Tyler."

Even beneath the bruises on his face and his black eyes, Kevin's face paled. "I can't talk about that. He told me not to." He sounded very small and very young, like a kid brother who's been beaten down most of his life.

"I know." Chris kept her tone quiet. "And you're trying to protect him. That's what you've done since you met him, isn't it?"

Kevin looked down at the carpet. His shoulders started to shake. He was crying. Harper shifted his weight, body language awkward and uncertain.

"He's tried so hard," Kevin said between sobs. "When he was little, his dad used to beat him for being queer. He called Chaz a sissy-boy. And a faggot. And whatever else." Kevin groaned, trying to breathe. He slurped some of his words as they gathered behind his clenched teeth. "Chaz told me that sometimes, his dad would force him to watch him have sex with prostitutes. This was when he was a little kid." He coughed then. Harper pulled a travel pack of Kleenex out of his inside coat pocket. He opened it and handed one to Kevin, who wiped his nose, wincing as he did so.

"Other times," Kevin continued, "his dad would drink and then tear up the house and he'd force Chaz to clean it. Then he'd inspect — his dad was in the Army — and if it wasn't good enough, Chaz would have to clean it again." He drew a sobbing breath. "It was never good enough and his dad would tell him he couldn't even be a decent faggot because he wasn't a good housekeeper."

No wonder Chaz has issues. If it was true. "What about his mom?" Chris asked as Harper handed Kevin another Kleenex.

Kevin shook his head. "She died when Chaz was born. I think his dad must've blamed him for that." He gingerly blew his nose, clearly trying to be careful. He was trying to talk, breathe, and cry with his teeth clamped shut and he coughed again.

"No siblings?" she asked.

Kevin shook his head.

"What happened to his father?"

"I don't know. Chaz said he left home after he graduated from high school and never went back. He said he's never talked to his dad since he left."

I'll bet no one else has, either. Chris had a feeling Daddy Dearest departed this earth about the time Chaz left home. "See?" she said to Kevin. "Chaz needs some help. All those terrible things that happened to him growing up — no child should have to go through that. Chaz needs help, Kevin. But he probably won't do it on his own. We can get him that help if you tell us what happened to you and Travis."

Kevin was silent for a long while. Tears rolled down his cheeks. "I can't," he said, sounding miserable. "You don't understand. I can't tell you."

"Because he'll hurt you?"

Kevin shrugged. "This? He's done this to me before."

Chris knew Harper was looking at her, but she didn't take her eyes off Kevin's face. "When?"

"A few times." Kevin's response was vague. "The last time was last summer, I think."

"That's not a nice thing to do to someone. Beat him up like that. Chaz needs help, Kevin. He needs help controlling his anger. What happened to Travis?" She shifted the focus quickly, a technique she had learned from Jerry.

Kevin shook his head.

"Did Travis make Chaz mad?"

"Chaz liked Travis," Kevin said. He wouldn't look at either Chris or Harper directly. "But Travis wanted more from Chaz. He wanted Chaz to come out. And he was jealous, too, because Chaz had friends in New Hope."

Chris briefly met Harper's gaze. "What kind of friends?"

Kevin gestured vaguely. "For sex. Chaz tried really hard not to like men. He even got engaged three times. He got married once, too. But he couldn't—you know. With women."

"Has Chaz ever had a steady boyfriend?" Chris kept her tone conversational, non-judgmental.

Kevin looked at her then, pain stamped on his face. "No. But I keep trying."

Jesus. Kevin's in love with Chaz.

"That's why I can't tell you anything." Kevin rubbed his right forearm absently with his left hand. "I can take the beatings. I can take his temper. But I can't take losing him. And he said if I told, he'd go away again, this time for good." Another tear ran down his cheek.

Harper handed him another tissue.

"Did Travis know that you care so much about Chaz?" Chris switched topics.

"Yeah. He found out before he—" Kevin cleared his throat, clearly nervous.

"How did he find out?"

"He said he had heard a rumor and he asked me. I couldn't lie."

Debbie. Chris waited a few moments for Kevin to regain his composure. "Did Travis like Chaz?"

Kevin nodded sadly. "Travis was a really nice guy. He was cute and funny and sweet. But he didn't know Chaz like I do. All Travis could give him was sex. But from me, Chaz got love, too."

Chris's mind was reeling through possibilities. "Why did Chaz kill Travis?"

"Travis said he'd—" Kevin stopped and gave her a look that was a mixture of anger and fear.

"He'd what?" Chris continued as if nothing had happened. "Out Chaz? Why didn't Chaz just beat Travis up like he did James Bates?"

If Kevin's jaw could drop, it would have. As it was, he stared at her, seemingly struck dumb.

"Kevin," Chris pressed, "we know Chaz killed Travis. And we're pretty sure he killed him here, in your house. The night of the movie. After everyone went home, Chaz showed up with Travis around four." She waited, letting that sink in. "We're also pretty sure you know all of this, which makes you an accessory to murder."

He sucked air through his clenched teeth and furiously rubbed his forearm.

"Chaz brought him here, didn't he?" Chris pushed her advantage. "And Travis wasn't lucid. He was drugged. Chaz undressed him and put him in your bathtub. He strangled him and then cleaned up. Then he wrapped him in plastic—I'm guessing a shower curtain—and maybe a blanket and took him out to his car. Is that how it went down?"

Kevin sucked more air through his clenched teeth and cried harder.

"Now," Chris softened her tone, "if you cooperate with us, the DA'll probably be willing to cut you some slack. Especially given the extenuating circumstances here. Chaz threatened you and you were afraid to say anything. If you don't cooperate, we will subpoena you—and I can have that within an hour or two—and we'll take you down to the station and charge you as an accessory." She sighed. "I don't want to have to do that. You're not a killer. You're not that kind of person. But Chaz could be in a lot of trouble and he's pulled you into it."

Kevin sniffled. He looked like a rabbit in the middle of a road watching a Mack truck approach at top speed.

"It's only going to get worse." Chris hoped she sounded resigned. "It's only a matter of time before Chaz does something else and drags you down even more. I know you love him. But you can't help him if you're sitting in prison."

Kevin shifted his weight from one foot to the other and dabbed at his eyes. Chris could sense he was wavering. Harper was writing in his notebook. Chris glanced over at him. Harper was so damn subtle with that notebook. She returned her focus back to Kevin.

"If I tell you," he said softly in his odd little boy voice, "will you help him?"

A sharp little jag of sadness pierced her heart for this man, who for at least twenty years had put up with God knows what kind of abuse because he thought Chaz was the best he could do for love. *What happened to you, Kevin? What caused you to think this is love?* "We'll do what we can to get him some help. You need to understand, however, that Chaz will probably be charged with murder. Because of his history, however, there's a possibility the courts might have him serve time in a psychiatric ward instead of a prison. He might be safer there." She moved a little closer to Kevin and forced him to look into her eyes. "But it can't start without you."

He sighed and another round of tears tracked down his thin, bruised cheeks. Harper handed him the remainder of the tissue pack. Kevin took one out and wiped his eyes—gingerly—before he swallowed. He looked at Harper, then at Chris, and the anguish in his expression was palpable, like the metallic tang of an impending storm.

"God forgive me," he finally whispered.

CHRIS SAT IN the front seat of her car, staring at the Styrofoam cup of coffee on her dashboard, thinking about the emotional train wreck that called itself Kevin Stillman. He'd gone on record when they brought him in and for another three hours Chris and Harper had listened to his descriptions of all the things Chaz did, and how he made Kevin keep quiet about them.

She looked up as Harper approached, his hands buried in the side pockets of his trenchcoat.

"How're you doing?" he asked as he stopped next to her car door and looked down at her.

"Tired. You?"

He rocked forward onto the balls of his feet. "Yep. Stillman's on his way to protective custody and the arrest warrant for Mumford is on its way over. You want in on the roundup? We'll pick him up as soon as the warrant's here."

Chris shook her head. "No."

He frowned. "You okay?"

She regarded him, surprised at his concern but also touched. "Just drained. You know how that goes. You ride the case and then sometimes you get that big break and everything you worked for comes together." She studied the coffee in her cup. "But Travis is still dead. Tyler's still dead. And what Chaz has been up to is going to affect lots of people. There'll be lots of media. Lots of shit. Court appearances. Snotty defense attorneys." She sighed and took a drink. "Why the fuck do I do this job?"

Harper smiled. "Adrenaline junkie."

"I could do without some of that for a while."

"Nah. Get some sleep. You'll be saddlin' up tomorrow again."

Chris laughed. "Thanks, Harper."

"Yep." He glanced back at the main entrance to the station then back at her. "I'll let you know how it all goes. Boss-man wants a briefing tomorrow at ten, by the way."

"Yeah, I know. I'll see you there."

"Okay, then. Take it easy." He turned and walked back toward the station's entrance. Chris watched him until he had gone inside. Hadn't been so bad after all, working with him. She adjusted her position in her front seat and stared out the windshield, hungry, tired, and wanting nothing more to do with Kevin Stillman's warped view of love, twisted religious convictions, Chaz Mumford's ultra-compulsive and psychotic streaks, or the blood on both their hands. She felt toxic, like some kind of vile sludge filled her veins.

Chris poured the coffee out onto the asphalt and tossed the cup onto the floorboards near the passenger seat. She should go home, get some sleep. Maybe eat. Her personal cell phone beeped in her jacket pocket again, reminding her that she had messages, so she removed it and checked. K.C. had called and so had Dayna. John's message was from earlier today and though she'd already caught up with him, she hadn't erased it. Dayna's message was the most recent, left about thirty minutes ago when Chris was still dealing with Kevin. She didn't bother to check it first and instead pressed twenty-five, the speed-dial code for Dayna's cell and Chris's high school basketball number.

Dayna picked up on the third ring. "Hey," she said, the warmth in her voice a cleansing comfort. "Where are you?"

"Still at the station. You?"

"Home. Are you done for the day?"

"Something like that," Chris said, thinking that she really wanted a shower.

"Come over."

"I've had a rough day." A lump formed in her throat.

"I know," Dayna acknowledged. "I can hear it in your voice."

Chris stared blankly at the dashboard. *I should go home. I shouldn't lay this shit on her.* "I'm not used to..." Chris paused and swallowed. "I don't know how to be with you when I'm feeling like this." *And I don't know how to keep you safe from it.*

"Come over and we'll start figuring it out."

The heat of tears gathered in her eyes and Chris wasn't sure whether relief, exhaustion, or a mixture of the two brought them to her eyes. "I need you," she whispered.

"I'm here." Dayna's smile raced right through the phone and wrapped itself around Chris's heart. "And I'm waiting for you."

Chapter
Twenty

CHRIS OPENED HER eyes, trying to figure out what woke her up. *What the fuck?* Her cell phone. *Shit.* She carefully and quickly extricated herself from both Dayna's embrace and the bed, glad the jar candle on the bedside table was burning because it afforded a bit of light. She had left her business cell phone attached to her trousers, which were on the floor at the foot of the bed. Dayna mumbled something as Chris pulled the phone off her pants and answered, moving quickly into the hallway.

"Yeah. Gutierrez."

"Chris. It's Dale."

The hairs on the back of her neck went up. He never called her by her given name. "What's up?"

"Our guy's bailed." He sounded tense.

Chris inhaled then exhaled. "Fuck. What happened?" She headed into the kitchen and leaned against the counter, ignoring the chill on her bare skin. She glanced at the clock on the microwave. Two-sixteen AM.

"Not sure yet. Stillman's with him."

"Oh, *hell*, no." *What is this? Bonnie and Clyde?*

"Stillman asked if he could get some clothes from his house, so Calloway drove him up there and went in with him and apparently Chaz was already there. Stillman opened the front door and went in first. Calloway was right behind him and Chaz did a little blunt force trauma on Calloway's head. We don't know if Stillman went with him willingly, but I'm betting Stillman got a call to Chaz and spilled his guts." He sounded frustrated.

"Fuck," Chris breathed. "Chaz probably manipulated Kevin into whatever the hell he's doing now. What are they driving?"

"Stillman's Ford Explorer. We've got an APB out and so far, no sign."

"How's Calloway?" Chris massaged her forehead.

"Concussion. He'll live."

Thank God. "Do you want me to come in?"

"Not yet. Are you at home?" His voice held a strange note.

"No."

"Good. Listen, I've got a bad feeling about this. Don't go home for a while, okay?"

A chill galloped down her spine. "Why not? What the fuck?"

"I don't think Chaz likes you too much. I think he might fixate on you, especially since you're the one who got Stillman to talk."

"I'm unlisted everywhere, Harper."

"Humor me."

"Fine," she relented. For all his quirks, he did have good instincts. "So what's the plan?"

"We've got his place and Stillman's under surveillance. I'm going to send a car past your place, too. Just in case. Nothing for you to do right now. I'm gonna try to get a few hours of sleep. We've got a command post up. I'll be there at seven."

"All right. I'll see you then."

"Okay, then. Keep your phone charged." He hung up.

Dammit. Chris closed her phone and absently stared at the outside of Dayna's refrigerator. She heard a rustle in the doorway and turned. Dayna, wrapped in a thin blue robe, watching Chris, questions and worry in her eyes.

"That was Harper. Mumford's on the run with Stillman. That's all I can tell you." Chris smiled tightly. "I'm sorry. Cop stuff. It comes up at really inopportune times."

Dayna snuggled into Chris's embrace. "I knew that going in." She rested her head on Chris's shoulder. "It's one of the things I love and respect about you."

Love? Chris tried to swallow but couldn't. She pulled Dayna closer against her, as if such were possible, and brushed her lips against Dayna's hair. "You say that *now*," she half-teased, "but give it a few months."

Dayna pulled away, hands on Chris's forearms, and stood regarding her. The expression in her eyes reminded Chris of Friday night. "I already have," Dayna said simply. "Come back to bed." She moved toward the doorway, holding Chris's hands. "Though I do enjoy the sight of you naked in my kitchen—" she smiled "we'll have to try that one out another time."

Chris released one of Dayna's hands and picked her phone up from the counter, then allowed Dayna to pull her down the hallway back to the bedroom. They cuddled under the covers and Dayna fitted herself around Chris, holding her. "Get some sleep," she said softly in Chris's ear.

Chris hugged her close. The last thing on her mind before she fell asleep was the look in Dayna's eyes and the sweet ache of possibility.

HARPER RUBBED HIS eyes for the hundredth time that morning and glowered. "Not at home. Not at work. Not at Stillman's. Nobody's seen the vehicle. Nobody's heard from him. We've got a media blast going, a nationwide alert, and nobody knows where the hell they are." He ran a hand over his head. "You'd think they caught a ride home with the goddamn Roswell aliens."

Chris took another round around the room, pacing. The largest conference room had been transformed into an impromptu command center. Tables now lined the walls and phones and computers were plugged into every available outlet. Personnel with headsets on were busy fielding hundreds of tips via phone and e-mail, after which they'd pass them to others who sorted through to determine which were the most credible. Nearly eleven. Chris had been here since 6:30 that morning. *Where the fuck are you?* She stopped pacing and sat down at the end of a table and studied Kevin's confession again, hoping maybe something would jump out at her, tell her where they were.

Yes, Chaz had brought Travis to Kevin's around 4:00 in the morning on Saturday, January 21st. Chaz was upset. Travis wasn't coherent. As Chris and Harper suspected, Chaz put Travis in the downstairs bathtub and strangled him with the electrical cord. Kevin admitted it was an extension cord that Chaz cut the ends off of. Chaz went out to his vehicle and returned with a plastic shower curtain liner. He turned the shower on and ran it on Travis's body for a while — Kevin estimated about fifteen minutes. Kevin said Chaz sobbed the whole time and stroked Travis's hair. Travis must have been sitting up, Chris figured, because Chaz didn't get that hair gel off of his body. Chaz also took the fake goatee off at Kevin's and told Kevin to get rid of it, along with Travis's shoes.

Chris stopped reading. She sat back, thinking. Fortunately, Kevin said he didn't. He said the beard was in the top drawer of his dresser though Travis's shoes were somewhere at a landfill. She read further. Chaz turned the water off in the bathtub and left Travis there for a while, maybe fifteen minutes, waiting for his body to dry a bit. He then lifted — lifted? Jesus, Chaz was strong. No problem carrying him from outside the Nature Center to the gravesite. It probably took him ten minutes, but he could do it.

She continued. Chaz lifted Travis out of the bathtub and placed him on the shower curtain liner and dragged Travis through the house. At the front door, he used the electrical cord to tie Travis's hands behind his back because according to Chaz, Kevin said, it was easier to wrap a body in something if the hands were tied. The arms wouldn't get in the way. *Good tip,* Chris thought sarcastically. Chaz wrapped Travis in the liner then rolled him in a length of carpet he'd brought. Harper asked where he got the carpet and Kevin said he didn't know. Chaz just showed up with it. *The church, maybe.*

Chris turned the page. According to Kevin, Chaz was very strong. *Obviously.* Kevin helped haul Travis to his feet in the carpet roll — not looking good for him as an unwilling participant — and Chaz slung the carpet with Travis in it over his shoulder. He put Travis in his Lexus. He then drove away and Kevin didn't know where he took Travis until the news broke about a body in the bosque, at which point Kevin said he had a feeling it was Travis though he didn't ask and Chaz didn't say. After Chris and Harper questioned Chaz at Wellspring the first time, however, Chaz called Kevin and told him not to say anything about Travis, that it could make things hard for both of them. So Kevin tried to keep his mouth shut, but thanks to K.C., Chris had a lot of ammo and she was able to extricate bits and pieces from him.

She started pacing again. Chaz had to make the Sunday service at Wellspring after he killed Travis. But he also had to get rid of Travis's body. Would an hour before dawn have been enough? Lots of people used the bosque trails for early morning work-outs, even in January. She tapped a pen against her thigh. It was possible that Chaz had waited to bury Travis Sunday night. Rigor might have come and gone since then. Given Travis's size and weight, he might have finished his rigor cycle by late Sunday night, early Monday morning. That might have been what Chaz did. Whether he buried Travis Sunday morning or Sunday night, Chaz had managed to get him into the ground and that's where Travis remained for at least five days.

She sat back down in the chair, oblivious to the controlled chaos around her. The bosque. Chris mulled that over. There were lots of places along the Rio Grande to hide. Anybody could conceal themselves right there within city limits for days. Hell, an entire shanty town of fifty homeless people had resided along the river for months, no one the wiser. No matter how dedicated the bosque rangers, they couldn't patrol all of it all the time. Shit, the Middle Rio Grande Conservancy District stretched for a good thirty miles, from Sandia Pueblo north of the city to Isleta Pueblo south of it.

"Harper," she called over to him.

He was standing over one of the phone monitors, hands on his hips. "Yeah?"

"The bosque," she said.

His eyes narrowed and he sucked his breath through his teeth as he rocked forward onto the balls of his feet. "I like it. I'll see if we can get a couple of patrols over there. Where do you think?"

"I think he might just access from the Nature Center." *Symbolism. Travis's final resting place.* "In fact, let's call over there and see if Stillman's Explorer is in the parking lot."

Harper actually grinned. "I'm on it."

Chris read through the rest of Kevin's statement. Yes, Chaz had also killed Tyler. But Kevin didn't know about it right away because at the time, he was in Albuquerque and Chaz was in Las Cruces. Kevin found out when Chaz confessed to him soon after he arrived at Wellspring and asked Kevin to please start an ex-gay group to help Chaz deal with his urges. Kevin asked him why he killed Tyler and Chaz said Tyler wanted too much from him. He had asked Tyler to meet him at a motel the night of Tyler's death. Chaz drugged Tyler, they had "carnal relations," as he put it, then he drugged him again. He put him in the bathtub and killed him the same way he killed Travis.

Harper had asked Kevin what the significance of "John 3:16" might be to Chaz and Kevin said it was Chaz's favorite verse. He liked to meditate on it, especially, but he rarely talked openly about it. Harper then asked if Chaz wore any jewelry and Kevin said yes, he liked to wear a small gold cross on a chain around his neck.

"Got it," Harper said, interrupting her thoughts. "Ford Explorer in the Nature Center parking lot. Maroon. We're running a check on the VIN, since the plate's missing. It's backed into a space, so you don't know the plate's missing right off." He studied her for a bit. "I'm not sure whether that's a good thing or a bad thing that you figured that out. Psychic bonding with a psycho and all."

"Think about it," she said as she set Kevin's statement on the table. "If he wanted to access from a more isolated area, the vehicle would be too obvious. He knows there's an alert for him. He knows we're probably looking for a maroon Ford Explorer and that anybody with half a brain is, too." She paused, thinking. "So if a car matching the description is parked on the side of the road near the bosque or parked at a pull-out that only holds a couple of cars, chances are, it'll get more notice. But in a place where all kinds of SUVs go, and there are lots of people around, Stillman's vehicle might escape notice right off. I'm thinking he drove over to that neighborhood by the Nature Center last night after he picked Kevin up and then parked near one of those houses over there. Or possibly got into one of the gated communities. He just waited until morning then drove into the parking lot at the Nature Center and took Kevin for a walk."

Harper nodded thoughtfully. "So what are they doing?"

"I don't know," Chris admitted. "Hiding? Butch and Sundance?"

"Each other," a rookie cop with a headset commented when he overheard Harper's question. Both Chris and Harper shot him a glare at the same time. He flushed and turned back to his computer screen.

Chris's business cell rang. She removed it from her belt and looked at the ID. She didn't recognize the number, but answered anyway.

"Chris Gutierrez."

"You weren't at home last night, De-*tec*-tive." The last word oozed with sarcasm.

Chris was on her feet in one motion. "Chaz," she said smoothly. Harper's eyes widened and he immediately began quieting everyone in the room.

"Where are you?" Chris asked.

"We waited for you, De-*tec*-tive. Waited for you to come home. But you were lucky and you didn't."

Had Chris swallowed liquid nitrogen, she wouldn't have felt as cold as she did at Chaz's words. *You son of a bitch.* Harper was right. Chaz must've followed her at some point. Or he was just playing her. Somehow, she didn't think that was the case. He might've been parked somewhere near her house all night. The thought galled her.

"Where are you?" She ignored his taunts and kept her voice level.

"Such a professional," he hissed. "Professional cop. Professional dyke."

He's one to talk. "Where's Kevin?" She strained to hear anything past him, to hear Kevin say something. Any kind of background noise to help pinpoint his location.

"Kevin is busy. He's weak. Allowed himself to be manipulated by a fucking dyke whore."

Chris felt her temper rise, reminded herself that Chaz was a fuck-case and psychotic and knew what to say to get a rise out of her. She wouldn't give him the pleasure. Harper was leaning in, listening. She held the phone slightly away from her ear to make it easier for him. "Chaz, it's over. We know what you did to Tyler and Travis. Turn yourself in. Don't make this harder for yourself than it already is."

"Come and get me," he said in a low, dangerous voice.

"Tell us where and we'll send a car over." She refused to let him bait her.

"No. *You* come and get me."

Chris locked eyes with Harper. *What the fuck?* He shook his head vehemently.

"You," Chaz continued, "only you. I'll come in if *you* arrest me."

What the hell kind of sick game is this? "Okay. But I can't do that if I don't know where you are."

"One hour."

"Where?" *Slippery bastard.*

"Where it all began with you, De-*tec*-tive."

Chris bit back an urge to tell him to fuck off. "Where you buried

Travis? Near the Nature Center?"

"One hour. Only you. If I see others, I'll finish what I started with Kevin." And he hung up.

Slowly, movement and sound returned to the room.

Harper was like a man frozen. "Kevin's a write-off," he said quietly. "This is bullshit. We're not sending an officer into a hostage crisis without back-up."

"This isn't about Kevin," Chris said quietly. "It's about a blaze of glory. Suicide by cop. And he wants *me* to do the honors." *Holy fuck.*

NOT FOR THE first time during the past hour, Mary Magdalene flashed through Chris's mind. Except she didn't shoot anybody, like Chaz apparently wanted Chris to do to him. Chris adjusted the Kevlar vest over her T-shirt. She could move well in a vest, and she made it a point sometimes to work out in one so she knew what she could and could not do and how to compensate. She pulled a plain grey sweatshirt on over it. She had changed into her tactical boots, which she kept in her office.

Chris was in jeans today because that was what she had in her gym bag in her car. She didn't go home to change that morning. Dayna had loaned her the T-shirt Chris was wearing, plain navy blue. It hugged Chris's body a little tighter than she was used to, but it wasn't unlike the tees she wore as a recruit underneath her button-downs. "It's a lucky shirt," Dayna said before she kissed Chris into next year and then poured her a sleek stainless steel thermos full of fresh ground coffee to take with her.

That's it, Chris remembered thinking. *I'm a complete goner. K.C.'s right. This is totally the "L" word.* And it felt wonderful and safe and completely real, though still a little scary. But she wanted to run outside and shout it to the entire city, to the whole state, and then the world. Instead she just pulled Dayna against her and held her close for a long moment.

And now here she was, on her way to the bosque to meet with a misogynist homophobic and ironically gay killer who apparently wanted her to redeem him for all his bad deeds. Chris slowed the unmarked police car at the entrance to the Nature Center and turned into the parking lot.

She quickly shut any other thoughts out of her mind, any thoughts about the people she wished she had called that day to tell them she loved them and how much they meant to her. *Fucking downer*, she told herself as she pulled into a parking space and shut the engine off. She put her cell phones into her glove box. *Cop stuff. This is cop stuff. All part of a day's work.* She took a deep breath and stepped out of the car. She locked up, like she was just one of dozens of other people who was headed out for a nice little stroll in the bosque on a brisk February day.

Chris crossed the parking lot and took the short walk to the bike path, over the pedestrian bridge. She saw a few walkers, two with dogs on leashes. Three cyclists cruised by. One she recognized from the force. Harper had worked fast, putting twenty cops on the ground here. The cyclists stopped just past the trail to the parking lot and dismounted, laughing and talking, seemingly taking a water break and inspecting their bikes.

Chris crossed the bike path and started down the trail toward the river. She wore a loose black windbreaker and she had holstered her gun under her left arm, butt pointing away from her so she could grab it easily with her right hand. She moved slowly, like she was enjoying the scenery and the air. A man and a woman passed, debating what kind of tree something was. Dressed in jeans and tennis shoes, both wore fleece jackets and looked for all the world like granola hippies from Santa Fe. Chris recognized them, too, as she walked past. They nodded at her, fellow wildlife enjoyers. Fellow cops. *Thank God.*

Afternoon sunlight lanced through the tangle of cottonwoods and smaller trees, splashing the dirt path underfoot in strange patterns. Chris kept her pace steady and relaxed slightly though she was on high alert. She walked halfway to the river, then turned left down a much narrower path that BMX bikes had carved out of the underbrush. Another twenty yards or so and she emerged into the clearing where Paul Woodfin had found Travis's body. She took in the whole clearing quickly. Sight, sound, smell. The crime lab had filled in the grave, but she knew exactly where it had been.

She had entered the clearing from the side closest to the river, thinking Chaz might expect her to take the more direct route. To her right stood the bike jump. Almost directly across from her was Travis's grave. No sign of Chaz. She stood on the edge of the clearing, waiting. Dead leaves rustled in the bushes around her as a breeze agitated them. Voices drifted from the main trail, clear in the crisp, dry air. She moved off the thin strip of trail behind a tree, its trunk offering some coverage should Chaz show up, guns blazing. From this new vantage point, she watched the clearing. Minutes crawled past. She forced herself to breathe evenly and maintain her position.

Movement in the underbrush from behind the bike jump. She reached under her arm and unsnapped the holster. Just in case. She didn't want to give this prick the satisfaction of getting his final wish. *If that's really what he wants.* Chaz appeared from behind the bike jump. He was half-dragging Kevin, who looked like he'd been worked over by a bunch of Thai kickboxers. Kevin's face was so swollen Chris doubted he could see. Blood had crusted at the corners of Kevin's mouth and his jaw looked off-kilter. *Jesus. That's got to hurt.* He was limping badly.

Here we go. Chris stepped out from behind the tree into the narrow path. She didn't enter the clearing, but she wanted to make herself visible. Chaz stopped when he saw her and a smirk played on his lips. He held his left index finger to his lips in an exaggerated show of telling her to keep quiet. In his left hand he held a knife. Eight-inch blade, Chris automatically estimated. Chaz touched the knife to the side of Kevin's face and held his finger to his lips again. He then motioned her to follow him back down the trail.

What in the holy fuck is he doing? "Chaz," she said in a low voice. Loud enough for him to hear, not loud enough to attract attention. "I'm here. This is over. Let's go."

"Just like a fucking woman," he hissed back at her. "Can't keep quiet. Won't listen." He drew the knife's tip along Kevin's left cheek. Kevin whimpered as a line of blood appeared. Chaz held the knife up for her to see. "Deeper next time."

In a quick motion, Chris drew her gun and trained it on Chaz. Forty feet between them. She needed a clear shot. She clicked the safety off. "Let him go. This is between you and me."

Chaz shifted and pulled Kevin between him and Chris, the knife at Kevin's throat. "I knew you wouldn't listen."

Chris kept her pistol trained on the little bit of Chaz's head she could see. She was a good shot. But she wasn't sure she was good enough for this one. She opted instead for Chaz's left leg. If she had to, she could probably put a bullet in his hip, but she needed a better angle. "Let him go, Chaz." She spoke a bit louder now, knowing the GPS tracker clipped to her vest was drawing Harper's hidden back-up closer. "I'm here like you wanted, to arrest you for the murder of Travis McCormick. I kept my end of the deal. Your turn." Her voice was calm, her gun steady. She was in full cop mode and the world had shrunk to just her, Chaz, and the distance between them. She could hear every sound in the clearing, from Kevin's labored breathing to the soft brush of Chaz's shirt against his skin as he moved.

"I never wanted to be like I am," he said in a strangely mechanical voice. "Never wanted it. I tried not to. Tell her, Kevin."

Kevin nodded once in agreement. Chris couldn't tell if he was looking at her, given his swollen eyelids.

"But God wouldn't hear me. I tried everything to get him to listen, to take the urge away, to stop my foul desires." Chaz was staring at her with his empty, reptilian gaze. "Nobody is supposed to be happy when they're this way. Nobody. Those who are—they're depraved. Evil."

"Is that why you killed Travis?" Chris prodded. "Because he was fine with who he was?"

Chaz watched her. "Travis didn't know that he was evil. He wouldn't listen." Chaz looked sad. "So I did the Lord's work."

Chris took another step to her left. Chaz mirrored with a step to his left, keeping Kevin between them.

"Maybe you didn't hear the Lord right," Chris said quietly. "Maybe He was trying to tell you that it's okay to be the way you are, and that it was your dad who was wrong."

"Don't you talk about my father," Chaz said between his teeth. "And don't you talk about God."

"Put the knife down, Chaz. Let Kevin go. It's over." Beyond Chaz and without having to move her eyes, Chris could see the male hippie granola guy, his own gun drawn, approaching Chaz stealthily from behind. Maybe thirty feet.

"No." Chaz pushed the knife against Kevin's throat and the tip slid into the flesh, drawing blood. Kevin struggled weakly, but Chaz was stronger. "Watch him die," he said flatly. "It's your fault."

"Cover!" yelled the hippie guy behind Chaz. Chris threw herself to her right and rolled as the hippie guy fired twice in quick succession. Chaz jerked at the sound of the voice and turned, releasing his hold on Kevin, who listed to the ground. One of the bullets tore into Chaz's right shoulder and he grunted. The second bullet missed and Chris thought she heard it hit a tree. She hoped that was what happened.

She was nearly on her feet when Chaz's full weight knocked her back onto the hard-packed earth of the trail. She struggled to catch her breath as he rained punches on her face and chest, even with his damaged arm. Chris struggled to fend off the blows. She still held her gun, but his punches were coming so close she couldn't position herself for a shot because of the speed of his fists and she wasn't sure she'd hit him. She might end up shooting another cop. Or herself. Somewhere, voices were yelling.

"Bitch. I told you not to bring back-up. Fucking bitch!" He grabbed the collar of her jacket and pulled so her head came off the ground and then he pushed, hard, slamming her head against the dirt. Needles of pain shot through her skull at the impact and she fought to maintain consciousness, working her right hand with her gun between his arms. Her eyes watered. He pulled on her collar again, probably for another head-slam. She rammed her hand and the side of her gun against his chin as hard as she could from her awkward angle. His head snapped backward and an exclamation of surprise and pain burst from his lips. He released her collar.

"Never had a bitch fight back, huh?" she rasped as she kicked, using her momentum to get out from under him. She gained her feet, slightly off-balance for a moment.

He lunged for her again and knocked her to her knees but this time, she had her pistol braced and ready. He stopped, his gaze moving from the gun to her face. He was panting and blood ran down his shoulder from the bullet wound and down his neck from Chris's blow. She kept her gun trained on his chest as she stood up. "Charles Mumford, you're under arrest for the murders of Travis McCormick and Tyler Henderson."

He glared at her, a cornered and wounded animal, as several people suddenly emerged from the surrounding foliage, guns drawn. Chris pulled a set of handcuffs out of her jacket pocket. Two officers — one the cyclist she recognized from the bike path and the other one of the dog-walkers — gripped Chaz's arms. Chris approached him with the handcuffs and with a quick motion of her left hand, she cuffed first his right wrist and then his left.

"You wanna do the honors?" the cyclist cop asked, smiling.

"Damn right I do," Chris said grimly. She reholstered her gun and adjusted her jacket over it before taking a firm grip on Chaz's left arm. She half-pushed him across the clearing to the narrow trail on the other side that would give them an easier time back to the Nature Center. Chaz said nothing and neither did Chris as they approached the parking lot. Her head throbbed and she quelled the urge to get one more punch in. The place was crawling with law enforcement. Any minute and the media would be here, too.

Harper met her at the bike path. He said nothing but he nodded once, a smile in his eyes. He followed them to a patrol car. Erin Halstead's. "Fancy meeting you here," she said as she opened the back passenger door.

Chris grinned in spite of the pounding in her head. It hurt to do so because her lip was swelling from one of Chaz's punches. She released Chaz's arm and maneuvered him onto the hard plastic back seat. "Make yourself at home," she said to him before she closed the door.

Erin smiled. "Just waiting on Jerry. And we'll get rid of Mumford for you."

"Thanks." Chris turned then to Harper. "And *muchas gracias* to you, *hombre*. I had no idea you were so good at that logistical shit."

He shrugged. "Military training."

"Well, who knew?"

"Not many." He motioned at her lip. "You're bleeding. When the paramedics get here for Stillman, check in with 'em."

She touched the back of her head carefully. A big knot and a dull ache.

"That was some damn good work," Harper said, hands in the

pockets of his trenchcoat.

"You were right," Chris said. "He did have some kind of issue with me. You're pretty good at reading people, Harper. Ever think about police work?"

He smiled. "Maybe. Seems like a lot of hassle, though."

Chris chuckled. Even that hurt and she winced. "Yeah. It does." She turned as an ambulance drove into the parking lot. "*Déjà vu* all over again," she muttered as it pulled up next to Erin's patrol car. Behind her, Kevin hobbled out of the bosque on his own power, a police officer on either side of him. *Damn. Tougher than I thought.* She headed over to the ambulance just as Jerry Torrez arrived in his own vehicle. And behind him, a media van pulled into the parking lot. Chris stood next to the open back doors of the ambulance, waiting for one of the EMTs to have a look at her head. A paramedic stopped what he was doing to examine her injuries. Chris described what had happened as he snapped on a pair of latex gloves.

"Yep. That's a nasty knock," he said as he carefully pulled Chris's hair aside. He took a pair of scissors and gently clipped a few strands to get a better look. "No bleeding. Lots of bruising. I'm gonna recommend you head on over to UNMH and get an X-ray. You can never be too careful."

She grimaced as he carefully prodded the back of her head. He then checked her bottom lip. "Won't need stitches on that. Too bad. Stitches on your lip are sexy. You'd get all kinds of dates that way."

She tried not to smile because it hurt her lip.

He examined her pupils and did some eye-movement tests. "All good there. You'll have a headache for a while. Big time. Try basic painkillers first. But get that X-ray ASAP." He smiled, teeth a flash of white against his dark skin.

"Thanks." She straightened.

"No problem. Good thing he didn't get a better grip on you. Could've done some major damage."

"No doubt." She grinned then, which hurt so she stopped. "But I do have my lucky T-shirt on."

"Oh, well, there you go. You oughtta market that sucker."

Chris gave him an I-don't-know-about-that look. "Can't. This shirt is one of a kind."

He nodded sagely. "Gotcha. I have my lucky drawers on my own self. Take it easy. Get that X-ray."

"Will do." She watched for a moment as they set to work examining Kevin, who sat on the gurney inside the ambulance. He looked like a meat-packing accident but he seemed functional. She went over to talk to Jerry about going to UNMH. Sometimes a call from him helped move things along a little faster. "X-ray first, statement later," Jerry told her sternly. "Call when you find out."

Ten minutes later, she was on her way to UNM Hospital in a patrol car. She relaxed as Officer Phillips drove, lights flashing but no siren. She watched out the window as the city raced past. Cop stuff. All part of a day's work.

Chapter
Twenty-one

CHRIS WASHED TWO Advil down with Diet Coke and surveyed her desk. The ache in her head she had downgraded from "oh, shit that hurts" to "just a little headache" over the past two days. She had organized all the files on Travis McCormick, including folders with information that K.C. had dug up. The originals were on file in the evidence room and the copies — what she had here — she locked in her file cabinet. She made sure that the files she had accumulated as a result of K.C.'s research included K.C.'s name and a list of her sources, which K.C. had supplied via e-mail at the beginning of the week.

Chris also called Tyler Henderson's parents to let them know that an arrest had been made in their son's murder and Mrs. Henderson had brusquely thanked her and hung up. Then Chris called Angela Griggs, who wasn't home, to let her know, as well, that someone had been arrested in Travis's death. Chris left a brief, polite message. She called Travis's father and left him a message, too. When she called Travis's Aunt Ellen and actually spoke to her, the relief and regret in Ellen's voice was tangible. Chris told her to call any time and she'd let her know when the trial started. She left the news on Jason Alvarez's voicemail, Josh Hopkins's, and James Bates's, too. When she finally hung up, she looked up at Al, who was standing in the entrance of her cubicle.

"Hey, good work," he said. He was one of many in a long line of well-wishers.

"Thanks. Couldn't have done it without Harper and my consultant, however. And your tip — thanks."

He shrugged. "Did you call Carl?"

"Hell, yes. He's ready to come up and review the materials for the court fight."

"He'll have a while," Al said dryly. "You know how long this shit takes."

Chris nodded.

"How's your head?" Al gestured with his hand.

"Sore. No scariness inside, though. Just surface bruising. They want me to check back Monday for another X-ray."

"Good." He nodded.

Chris waited. She had a feeling he wanted to say something more. Instead he waved and moved away and Chris went back to organizing. Starting in about an hour, she was on medical leave for a few days, Jerry's orders. She had spent all day yesterday — Thursday — giving statements and typing up her notes, popping super-strength ibuprofen that the doc at the emergency room provided. Her lip still hurt, though the swelling was down. Her tooth had caused the split when Chaz punched her and she still couldn't smile too much without a little sting of pain.

She thought about dinner that night with Dayna, Sage, and K.C. Sage immediately told her they could reschedule but Chris really needed to be around good vibes, so Sage shifted the venue. Rather than going out, they'd eat at K.C. and Sage's. Dayna loved the idea, as Chris knew she would. *I think I might be in love.* Or at least in serious like. Chris struggled not to smile because it hurt.

She finished stacking the files of the other cases she was working on in a neat pile on her desk. Something to keep her busy over the next few days. She put her leather jacket on and picked up the files. Everything was shut down, her coffee cup was empty, and all the files that needed to be locked up were. She stopped by Harper's cubicle on the way out. He wasn't in, but he was around somewhere. His trenchcoat was slung over a chair in the corner and his computer hadn't gone to screensaver mode yet.

He was working on the McCormick case, Chris noticed from the file that was open on his desk. His pocket notepad was lying open next to it. He was typing up his report, probably. Other than that, his desk was nearly pristine. A pint glass with a beer logo on it stood near his computer stuffed with pens and pencils. He had an APD recruiting poster on one of his cubicle walls. She noticed a coffee cup on his desk with the logo turned toward her. *Navy. Huh.* Chris sat down in the chair in front of his desk. A framed photograph sat on the corner, facing away from her and toward the computer screen. She picked it up. A young woman, probably in her early twenties, smiled back at her. Long blond hair and pale blue eyes. Nice cheekbones.

"That's Terri," Harper's voice said behind her.

Chris put the photo back on his desk, facing toward him as he sat down across from her. He was in typical G-man form. Grey slacks, white button-down shirt, and dark blue tie.

"She looks like a very nice young woman. And she looks like you, too." Chris studied him.

He snorted. "Let's hope not. This mug'll scare the stripes off tigers."

Chris managed a little smile without hurting her lip. "What's she majoring in?"

"Engineering. She wants to do NASA stuff." His pride was unmistakable.

"Does she want to follow your footsteps into the military?" Chris gestured at the Navy cup.

A faraway look entered Harper's eyes. "Her mom said she was thinking about the Air Force, which would be a good fit with what she wants to do. But there are some things to think about." He leaned back in his chair. "We're divorced," he said, responding to the question in Chris's eyes. "Eight years now. Allison — my ex-wife — is in St. Paul."

Chris nodded and held her stack of files up. "I'm about to take off. I just wanted to let you know. Call if you need any follow-up. All my notes are in the evidence room." She stood.

"I'm taking a few days myself," he said quietly, regarding her from his chair.

"Good for you," she responded, surprised. He was usually such a workaholic. *Avoiding shit.* That thought made her uncomfortable because she recognized the tendency in herself.

He shrugged and glanced at the photo of his daughter. "I'm going to visit Terri."

"That's great," Chris said noncommittally. "Hope it's a good trip."

He pursed his lips and ran a hand over his crewcut. "It'll be...interesting. Probably good for both of us." He cleared his throat. "I'll be meeting her — um — partner," he finished. The last word was hard for him to say.

"That's tough for a dad," she said quietly. "Nobody's ever good enough. Especially if it's a daughter."

He sat looking at her for a long moment. "Okay, then." He stood as well, changing the subject. "It was a pleasure working this one with you. I hope we get the chance to do it again."

Chris rolled her eyes. "Yeah. Nothing like bonding over homicide, preachers-gone-wrong, and obsessive compulsive disorder. For sure, Harper. Let's definitely do this again." She managed a tiny smile. "Take it easy and good luck with the visit." She started to leave his office.

"Chris—"

She stopped and turned, eyebrows raised expectantly.

"I hope Terri's partner—" his eyes clouded a bit. "I hope she's a lot like you."

Chris's voice caught in her throat momentarily before she responded. "I hope she loves and respects Terri and that she gives her space and encouragement to be her own woman."

Harper nodded once, a softer look in his eyes. "See you around."

"Yeah. You will." She touched two fingers to her forehead in a little salute and left his cubicle. She stopped by Jerry's office and he told her to get the hell home and get some rest, with laughter in his voice. Chris said goodbyes to Theresa at the front desk and other cops and detectives hanging around. Mark was out in the field but he had come by yesterday to congratulate her on a job well-done and to tell her that he had called K.C. to tell her what a great bunch of research she had contributed. As Chris exited the building, she felt as if a weight sloughed from her shoulders, as if rough edges of her spirit had filed themselves down. She drove out of the parking lot and headed toward home, thoughts of dinner with her posse keeping her company.

"FOR REAL? HARPER'S daughter is gay?" K.C. gaped at Chris.

Chris nodded as she served herself some rice out of the bowl Dayna passed to her. "Yeah. Which explains a lot."

Sage smiled. "I think it's really sweet. You changed his mind about a lot of things and now he's going to try to get to know her and her partner. That's pretty damn cool."

K.C. picked up the wine from her end of the table and stood so she could refill Sage's glass. She then walked to the opposite end and refilled Dayna's glass. "It is cool, *amiga*," she said to Chris. "Well done."

"Thanks," Dayna said appreciatively to K.C., smiling up at her.

K.C. flashed an answering smile and disappeared into the kitchen with the empty bottle.

"I'm with K.C. and Sage," Dayna said to Chris. "That's cool."

Chris shrugged, embarrassed, and mixed the chicken with the rice on her plate and took a bite. Flavor exploded on her tongue. "This is so damn good. Sage, I swear. You and John should open a restaurant."

Sage giggled. "Maybe my second career."

"Or third. Or fourth." Dayna looked at her. "This is excellent. Thanks for having us over."

K.C. reappeared with a fresh bottle of wine. "Absolutely. It seemed so much more mellow to stay in." She looked meaningfully at Chris. "Especially with Wonder Woman here thinking she could kick some psycho fundie's ass in the bosque with her head."

"Yeah, well, it worked, didn't it?" Chris shot K.C. a "nanner nanner" look.

K.C. set the bottle on the table and resumed her seat to Chris's right. "I'm just glad you're okay and you're here right now."

Sage raised her glass. "To Chris, for using her head to kick an ass. To Dayna, for pulling Chris's head out of her ass. And to K.C. — "

"For watching *your* ass," Chris interrupted.

"Nice, Gutierrez. Really nice," K.C. growled, teasing.

Dayna raised her voice slightly. "To Sage, for putting up with both Chris's *and* K.C.'s asses."

"You *go*, girl," Sage said, laughing, as she touched glasses with Dayna.

Chris and K.C. followed suit, touching glasses all around, laughing and talking. Chris finished eating, watching Sage and Dayna interact. K.C. bantered back and forth with them for a while before she stood and started gathering dishes. Chris started to get up but K.C. gave her a stern look. "Nuh-uh. You're head-injured, girlfriend. This here's my job tonight."

Dayna stood and picked her plate up over K.C.'s protests. She reached for Sage's plate as well and followed K.C. into the kitchen. Sage watched her then turned her head to look at Chris.

"How are you feeling? You want some Advil?"

"No, thanks. I'm okay. Just kind of tired." Chris offered the barest of smiles.

Dayna and K.C. returned to the dining room and cleared off more dishes. Dayna shot Chris a look that could have melted steel before she followed K.C. back into the kitchen. Sage smiled.

"So things are going well, I take it?" Sage teased.

Chris felt a flush on her cheeks.

"I'll take that as a yes." Sage took a sip of her wine. "She's very good for you. Very, very good."

Chris held Sage's gaze with her own. "I know." *I'm head over heels for her.* The words echoed through her mind. She listened to Dayna and K.C. laughing in the kitchen about something. It warmed her heart, seeing how K.C. and Sage welcomed Dayna into their lives and how Dayna seemed to fit the comfortable circle of friendship.

Sage grinned. "Yes, you are. Don't forget to let Dayna know, too."

Chris's jaw dropped. "I didn't — "

"Chris, it's all over your face. It's in your eyes. It's in the way you look at her." Sage raised an eyebrow. "It don't take no damn rocket scientist to see how you feel about her." She stood up. "Coffee time. Can I count you in?"

"Totally."

"Go sit down on the couch." Sage picked up her wine glass and Chris's empty water glass. "Don't worry. I'll be gentle with the interrogation." She laughed when Chris groaned.

K.C. appeared in the doorway. "Hey, I've got those." She took the glasses out of Sage's hands and looked at Chris. "You are so keeping her, *mujer*," she said in a low voice, half-serious. "I will kick your ass if you let this one go."

Chris groaned again. "Great. Dayna was the one who was supposed to pass some kind of test and here I am getting the third degree."

"It's only 'cause we care." Sage blew her an air kiss. "Dessert's up soon. Go sit." She and K.C. went back into the kitchen.

Chris sighed plaintively and stood so she could follow Sage's instructions. She was pretty tired, she decided, as she sank onto the couch facing the fireplace, the small stack of logs still burning. She smelled incense—Sage favored lavender and jasmine—and the flames from the big pillar candles set strategically around the room bounced lazily in the warmth. Chris closed her eyes and leaned her head carefully against the back of the couch, resting.

"You okay?" K.C.'s voice.

Chris opened her eyes. "Yeah. Just kinda tired. And relaxed, actually. This was great. Thanks for having us over. I wasn't up to going out."

"I figured. So how are you really?"

"I'd smile more but it hurts my damn lip," Chris said. "I'm glad this whole thing is over and I'm glad we got him. But I'm drained, too. And it'll take basically forever before this guy gets convicted. That's how it works." She shrugged.

K.C. didn't respond right away. She instead put another log on the fire and made some adjustments with the poker. When she had completed that task, she plopped down onto the other couch. She was about to say something when Sage entered with two cups of coffee. One she handed to K.C., the other to Chris. She brushed a kiss across the top of K.C.'s head before returning to the kitchen. K.C. watched her.

"Damn. She still gets to me," she said, wonder in her voice.

"She'd better. And for a good long time." Chris sniffed the coffee. *Yes.* Mexican spice and cinnamon included. She took a sip.

Sage reappeared carrying a plate of *bizcochitos* in one hand and four smaller plates in the other. Dayna followed her, a cup of coffee in each hand. She sat down on Chris's left and Sage took a seat on the other couch, to K.C.'s right. She handed two smaller plates to Dayna, who had set the coffee cups down. The coffee table between the couches was going to serve once again as a dessert rendezvous.

Chris reached for a *bizcochito* and bit into it. "Oh, my God. They're still warm." She chewed, the cookie's warm dough enhancing its flavors. "Wow. I think I taste chocolate. Did you put chocolate in these?"

"Chris, you always surprise me with your culinary gifts." Sage laughed. "Yes. A twist on the traditional. Anise and cinnamon actually taste pretty good combined with Mexican cocoa. *Abuelita* and I tried several variations and finally got this one. She likes the diamond shape, too."

Chris swallowed before answering. "Hell, maybe you, John, and *Abuelita* should just open a *panadería*."

"Second that," Dayna said. "Sage, these are absolutely unbelievable. And if you served this coffee at your bakery, I'd be there every damn morning."

Sage smiled, shy. "Thanks."

"And you were worried that I'd freak out and head for the hills when I met her," K.C. scoffed at Chris. "I know a good thing when I see it." She leaned over and kissed Sage on the cheek.

"Whatever," Chris retorted. "You know a good meal when you taste it."

"Yes, she does." Sage batted her eyes innocently and took another cookie.

Dayna smiled and leaned against Chris, who shifted to accommodate her.

"So, Dayna," K.C. started.

Chris rolled her eyes with an "oh, no" expression.

K.C. shot Chris a "get over it" glare. "I just want to thank you for taking a chance on my best friend. I know she's not the easiest person to deal with —"

Sage laughed, then took a sip of coffee. Dayna grinned.

"And I know she can be a total pain in the ass and sometimes you need pliers just to talk to her, but —" K.C. leaned forward, serious. "She's worth it."

"Jesus," Chris muttered. She felt heat on her neck and cheeks. "Kase —"

"She is," Dayna interrupted. "Thanks for being so open and for including me tonight. Chris was really nervous about it." Chris groaned softly as Dayna smiled at her before continuing, "Because your opinions matter so much to her. She's really, really lucky to have you both in her life."

"She's really, really lucky to have *you* in her life." Sage looked at Dayna, one of her enigmatic expressions in her eyes. "And I hope to see more of you both."

"For these *bizcochitos*, I'll be moving in," Dayna quipped.

"Oh, yeah! I like her!" Sage giggled and waggled her eyebrows.

"Can you make it to Sage's birthday soiree next week?" K.C. asked, hopeful.

"Saturday?" Dayna reached for her coffee, looking at K.C.

"Yep. I asked Chris a while back but her busy social life and all..."

"Wouldn't miss it." Dayna turned to Chris. "You?"

"With an invite like that, how could I possibly resist?" Chris said with mock sarcasm as she placed a light kiss on Dayna's cheek.

"Most excellent. Festivities begin around six." K.C. reached for another cookie.

"No gifts," Sage said sternly. "I just want your company and good vibes."

Chris smiled slightly, careful about her lip. Dayna leaned into her more, sending waves of warmth through Chris's body. K.C. and Sage were teasing each other and invited Dayna in and the conversation moved to other matters. Chris offered a comment now and again, but she was more content listening to the others, feeling the heat from the fireplace and Dayna circulate through her veins. *I'm completely loco for her.* As if she heard, Dayna interlaced her fingers with Chris's, a seemingly automatic but completely natural gesture. She didn't miss a beat in the discussion about Sage's upcoming photo excursions in March.

"I'm going to leave a sign out front," Sage was saying. " 'Please feed bachelor'."

"We'll make sure she's fed and clean," Dayna assured her. "And we'll take her out for some exercise, too. And make sure she goes to bed at a reasonable hour."

"Speaking of which—" Sage gestured at Chris. "I think it's almost lights out for Supergirl."

Chris's eyes, which had been at half-mast, opened. "I am a little tired. Sorry."

Dayna extricated herself. "Sage is right, hon. It's time to get you home and tuck you in."

"You're hired, if you want the job," Chris said, another flush racing through her nerves at Dayna's use of "hon." She slowly stood up, surprised at how stiff and tired she was.

"Nothing to be sorry for," K.C. said as she, too, stood. "You two just run along and stay out of trouble. I need you, after all, to feed me while Sage is out of town." She followed Dayna and Chris to the front door while Sage went to the spare bedroom for their coats.

"Thanks," Chris said as she helped Dayna with her coat. "I love you both and I'll talk to you later." After hugs all around, she followed Dayna to her truck and settled into the passenger seat, Dayna waiting for her to buckle up before she closed the door and went around to the driver's side. She buckled up as well and started the engine.

"Thanks for driving." Chris sighed as she leaned back.

"No problem," Dayna said, smiling, as she pulled away from the curb. Chris wanted to say something in return but she was so tired. Sophie B. Hawkins was crooning "Damn, I Wish I Was Your Lover" over Dayna's sound system. *I'll just close my eyes for a minute.*

She didn't remember falling asleep but she obviously did

because she jerked awake as Dayna slowed and eased into Chris's driveway. She pulled up behind Chris's car and turned off the engine. Chris got out and walked into the carport so she could go in through the side door. She heard Dayna locking her truck and she waited until she joined her at the door. Chris unlocked the door and flipped the light on before heading across the kitchen into the living room so she could turn the alarm off. A light in the living room was on, triggered with a timer. Chris turned around, managing a tiny smile at the sight of Dayna watching her from the archway into the dining room.

"I'm sorry. I guess I'm really tired," Chris said apologetically.

"Give me your coat and go get ready for bed." Dayna crossed the room and took Chris's coat from her so she could hang it on the rack near the front door. She added her own coat to the rack, as well.

Chris stood looking at her, struck again at how much she liked the idea of Dayna in her house.

"I think you might be falling asleep on your feet," Dayna said gently as she took Chris's hand and pulled her back toward the dining room and the short hallway to the master bedroom.

"Will you stay?" Chris asked as Dayna turned the bedside lamp on. "I mean — unless you have something to do or...something." *Shit, I'm tired.*

Dayna smiled and it melted any misgivings Chris might have had tucked away in the neglected recesses of her heart.

"I was hoping you'd ask that." Dayna ran her fingers lightly along Chris's jaw. "I'm going to get you some Advil. I'll assume you can undress yourself." she quirked an eyebrow. "Not to suggest I wouldn't do it for you." She turned and headed down the hall back to the kitchen.

Chris stood dumbly in the middle of the room then followed her, not really thinking. "Dayna," she said as she entered the kitchen.

Dayna was pouring a glass of water from the pitcher in the fridge. She set the pitcher on the counter and looked up, a question in her eyes.

Chris took the glass of water from Dayna's hand and placed it next to the pitcher. She cupped Dayna's face in her hands and leaned down to brush a light kiss over Dayna's lips, careful about her own lip. She pulled back slightly, mesmerized by her eyes. She was aware of Dayna's hands at her waist, resting there. Secure. Warm. "I know I'm not the easiest person to get to know," Chris said quietly. "And I know that sometimes I drag the cop stuff out and use it as a wall." She stroked Dayna's face. "And I can be overbearing and overprotective and just plain bitchy." She sighed, a "God help me" sound. "But I'm completely crazy about you."

"Completely, huh?" Dayna looked into Chris's eyes, a smile

pulling at the corners of her mouth.

"Totally. So you think you might give me a chance?"

"Hmmm. Are you sure about this?" Dayna said it gently, teasingly. "After all, I have that damn lawyer stuff that comes up. And some issues in my past that haven't settled. Plus, I can be really pushy." Her eyes sparkled like sunlight on water. "And I'll expect you to do things like communicate with me. And tell me when things bother you. Are you up for that, Detective?"

Chris grinned, ignoring the sting in her lip. "Definitely."

"It's not just the exhaustion talking?" Dayna ran her lips delicately along Chris's, mindful of the injury. "You're not just getting all caught up in a Florence Nightingale thing, are you?" She nuzzled Chris's neck and Chris slid her arms around her, pulled her as close as she could.

"Positive. Though I'm sure you'd look hot in one of those starched, old-school nurse's uniforms."

Dayna pulled back slightly. She opened her mouth to say something but Chris put her fingers gently against her lips. "I think I might be head over heels for you, Counselor."

Dayna kissed Chris's fingertips then gently pulled them away from her mouth. "It's mutual." And the look in her eyes sent shockwaves from Chris's head to the soles of her feet. "So," Dayna continued, "how about I tuck you in and we try these revelations out for the next—oh, I don't know. Ninety-seven years or something?"

"That might not be enough," Chris whispered against Dayna's ear, breathing in the smell of her, encouraging Dayna's essence to permeate every cell of her body.

"Not to worry. There's an extension clause." Dayna moaned and ran her hands up Chris's back.

"I don't think I'm so tired anymore," Chris said softly, backing toward the doorway and pulling Dayna with her. "But I would like that *tuck*, if you're up for it." She grinned again and this time, her lip didn't protest so much.

Dayna's smile stopped gravity. "Definitely."

Aw, geez. That's the end.
Until the next time.

FORTHCOMING TITLES

published by
Quest Books

Hanging Offense
by Cleo Dare

Mandy Barnes, her trust betrayed by her husband Jay, needs a summer away to think about her marriage. She opts for a seasonal job at Bryce Canyon National Park in remote southern Utah and there meets Jo Reynolds, a lesbian park ranger from California. Mandy is attracted to Jo, but uncertain of her own sexuality.

On a hike into the wilderness, Mandy chances upon some vintage coins in a rusted can and is then plagued by violent dreams of a murder from the past. Are the coins connected to the dreams? Will deciphering the mystery of the past help her unravel the tangled knot of the present? Can she overcome her fears to find renewed trust and true love in Jo's arms?

Available May 2009

Tunnel Vision
by Brenda Adcock

Royce Brodie, a 50-year-old homicide detective in the quiet town of Cedar Springs, a bedroom community 30 miles from Austin, Texas, has spent the last seven years coming to grips with the incident that took the life of her partner and narrowly missed taking her own. The peace and quiet she had been enjoying is shattered by two seemingly unrelated murders in the same week: the first, a John Doe, and the second, a janitor at the local university.

While Brodie and her partner, Curtis Nicholls, begin their investigation, the assignment of a new trainee disrupts Brodie's life. Not only is Maggie Weston Brodie's former lover, but her father had been Brodie's commander at the Austin Police Department and nearly destroyed her career.

As the three detectives try to piece together the scattered evidence to solve the two murders, they become convinced the two murders are related. The discovery of a similar murder committed five years earlier at a small university in upstate New York creates a sense of urgency as they realize they are possibly chasing a serial killer.

The already difficult case becomes even more so when a third victim is found. But the case becomes personal for Brodie when Maggie becomes the killer's next target. Unless Brodie finds a way to save Maggie, she could face losing everything a second time.

Available July 2009

OTHER QUEST PUBLICATIONS

About the Author

Andi Marquette was born in Albuquerque and grew up in Colorado. After completing a couple of academic degrees in anthropology, she returned to Albuquerque where she completed a Ph.D. in history. She fell into editing in 1993 and has been obsessed with words ever since, which may or may not be a good thing. Currently, she resides in Colorado where she edits, writes, and nurtures a fascination with New Mexico chile.

VISIT US ONLINE AT
www.regalcrest.biz

At the Regal Crest Website You'll Find

- The latest news about forthcoming titles and new releases

- Our complete backlist of romance, mystery, thriller and adventure titles

- Information about your favorite authors

- Current bestsellers

- Media tearsheets to print and take with you when you shop

Regal Crest titles are available from all progressive booksellers and online at StarCrossed Productions, (www.scp-inc.biz), or at www.amazon.com, www.bamm.com, www.barnesandnoble.com, and many others.

Printed in the United States
132208LV00004B/4/P